THIRD ROTATION

GEORGE HAWKINS SPACE CAMPER

•

Dark Secrets

L. A. BISSONNETTE

BISMIL LLC

2011

Also by L.A. Bissonnette:
It Comes From Within – 1st Rotation
Past and Present Fear – 2nd Rotation

For previews of upcoming books by L.A. Bissonnette and more information
about the author, visit **www.georgehawkinsspacecamper.com**

BISMIL LLC

GHSC Book Group

Visit our website at **www.georgehawkinsspacecamper.com**

Illustration by Tyson Mangelsdorf

ISBN 978-0-9823961-2-4   0-9823961-2-0

Printed in the U.S.A.
First American edition   August 2011

*For all that believe in the dream
and the depth of the words.
Thanks, Mom and Dad.*

Peace.

Contents

Prologue

2ND ROTATION

George's birthday and the beginning of summer vacation had fallen on the same day last year. In his wildest dreams, he never imagined he would be going to a summer camp in space on a faraway moon filled with summer campers like himself. In one short day he went from being a regular teenager on Earth to being a cadet on a space station.

After his first summer camp on Jupiter station, he and his new team had stopped a Zeleion invasion. The five other members on his team were amazing new friends and George was learning to trust their instincts and his own. On Jupiter's moon, Ganymede, George met up with the five other camper cadets who were now part of his Red J team.

Andy Penteado was a tall muscular boy with dark brown hair. He had grown up in the wilds of Brazil on the family's ranch. Over the summer, Andy was learning to be George's second in command and the defender of their team.

Gus Reiter was from central Germany, a bit rounder than the others and was as strong as an ox. Andy seemed more seasoned than Gus, like he had grown up faster. Gus was their cook and keeper of their strongest weapon, the seeds of hope.

Emily Miller was from Great Britain. She was about George's height, with light brown hair that curled over her shoulders. Her mom had died when she was very young; the closest thing Emily had to a friend was her computer. Over the summer, Emily created intricate computer programs that would help save their lives.

Anna Jhang was a short girl from Japan with long, straight black hair braided down her back. When she was very little, her grandmother had taught her all about the universe and the stars. Anna had become their navigator through the caves of Ganymede moon.

Sara O'Conner was from Ireland and was from a large family of six older brothers, with no sisters. She had learned about medicines from her grandfather, and herbs from her grandmother. She was now the team's healer.

Pete Petrosky was their team captain and in charge of their training. He and his team of captains had become their friends over the last year. Yet George knew there was something their captain had not told them, something was missing, unsaid. George and his team had taken the Oath of Odin with Pete's team and his older brother Frank's team. It was serious business and Frank had taught George a lot about the cadets, CORE, their new triad over the school year. Now on their second rotation, they were on a mission far away from Jupiter station, and Captain Stiles was their new captain!

Before long, Jupiter station was under attack and the Thoreans who had helped George and the others on their first rotation rescued them from Jupiter station. They cloaked the tiny training ship as they headed across the galaxy into open space for the Thorean Cadet station, Indus.

Emily's computer programs stopped the invaders on Jupiter station; however, there were spies in high places on Indus station. Disguised as Thorean cadets, George and his team stayed on Indus station to learn a new culture and the Thorean language. Toma and his team of captains completed their triad and Toma became their new captain leader while Pete was away.

Yet the team had an odd feeling something was wrong on Indus station too. Late into the night, the Thoreans on Indus station disappeared. By early morning, the station was being flooded with deadly gas. Emily's programs slowed the spread of the deadly gas, however, she could not stop it. George and the others were humans and did not show up on the scanners so they stole three enormous galaxy class cruisers loaded to the brim with tunnel hogs and lifted off Indus station, escaping the new invaders.

Anna, Emily and Sara flew the three enormous galaxy cruisers across the galaxy to a planet Senior Viceroy Petrosky said was safe to drop off the tunnel hogs, before going on to the 'second kitchen' trading post to pick up Pete, Frank, and their teams. Soon they were racing across the galaxy with Pete, Frank and their teams, chasing the Mahadean slave traders who had captured the Thorean station cadets and officers on Indus station. They were on their own, with galactic help three days behind them.

George and Andy formulated a plan, Sara created Mahadean viruses, Emily created computer control programs and Anna navigated their enormous ships. When they finally caught up to the Mahadean slave ships, the teams were ready. In their triad mind link, they told Toma their plan. Within eight hours, the Thoreans were free and the Mahadean warships, who had fired on their own spaceships, were limping home without their Thorean cargo.

When they returned to Indus station, they exposed the Zeleion spies on Indus station. George and Andy stood in the center of power with the Galactic Council Viceroys watching and learning about the energy of the universe. In flight training class, Anna, Sara, and Emily led their team to victory, beating the Calshene space race record that held for more than two hundred years, becoming heroes across the galaxy.

Toma and his team played in the final game of Sport on Indus station. George and his team were invited to sit in the Viceroy's box for the game. It was an epic match; however, George and the others were quiet, and sitting in the back of the Viceroy's box, as protocol prevented them from hopping and hollering. Yet they were there watching Sport on a cadet station far from home on the adventure of a life time.

Chapter 1

FINDING SAFETY

The final school bell of the day rang and the high school students poured out of their homerooms and into the hallways, racing for their lockers. Quickly, the students began their mad dash out to the school buses for their ride home. At his locker, George carefully slid his three-ring history binder and books into his red backpack and stuffed his older brother's hand-me-down green hoodie on top. The bright yellow buses never left without all of their students, but you had to be fast or you could end up sitting in the front row or in the last row of the bus. The students in the last row were always getting yelled at by the bus driver and ended up with detention. The students in the first row didn't talk for fear of being overheard by the bus driver. The middle of the bus was the place to be!

Like a stampede of wild horses, George and the other students hurried through the school hallways, careful not to actually run for fear of being caught by the vice principal and getting detention. A warm spring breeze swept across the students as they rushed through the high school's glass doors and ran across the sidewalk to the waiting buses. George leapt over the bus steps and easily threaded his way passed the other students' backpacks and bags that half covered the floor. Carefully, he slid into the seat his friend had saved for him. He groaned a heavy sigh of relief as he sat down on the dark blue seat. It was Friday and George had no homework to finish by Monday morning. A weekend without homework—excellent!

He sat with his friends in the middle of the bus as it bounced off the bus circle curb, leaving the brown and red brick high school behind. There was a home baseball game tonight and the high school baseball field lights were already on, as if calling the students back to school to cheer on their team. Tonight, he would be there with his friends, if his mom agreed. All he had to do was talk his dad into dropping him off—a simple drive-by, drop-off, kind of thing. Keeping him from being embarrassed by being seen with an actual parent. After all, George was a sophomore in high school this year and image was everything.

On the way home, George and his friends finished their plan for their Friday night adventure as the bus passed over a small bridge and slowed down. George was the third bus stop on Route 37. The school bus stopped with a jolt. George and three other students hurried through the narrow aisle, bumping as many friends as they could before they got off the bus. He watched the yellow bus disappear around the next corner as he walked down Lily Street towards his house on the bright sunny afternoon in early May.

There were only four weeks left of the school year - a thought that made him happy as he walked. Yet, he had been a little lonely all year. His older brother, Frank, had graduated high school last year and this was the first year George had to come home to a quiet house. Frank had always been there and they had become good friends in the last year. They had talked about the cadets, the CORE, outer space and the value of water in the galaxy. Now Frank was living on campus at the university, and George was home alone with his mom and dad.

It wasn't that George's mom wasn't there when he got home. She was always there and she would do anything for him. Well, anything except answer questions about space, the cadets, the CORE, the Galactic council and the Union. He loved his mom and dad—they just weren't Frank! What was an odd thought… it seemed to George, as he hopped over the neighbors white picket fence, to cut across the yard?

Two years ago he would not have thought twice about trading in his older brother for a new skate board or stunt bike. Now he actually missed Frank's company and advice. He jumped over the short leafy hedge his mom had planted a few years before in front of the sidewalk leading up to the front steps of his house. It may have screened the sidewalk from the street, but it was in the way as far as he was concerned. In the fall, it was always stuffed with tree leaves that his mom wanted cleaned out.

The year before, he had to walk around the bushes, now they were like a low hurdled for him. He had grown over the last school year. George hardly touched the front porch steps as he leapt onto the front porch, landing quietly, practicing his stealth moves. His mom always seemed to yell when he crashed onto the floor after leaping from the upstairs steps.

Now he wanted to surprise her; sneak up on her. He smiled as he swung open the front screen door and slammed face first into the glass window in the front door. The window in the door bounced him back to the middle of the porch!

"That's weird, our front door is never closed in the spring," he mumbled.

His mom loved the fresh air and the smell of fresh spring flowers. She always kept the doors and windows open as much as possible. This was a warm spring day in early May with a light spring breeze. His house should be so open the flies and bees could fly though and not even know they had been inside. He reached for the door handle; however, this time, a bad feeling crept into the pit of his stomach the closer his hand came to the doorknob.

"Run," it seemed to say.

He backed up quickly and with one hand planted on the wooden railing, he vaulted over the porch railing, gliding down between the big green Juniper bushes that surrounded the front of their house and the porch's brick wall. His arms scrapped along the stiff Juniper branches, and his red T-shirt sleeve tore open. He landed silently on the soft ground, raising a cloud of dust and dirt that covered his year-old tennis shoes. The sweet smell of newly crushed Juniper needles filled the air as the branches stopped moving.

He turned around, slowing as the hairs on the back of his neck stood up. Rising up a little, he peered between the bottom board on the porch railing and the gray floor boards. Silently, he watched two dark shadows inside the house pull back the old white lace curtains covering the window on the front door. They peaked out over the porch. Patiently, he waited until the curtains swung back into place before he moved. Quietly, he lowered back down below the porch floor, twisting around beneath the thick Juniper branches. He dropped his backpack in the dirt and rubbed his arms to stop a few small cuts from bleeding after his leap into the Juniper bushes. On his hands and knees, he crawled along the brick wall to the corner of the porch. The windows in the dining room were lower and it would be easier to look inside without being seen.

He stopped at the corner of the porch, scanning the side of the house and the neighbor's house for anything out of place before climbing out from behind the Juniper bushes. There were no bushes on the side of the house; only, one long continuous flower garden George's dad had made one year for his mom. At this time of year, the flowers were low to the ground. There would be nothing to hide behind. He noticed nothing out of place as he looked around the side yard. Everything was exactly where it should be—except it was oddly quiet.

He paused, his hand holding onto the corner of the bricks as he leaned forward popping his head out from behind the Juniper bushes. "Something's really not right," he muttered, as he rolled back into the Juniper bushes to make a new plan. "It's spring, bees should be buzzing in the little flowers and there should be birds making annoying noises. This is wrong, it's like a..."

A moving figure on the sidewalk caught his eye and he snapped his head around to see who it was. George's dad was walking up to the house and into a "trap!"

In a moment of desperation, he grabbed a clump of dirt from under the Juniper bushes and lofted it high into the air at his dad. The dirt ball hit the sidewalk near the street and rolled across it leaving a path of dirt and needles a few feet in front of him. His dad stopped and stared at the clump of dirt and then at their house. George bent his body around the thick stems of the Junipers, pushing his way past the prickly branches.

His hand popped out in front of the bushes. "Trap," he signed.

Mr. Hawkins bent his arm and touched his shoulder with his finger tips. He disappeared. The grass bent down and a blur appeared over it as he walked quietly over to the Juniper bushes to where his son was hiding. Carefully, he stepped into the Juniper bushes bending back the thick branches. Sitting down in the dirt next to George, he reappeared. His dad had a wrinkled forehead and a funny tilt to his head as he sat in the dirt in his work clothes beneath the Juniper bushes with George.

"Dad, the birds are gone," George replied, using the common sign language all cadets learned on their first space camp rotation before they made up their team sign language.

"Good observation, son," his dad signed back.

"Dad, someone is inside our house with mom. I saw them pull back the curtains. We need to rescue her?" George signed quickly.

His dad concentrated for a moment. "She's not here, George," he signed back.

He wanted to ask another question, but his dad waved him off. Touching his shoulder, they both disappeared just as a man and woman, dressed in black suits, stepped around the corner of the house. They made no sound as they stepped softly through the grass. George and his dad sat very still; his dad's holographic projector was simple and could only reflect their surroundings.

The holographic projector bars they had used during their second rotation on Indus station, the Thorean cadet station, had been much more sophisticated. George had not fully appreciated the projectors until this moment. The two people in the black suits walked past the Junipers bushes and stepped up onto the first two porch steps. The wooden steps creaked as they paused to look around the front yard before walking across the porch to the front door. Two taps on the front door by the woman and the door cracked open. They nodded and entered the house. The latch on the front door clicked, echoing in the still air around the porch.

His dad touched his shoulder again and they reappeared. He looked tired. George recalled one of Toma's warnings about the holographic bars. It could hide two cadets if one of the cadet's bars broke or failed; however, the energy draw was much larger and they would need to get to safety quickly. His dad would not be able to use the holographic bar again, as it was oddly too much of an energy draw on his dad, as a Viceroy.

"How was that possible?"

At that moment, he thought of Sara and wished he could heal like she did.

"We will stay until it's dark," George signed, and his dad smiled weakly.

He leaned on his dad's shoulder, yet something was wrong. It was as if his dad's strength was being drained from him as they sat in the dirt beneath the Juniper bushes. George didn't know how he knew. It was a bad feeling he had, like the front door—a warning, telling them they had to leave.

Dusk came late in the spring, and George slipped the holographic bar off his dad's shoulder and onto his shoulder. In only a few hours, his dad had become much weaker. It was as if someone was in a mind link with him, sucking the energy right out of him. Yet, George couldn't sense a link within his dad. Maybe, it was one of those stealth-type links where someone slips into your mind, and now his dad was losing strength, having to fight off the attacker.

He was worried about his dad as he flicked on the holographic bar and helped his dad standup. Together, they pushed through the thick Juniper branches. However, what made them good for hiding behind made them hard to push though to escape. George's blue jeans caught a branch and tore open. His dad's shirt caught another branch and ripped a hole in his sleeve.

"Mother will not be happy," he and his dad thought at the same time. George smiled. His dad and he were in a link! When did that happen? It was an amazing way to communicate, yet George didn't remember making the link with his dad.

"Stay focused George," his dad thought back. "These people can't be good. They will do anything to distract you to get you to make a mistake so they can capture you, son," his dad added.

"Yes, stay focused. Yes sir," he replied without thinking.

George didn't hear all of his dad's words or he would have questioned why his dad had warned him about being captured, and how he knew they were bad people.

Free of the Juniper bushes, they walked together in a straight line across the front yard over to the end of the neighbor's white picket fence. Only their footsteps bending the grass blades showed their location. Quickly, they crossed over the front sidewalk, passing George's clump of dirt. Off the curb and out onto Lily Street, George and his dad hurried, arm and arm. His mom was not at the house, and now he and his dad had to get away.

The further they walked away from the house, the stronger his dad seemed to be getting. He was still wobbling and stumbling a little. Yet leaning on George, he could walk better. Max had said his dad was in one of the strongest triads in their sector of the universe, but right now, something was draining his strength. He knew his dad could use the raw energy of the universe, which gave him strength, but George wondered if the people dressed in black could track them if he used it. Maybe that was why his dad was getting weaker, because he hadn't used any of the energy of the universe to power the holographic bar, only his own strength. Soon Toma's warning would be all too true for George, and he too would be getting weak from using the holographic bar to hide two people.

As they crossed the street, George worried he would not have enough energy and strength to keep the holographic bar working and help his dad until he could recover. Through the neighbor's side yard and across two backyards, George and his dad hurried, a mere blur to anyone looking outside.

Two blocks away from his house, there was a small park and a covered pavilion hidden by trees and bushes on the backside of the park. The drainage ditch that flowed behind the park became a small stream each year with the spring rains. He had to get there to hide himself and his dad and soon; as he too was beginning to feel tired. His dad was still walking, but he was starting to slow down. George cut through another neighbor's side yard and then through the front yard of another, pulling his dad along.

One more street to go and they would be there. A cold feeling crept over George and the hairs on the back of his neck stood up again. His stomach ached and he wanted to bend over, yet he couldn't—his dad needed him. George stopped at the edge of the sidewalk and slipped his dad under a clump of large spruce trees on the edge of the road. A black car drove slowly down the street passing only a few feet from the spruce trees. He cleared his thoughts and concentrated on being the tree, nothing but the tree.

The car drove slowly by the trees and turned at the corner. The stop had cost George and his dad precious seconds. With the car out of sight, they moved on slowly out into the open and crossed the street. George was nearly carrying his dad now.

"Hurry dad, we have to keep moving," he whispered.

The men in the car seemed to have sucked what little energy and strength his dad had left out of him. George stared at his dad, shaking his head. Somehow, their link was stronger. He could feel it in his mind. His dad's mind was so focused and strong, even now as weak as his body was becoming, his mind was still focused and strong. George paused.

"The men in the car hadn't weakened his dad. His dad was blocking them from reading his thoughts and George's thoughts, and it was weakening his dad. The same as it had weakened Toma on their second rotation on the Calshene station, when Toma had protected the cadets from the strong minds searching for information on the cadet station," George thought.

"Focus, it is only a distraction, George," his dad thought to him.

George looked up. It was a distraction meant to stop them so time could slip away, and they would get weaker. As quickly as they could, they crossed the last yard and street. They hurried into the park and his dad sat down to rest at the first picnic table.

"Not here, Dad, there is no cover," George whispered, motioning toward the other picnic tables in the open. "Back there." He pointed to the far side of the park. "We need to get as far from the road as we can get, Dad."

George helped his dad up and together they headed for the far side of the park, weaving around the tall trees. By the time they reached the pavilion, he was almost carrying his dad over his shoulder. It reminded George of their first rotation, when they had carried the yellow captains from the caves on Jupiter station.

"Focus," was the only thought that popped into George's mind. He nodded. His dad was weak but still blocking their thoughts.

He sat his dad down in the dirt behind the small half-brick wall of the pavilion. Turning off the holographic bar, he slumped down next to him.

"Dad, are you OK? Can you call the others? We need help," George whispered.

His dad nodded slowly, he strained to concentrate and then drooped over. Whatever had drained his dad at their house on Lily Street, was still affecting him now.

"Think, George, think strategy," he thought to himself.

He needed to focus and call for help, but who could he call? His dad was a Viceroy, and yet, his strength was slowly being drained from him. George was not strong enough to call across a solar system looking for Pete's dad or grandfather—well, at least not alone, not yet. The last time he had called the Senior Viceroy by himself from a great distance, it had been intercepted, and he had almost died. Max had saved him and sent the energy trapped within the link back to its evil sender. This time Max was not here to save them.

"Think, think, what else?" George muttered, racking his brain for an idea, anything to save them. There was Frank and Pete off at the University and of course his team; yet, they were all too far away to help or were they? He focused his mind and thought of Frank and Pete. In the past, he and Andy had been able to find them over light years of distance. However, this time he found nothing. Was he too far away and too weak to reach them?

"How is this possible?" George puzzled.

Slowly, his thoughts came back to Max, who had saved their lives more than once. Inside, George knew Max was a different kind of being from them.

"Maybe Max?" George wondered.

He wasn't human or Thorean or Calshene, he was something else; maybe he could hear George's message. He thought of Max and Max alone.

"Help, Max. Dad's hurt, help," was his short and cryptic message. He thought it over and over, concentrating and focusing his thoughts as hard as he could. Yet, he could not sense Max and he heard no answer in a link in his mind.

"Maybe communicating with thought was not possible except on one of the cadet training stations, or in a tunnel hog, or on one of the CORE starships?" he wondered.

His dad lifted his head, tilting it ever so slightly, "Keep trying son, it is possible," he whispered and slumped down again.

A rustle in the bushes by a pair of birds landing near them reminded George they were still in the open. Slowly, he peeked around the edge of pavilion's half wall. The black car that had passed them earlier in the street was slowing down now by the park. Suddenly, George's head started to hurt. His dad was no longer able to block his thoughts. He focused on nothing and emptied his mind of any thoughts. Slowly, the pain slipped away as it had the year before when his triad had helped him. Yet, he feared he was too late and the people in the black car could somehow track them now.

The black car drove slowly into the park's small parking lot, its brakes squealing as it stopped. "Click." The doors opened, the sound echoing through the now silent park. Two men in dark suits got out, each scanning the area with small silver boxes as they walked to the back of the car. "Click." The trunk popped open. Silently, they pulled out two small machines and unfolded long rods with glistening copper disks on the ends. They held the small machines close to their bodies as they scanned the small park with the spinning copper disks. It reminded George of the scanning machines they had seen the guards use on Indus station during their second rotation. The circular disks hummed and reflected the fading light of the twilight sky as the two men in dark suits spread out, scanning across the park.

George ducked back down behind the pavilion's half wall. They had to move. The men from the black car would soon be close, and he was not that great at hiding his thoughts. At least, he didn't think so. His dad was weaker now and could no longer stand. George knew he was too weak to use the holographic bar again, and he was not strong enough to lift his dad totally off the ground!

Sitting in the dirt, he rolled his dad over and wrapped his arms around his dad's chest. Quietly, George dug the heels of his tennis shoes into the soft ground and slid backwards pulling his dad along the gravel-covered ground toward the drainage ditch that ran through the park. It was spring, and the drainage ditch had filled with rainwater, becoming a fair-sized stream.

George reached the leafy green bushes at the edge of the stream bank. Carefully, he rolled his dad under the branches and left him near the waters' edge. He flipped over onto his stomach and crawled back and forth between the gray bricks of the pavilion half-wall and the steep stream bank, brushing the ground with a small branch to hide the marks he had left dragging his dad. Dust curled in the air, and George held back a hard sneeze. He returned to his dad, as a branch snapped from a bush near the front of the pavilion.

"Think tree, George, only trees," he told himself over and over. Through the thick branches of the bushes, he could see one of the men in dark suits walking slowly toward the outer half-wall of the pavilion where they had just been hiding. In the distance, George could see the other man waving to the second man by the pavilion to come over to the tables at the front edge of the park. It was the picnic table his dad had sat on when they rested!

With both men's backs turned, he slid his dad into the cold clear water of the stream without a sound. George slid in after him and pushed off from the bank holding his dad's head up just above the water. Without making a sound, they drifted with the stream's current along the bank, hiding beneath the overhanging branches at the waters' edge. Slowly, they left the men and the park far behind.

Sticking close to the shadows, they drifted under the 3rd Street Bridge. George pushed at the edge of the stream bank to move them along faster as they passed under the 2nd Street Bridge. He had never paid much attention to the stream before, something that he now kicked himself for. He crossed the stream twice a day to go to school and home again; and yet, he didn't even know its name or where it went.

"Sure wish I'd been more observant of my surroundings, might be important. Duh!" he thought feeling stupid.

He would have hit his head with his hand, but he was still holding his dad's head up above the water as they continued drifting quietly along. The runoff water was cold from the spring rains and he knew they would need to get out soon.

"But where, where was it safe?" he thought.

Never had he trained for this situation. In all of his memory, he had only crossed streams, rivers and lakes at summer camp, never actually floated in them for escape. But escape to where? There were no Thoreans here to rescue them in a starship or his older brother Frank and his team to lift them up and out of harm's way at a Sport arena.

He needed Gus's strength, Sara's healing abilities, Emily's way with the ground, Anna's directions, and Andy's tactics. He wished Max were there. His dad seemed better, but maybe that was because he was getting worse himself and his judgment was getting bad. The sun had gone down and the spring air was cool. He shivered.

They were approaching another bridge. There was a cement walkway underneath it, and a small fire burning in a half-barrel with some people standing near the fire to keep warm. George tried to push away from the people, to drift by unnoticed on the opposite side of the stream; but his legs were getting weak, and he was having difficulty keeping his dad and himself afloat.

Chapter 2

HELP ARRIVES

A woman on the walkway spotted the two people in the water and waved her hands at them. One of the men with her slipped into the waist-deep stream to grab him and his dad. He lifted George and his dad up a little by their shirt collars and floated them to the other side of the bridge.

He was strong and handed his dad up to another man and the women standing on the walkway under the bridge with one arm. Then he lifted George up into his arms and walked silently out of the cold stream. Under the bridge, the other man set his dad down on a small log while the woman tried to warm him by the fire. The man in the stream sat George down on another small log near the fire to warm him too.

"Boy, can you talk?" asked the man who had pulled them from the stream.

"Ah, yes sir," he answered, quietly shivering, his teeth chattering.

"Who are ya and who's he? Why are you in the water, boy? It's cold, you shouldn't be in there, boy," he whispered, pointing at the stream.

"He's my dad. I need to get help; he won't wake up. There were these men in black suits and a black car that was following us and my dad collapsed. I had to get away with him. To somewhere safe," George said as cryptically as he could, his voice still quivering from the cold.

"You could have left him and got yourself somewhere safe. I mean if he's, ya know, already unconscious and all. No harm in that, boy," the man whispered, waving his hand toward George's dad.

"No, sir, you don't sacrifice someone else to save yourself. You both get out together, cause you wouldn't ever want to be that other person. If the people around you can't count on you, well then," George replied shaking his head, worried about his dad.

The man stopped George mid-thought and pointed. His dad drew a long breath and raised his head. Opening his eyes, he smiled weakly. The woman was holding a glowing yellow sphere over his dad's head. George's mouth dropped open. The first man nodded and the second man slid open a rust-stained, white steel door in the center of the walkway under the bridge. The two men carried George's dad inside, while the women helped George up from the log. She led him inside, through a narrow mossy tunnel, into a dimly lit room about the size of a classroom at school. She helped George sit down on one of the musty-smelling brown cots in the corner of the room.

With George resting, the women switched places with one of the men and walked over to a small table with a silver box sitting on it. Softly, she moved her hand over the box, touching the different colored panels. The lid slide open, and she lifted out a small scanner like device with glowing green lights. The woman now looked like a doctor as she came toward them; first, she knelt down in front of George to make sure he was alright.

"Please ma'am, my dad is worse off than I am, please help him," he said, waving his hand and blocking her. He motioned toward his dad on the next cot.

She stood up and stepped over to the second cot to help his dad. In the dim light behind her, George could now see the face of the man who had pulled them from the stream. Still shaking from the cold, George fell forward and then backward on the wobbly cot as he tried to stand up and reach out for Max! Max rushed forward and caught George in his arms as he stumbled.

"Max, how did you get here?" George stammered, his teeth still chattering from the cold as a pool of water spread across the floor from his dripping clothes.

"You called," Max replied and smiled warmly, sliding an old musty brown blanket over George's shoulders.

He did not remember getting an answer when he had concentrated on contacting Max. Yet here he was.

"You're not a Viceroy, but I'm sure you must have been. It's the only way you could have heard me," George whispered his arms wrapped around Max.

Max lifted the musty brown blanket back up over George's shoulders. "Oh, I don't think so, George. We are connected, that's all. Besides, can you really see me living with all those rules and regulations?" Max replied with a smile.

He helped George over to an electric heater near another wall of the room and sat him down on another old and tattered, musty green cot. A puff of dust rose from the cot as he sat down.

"Rest now, George. It is safe here," Max whispered kindly.

It was all he heard before falling asleep under the musty brown blanket. A thin shaft of sunlight woke him in the morning. His dad was standing off to one side of the small room with three new people surrounding him. There was a faint yellow glow around them. His dad looked well again. Max was sitting on the floor next to George's cot staring at George's dad too. Without turning his head, Max handed George a ration pack as George lifted his head.

"Eat, it's your breakfast," Max whispered.

"What are they saying, Max?" he asked quietly.

"The guys in the black suits are really bad. They were sent here to, oh no, by who? No, that can't be right?" Max said, talking to himself more than to George. His words faded as he stood up and walked over to the circle. George's dad lifted his arm up and welcomed him into the circle of yellow light.

"No, it's not a healing circle, it's a link. They're in a link, talking to someone," George said, talking aloud to himself like Max.

George slit open the ration and took a bite. It was stale, yet he was hungry. He bit off another bite as he looked around the small room. Aside from the people in the link, the room was nearly empty. A few more old tattered green cots were stacked over in one corner with some ration packs on the floor nearby. The walls were a dirty whitewash color that seemed to glow, emitting a soft white light. He smiled and thought Emily would enjoy talking with the glowing fungi. However, without her here, it was probably not wise to touch it as he didn't know how to ask it not to nibble on him. Emily had such a way with creatures. He really missed her.

The fan in the electric heater hummed softly as he drifted off to sleep again for a few more hours. The sounds of shuffling feet woke him up. In a haze, he stared at the walls looking for a door. His dad walked up next to him and reached down nudging George's shoulder to see if he was still sleeping. Startled, George twisted, flipping the old cot over and landing hard on the floor with a loud thud.

"Ugh."

"George, it's OK, it's Dad," his dad said, kneeling down to help him up.

"Dad, you're OK?" George said, grabbing onto his dad's arm.

"Yes, George, you did well. They would have hurt us if you hadn't gotten us to safety," he said, lifting his son from the floor with one arm and wrapping his other arm over his shoulder as they stood up together. "We can leave now. It is safe again," he whispered, hugging his son.

"Where will we go? Where's mom? Is she safe? Did they get her?" George asked, worried about his mom.

"Slow down, George. Your mom is safe, and I would be willing to bet she's going to be making a pie for us," he said, chuckling, trying to distract George from worrying.

"Funny how that is, her making pies when there's trouble. Does that mean, Pete's grandfather is coming, like when Mrs. Petrosky makes a pie and he appears?" George asked.

"George, you think too much; however, yes, they are all coming," his dad replied laughing, also knowing that pies were the cosmic signal that company would be coming.

They walked up to Max in the small room, and his dad shook his hand.

"Thank you, sir," his dad said formally, dipping his head in respect.

George may not have understood who and what Max really was or what his place in the universe was; but his dad did, and he was happy Max was looking out for his son. George wanted to ask Max to dinner; however, he knew Pete's grandfather and Max did not exactly see eye to eye so asking him to dinner was out of the question. Instead, he reached out to shake Max's hand. Max grabbed George and hugged him like a son.

"Now you know where to come if there is danger again. Keep your eyes open, George; they have found us and they do not give up so easily. Remember 'trust only those that bind you.' Never forget," Max whispered, repeating George's father's words from the summer before.

Then he released George from his bear hug, placing his feet back on the ground!

"Will we see you again?" George asked.

"Perhaps; I will stay near enough for you to call. To answer your question from Friday, you can call, and you hide your thoughts well when you focus and are not distracted," Max replied, smiling.

George's dad waved for George to follow him out the small tunnel they had entered two evenings before. He crouched down and followed his dad out onto the little cement walkway under the bridge. Two new men he had not seen inside the little room were standing on the walkway under the bridge when they emerged. George knew instantly they were CORE officers simply by how they stood and acted.

"Sir, this way, sir," the lead CORE officer said to Mr. Hawkins.

It was late afternoon, and the bright sun sparkled across the water as the stream flowed under the bridge. One man walked in front of George's dad and one walked behind George as they climbed the steep stream bank up to the road.

There was a beige four-door car waiting for them as they stepped out of the brush onto the side of the road. The lead man opened the rear door, and George's dad slipped into the backseat. George followed his dad inside, and the second man sat next to George. The first man sat in the front seat. The doors closed, and the car pulled out slowly onto the road, crossing over the bridge.

He looked up to see what street they were on and glanced in the rearview mirror. The driver was Frank! He wanted to yell out, but he remained quiet, although not calm. His dad smiled. Oddly, Frank drove right to their house on Lily Street. George felt uneasy and started to fidget in his seat as Frank pulled into their driveway and parked the car.

"It will be OK, George. It's safe again," his dad whispered, patting his son on his shoulder.

Two car doors opened and the two CORE officers stepped out first and looked around. They nodded and George's dad opened his door and got out. For a brief moment, George and Frank were alone in the car. He started to speak, but Frank spun around and raised his hand. A small yellow sphere glowed over his palm, he high-fived his brother; and George joined his brother's link.

"Keep it until tonight. We'll talk then," his brother signed.

George nodded and slid out of the car to join his dad as they walked to the front steps of their house together.

"Everything OK, George?" his dad whispered, sliding his arm over his shoulder.

"I'm good, Dad. It's all good," George whispered worriedly from the front steps of their house, watching Frank back out of the driveway.

They walked across the porch and entered the house as Frank drove down the street. George's mom was waiting inside the front door. She hugged the stuffin' out of George and his dad the minute they were inside.

"George, I am so proud of you, you are so brave," she said, gushing on and on, hugging and kissing both of them.

"Mom, Mom—air, I need air!" George said, struggling to free himself from his mother's grasp. "Besides, I'm kinda hungry, Mom," he said in his hungriest way.

Oh, yes, well, dinner is nearly ready," she said, releasing them from her grasp.

After all, he was almost fifteen now, and the whole gushing mom thing in front of other people was embarrassing, to say the least.

"Up the stairs with both of you, now. You both need to get changed out of those dirty clothes. They smell like musty old rags," she said, smiling, walking down the hallway, and disappearing into the kitchen.

George hurried up the front stairs to get changed while his dad talked with the two CORE officers a few minutes longer before he went up the front stairs too. Their escape had been a lot to deal with, and George was still a little shaken. Losing his dad to something he didn't understand— to people in black suits—had never even crossed his mind. He stopped his dad as he walked out of the bathroom.

"Dad, Max said they can find us now. I'm worried about Mom," George started to say; however, his dad raised his hand, stopping him in the middle of his sentence.

"George, your mom will be fine. It's you we are all worried about," he whispered. "There will be secret guards for her. However, they will stay hidden so she doesn't get upset. Now don't say anything about the guards to your mom. She will be safe," he said, holding his son's shoulder to help calm the fear rising in his mind.

His father strength had returned. George felt better and went into his bedroom to change. He dropped his dirty clothes in a heap in the middle of the floor and pulled clean clothes from his drawer. Quickly, he left his room, meeting his dad on the back stairs. His house had two sets of stairs. He had not thought about it until he had gotten older and slept over at a friend's house for a party. They only had one staircase. How odd, George had thought, to have only one set of stairs.

George and his dad walked down the back stairs and turned the corner into the kitchen. Suddenly, they stopped, staring in disbelief! There was a feast fit for a king laid out over the kitchen table and countertops with real mashed potatoes, green beans, carrots, two salads, and fresh steaming rolls.

"Mom, what army did you cook for?" George asked, sitting down in his regular seat. His mom smiled.

"It's a regular Sunday dinner, nothing special," she replied, winking.

"Sunday, no Mom, it's Saturday!" George said, franticly looking at his dad as his mom moved over to the oven to get the roast off the top of the stove.

"No. It's Sunday, George. You and I slept all of Saturday. We expended a lot of energy in our escape. Don't worry your mother with the details now," he said, nodding toward his mom.

George's translation of his dad's comment; 'Don't tell your mom all the details. She'll be even more worried than she is now, and she cooked a huge dinner for the three of us. If we want to get out of the house in the morning, I should not say too much.' Yes, that sounded about right to him.

His mom returned to the table with a five-pound roast and enough carrots and green beans to feed an entire hungry soccer team.

"I'm so happy you are both alright. I wish Frank was here and not so far away at school," she said, as she passed George the rolls.

His dad rolled his eyes at George.

"Ya, Mom, I wish he could be here too," he replied, starring at his dad. His dad smiled.

Dinner continued with George almost answering the questions his mom asked and his dad definitely dodging every question she asked.

"I made pies for dessert," she said, smiling as George cleared the dinner plates.

"Are we having company, Mom?" George asked, chuckling.

"George, I make pies when we don't have company" she said, clearing more dishes off the table.

George glanced at his dad and they shook their heads. If she made pies, they would be having company; the pie-eating kind of company. The kind of company that say, 'Oh, I was in your solar system and thought I'd stop by for pie,' kind of company. He had always thought that pies were really some sort of coded message sent between moms across the galaxy in times of trouble.

They walked into the living room as his mom set three pies on the kitchen table to cut. His dad turned and looked George directly in the eyes.

"George, you can't ride the bus for the rest of the school year. There will be a driver for you from now on and security in your school. You are being allowed to keep your schedule until the end of this school year. However, you need to be aware of your surroundings at all times," his dad said very seriously, Viceroy like. Kinda spooky.

"Yes, sir," he said, replying by instinct.

A knock on the door brought his mom out of the kitchen with the flowered tray of pies and plates before George could ask why. It was Pete's grandfather, and his mom, and dad.

"Great, this is really not good if they are all here," George muttered.

However, he had spoken too soon. Behind them was Andy! George nearly fell over.

"Now, this must be really, really bad if they flew Andy up from Brazil, one month early, in less than one day!" George thought to himself.

Pete's mom hugged the stuffin' out of George. Mr. Petrosky and Mr. Petrosky senior only shook his hand.

"Pie?" Mr. Petrosky senior said, with surprise in his voice, as he glanced at George's mom.

"I'll get some more plates," his mom said, as she and Mrs. Petrosky slipped into the kitchen.

"Andy, what are you doing here?" George asked. His mouth was still hanging open.

"Apparently, I am enrolling in your high school for the last month of school. I have been a troublemaker at my high school and need to be watched more closely," he said with a bit of sarcasm in his voice, shrugging his shoulders. "So what did you do, George? How bad was it?" he added, rolling his eyes.

They shook hands, and George shook his head. "Later," he whispered, starring at Pete's grandfather.

The moms returned with more plates before he could say anymore. Mrs. Petrosky commented on how much she liked the flowered dishes as the plates were set on the dining room table, and everyone sat to eat the pies. All the while, they only talked about the spring weather. When the pies were nearly gone and everyone was full, the moms carried the dishes into the kitchen and grandfather, Mr. Petrosky senior, called George and Andy over to the living room couch. George and Pete's dads moved closer together, concentrating on something in the dining room.

"They're blocking our conversation for us, George," Andy signed, reading their lips.

Grandfather sat on the couch, and the boys sprawled out on the floor with the green and yellow pillows from the couch, propping themselves up and leaning in toward him.

"George, the men in the black suits are very bad people. Do you and Andy remember last summer and the darkness you felt on the warship on Indus station?" His voice was warm and yet serious.

"Yes, of course, sir," George replied, shaking off the bad feeling.

"I don't think we will ever forget, sir," Andy added, nodding in agreement.

"The men in the black suits are connected to that evil. They have found you and your families. For now, your team and your families will be protected so you can all finish your school term on Earth," he said, his voice was low and calm.

George and Andy wondered why it was so important for them to finish the school year; however, they didn't ask. Instead, George pressed for a bigger answer.

"What about this summer and next year, Sir?" George asked.

"The Galactic council has not yet made that decision. We'll see," he said. He was serious now, not the warm and caring grandfather- instead, more of a seasoned veteran, a Senior Viceroy, giving out information and issuing commands.

"The two of you must not be separated for the rest of your time here on Earth or during your rotation. Not even for a minute," he said firmly.

"But, what if?" George started to say.

"No!" the Senior Viceroy said, cutting George off.

His face was tense, and his voice had changed faster than Pete, Frank, and Toma's. This was serious business and the boys had to respect this order.

"Yes, sir," they said, lowering their heads in respect.

"Not even for a minute. You are only safe together. I warn you now. If you break this rule, the Galactic council will know; and they will act swiftly to protect your team and your families. You will not like their decision or the isolation they will put you in for your protection. You are only here because of Max. He spoke to the Galactic council on your behalf. Do not betray his trust in you," he said, ominously staring at the boys.

"Yes, sir, we will not betray his trust, sir," they answered together. "Or yours," they whispered under their breath.

They thought it would take more than Max's word to convince the Galactic council to let them stay. It would take the Senior Viceroy speaking on their behalf. Andy and George knew they had to keep their word and show that they could be trusted.

"I know you will do your best. Off you go now, it's getting late," Grandfather said, his voice softening as he, and the boys stood up. He motioned them towards the front stairs. They left him, walked slowly over to the front stairs to go up and stopped. Andy was again facing the dining room. George leaned over and picked up Andy's red suitcase.

"So, what are they talking about?" he whispered.

"Us, and they are worried about whether or not they can protect us on Earth. The Galactic council wants us to leave immediately; and the Senior Viceroy, I mean Grandfather, argued against them taking us away. There is a destiny or prophecy or something they keep mentioning, and then they refer to our team. There is something about Pete, Frank, and Toma's teams too. They are too cryptic, George, I can't make sense of it," Andy whispered.

"Don't think about the words, Andy, simply repeat them," George whispered.

"The evil entity is strong and growing again. It is close and bold, stronger than the Zeleion. The Zeleion are running from the evil entity that's why the Zeleion attacked Jupiter station. They're afraid and wanted the evil entity to go after us instead of them. The Galactic council wants to send us away, not to Jupiter station for our third rotation. Pete's grandfather keeps saying no, he's repeating a line from the prophecy. It's 'hide not in a place of hiding, hide instead in the open, among friends.' What the heck does that mean?" Andy whispered.

"Boys, it's late," George's mother said.

George and Andy nearly jumped out of their clothes as Mrs. Hawkins came around the corner from the kitchen. They gasped, trying to stop their hearts from racing.

"Ah, yes Mom, we're on our way up now. Goodnight, Mom," George said, hugging his mom.

"Goodnight, Mrs. Hawkins," Andy said as they crept up the front stairs in stealth mode.

They rounded the top step, and George spoke up. "Frank was here; he drove the car that picked us up. I'd have given you his room to sleep in, but we promised Grandfather," he said, shrugging his shoulders and pointing to Frank's bedroom. They entered George's room and the smell from his musty clothes filled the air.

"Man, what died in here?" Andy asked, backing up into the hallway.

"Oh, it's just my clothes from under the bridge," he replied laughing, picking them up and carrying them to the laundry chute in the hallway.

He came back, and Andy was fanning the room with the door. George pulled a sleeping bag out of his closet and tossed it into the center of the room as Andy fanned the door some more.

"Don't worry about the sleeping bag. It's OK, George, so what really happened? I mean, I didn't fly up here on the grandfather energy express just to say 'hi,' if you know what I mean," Andy asked.

"What?" George asked as he turned around, pulling the shade closed on his window.

Andy closed the door, and they sat down on the floor.

"Well, Max isn't the only one who can use the raw energy of the universe and transport across space," Andy said seriously.

"What? What are you talking about? I figured Grandfather sent a spaceship or something for you," George replied, surprised.

"No, George, you don't understand. One minute, I was in my room at home doing homework on a Saturday night, and the next, Grandfather appeared outside our front door. He spoke with my parents, and then they came to my room, and I disappeared with Grandfather. I reappeared in Pete's mom and dad's house with Grandfather," Andy said, still amazed as he said the words.

"We need to learn how to use the raw energy of the universe, Andy," George replied, nodding thoughtfully.

"I don't know, George. It really seemed to weaken him," Andy replied, shaking his head. "So tell me. What did you do? Really, it had to be bad," he pressed, changing the topic.

George flipped his hand over, and the small yellow sphere Frank gave him reappeared.

"You're in a link? With who?" Andy asked, his mouth hanging open.

"Frank. He gave it to me before he left today," he answered.

Andy held his hand over George's, joining the link. They concentrated hard, calling out to Frank and Pete and Toma. They found them, and their link became stronger.

"Report," was Pete's only word.

George relayed the events of the last two days to Pete, Frank, Toma, and Andy. Then Andy repeated George and Pete's parents' conversations.

"What is the prophecy, sirs? What is our destiny? Why is everyone trying to protect us?" George asked, wanting answers.

"And the whole 'traveling- with- the- raw- energy-of-the- universe' thing? What's with that? It really seemed to weaken grandfather," Andy added, wanting more explanation.

"I cannot say what your destiny is; it is not for me to answer, but for you to discover," Pete replied with Grandfather's words that had been said to him.

"It is late now, you both will need your rest," Frank added kindly.

"But," George said, trying to stop them, to get any kind of answers.

"It's late," Toma repeated firmly.

"Yes, sir," George and Andy mumbled.

They knew they could push Pete and Frank a little; however, Toma was seriously serious and would not budge. No arguments allowed. Rachael appeared in the link and walked George and Andy out. George lay down on his bed, and Andy grabbed one of George's pillows for the sleeping bag on the floor.

"We need Emily," George said.

Andy nodded.

"We need to find out about the prophecy before it is hidden from us," George added, and they drifted off to sleep.

"You know they will find out about the prophecy very soon," Frank thought through their link as Rachael had only taken George and Andy out.

"Why didn't you tell them about the prophecy?" Toma asked.

"Like both of you, I took the same oath," Pete replied and sighed, worried about their young team of cadets.

"I had hoped you had found a way around our oath," Frank said.

Pete shook his head. "No, not yet; however, for now we need to warn the Senior Viceroys," Pete added.

"I don't know why we should be worried. They have no way of getting to the real prophecy, only altered copies," Toma said plainly.

"And six 2nd rotation cadets can't fly three Thorean galaxy class starships halfway across the galaxy to save an entire Thorean station, cadets, officers and Viceroys?" Pete replied, shaking his head.

"Good point. They will find out and they will know the copy is a fake. I don't know how, but I agree, they will know," Toma said, suddenly worried what they might do if they discovered it was a fake.

"Then they will figure out a way to read the original prophecy," Frank added, shaking his head.

"And they will know their destiny," Pete said somberly.

"Are they the ones written about in the prophecy?" Toma asked.

"Sure looks that way from what I know of the prophecy," Pete said.

"Now what do we do?" Frank asked.

"Warn our fathers that they know about the prophecy. Then we watch, we keep them safe and guide them as best we can," Pete replied, and Rachael ended the link.

Chapter 3

THE PROPHECY

The alarm clock was buzzing as George reached for the snooze button. Andy hit it and flopped back down on the floor, groaning. Monday morning had come early, and George and Andy really didn't want to get up. It had been a late night Sunday; and they wanted to sleep in, if only for a few more minutes.

"George, Andy, are you getting up or sleeping all day?" George's mom called up the back stairs.

"Coming, Mom!" George yelled as they got up and dressed.

They ran down the back stairs to the kitchen, hitting every other step as they landed in the first floor hallway and bolted through the kitchen doorway.

"You sound like a herd of wild elephants, boys," George's mom said, raising her eyebrow and staring at the boys as they slid across the kitchen floor, plopping onto the green chairs around the kitchen table. In front of them sat heaping bowls of brown cereal.

"Just like home, and just as delicious," Andy grinned.

George smiled, taking his first bite.

"I packed lunches for both of you," she said, setting two brown paper bags on the kitchen table. "I'll pick up a new backpack and some more clothes for you, Andy, on my way home today," she added.

"Ah, thank you, Mrs. Hawkins, that would be great," Andy answered, gobbling down his cereal.

He ate it as fast as he could because he really didn't like it. They finished quickly and carried their dishes to the kitchen sink.

"You both need to get going, your driver will be waiting," she said kindly, hiding her worry.

They walked back to the table, gulped down the rest of their milk and hurried to get the glasses to the sink. George's mom hugged each of them as they grabbed their brown bag lunches and headed for the front door. As planned, a driver was waiting for them in the driveway.

"We need Emily," George signed, closing his car door.

It was a beige four-door car, like the one Frank had picked them up in. Slowly, the car backed out onto Lily Street and headed for school. It was a short ride to George's school. In Brazil Andy had been home schooled. For high school, he was sent away to a private boarding school, going home only on the weekends.

Andy was stunned when they arrived at the drop-off circle in front of the high school. He thought the high school was huge. It seemed odd, being in such a large public school with twenty- five hundred other students coming and going. To Andy the noise in the hallways was nearly deafening.

George dragged Andy through the hallways as Andy stared at all of the students, hurrying from their lockers to their first-hour classrooms. Somehow, Andy's new locker was right next to George's locker. The school principal met them at George's locker and introduced Andy to his new school from the hallway, and then he disappeared into the crowd of students going to their first-hour class.

Andy borrowed a notebook and pencil from George, and they left for their first-hour class. Andy was introduced as George's cousin from Brazil and that he would be with them for the remainder of the school year. He was in every class George was in. They were inseparable.

By noon, Andy was ready for a break. With a crowd of students right behind them, they pushed open the double doors and walked into the cafeteria. Andy spun around and, like salmon swimming upstream, pushed his way out of the cafeteria, leaving the room as fast as he could. He ran into the lockers across the hallway, gasping for fresh air.

"What's wrong?" George asked, following Andy into the hallway.

"How can you eat in there? It's so loud, and there's food everywhere. It stinks!" Andy said, crinkling his face as he leaned back on the lockers, gasping for more air.

"Oh, you get used to it after a while. I can't even smell it anymore," George said, joking.

"We need to go somewhere else. Does your school have any student computer internet access? Do you have a library or computer lab we can use at lunch? Anything but go back in there?" Andy asked, changing the subject and pretending to beg.

"OK, but we're not going to the library. Too many eyes and ears, I have a better place," George replied, grinning.

Hurrying through the hallway, past the school office, they ran up the stairs to the second floor. George's public high school looked like any other public high school across the country. There were two floors of classrooms—all tiled in creams, beiges and the occasional green, red or blue tiles. Nearly every inch of hallway was covered with lockers. The floor plan was one addition after the next, in seemingly random order. The newer sections had whiteboards and a few of the older classrooms, not yet renovated, had blackboards. The gymnasiums were huge. George's high school also had a huge swimming complex and auditorium. He had used a map his first week in high school to find all of his classes. Now, as a sophomore, it seemed so easy.

George stopped in the middle of the second floor hallway and opened a small door that Andy was sure was a janitor's closet. They entered a small musty room with water dripping into a rust- stained white utility sink. Some mops and buckets leaned on one wall, and a small shelf filled with paper towels was on the other wall.

"Yes, much better, a closet with a leaky sink!" Andy said, shaking his head.

George only smiled. On the wall, opposite the hallway door was a battered brown door. George twisted the handle. Click! He walked through it into a small classroom filled with old desks, two worn brown leather couches, and large wooden shelves held to the wall by the shear mass of papers stacked on the shelves.

Four older computers, a printer, and a scanner sat on two wooden desks in the center of the room. The wires weaving in and out amongst the stacks of papers reminded George of the Cadet Sector Commanders office on Jupiter station. A large flat board lay against another wall. It was covered with pictures and colored notes. The other walls were covered with newsprint and banners of every kind. A wall of windows covered the third wall; however, it was nearly obscured with posters and banners taped to the glass.

"Welcome to the newspaper and yearbook office," George said to Andy as he stepped through the second door.

"Andy, everybody, everybody, Andy," George said, introducing him with his arm held out to half a dozen or so people in the room.

"Hey," everyone replied, looking up for only a moment then returning to his or her work.

"Hey," Andy replied. "And this place is less crowded than the library and the computer lab? How do you figure?" Andy asked, shaking his head again.

"It may be crowded, but it has one thing the library and computer lab doesn't have," George said, teasingly as he led Andy into the room.

"And that is what, space?" Andy replied, frowning.

"No. Unsupervised access of the internet," George replied and dipped his head toward an empty computer terminal.

Andy smiled ghoulishly and sat down at an empty computer. His hands flew across the keyboard as he opened window after window. He searched the web and downloaded a few programs Emily had taught him. George followed his keystrokes.

"Emily?" George asked, wondering how Andy knew about the freeware software.

"Oh, ya. I don't think I could have figured this out without her," Andy whispered.

In a few minutes, they were connected. Andy had routed himself through multiple servers and ended up at Emily's computer's back door. If she was online, the door would open. If not, he would leave her computer a path to follow.

Andy wrote a short cryptic note. "Must talk. Need prophecy notes for new school assignment. Access local solar network. Highest priority. TTFN G&A."

"Was she in?" George whispered.

"No, but the message is sent," Andy replied.

"When will the reply come?" George pressed.

"Knowing Emily, in a few minutes; I think she is hardwired you know," Andy said, chuckling.

Not a minute passed before the computer beeped.

"That's for us," Andy whispered, taking a bite of his sandwich. "Emily doesn't use e-mail, only flash. It can't be traced, and it's like having a conversation without having to talk," he said cryptically.

Andy slid off the chair, and George sat down.

"I hope you have been practicing—Emily's fast," Andy added, chuckling.

"I've been practicing," George replied as his hands also flew across the keys.

Andy's mouth dropped open; George had been practicing. In fifteen minutes, Emily knew what had happened and what was needed. George turned to Andy to see if there was anything else to add.

Beeeep.

Emily was gone.

"What happened? When do we contact her again?" George asked, staring at the blank computer screen.

"Someone must have found her or us. The beep is Emily's warning device. Look in your flash memory, she would put a note there if she was traced," Andy answered confidently.

"My what?" he asked.

"Flash, George, flash."

Andy switched seats with George and opened what looked like a public folder on the internet in the public domain. It said, "G&A 1WK U Sam ADR E."

"Cryptic and totally undecipherable," George muttered over Andy's shoulder.

Andy shook his head. "OK, I'll make a deal with you, I'll decipher Emily and you decipher Pete, Frank and Toma," he grinned, thinking he was getting the better of the deal.

"Agreed," George replied, thinking he was getting the better of the deal.

"It says, 'George and Andy, 1 week, use same address, Emily.' Now we wait," Andy said, deleting the file folder.

"No, I think we have some work to do too. But first we have to get back to class," George said, glancing up at the small wall clock.

The school bell rang as he finished his sentence and half a dozen students rushed for the brown door. Through the janitor's closet, they hurried, pouring out into the second floor hallway.

"Do the teachers know about this place?" Andy asked as they rushed though the upstairs hallway, without actually running, to their fifth period class.

"Oh, they know. They just don't know about the internet connection," George whispered. "Kind of a student secret, no one tells this one. Only the yearbook team and newspaper team know. They pass it down from class to class. Very hush, hush, no one wants to lose the privilege for the next year's team," he added, leaping down the last few stairs to the first floor. Andy slid down the railing and ended up next to George.

"Man, in my school, we would be in so much trouble if the teachers found out," Andy said quietly.

"Here too, Andy, but it's worth the risk. No one messes with the privilege. The two groups see to that," George replied as they slipped into their fifth hour class before the second bell rang.

The afternoon passed quickly and soon the last class bell rang. Andy's and George's lockers closed nearly simultaneously, the force shook the other lockers in the row. Through the hallway they hurried to their star homeroom to wait for dismissal. There was no real reason for a five-minute homeroom class at the end of the day other than for the teachers to get a head count at the end of the day to see if anyone had skipped out that day.

"One day down, twenty-one more to go," Andy whispered, sliding into the desk next to George. However, George didn't laugh or look up. It looked like he was lost in thought. Two bells and the students were released. Andy nudged George.

"Where are you, George?" he asked; but George didn't answer.

The classroom emptied as Andy tried to lift George to his feet. The driver would be waiting for them when they left the school building. Andy needed George back from wherever he was so they could get to the waiting car without the driver knowing something was suddenly going wrong on the first day they were left alone.

Andy was a bit afraid of the Galactic council and what they might do if anything went wrong—well, more wrong than it already had this last weekend. In desperation, Andy made a small yellowish-reddish sphere—a link, not his first; but wobbly all the same. He carefully held George's hand out over his. The connection was made. Andy's mind was suddenly joined into a new link. George's mind was racing as if he was trying to calculate a difficult math problem all in his head.

However, it wasn't a problem at all, and Andy knew it. George was fighting against a stealthy invader's mind link. It was like the year before, when they had been attacked on the transport ship. Andy couldn't see the attacker, but he could sense her. In his mind's eye, Andy shared his energy and strength with George. It was the edge George needed to fight back and stop the mind invader.

Andy created a large, red energy sphere and gave it to George in their link. George sent the red energy sphere zinging through the link at the invader with Andy's help. It was a smaller version of one of Andy's full-sized blazing red spheres. It worked! The invader was caught off guard! The link broke suddenly, and the invader was gone.

George snapped his head backward and forward. Finally, he looked up, holding his head between his hands. Andy shook his head.

"George, are you back?" Andy whispered, shaking George's shoulder carefully as his head was also hurting from the link suddenly breaking.

"What's going on? What was that glowing red sphere?" George asked, staring at Andy, still a little stunned as he rubbed his head.

"There was an invader in a link with you, George. The red energy sphere I gave you was real, and it broke the invader's stealthy mind link when you sent it through the link," Andy whispered cryptically.

George's mouth dropped open. "What do you mean 'real,' Andy?" he said, staring at Andy as if it had been a dream.

"It was real, George. I don't know what kind of link it was, but it wasn't a dream. It was a real mind link, and the red energy sphere I gave you was real too," Andy said seriously.

"It was as if we were on the Thorean ship again; like last year," George said a little puzzled.

"Yes. When you were attacked, the energy sent through the link had to be dissipated or we would have been destroyed. George, did you try and make a link with someone?" Andy asked, looking at George for an answer.

"No, someone slipped into my mind in stealth mode. It was like the attack on the Calshene cadet station. Just like Toma and Pete had said, very strong minds searching. Now someone has found us again," he said, shaking his head. "What time is it, Andy?" he asked suddenly, looking around at the empty classroom.

"The second bell rang ten minutes ago. Do you know who or what it was?" Andy asked.

George shook his head, still trying to understand what had happened.

"No, but I think whoever she was, she was trying to capture my mind—hard to tell. I need to think about it," George replied, still fuzzy.

They heard footsteps, echoing through the hallway. Each step getting louder, the closer the person got to them.

"The driver!" they whispered simultaneously.

In a moment of desperation, George pulled his three-ring history binder from his backpack and threw it high into the air, barely missing the hanging florescent lights. It was an immense three-ring binder and had been protected at all costs through the entire year. His history teacher graded their binders and their ability to keep them neat and orderly. Everything had to be in exactly the right order and under the correct heading. In George's binder, every paper was in exactly the right place and nothing was wrinkled.

The thought of its destruction terrified George, but the fear of what the Galactic council would do to them was worse. The binder hit the classroom floor on its edge and burst wide open, flinging the history notes across the room. They dropped to their knees, chasing after the pages.

"Don't crumple any pages! Be careful!" George yelled loud enough to be heard out in the hallway.

"Do you remember the order they go in?" Andy asked frantically.

"I think so, try and pick them up in neat clumps if you can. Bend nothing!" he answered as the driver entered the classroom.

George and Andy looked up. The driver was shaking his head.

"We have almost all the pages, sir. Please don't step on anything. Please, sir," he pleaded, returning to the pages scattered across the floor.

Soon all the pages were gathered up. George cradled the papers, trying not to bend any pages, as Andy picked up the rest of their books; and they walked to the door with their driver. He looked sad.

"It'll be OK, George. Is there anyone who will lend us their notebook?" Andy said, trying to hide the smile on his face and console George.

They had made it, George's quick thinking had the driver on a different track, and he had no idea why they were really late. The morning driver was also the afternoon driver. When the doors of the car closed, he looked into the rear view mirror.

"Will you always be our driver, sir?" George asked, carefully straightening his pages.

"Yes, Mr. Hawkins, I will. You are to leave with no one else. Is that understood, gentlemen?" he said firmly.

"Yes, sir," they chorused.

They rode through the streets in silence to George's house, all the while thinking of nothing except the history binder, for fear the driver could read their thoughts. The driver stopped in George's driveway and spun around before they got out.

"Don't worry, I'm sure you will be able to reassemble your history binder in time," the officer said, trying to console the boys.

"Thank you, sir," George replied kindly, and they raced across the front lawn and up into George's house.

"Hi, Mom!" George yelled.

"Hi, Mrs. Hawkins!" Andy yelled as they raced up the front stairs and into George's room, closing the door behind them.

"He was reading our minds," Andy said, catching his breath as he leaned on the desk.

"Well, duh," George replied and raised his eyebrow.

He set his notebook down on his desk and pulled down the window shade in his bedroom.

"That was close, George. Excellent. Fast thinking with the binder. I can't believe you sacrificed it," Andy said in awe. "So, who linked with you, George; or maybe the better question is, how did they do it?" Andy pressed.

"I don't know. One minute, we were walking down the hallway, and the next, I remember seeing you in the empty classroom. It was like a dream, Andy," George replied and paused. "We hurt someone bad, didn't we?" George asked, yet he sounded oddly concerned, considering whomever they hurt was trying to hurt him.

"I don't know for sure. I don't think it was enough energy to do any real damage. But I'm sure whoever it was, she will have one nasty headache," Andy said, grinning and rubbing his own head. "The invader wasn't expecting a red energy sphere from you, that's for sure," he added, chuckling.

"We need to talk with Max," George whispered, sitting down on his bed and resting his head in his hands.

"George, don't you mean Pete or Frank or Toma or your dad?" Andy said, correcting George and frowning as he sat on the desk chair.

"No, I think Pete and the others are bound to protect us, and they would think the mind invasion was really bad. Which, of course, it is; but they will act to protect us when what we need is information," George said, trying to reason his way around doing the right thing.

"So, do you know where Max is?" Andy asked concerned George was not making a good decision.

"Yes, Dad and I were there Friday and Saturday night," he said, starting to make a plan.

"There are guards outside, George, and I don't think they are regular guards either. It's not just the CORE officer in the car. So that means we would have to sneak out tonight and ditch the officers and the guards? They are going to know, George," Andy said, questioning the wisdom of his strategy and wondering if the Galactic council would understand.

"We are going to call Max and bring him here. I have no intention of breaking our word to the Galactic council. We need a pie!" George said, plotting with a devious grin on his face.

"Does that really work? I mean the whole make-a-pie-and-have-company thing?" Andy asked, skeptical.

"It's a cosmic signal, Andy. A cosmic signal." George whispered, his eyes wide as saucers. He walked to his bedroom door and opened it. "Hey, Mom, can we have a pie tonight to celebrate Andy's first day at school?" he yelled down the back stairs to the kitchen.

"Would you like apple or strawberry rhubarb pie, Andy?" his mom called back.

"I get a choice?" Andy answered, surprised. He had never got to choose his pie before. "Apple, please. Thank you, Mrs. Hawkins that would be great. Thanks," he yelled back.

George closed the door and walked over to the middle of the room to think.

"You get to pick the kind of pie you want?" Andy said, still in awe.

"Focus, Andy, it's a pie. We need Max," he said, spinning Andy around in the desk chair. George held out his hand and Andy held his hand over it—their link was strong. They started to focus and clear their minds. "Max we need you," they thought repeatedly.

An hour passed, and George's mom called up the back stairs again. "Dinner, boys."

They lowered their link and walked to the door.

"George, we need to stay connected in our link. I can't risk you getting ambushed by another stealthy mind invader and me not being able to help. Besides, the whole making-a-link thing is really hard," Andy whispered, as they walked down the back stairs.

"Good, cause I'm not sure I know how to stop the link without giving us one heck of a headache right now, and your weird yellow-reddish sphere link really hurt," George whispered, rubbing his hand.

George's dad was in the kitchen when the boys entered the kitchen.

"Hi, Dad," George said.

"Good evening, sir," Andy said as the boys sat down at the kitchen table to eat.

Andy sat in Frank's seat. George's mom smiled and got up from the table, hurrying to get a tissue from the downstairs bathroom.

"She misses Frank," George whispered.

"Oh, I can move," Andy offered and started to stand up when Mr. Hawkins motioned him down.

"No, stay where you are, Mary will be fine. So boys, your mom made a pie, who's coming over?" he asked; his voice was not dad-like, it was Viceroy-like.

"Max, sir," George replied formally.

His dad raised his eyebrow. "Sons?" he said firmly.

"You are bound to the Galactic council, sir. If we say anything, you have to tell the Galactic council. Max is not so bound, sir," George whispered.

"You are using a loophole—George, Andy. Be careful you do not cross the line. You must not use Max to get around the rules you don't like," he said, his words ominous and serious.

"Yes, sir, he is our friend first," George replied, yet he wondered if they were crossing the loophole line. He had not thought about crossing the line before they had called Max for help.

His mom was coming back; and his dad waved his hand at the boys, cutting off their conversation abruptly. Quickly, they all slid food onto their plates. The boys had food in their mouth by the time George's mom sat down at the table again.

"Good hot food, Mrs. Hawkins," Andy spoke between bites, gobbling down his homemade hamburger.

"Sorry, I don't mean to be so emotional," she said, sipping her iced tea.

"In my house people come and go from the dinner table all the time, Mrs. Hawkins. Besides I'm actually eating hot food, so it doesn't get any better than this," Andy said, trying to distract George's mom from thinking of Frank.

"Your mother made a pie, I see. We should have company more often," his dad said, adding to the distraction.

"Hump, I make pie when we don't have company," his mom replied.

George and his dad looked at each other, shook their heads, and laughed out loud.

"Honestly, you two," she said, scolding them.

He thought his mom was probably the only person in the galaxy that could scold his dad and get away with it. Dinner disappeared with George and Andy eating as much as they could so they couldn't answer any questions. Quietly, they cleared the plates.

His dad usually cleaned up the dishes and loaded the dishwasher. He thought if Mary went to the effort of cooking a homemade meal after working all day, then the least he could do was clean up after the meal was over. George thought it was part of what had kept them married for more than twenty-five years. They respected each other, George mused, walking into the living room.

"Where's Max?" Andy signed.

He was anxious. He wanted to believe in the cosmic power of pie; however, he had his doubts.

"Patience, Andy. You'll see, the pie won't fail," George said, smiling and leaned back on the couch.

His dad entered the dining room carrying plates, and his mom was right behind him with a tray of napkins, forks, and a steaming apple pie. The sweet smell filled the air in the room. She set the tray down on the table, and the door bell rang. George smiled. Andy's mouth dropped open.

"No way, man, no way," Andy signed as they stood up.

"I told you, it's the pie. It's a cosmic calling card," George whispered as his mom and dad went to the front door.

Max and Pete's dad were standing at the front door.

"Thought we would check on Andy and see how his first day went at the new school," Max said, entering the house.

"It's good to see you both. You are always welcome," George's mom said, hugging Max and Pete's dad. They entered the living room, and George and Andy stepped forward to shake their hands.

"Welcome, sir," George said.

"Pie?" was Max and Pete's dad's greeting.

"We'll need more plates," Mary said, disappearing into the kitchen.

"We don't have a lot of time boys, what's going on?" Max said seriously.

George's dad and Pete's dad turned their backs to the three of them, and Max held out his hand. The boys flipped their palms over, revealing their yellow-reddish sphere. Max stared at the unusual reddish-yellow sphere and then quickly joined their odd link.

"How did you make this link?" he asked, staring at the glowing sphere.

"I don't know, sir. I needed to help George so I just did it. We don't have Gus so we're kind of stuck on the whole breaking- the-link or walking-out-of-the-link part, but then I can't let him alone anyway. Not again, not now," Andy spoke only through the link.

"What happened today, George?" Max asked kindly.

George looked down. "Max, we don't mean to drag you into this; we are exploiting a loophole in our deal with Galactic council. You can back out. We're sorry; we shouldn't have called," George said sadly.

"Report, Cadet," Max said sternly, staring hard at the boys. Precious seconds were slipping by, and George and Pete's dads could only block their thoughts from the Galactic council for so long before they were discovered.

George and Andy spoke hurriedly though the link and told Max everything that had happened that day in what seemed like an instant.

"Keep your link for now, it will protect both of you," Max said, backing himself out of their link. Max touched Pete and George's dad's shoulders and nodded. They all sat down in the dining room as George's mom reappeared with more plates.

"Sorry for being so long. Martha called and wanted to know when you would be home." she said to Mr. Petrosky as she sat down and started cutting the apple pie. The apple pie disappeared in record time, and George's dad glanced at his mom and nodded.

"It's time for bed—George, Andy," Mom said. The boys stood up and collected the empty plates, carrying them and the pie tray into the kitchen. Andy spun around and saw Max, and Pete and George's dads make a link the minute the boys were out of the room. George's mom touched his dad and Max's shoulders and then stepped back.

"They made a link. Your mom's like Gus," Andy whispered and George nodded. "Max is going to tell them what we said," Andy whispered, worried.

"No, he won't. We need to trust Max, Andy. He trusts us," George whispered.

"Ya, I guess you're right. He did stand up for us with the Galactic council," Andy replied, nodding thoughtfully—yet he was worried.

George and Andy walked up the back stairs. They had to trust Max, yet in the back of his mind, George was sure they had crossed the loophole line.

Chapter 4

KNOWLEDGE

Morning came early on Andy's second day at George's house. They half expect a bolt of lightning to strike on their way to the car that morning.

"So the pie thing really works," Andy said, still amazed.

"Yes, it really works. It's cosmic," George said as they walked to the car in the driveway.

"Good morning, sir," Andy said, opening the door.

"Did you sort your history notebook out?" the driver asked as they closed their car doors.

George looked down and opened his backpack. In all the activity last night, he had forgotten. Yet, the notebook was reassembled.

"Ah, yes, sir?" George said.

Andy was shaking his head, wondering how it got fixed.

The school day flew by and soon the second bell at the end of the day was ringing. They left their star class and headed for the car on time today, no need for a diversion. Their driver was waiting for them on the school steps when they stepped out of the school doors.

"Hey, George, what's with the limo ride?" a friend called as he walked to George's old bus.

"It's my driver. We don't have buses where I'm from in Brazil, we share rides or have a driver if you're lucky. Otherwise, you have to walk five or ten miles to and from school each week," Andy yelled back.

"Whoa," George's friend nodded and got on the bus, waving goodbye.

George smiled and waved back. "Good cover story," George whispered.

"What cover story, it's true," Andy replied, frowning.

The driver took them straight home. It was a quiet ride again as they focused on the history exam for tomorrow. The boys bolted from the car, racing across the yard, up the front porch steps, and through the front door in seconds.

"Hi, Mom!" they yelled as they raced up the front stairs to George's room.

Between Andy and George, they only used every third stair, saving the wear and tear on the stairs' carpet. They bumped each other as they rounded, the corner at the top of the stairs and slid into the hallway wall with thuds. Andy grabbed for the door jam on George's room and missed his grip. He sailed through the air, landing on the floor and tripping George.

George dove over Andy trying to miss his body but clipping the desk in his room. Rolling across the floor, he stopped with a thump when he hit the bed. Andy rolled over in the middle of the floor, laughing. George flipped back over and slid his legs off the bed, sitting on the floor laughing. When he opened his eyes, he was face to face with an old pair of brown shoes. He looked up.

"Oh crap! I mean, sir, sorry, sir, we were…," George said, scrambling to his feet while pulling Andy up by his free arm. "Sir, how can we help you, sir?" George stammered.

"Sit down, boys!" the Senior Viceroy said firmly, motioning to the bed. His voice was stern.

The boys barely sat down on the edge of the bed. The Senior Viceroy stood the desk chair up and sat down. The silence was deafening.

"Sir," George said, trying to speak; however, Senior Viceroy Petrosky, Pete's grandfather, raised his hand.

"I have spoken with Max," the Senior Viceroy said abruptly.

Andy glanced at George, but George shook his head.

"Your trust is well grounded, George, he did not give the details of your discussion. However, he is concerned to such an extent that he called me!" he said, raising his voice.

George and Andy knew the Senior Viceroy and Max did not get along. What they told Max must have meant more than they thought.

"The gravity of the situation has changed. The Galactic council is greatly concerned," he said when George cut him off.

"Why is the Galactic council concerned, sir?" George asked, jumping in before the Senior Viceroy could stop him again. "Nothing has changed. They don't even know what happened sir!"

"We stopped the invader, sir." Andy added quickly. "Whether we are here or there, they will not stop coming after us. You know this, sir. I am here now, and I am protecting George!" Andy said boldly.

"They know about the prophecy, sir, and we know that is why the ones that hunt us are here. It is why you are here and why we have Pete, Toma and Frank in our triad, sir," George said as boldly as Andy.

Suddenly, he began to understand what was really going on as the words blurted out from his mouth. He was connecting the puzzle pieces on the fly, guessing, and his words were making sense. Now he only needed the Senior Viceroy to confirm his words.

"George, Andy, you need to tell me what happened," Senior Viceroy Petrosky said firmly.

George and Andy may have been allowed to speak to as equals. However, the Senior Viceroy was in control, and his words were final. George looked at his second in command. Andy nodded.

"We did what we agreed to do and now we will see if the Galactic council can keep their word as well, sir," George replied harshly as they stood up.

They held out their hands side by side and a small yellow-reddish sphere glowed above their palms. The Senior Viceroy stared at the odd sphere. Suddenly, he stood up and the chair rocked back, leaning on the edge of the desk.

"Thank you. I will take my leave of you now," he said firmly.

He opened George's door and walked down the hallway to the back stairs that lead to the kitchen. They were left with their mouths hanging open, staring at the empty chair.

"So that was a test?" Andy asked, stepping over to the desk chair and looking down the hallway.

"I guess?" George said, staring at the door and hallway.

"What just happened?" Andy pressed. "Why did he leave?"

"I don't know," George replied, plopping down on his bed to think.

They were stunned.

"So explain the thing you said to grandfather," Andy asked, closing the door and turning to face George.

"What thing?" George muttered still thinking about what happened.

"George, you figured it out, the prophecy, yes?" Andy pressed, looking hopeful as he sat on the chair.

"No, not really. But as I was talking, all the pieces we know about the CORE and the officers started to fit together. Emily said few beings can actually form a triad. Many officers cannot form the bond and trust needed between the members for a triad even after years of work. It is special and unique. When a triad is formed it comes from years of working with other officers in your sector. We had two teams of our triad in our first rotation and completed our triad in our second rotation," he said, pausing to think.

"It was easy. And the only thing that slowed us down was knowing what a triad really was," Andy added, thinking about it.

"Our team is strong, and with Pete, Frank and Toma's skills, we are unbeatable. All three of their teams have made it into the Sport finals and won. They guide us more than order us. They let us lead and take responsibility. And now, in spite of the Galactic council's obvious concerns, they give us a test and let us stay? Max did not roll over on us, Andy, and we didn't roll over on him. I'm sure Pete's dad and my dad were blocking for us yesterday so we could talk with Max in private," George said, connecting more points.

"I wonder if they got in trouble for that." Andy asked, worried they would be punished for his and George's actions.

"I'm sure the Galactic council knew, and I bet they weren't happy or grandfather wouldn't have been brought back so quickly," George only half said. "We need to read the prophecy, Andy, more now than ever before. Somehow they all seem to think there is some information in this prophecy; and whatever it is, it's about us."

"If this prophecy thing is about us then, maybe it can tell us who is after us and how to defend against it," Andy said, thinking of tactics and strategies.

"And why they want to capture us so badly," George added, thinking more about the pieces and information they did know.

Andy nodded in agreement. "So do you think grandfather will stay for dinner?" Andy asked.

"Only if my mom made pie for dessert," George replied.

They laughed so hard they nearly fell to the floor. An hour passed as the boys planned their next set of questions.

"Andy, George, dinner is ready," his mom called up the back stairs.

George and Andy stood up and walked to the door.

Andy grabbed George's arm. "Thanks, George."

"For what?" George asked, staring at his friend.

"Patience," Andy replied.

"If you say so," George said walking, down the hallway; but inside, he smiled.

Andy was skeptical of Max. George had let him figure it out for himself that Max really was part of their team, and their trust was not misguided. They hurried down the back stairs and walked into an empty kitchen. They glanced at each other.

"He stayed," they chorused together, laughing.

"The pie must still be in the oven," George whispered.

They grinned, spun around and headed into the dining room.

Pete's grandfather was talking with George's parents in the dining room. George's mom looked a little worried to the boys She was a brilliant scientist who was use to fairly routine and orderly events. Now her oldest son was far away at the university, her younger son had been attacked twice in two days and there was little she could do but make pies. How unfair it seemed to George. She worried and cared so much, yet everything was out of her control. He thought about his mom, and how sad she would be until she could adjust as he, too, would eventually leave for the university. He would have to remember to be extra kind and helpful to her.

"George, Andy, look who has stopped by for a visit," George's mom said with a smile and a nod for them to mind their manners.

"Welcome, sir," they said in unison.

George turned to his mom and whispered, "Did you make pie?"

"Honestly George, that's not true, we have visitors without making pie," she replied.

Maybe, but George couldn't ever remember when. The dinner conversation was dull to say the least, with nothing interesting to George and Andy. All very serious and proper with a lot of discussion centered on the spring weather and when his mom would start planting her flowers. After dinner Andy, George, and Pete's grandfather walked into the living room as George's mom and dad retreated to the kitchen with the dishes.

The Senior Viceroy, their grandfather, was a very powerful being. His rank put him in the top of the Galactic council circle, on the center four white light spaces. On their last rotation, their team had stood in the center of the circle and felt the energy of the universe ebb and flow through the Senior Viceroys and the Galactic council. Yet, to George and the others, he was their grandfather first, protecting them and keeping them safe.

"Why didn't you take our link upstairs, sir?" George pressed as they walked into the living room—right now was not the time for protocol.

"I asked you for it and you obeyed an order. It was not your choice, it was a protocol answer," he replied firmly.

"Why do you treat us so differently, sir?" George asked, staring at the Senior Viceroy.

"Because you are different," he replied seriously.

"Are we the team in the prophecy , sir?" George asked bluntly.

The Senior Viceroy raised his eyebrow. "What do you know?" He asked, staring at the boys.

"The prophecy talks about a team who will balance the universe again. It has been many years, and the galaxies are weary," George said bluntly. He was lying; he had no idea what was in the prophecy, but he had to try.

The Senior Viceroy smiled. "Indeed you are a resourceful team. I do not know if you are the team of the prophecy; however, your team is very strong and needs guidance to find the path that has been destined for you. You all have great strengths and a compassion for the welfare of others. That has not been seen or felt in the Galactic Union council in over 500 years," he replied, actually answering his question.

George stared at the Senior Viceroy; he wasn't used to anyone answering his questions. Usually, he figured out what was going on by what they had not said.

Andy changed the subject to give George time to think. "Great, I'm compassionate, just what a guy wants to hear, sir," he said a little sarcastically.

"Andy, there are many forms of compassion and inner strength," the Senior Viceroy said, scolding Andy. "George, the evil that hunts you and your team is very bad. It will do anything to turn you and your team into one of its minions of evil. You felt its pull on you in the Thorean ship and it believes you are the team of the prophecy," he said, his voice low and quiet.

He paused, choosing his words carefully. "George, Andy, within all of us is the capacity to create great good and the capacity to create great evil. The choices we make along our path of life direct us towards one goal or the other," he said, trying to get them to think.

"Does that mean once we start down a path we can't ever change paths?" Andy asked, leaning in close to hear his answer.

"No, Andy. Each day we make a choice of how we want to live our lives. If you have chosen a life of good, happiness, and trust in each other, then it is easier to wake up each day and stay on that path. If you are on the other path, the same is true. However, every day people and creatures make a conscious effort to change the path they are on and become a better being today than they were the day before. It can be as simple as opening a door for someone whose hands are full or as complex as learning to volunteer and finding the place you belong. It is hard to start, and it requires work. Yet, it is done every day. The evil side makes everything look easy, as if, you can get great rewards without any work. However, to get those rewards, you must surrender your freedom, your right to choose your own path and submit to the will of the evil that will consume you. Often we travel on a very narrow path, trying to split good and evil. My words sound simple, as if everyone should be able to easily make the choice of good, but until you come face to face with a difficult choice, you will truly never know. It is a defining moment in your life. Therefore, each day we practice by making simple choices to build our character and inner strength. Then if the unthinkable does happen, we can be prepared as best we can to be able to make a good choice and not a choice we will regret later. Does this make sense to the two of you?" the Senior Viceroy asked kindly.

He had said a lot and told them the truth. George and Andy were numb from the words the Senior Viceroy had said. They believed him and wanted to understand the meaning of his words, yet in reality what they heard was 'Choose each day to be good or bad, bla bla. You can change your path, bla bla bla bla. Practice your path and there are defining moments in your life.'

"Yes, sir," they answered in unison.

"Perhaps it is a lot to absorb on a full stomach," he said, patting the boys on their shoulders.

George held out his hand. Andy pulled his hand out of his pocket and held it next to George's hand. A small yellow-reddish sphere formed. George lifted the Senior Viceroy's hand and placed it over theirs, and the link was made.

"We're sorry we did not call you first. You and Max have often saved us from our mistakes and have always been there when we needed you. It was not the best choice to hide what really happened from you because of our fears, sir," George said as Andy nodded. They both knew they had crossed the loophole line.

"We all make errors in our choices. The Galactic council is not immune to this. We simply do the best we can," the Senior Viceroy said his voice softening.

"Yes, sir," they replied together sheepishly.

George told him everything they had told Max, and Andy added his part too.

"Andy, the red energy sphere you gave George?" the Senior Viceroy asked.

"Yes sir, it was real," Andy replied, cutting off the Senior Viceroy's question. "Not as strong as on the Thorean ship, but just as good none the less. The person on the other end of the link wasn't destroyed, but she wasn't expecting it and the link broke abruptly, sir," Andy said seriously.

"Thank you cadets," the Senior Viceroy said sincerely. He ended his link with them like Max did and left them connected. "I believe you are right, it is safer for now if you are both connected in your link. Andy, I will arrange additional training for you on your third rotation," he added with a little grin, knowing Andy was not fond of extra training.

"Ah, thank you, sir," Andy replied with a 'how'd that happen' kind of look, more special training, again!

George wondered what additional training Andy needed. In reality, Andy had created and launched more high-energy red spheres than most CORE officers. The Senior Viceroy knew the energy spheres would only get stronger and Andy would need training to be able to control them.

"Cadets, you are dismissed," he said as George's parents entered the room.

George and Andy said goodnight and headed up the stairs. George's mom followed them partway up the front stairs to make sure they went up this time. They entered George's room and George laid down. He threw Andy a pillow.

"What's the extra training for?" he asked, leaning back on his bed.

"It must have something to do with the red energy spheres I've been launching," Andy replied, hanging his head low. "Man, I hate extra training," he whined.

George stared at Andy. "Andy, how bad are the red spheres? I mean really?" George pressed.

"It's like a gun—you only take it out if you are prepared to use it. The police and the armies carry guns, and they are trained to use them. You only draw your weapon if you intend to use it. You know, for self defense, to stop a crime, or protect someone, that type of stuff. The red sphere is no different. If you create it, the energy inside is huge, and it's difficult not to launch it at your target. The control required is, well… it's a lot." Andy paused and stared at George. "You know, George, we can't let Gus create the red spheres. He is not prepared well enough to defend with it to… well you know, to destroy whatever. And trying to collapse the energy and dissipate it once it's drawn out can destroy you," Andy said as seriously as he could.

"Then we will discourage Gus from creating any red energy spheres for now," George said, agreeing.

"Good try with the whole prophecy thing. I thought the Viceroy was going to confirm your story for a minute there," he added.

"Me too. Yet, in a way, he did. You know?" George replied cryptically.

"How did you figure out the whole team in the prophecy thing?" Andy pressed.

"I didn't. I guessed. But he did confirm there is a prophecy. Something evil is now hunting us, and that evil and the Galactic council, both think the prophecy is written about us," George said, grinning. "But there is something more we are missing, Andy," George said, leaning back on his bed.

"I hope Emily can find out what it is before they try and stop her. I mean, you know, now that they think we know stuff about the prophecy, George,"

Andy added, yawning.

"Emily's good, Andy. She'll find a way," George said as they drifted off to sleep.

The next few days at school passed quickly. Each day, George and Andy entered the school newspaper and yearbook office to check for a message from Emily, and each day no message came.

"Either she's been quarantined or she is having difficulty finding out about the prophecy," George whispered, walking through the janitor's closet back into the hallway heading to their fifth hour class.

The weekend came and went and another school week dragged on. It had been nearly ten days since they had first contacted Emily and sent her on her quest. Soon it was Friday again, and they would have to wait until Monday before they were able to check the computer again. Hurrying to their fifth hour class, Andy suddenly spun around in the middle of the second floor corridor and ran for the closet.

"I got it!" he yelled, skidding into the small classroom.

He fell into the wooden chair in front of the computer terminal and started typing with wicked speed.

"What?" George asked when he caught up to Andy.

"The computer's IP address and server connection, I don't know why I didn't think of this before," Andy said as he downloaded a computer program from the web and then opened up the computer's control screen.

Scanning the page, Andy stopped and scratched some numbers on a scrap of paper. He stuffed it in his pocket and locked out a section of the computer. He turned off the screen but not the computer. He jumped up from the chair and motioned to the door. They ran out of the classroom again, skidding around the hallway and scrambling into their fifth hour class as the bell rang.

"Mr. Hawkins, Mr. Penteado, do you have a written excuse for being tardy to class after your lunch period?" the teacher asked firmly.

George looked up. "No, sir," he answered sheepishly.

"Then I will assume you and Mr. Penteado will be collecting demerits today," the teacher said, handing the boys two yellow slips of paper.

"Yes, sir," George said, swallowing hard and plopping down in an empty chair next to Andy.

George had not gotten a demerit before and had no idea what being tardy was worth in demerits. It was a new system this year, and he had not actually paid attention at the beginning of the year when the school staff rolled out the new plan in an school-wide assembly. Right now it seemed like an important detail. Maybe the school grade and homework computer system had some information on the whole demerit thing. George was lost in thought.

The class bell rang and students handed in papers as they left the classroom. George looked up and Andy waved him off.

"I wrote two pages. You owe me big," he said, grinning as he set the two pages down on the stack of papers growing on the teacher's desk.

"So what did I write about?" he asked, walking quickly to their next class.

"Responsibility," Andy replied, stepping into the crowded hallway.

"Did I do well?" George asked as they walked to their next class.

"Not as well as you may have hoped," Andy replied, grinning.

Their last two classes passed quickly with George actually paying attention. At the end of the day, they returned to their star homeroom to be counted, then two bells and out the door they went.

Their driver was there waiting for them at the school door. George and Andy smiled; demerits were the topic of focus on the car ride to George's house. They knew the driver was not just any old driver but a trained CORE officer who scanned their thoughts each day.

"A rather stealthy mind invader; smooth as silk, not one of the standard brutes. They would need to get better at hiding their thoughts. However, for now it's good practice each day," Andy muttered as they got in the car.

He rather admired the driver's abilities.

It was Friday and the whole weekend was ahead of them. They had spent the entire weekend indoors last week, and they assumed they would be just as watched this weekend.

"Keep practicing, you are getting better," the driver signed to Andy as he stopped in George's driveway. Andy smiled.

"See you Monday, sir," George said as they raced across the front lawn, up the front porch stairs and into the house like every other day.

"Hi, Mom!" they chorused, bolting up the front stairs to the second floor and sliding into George's room.

"So why did we get the demerits today and what did you do on the computer?" George asked as Andy turned on George's computer.

Andy sat down at the computer and called up the internet as George closed the door and pulled down the window shade.

"What are you doing? You know they will trace the computer's internet connection," George whispered.

"True; however, we are not logged in as us—we are the computer in the school's yearbook office," Andy replied with a sneaky grin.

"How'd you know how to do that?" George asked, leaning in over the computer.

"I don't, but Emily sent me this great program that was free on the internet. I need the computer's address and server name. Then I add the free program to the school computer's hard drive and leave it on. I log on somewhere else and control the other computer from here. They can trace our house internet call, but it looks like I'm calling the school computer network. The school computer is logged onto the internet and they can't trace it because I'm sending it instructions from here and my computer doesn't change its internet connection. Well, something like that, maybe something more, I didn't exactly understand everything Emily said," Andy said as he searched for the school computer's internet connection.

"You understood enough. I'm impressed," George said, staring at the computer screen.

"Don't be, it's all Emily. I'm only replaying what she created," Andy said, traveling from server to server to get to Emily's back door. "She is a whiz at this stuff ya know," he added more seriously.

"I know she is a whiz. Like you and the others on our team," George replied, studying the computer screen with Andy.

Andy sent a message to Emily like before, except this time he stayed on line and waited.

"I don't know if Emily will even be awake. It's 5:50 pm here so add six hours and you get 11:50 pm in England. Or is it five hours... no four," Andy mumbled, questioning his own math.

George smiled.

"What?" Andy looked up and stared at George.

"Emily's awake," he answered, grinning.

"How do you know?" Andy pressed, frowning.

"I don't know, I just know," George said, smiling as he thought of Emily.

The computer beeped. Emily flashed a message to Andy and George. "One more hour should have homework done. You will want to study this. TTFN," and the screen went blank.

George's mom called—it was dinner time. They walked down the back stairs into the kitchen.

He looked at Andy. "No pie tonight?" George whispered.

"No company," Andy replied.

George's dad overheard him and grinned. They sat down to a table of steaming food.

"I could get used to hot food," Andy said, scooping up some steaming mashed potatoes.

With their dinner plates full, George started to ask questions. "So Dad, can you tell us about the prophecy? I mean, you know, Pete's grandfather will not tell us, Max will not tell us, and Pete and Toma and Frank will not tell us, and well, you're my dad and all and I thought maybe you'd tell us?" George asked, boldly scooping some mashed potatoes into his mouth.

George's dad stopped midway through a bite of carrots and set his fork back down on his plate.

"I don't think Pete, Frank, and Toma know as much about it as you think they know. Pete's dad, Toma's dad and I are bound to the Galactic council and to our triad. We cannot tell you either. You need to find out over time. It is too soon to say for sure one way or the other," he said, picking up his fork again.

George swallowed and pressed his dad further. "Max and the Senior Viceroy, I mean Pete's grandfather, well, sir, we know they know a lot more than they are trying to let on. And we know they don't get along, Dad. Oddly, we don't really care why anymore. But if this evil thing is trying to hurt us, I think we should know why. So we can defend ourselves against it," George said hopefully, munching on his carrots.

Andy smiled and nodded, scooping more mashed potatoes onto his plate.

"Son, your argument is well thought out; however, I cannot answer your question. You are my son and Andy is a new member of our family, but I cannot give you the answer you seek. It must be a process of discovery for you and your team," he said, choosing his words very carefully.

"So, Mr. Hawkins, sir, how much do you know about the prophecy?" Andy asked, pressing in a different direction.

George's dad turned remorseful. "More than I ever wanted to know, Andy," he answered sadly.

"Dad, have there been other teams like ours in the past that the evil thing, that is trying to harm us, has successfully destroyed?" George asked, trying yet another approach.

"Yes, Son," his dad answered, raising an eyebrow but did not stop him.

"Did the Galactic council try and protect them as they are trying to protect us now?" he pressed.

"Yes, Son," his dad added seriously.

"Was Max or grandfather on one of those teams or was grandfather or Max suppose to protect them and failed?" George asked, hoping for an answer.

"You will have to ask them yourself, George," his dad replied.

Yet both Andy and George knew they would not answer the question either.

"What if we ask the evil that hunts us?" George asked, pressing for another answer.

"Then you will have to pay the price for the answer, and you may only hear one side of the prophecy," his dad said, finishing his sentence.

"But you will not tell us, sir," Andy asked, whining a little from frustration.

"No, that's not what I said. I said it was a process of discovery for you and your team," he replied, tipping his head and raising his eyebrow as if he had asked the right questions but not really heard the answers given. He glanced at Andy.

"Pete's standard answer, sir?" Andy said with a little sarcasm.

George grinned and nodded to his dad. He figured they had pressed him about as hard as they could get away with. They finished eating and cleared their plates. Then George and Andy retreated to George's room.

George's mom turned away as she listened to the boys' thumping footsteps bang up the back steps and down the hallway. Tears filled her eyes as she started clearing the remaining dishes from the kitchen table.

"It's just a game to them. They don't understand. They are so young. All of the other teams of the prophecy have died," she said, tears streaming down her rosy cheeks.

"Now, Mary, we don't know if they truly are the team of the prophecy. We do not know that history will repeat itself," George's dad said, walking up to his wife and hugging her in the middle of the kitchen. "They are very young and very strong. The teams of the past were older and much more stayed, not as flexible. I think they break rules faster than Pete's grandfather Alexander can make them," he said, trying hard to comfort Mary.

"You and I both know it is precisely because they are young that they are the team of the prophecy. James, I cannot lose them, not any of them. The evil that hunts them will not stop even if they are not the team of the prophecy. It will try to capture them, or it will try to destroy them. And if they are not the team of the prophecy, then they will be defenseless and they will all die," she said unable to stop her tears.

They stood in the kitchen for a long time. George's dad was worried too; however, at that moment he needed to hold his wife close and comfort her as best he could.

George and Andy were oblivious to his mom and dad down in the kitchen. Instead, they were mesmerized by the information Emily had found on the prophecy. As it turned out, no one quite remembered who had written the prophecy, yet it had guided the lives of billions and billions of humans and aliens since the beginning of everyone's recorded time.

Many of the events foretold in the prophecy had come true or at least had been attributed to the prophecy after the events had occurred. It made Emily wonder if the prophecy was all knowing. If the leaders knew when bad things were going to happen, why didn't they plan better to prevent the bad things from happening in the first place?

The prophecy foretold of great famines, earthquakes, asteroid impacts, and invaders from space. It also told of times of great prosperity, civilizations, and space exploration.

"All the things that have been foretold by the prophecy have happened on many of the planets. It seems to me to be a process of human and alien cultural evolution more than some grand prophecy thing," Emily wrote with distrust in her words.

"We agree," they flashed back. It seemed to be more an evolution of the different cultures on the different inhabited planets in the universe. The older the culture, the more of the things listed in the prophecy had happened.

"So why, then, do they think we are some sort of unifying team?" George flashed.

"Some planets are simply further through the writings of the prophecy than others, that's all," Andy added.

"True. And there is nothing here that even talks about a galactic unifying team," George flashed back.

"As if it was somehow removed from the document we found," Emily flashed back and then paused, thinking about the words she had written.

"Emily, where did you get this document?" George flashed, as sudden worry entered his thoughts.

"From the main computer archive directorate in the CORE," Emily flashed back.

George was stunned. It was like hacking into the Pentagon's or the KGB's main computer system undetected. He paused.

"Where is that?" he pressed.

"Well, here on Earth," she replied and then paused a long time. "Where we are, where they knew we would look!" she flashed, suddenly annoyed at being tricked.

Andy glanced at George, and he shook his head hard.

"Emily, Emily, it's OK. We did learn a lot. We fell for their trick, that's all. We can't hurt them for trying to stop us. We need to be patient with them, you know. You're not going to hurt them, right?" George wrote back quickly and calmly. He was worried. He could somehow sense Emily's rising anger at being tricked by the CORE. "I mean, we knew they would try and keep the truth from us. You cannot delete their database or send a worm or something not nice, right?" George wrote carefully.

"Hump, fine, have it your way," she flashed abruptly. "I can crush them, you know. Their computer system is barely protected."

"Yes, we know, but they will not learn and grow if they are crushed," George added as kindly as he could. "Can you recover the deleted data? I mean, they may have only removed data from the open files." George's mind was racing; he knew Emily was angry. He needed to find a new problem for Emily to solve, a distraction. "The real prophecy has to be somewhere, right? You know, written down in some language and what we see is only a translated copy. We need to find the original document, not a translated computer copy. Any thoughts on where we would look for that?" George flashed as kindly as he could, trying hard to change the subject and protect the CORE's main computer system on Earth from Emily.

"Where is the Galactic council? Find the Galactic council, and we'll find the original prophecy," Emily flashed back, becoming interested in the new challenge.

Andy leaned forward and George slid back. "If only the Galactic council knows what is really written on the original prophecy document, then does that mean the evil that hunts us was once on the Galactic council?" Andy asked Emily, typing as fast as he could.

They had been connected for twenty minutes and Andy was sure their time was running out. The CORE computer hackers may not have had Emily's skills; however, they were talented and formidable as a team. George patted Andy on his shoulder, amazed at his insight, then slid forward to the computer keyboard.

"Emily, can you find a history of the Galactic council?" George asked when he was suddenly cut off.

One long Beep sounded and their connection died.

"They found us. Well, they found the school computer," Andy said, shaking his head.

"And the beep?" George questioned, frowning.

"An Emily earlier warning device before they can lock onto either computer's location," Andy answered quickly, closing the internet connection between their computer and the high school.

"Now we wait," George added.

"I hope Emily doesn't hurt anyone for tricking her. She seemed a little angry," Andy said, a little worried.

Emily was good, and the CORE's main computer system was an easy target for her.

"No, she is more intrigued now than vengeful," George whispered, looking into the air.

"Again, I ask, how do you know?" Andy asked, crinkling his forehead.

"I have no idea, I just know. I know Sara, Anna and Gus are fine, too, and sleeping right now," George replied with a smile.

"How do you know?" Andy puzzled, lying down on the sleeping bag on the floor and leaning back on his pillow.

"It's a sense of them, like a connection in my subconscious. It's getting stronger," George replied with a smirk. "Like making your red energy spheres; you do it when you need to. How you do it is still a mystery. This is the same. It's like I need to know if they are OK and then I can somehow sense them," George whispered and shrugged.

"OK, cryptic, but I can live with it," Andy said, falling asleep as George shut down the computer.

Chapter 5

SIMPLE TRAP

The last two weeks of school passed quickly with no other word from Emily and no more odd occurrences. Soon, they would be leaving for summer camp in the stars—their third rotation. George wondered if they would be together on Jupiter station or some isolated rock far away.

The last day of high school and the last day of university finals were the same day. Frank and Pete arrived at the Hawkins house around mid-morning with all of their college books, bedding, and clothes crammed into garbage bags in the back of an old beige car. Mrs. Petrosky had arrived early to help Mrs. Hawkins sort out Pete and Frank. The moms had Frank and Pete doing laundry for most of the day.

"There are washers and dryers at the university," they kept, saying while they made a birthday cake for George and Andy's 15th birthdays.

Pete and Frank were waiting for them on the front porch when George and Andy's driver arrived. The boys carried two huge, clear bags of books and locker stuff between them as they crossed the front lawn. They nodded to their driver as the officer drove away for the last time.

School was over. They had made it, they thought as they carried the school bags to the front porch. Frank held the door open for them to carry the bags directly inside without stopping. They dropped their bags of books inside the house next to the front stairs with a loud thud. Mrs. Hawkins and Mrs. Petrosky came running as if they heard a small explosion. Seeing the two stuffed bags with a heap of books on the floor in the front entry, they looked up.

"You boys carry your books upstairs immediately. You're not leaving your books stacked in the front hallway," George's mom said, motioning the boys upstairs.

"Yes, Mom," they chorused.

George and Andy grunted, lifting the bags and heading up the front stairs. The bags seemed heavier on the stairs than on the level ground. Up to George's room they went, dropping the bags on the floor with another thud. George and Andy plopped down on the floor with the books to rest. Pete and Frank entered George's room. They jumped up immediately.

"Relax," Pete said, motioning them down as he walked over and pulled the window shade down. He turned and leaned on the window sill, sitting down on the edge as Frank closed the door and flicked on the desk light. "So what have we missed?" Pete asked.

George held out his hand with Andy and their glowing yellow-reddish sphere appeared on their palms. Pete raised his eyebrow, and placed his hand over George's. Frank joined them, completing the link. They caught Frank and Pete up on all the happenings of the last few weeks at home and school.

Then, Pete glanced at Andy. "What Andy?" he asked, knowing there was something they had left out.

"It's about the prophecy, sir," Andy said seriously.

"Continue," he said kindly, studying Andy's face.

Andy told them what they had figured out about the prophecy, their ideas about a secret invader on the Galactic council, and the evil that hunted them. Pete and Frank walked out of the link with help from Rachael, who was not there. Pete and Frank stood there staring at George and Andy, hardly knowing what to say.

"How did you figure all this out?" Frank asked, a little stunned by the depth of their knowledge.

George and Andy just shrugged. "We have no idea," Andy replied, fiddling with a pencil from the book bags.

"It just seems logical and the pieces fit like a puzzle," George said, shrugging his shoulders again.

Pete's mom called upstairs that dinner was ready. Together, they tromped down the back stairs toward the kitchen. The smell of hot food wafted through the air.

"Do I smell a pie?" Andy asked, now believing in the galactic power of pie.

"Pies," Pete said and smiled.

"More company," Frank said, inhaling the air.

They all laughed—it was a Galactic visiting signal in Pete's house as well.

Rounding the corner into the dining room, they were suddenly stopped by George and Pete's dads.

"There will be no discussions upsetting your mothers this evening," George's dad said sternly.

"Yes, sir," they all answered in unison. Smiles affixed to their faces, they entered the dining room. Their moms were finishing setting the food on the table. Everyone sat down politely. It looked like enough steaming food for twenty cadets, yet somehow all the food disappeared. Hardly a word was spoken except about the lovely spring weather and to thank the moms for the great dinner. George and Andy stood up and cleared the dishes when they were done.

The moms came into the kitchen and sent the boys back into the dining room with the plates while they slipped out the cake.

"The smell of pie was an illusion," George whispered. George and Andy stopped in the dining room archway and watched the Viceroys and the captains talking.

"What are they saying?" George whispered.

"They are discussing the upcoming rotation and the Galactic council's decisions," Andy replied in their half-new sign language.

"So where are we going?" George asked, staring into the living room.

"Go ask them," his mom said, pushing the boys out of the hallway into the living room.

George and Andy knew better than to ask the Viceroys, even if they were their dads. They would ask Pete and Frank later. Everyone walked into the dining room as Pete's mom came around the corner carrying a large, red birthday cake. George and Andy were spun around by Pete and Frank as the others started singing an off-key Happy Birthday. With the cake on the dining room table, the boys locked arms over shoulders and leaned forward, blowing the candles out together.

Laughing and joking around, the cake disappeared almost as fast as it was served. Soon Andy and George were shooed upstairs with Mrs. Petrosky and George's mom following close behind. Frank and Pete stayed with their dads in the living room.

"Dad, they know a lot more than you think about the prophecy and the Galactic council, and they have figured out a couple of things we never even thought of," Frank signed. Their dads flipped their hands over and opened a link between them. Pete and Frank shared what George and Andy had told them. Pete and Frank were really worried, or they would never have shared

George and Andy's confidence with their dads.

As a child growing up on the Calshene asteroid colony, Pete had heard the stories of the last two teams the Galactic council had thought could have been the teams of the prophecy. They had all died. The first team died alone and the second team died fighting with their triad.

It was how Pete's uncle was killed; and George's grandfather and great aunt, Andy's uncle, and Toma's uncle were killed too. George and Andy already knew more than Pete and Frank had been able to figure out. Of course, they didn't have Emily. The implication of the members of the Galactic council, however, was a different matter. There was a hole in their defenses, a spy on the inside. The Viceroys would need to do some covert investigating.

Saturday morning came early for George and Andy. They had enjoyed sleeping in on the weekends after having to get up early each day for school during the week. Frank yelled into George's room, and Andy sprang up from the floor, ready to attack.

"Stop screwing off. It's time to get up," Frank yelled, continuing down the hallway to the bathroom.

George glanced at Andy.

"Breakfast is ready boys!" Pete's mom called from the kitchen up the back stairs.

George and Andy scrambled to their feet, dressing as they got up. Across the hallway they went rushing down the back stairs together, nearly toppling over each other in their hurry, then slowing down behind Pete and Frank. No mushy cereal this morning—instead, the sweet smell of maple syrup and pan-cakes filled the air.

"Our last supper," the boys said in unison, laughing and grinning.

Pete spun around at the bottom of the stairs and grabbed both boys on the last step. He slammed them hard up against the hallway wall so fast their heads hit the wall with a thud. Frank continued walking through the kitchen door as a distraction for their moms.

"Less than a poor choice of words cadets! Our moms have broken a dozen rules in making us this breakfast. Based on how closely we are being watched, I'm sure they will pay dearly for it. Just as our fathers have paid for blocking for you and Max's conversation. You diminish their sacrifices with your callus, un-appreciative comments," Pete said firmly.

His eyes were steely cold when he released them and they dropped to the floor. He had lifted them off the ground, and their feet had been dangling in mid-air.

Pete's dad rounded the corner from the kitchen. "Everything OK, boys?" he asked.

"Yes, sir… ah, slipped on the last step, sir," George replied weakly.

Pete followed his dad into the kitchen, leaving the boys at the bottom of the stairs to ponder his words. George and Andy followed a few moments behind.

"Thanks, Mom. You didn't have to do this," he whispered in his mom's ear before sitting down.

The stack of pancake disappeared in record time. With so many helping hands, the dishes were washed, dried, and put away quickly. Soon they all headed out to the two cars in silence.

George had a bad feeling about this rotation; perhaps he was just nervous, perhaps not. It had been a difficult the last month of school without a true moment of rest. He wanted to know if the Galactic council was going to let them go to Jupiter station or quarantine them on some rock for their own safety.

There had not been time last night to talk with Pete or Frank; and judging by their serious mood this morning, they were a bit too afraid to ask. Whatever had happened last night, after George and Andy were sent upstairs, obviously did not make Frank and Pete happy.

They arrived at the airport as usual, and their dads parked in the expensive, short term lot. George was sure it irritated his dad; however, he was also sure he was trying to minimize their exposure. Quickly, they unloaded the red, blue, and green suitcases that George and Andy did not remember packing. The suitcases glided along easily as they walked into the gleaming silver and white airport terminal.

Pete's dad glanced at everyone. They knew what that meant. "Say nothing, I'll deal with security."

Mr. Petrosky went on ahead, walking up to the gated side entrance. The guard looked like one of those tough guys who was having a bad day. Mr. Petrosky started speaking, and the guard pointed to the long security line and motioned him away.

"Bad choice today, Mr. Guard," George thought in their link and Andy smiled.

Mr. Petrosky slid his identification card out of his shirt pocket, and the guard nearly collapsed. A second guard came running to investigate the commotion. Now there was a stir, a commotion, too much attention for George's dad to go near them until things calmed down. George's dad turned their group and headed down the terminal as if on a sightseeing tour. Some other guards, who were not watching Mr. Petrosky, saw their group turn and walk away. The guards started tailing them. George's dad directed Pete and Frank to make a loop and come back while he stopped the second set of guards from following them.

Further down, there was another guarded entrance to the main terminal on the main floor. The group stopped to rest as they had now walked the better part of a half-mile, pulling their heavy suitcases. George was sure there were bricks in his suitcase; the two rear wheels were wobbling. At the far end of the terminal, Mrs. Petrosky, and George's mom left the group for a quick stop in the ladies room, while the boys rested on their suitcases in the middle of the terminal.

Frank and Pete stood scanning the terminal as George and Andy sat on their suitcases in the middle of the terminal floor in the open, fully exposed. George felt uneasy, his stomach actually hurt. He held it with his right arm and bent over.

"George, are you OK?" Pete asked.

Distracted, he took his eyes off the crowd in the terminal and looked down at George. At that moment, screams rang out. George's mom and Pete's mom were lying on the terminal floor, covered in luggage.

"Go help Mom. I'm OK. I have Andy," George said, straightening up as he pushed Frank and Pete away.

They rushed to help their moms untangle from the mound of spilled luggage. The trap was set. A large group of twenty or more exchange students passed between Pete, Frank, their moms and George and Andy. Suddenly, Pete turned and stood up, scanning the terminal.

"It's a diversion! Noooooo!" he yelled at the top of his lungs.

He was too late; George and Andy were gone. Mrs. Petrosky and Mrs. Hawkins scrambled to their feet as Frank and Pete ran between the people in the main terminal to the place they had left George and Andy. The boys were gone. Frantically, they looked around, scanning the terminal for clues. Across the main terminal Frank spotted one of George's red wheels. They started to run, this time pushing people out of their way, racing across the terminal to the red wheel.

The metal axle on George's suitcase left a thin scratch mark in the waxed granite floor of the terminal. They ran on following the scratch as their moms called for help. At the elevators in the center of the terminal, the second red wheel lay next to a silver trash bin. The kidnappers had waited for the elevator!

Pete hit the wall in frustration. "Why didn't someone stop them?"

"What floor, what floor did they stop at?" Frank said, echoing Pete's frustration and pushing the elevator button a dozen times, trying to get the doors to open.

Mr. Petrosky and Mr. Hawkins joined the four by the time the elevator doors opened. The elevator went to six floors, not including the main terminal floor. Each of them took a floor to search. Mr. Petrosky had the airport and spaceport shutdown in a matter of minutes.

Far below the main terminal's public spaces, George and Andy were struggling to break free from their captors and knock holographic projectors from their shoulders. Two men had crushed George and Andy's arms and legs together, carrying each of them over their shoulders-like a shepherd carrying a young lamb. Their mouths were taped shut, yet the boys struggled and squirmed. The elevator stopped with a bump, and the silver doors slipped open silently.

As the two men stepped out of the elevator onto the basement floor of the terminal, the boys' arms broke free from their captors. They frantically grabbed for the elevators door jam, holding on with all their might. Their captures pulled hard on the boys, twisting and turning to break their grip, their fingers scraping along the sides of the door. The captors finally broke the boys free from the elevator doors, leaving only finger prints and small scraps on the door jams as it closed.

George and Andy spun around, pushing against the two men carrying them with their free hands. The men grabbed their free arms and twisted them over their shoulders again. The boys were trapped once more.

They were in what looked like the luggage handling room. Over their heads, conveyors with colorful luggage whizzed by, snaking their way through the underground maze of pillars and conduits. Another man came up to George and Andy and smiled an evil grin. He threw their luggage up onto one of the conveyors and laughed as it whizzed away for parts unknown.

"Easy as cake, easy as cake" he said, motioning the two men to follow him through the labyrinth of conveyors and walkways.

The other two men laughed as George and Andy struggled to break free. However, this time the two men had a better grip on the boys, and they were not going to lose their prey. At another set of silver doors, the third man spun around and held a small blue rag in front of the boys faces. George and Andy collapsed, dangling over the men's shoulders. Then he placed another holographic bar onto each boy's open shoulder. Turning it on, the boys' images disappeared. The two men laughed and carried the boys across the terminal floor to a small transport ship on the edge of the main spaceport. Up the gangplank and into the cargo hold they went with their sleeping cargo. They dropped the boys into gray shipping crates, pulled off the holographic bars, and locked the crate tops, leaving them in the transport ship's cargo hold-alone and unconscious. All the time, laughing and joking at how easy the capture of the boys was for them. No one saw the boys under the holographic disguise. They were gone!

On each floor of the terminal, the Hawkins and Petroskys were frantically searching for the missing boys. George's dad found the boys' handprints on the elevator doors and broken projectors on the basement level of the airport. However, there was no sign of George or Andy; they were gone.

The boys' captors waited patiently until the spaceport was eventually reopened. With their ship's cloak on, they launched the small transport at the same time all of the summer camper transport starships launched for their journey to Jupiter station.

Chapter 6

WRONG TRANSPORT

Several days later, George woke up crushed inside the gray plastic shipping crate. He heard the faint hum of a starship's engines as he opened up his link with Andy, jostling him until he regained consciousness.

"Where are we?" Andy asked, twisting inside his shipping crate to turn right-side-up.

"Don't know, can't be good," George thought back.

"Whoever it is, they laid a good trap to separate us from the others," Andy whispered.

"Yes, we must remember they like traps," George said, agreeing.

They were not tied up inside the shipping crates but there was very little room to turn around or sit up.

"We need spacesuits or uniforms, George. Our bodies wouldn't take a long space journey without them," Andy whispered in their link.

"Why not? There's gravity inside this starship," George asked, not understanding.

"A lot of reasons—mostly, we'll die from dehydration, radiation exposure, and muscle atrophy," Andy replied.

"Muscle atrophy?" George asked, surprised Andy knew so much.

"You know, your heart muscle gets too weak to pump. Well, something like that. Sara was talking about it one time. She's good at that kind of stuff, George," Andy replied, suddenly missing Sara.

"I know. I hope they are all safe. I can't sense anything or anyone right now. Someone must be blocking us or something," George said sadly.

"We need to get out of these boxes and get suits on before, well, you know, or Sara will be angry," Andy thought, trying to clear his thoughts and focus.

It was odd that George couldn't sense the others as he had been sensing them all year. George's mind was concentrating now, and Andy didn't want to stop his train of thought. Andy hoped he was making a plan. George started to concentrate on the silver lock of the shipping crate he was in. He thought of it as weak and soft. He didn't try to break it, only make it soft and bendable.

Andy didn't understand, as one good-sized red energy sphere could have easily blown the lock apart quicker. All year he had read about and worked on his armaments and stealth movements. However, George had worked on his mind, on controlling his thoughts and guiding those around him.

His friends at school had been unknowing participants. His family had attended nearly every sporting game this year so he could practice listening to individual thoughts. His favorite game had been listening to one coach and then the other coach and then seeing how the plays each had called unfolded. He was careful not to tell each side what the other was doing, even if it meant his team would lose.

Andy felt the pull of energy and shared his red sphere energy with George. He had gotten significantly better at controlling the flow of energy. Not as good as Cal, Nick or Niels but better none the less. George held his hand over the lock and formed a small glowing red sphere. The sphere slid into the lock, and the lock softened and stretched, dripping silently onto the floor. George was free; however, he stayed inside the shipping crate.

"Andy, hold your hand over the lock on your shipping crate," he whispered.

"I can't do this, George. I really don't have the control you have. You know my red energy spheres are bigger-you might say," Andy replied, shaking his head.

"Then I will give you my control, Andy. You can do this. Besides, it's your red energy spheres I'm using," George replied and chuckled.

"Oh, ya," Andy answered, surprised.

"You didn't actually think I could make a red energy sphere on my own, did you?" George grinned.

Andy shook his head and held his hand over the lock. It took a bit longer, but the silver lock finally softened and stretched out as it puddled on the floor. The crate top was opened without a sound. Slowly, they lifted the shipping crate tops up. The crates were lying on the floor against the back wall of what looked like a cargo hold.

As they cracked open the tops a little more, they saw two guards standing in the room by the main door. There were a few other boxes in the room and what looked like canisters of compressed gases and a few silver barrels of water.

"We will need a plan, a diversion to get free from these shipping crates," George whispered. "Andy, what don't you like?" he quizzed, looking for an idea.

Andy thought and then smiled, "Bugs. Yes, bugs. I know we need them for the environment, but I really don't like bugs. Space doesn't have bugs. I like it."

George smiled. "Maybe we just haven't seen any of the bugs out here yet," he replied, stopping Andy's happy thought intentionally.

Andy shuttered and imagined monstrous creepy-crawly bugs. George used Andy's thought and sent creepy crawling bug messages to one of the guards. The guard jumped, brushing an imaginary bug off his shoulder.

"We can use their suits. Somehow we need the guards to take them off and give them to us," Andy whispered, beginning to understand what George was doing.

"Then we will need more bugs to get them out of their suits," he whispered devilishly.

"I hate bugs. Does it have to be bugs, George? They creep me out. Don't know why, just always have. I especially hate the big ones that crunch. In Brazil, we have some little tiny crunchy ones that are hard to smash too. They hang on and don't brush off easily," Andy said carrying on.

"Keep thinking that way, Andy. Its working," George said, concentrating hard.

Andy looked up and the two guards were wiping the imaginary bugs from their suits.

"Ugh." Andy winced and George made the bugs go under their suits.

"I need more, the ones that really creep people out, Andy," he whispered.

Andy thought of the bugs crawling all over his skin and biting from time to time. The second guard tried to smash them, but he couldn't get a good hit. He hit an imaginary bug on the other guard's back, and George made it squish.

"Do it again," he whispered.

The first guard yelled in pain; yet, they kept hitting each other, squishing the imaginary bugs. George and Andy had the two guards knocking each other down trying to squish the imaginary bugs beneath their suits. For every bug they squished, George made two more. The guards couldn't take it. They nearly tore their suits off, trying to get them off as fast as they could. The guards were jumping on their suits on the floor, squishing their imaginary bugs.

With the guards distracted, George and Andy slipped out of the shipping crates and hid behind some of the boxes. Carefully, Andy slipped out a bluish staff weapon from his sleeve. It was his uncle's and Andy had used it last year when he helped remove the evil from George. Now he was never without it.

George circled around, wondering why Andy had a staff weapon up the sleeve of his regular clothes, not knowing what had happened last year when the evil was removed from him. George climbed up a small stack of boxes and waited.

At Andy's nod, he jumped off the boxes and landed on one of the guard's shoulders. Andy charged forward with his staff weapon held out at arm's length and tripped the second guard. The second guard stumbled and fell forward into the first guard as the first guard spun around, trying to unhook George from his back.

George had his arm over the first guard's eyes and grabbed onto the door frame with his free hand. Andy spun around, jerking the second guard hard as they fell to the ground. The second guard hurriedly got up from the floor to stop the freed prisoners. Quickly, Andy vaulted himself into the guard's chest before he regained his balance. He fell backwards, waving his arms wildly trying to stop his fall. George jumped off the back of the first guard as the second guard crashed into him. Smack. Smack. The guards knocked each other out, falling to the floor.

Quickly, Andy and George dragged the two guards over to the shipping crates. They pulled off their t-shirts and tore them apart into thin strips. George tied the strips of cloth from their shirts across the guard's mouths, and Andy tied their hands and feet together like a rancher roping cattle with more shreds of the shirts. They rolled each guard into a crate. Quietly spinning the shipping crate around, they blocked the crates up against the wall so they could not be broken open by accident.

Running across the room, the boys slipped into the white suits the guards had removed. Amazingly, the suits changed form and molded to their bodies. The boys were surprised; they didn't know the suits could do that! They stood at the cargo door ready to leave, when it suddenly opened. They jumped back into the original positions of the two guards. Two officers entered in a hurry, barely noticing the new guards. George and Andy froze next to the door!

"Guarding, guarding crates, guarding," was all they thought about.

The two officers looked like CORE officers they had seen before. The older CORE officer bent down and placed his hand over one of the shipping crates.

"Still asleep! Hump, I do not think they are the team of the prophecy. They are weak without their protectors," he said gruffly.

The other officer nodded. "I don't know what all the fuss is about," she said.

"This wasn't even difficult."

The older CORE officer stood up and walked back to the door without noticing the two guards.

"We will be greatly rewarded for capturing them, even if they are not the team of the prophecy," he added, grinning.

"The rest of their team will fall easily without their leader," the other officer chuckled, walking to the door. "Stay alert!" she yelled, following the first officer out the door.

They gasped, breathing hard when the door closed.

"That was close," Andy whispered.

George nodded and moved to the ship's wall. A change of plan was needed. He waved his hand, and a computer terminal appeared.

"It's a CORE transport ship!" George whispered a little surprised.

"The size Pete and Frank used to rescue us on our last rotation?" Andy asked.

George nodded as Andy started to search the walls for a weapons locker. George opened a computer window and did Emily's trick of rerouting himself through the computer system so it would be difficult to trace his work. He set up a small beep for an alarm and then dove into the navigational system of the transport ship's main control computer.

"The course is set for the Zeleion trading post, the second kitchen," he said to Andy who was still searching the cargo bay for weapons.

They had been there on last year's rotation when they had been looking for Pete, Frank, and their teams to help them rescue the Thoreans from the Mahadean slave traders.

"How many officers are on this ship?" Andy asked as George scanned the database for the navigation controls.

"Only eight left, not counting the two in the shipping crates. According to the log, we have seven days before we get to the Zeleion traders station," George replied.

"How long have we been asleep?" Andy asked, moving some boxes to get to the wall.

"Nine days! But we are moving really fast. Faster than this transport can go on its own," George said, checking the navigation and engine programs. "It's weird, Andy."

"Is there anyone friendly and close to us out in this part of space?" Andy asked, searching the walls.

"Only the Calshene cadet station, Asteria," George said, grinning.

"Man, they really don't like us. Are you sure there isn't anyone else? Anyone actually friendly, I mean anyone at all? The Zeleion outpost didn't look that bad when we were there," Andy whined.

George grinned and walked over to the two shipping crates. He thought of a deep sleep, a very deep sleep. He left them and returned to the computer terminal as Andy continued to search the room.

"The two guards are human, but I think the other two CORE officers were Calshene. They looked familiar somehow," George said, trying to remember where and when he had seen them before.

"I am not even going to ask how you know that," Andy said with a big grin.

He raised his hand and pointed at the ship's wall. With great fanfare, he swung his other arm through the air, and with a single pointer finger extended, he touched the wall. A small armory appeared in the wall. He threw George two staff weapons and slid one more into each sleeve of the suit he was wearing. George smiled, catching the staffs and following Andy's lead, placing one staff weapon in each sleeve. Andy closed the armory door and walked over to George.

"We need to shut down one system at a time and concentrate their activities. First, we need to slow this ship down without destroying its engines, then we need to make them all sleep until we can get more help," George whispered.

"Sara!" Andy whispered and smiled, thinking of her medicines from their last rotation.

"And lastly, with the officers asleep, we need to get to someplace where our real officers can hold them properly," George said seriously.

"I know, Asteria cadet station, here we come. Yahoo!" Andy replied mockingly, still not happy about going to Asteria station.

Within the hour, George had reproduced Sara's cold virus in the computer system and converted it into a sleeping virus. George added it to the food system and then sent one of Emily's engine programs into the main computer system. Emily's program could stop the transport ship's engines, but he needed the master computer access codes to gain full control of the main computer system. Next, he added her programs to change the ship's outside sensor reading and engine output to match that of a fast comet when they gained full control of the computer system. The moment one of the officers entered a master command code, Emily's programs would start and the transport ship would become a speeding comet.

Motioning to Andy to come and look, he added one final program. Andy glanced at the computer screen and nodded—it would be their last defense… the total destruction of the transport ship!

"We are as ready as we can be," George said, and Andy nodded.

George pushed the execute key on the computer terminal, and the ship lurched forward, then slowed to half its original speed. He would force the CORE officers to enter the master control codes and start Emily's programs. Andy opened the door, and two CORE officers ran by.

"Get to the engine room and help out!" one of the officers yelled as she disappeared down the hallway.

George locked the cargo bay doors with one of Emily's programs, and they ran down the hallway toward the engine room. Four officers were working on the engine computer controls when they arrived. Without thinking, George left Andy and ran to the hospital.

Andy spun around to stop George, but an officer grabbed his arm and pointed to some new dangling wires under one of the control consoles. George had not been out of Andy's sight since they had made their promise to grandfather and Andy wasn't happy, especially here.

Once inside the hospital, George scanned the room and headed for one of the silver cabinets covering the far wall. He pulled out two vials of their new sleeping medicine from the medicine distributor machine. Quickly, he loaded the vials of the sleeping virus into a small shot dispenser, similar to the ones Sara had used to give them vitamins. Spinning on his heels, he ran back to the engine room.

Andy was twisting loose wires together and moving closer and closer to one of the open engine computer control panels. The transport ship jolted again, and they all fell to the floor of the engine room. Andy rolled over and stood up behind the empty computer terminal. An officer pushed him aside and entered his master access code. Andy smiled as Emily's programs started, and the ship's sirens roared to life and then stopped suddenly. The life support systems turned off and then on, over and over again. The officers started yelling command after command, trying desperately to stabilize their starship.

Andy ducked down and disconnected a cooling tube under a control console. Quickly, thick blue smoke filled the air in the engine room. George ran in through the blue smoke tossing Andy one of the sleeping dispensers. In the commotion George and Andy struck two officers in the neck, injecting the dispenser's contents. The officers collapsed, dropping like rocks.

"How strong is this stuff?" Andy signed, but George waved him off.

"Help! Help!" George yelled, pretending to help the two unconscious officers. The other two officers in the room left their posts and ran over to help carry the two sleeping officers to the hospital. The officers helped George and Andy load the unconscious officers into stasis tubes in the hospital. Spinning quickly around, George and Andy tagged the two officers and injected them in the neck with the sleeping medicine. They fell to the ground like rocks too! Andy shook his head and together they loaded the two new officers into stasis tubes.

"Four down. Two in the crates and only four more to go," Andy whispered, high-fiving George.

Quickly, they returned to the engine room to fix the coolant leak Andy had caused earlier. He reconnected the hose and the room was clear of smoke when a bridge officer entered the engine room. The engine lurched forward again, sending everyone to the ground.

Andy stuck the bridge officer in the neck, and she passed out. George ran to the computer terminal and started another of Emily's programs as Andy dragged the bridge officer to the door. The four officers and bridge officer's bio signs suddenly appeared at their assigned duty stations on the computer.

Together, they carried the bridge officer between them to the hospital. George smiled as they slipped the fifth officer into a stasis tube. George locked the stasis tubes with another of Emily's locking programs stored on his pad.

"Where are you getting all of these programs?" Andy asked.

"Emily, of course," George replied with a little grin.

"Max is right, we are never alone," Andy added.

"Even without them here, they are here," George said, grinning as he slid his pad back up his sleeve.

They reloaded their dispensers and returned to the engine room. The last two officers fell without a struggle. Quickly, the officers were put into the stasis tubes. Then, for the third time, George and Andy reloaded their dispensers, locked the stasis tubes, and locked the hospital room door.

"We need to search the ship again and make sure we really only have one officer left," Andy whispered.

"Yes, and I'm sure the last bridge officer will be the most difficult to stop," George replied with a sigh, nodding.

They ran to the main computer terminal in the engine room and scanned the ship. The computer reported twelve life signs present. Seven in the hospital, two in the cargo bay, the bridge officer on the main command bridge of the transport ship, and the two boys. George added another of Emily's programs and made the ship's computer report that they had returned to the original course and speed. Emily's program, again, added all of the officers in the correct locations in case the one bridge officer left was interested and looked for his crew.

Finally, the computer blinked, waiting for a new heading. George looked at Andy. Andy shook his head.

"They really do hate us, you know. How about the second kitchen, how far can it be? At least the Zeleion only want to destroy us. Or maybe the Mahadean? I mean they only want us as slaves," he whispered hopefully.

He tried to look convincing; however, his face just looked goofy. George wanted to laugh, but he typed in the heading Anna had given him on the last rotation to the Calshene cadet station on Asteria, instead.

"Hate is such a strong word. Perhaps we should say, dislike intensely?" George whispered back, chuckling and closing the computer terminal.

They ran down the corridor toward the main command bridge. Outside the main door they started thinking "guarding, guarding, must guard," over and over in their minds. The door slid open, and they stood in the entrance waiting to be let into the room. Protocol training did have its uses from time to time. The bridge officer did not even turn around.

"Report!" the bridge officer yelled, still looking at his navigational array.

"Back on course and speed, sir," George answered, mumbling as they walked into the main command bridge.

Andy slid out his two staff weapons and George followed his lead. They held them vertically at arm's length. Suddenly, the lead bridge officer spun around, but it was too late. Andy leapt behind him as they spun their staff weapons horizontally. When the ends touched, there was a flash of white light and a controlling energy field from the staff weapons formed around the officer.

It was like last year's rotation when Andy, Max and grandfather had surrounded George. Now on the bridge with the controlling energy field in place, the bridge officer could not escape; however, it took a lot of strength and focus to maintain the field-neither of which George and Andy were good at.

Andy yelled nonsense, and the bridge officer turned toward him. George thought of the medicine dispenser. He tossed his staff weapon up into the air and threw the dispenser into the field, stabbing the officer in the neck. "Need more!" he yelled, catching his staff weapon as the bridge officer spun around to yell at George.

Andy tossed his staff weapon into the air and threw his dispenser at the neck of the bridge officer, but the officer jumped. It missed his neck, but hit the officer's upper arm and the bridge officer fell to his knees. Instantly, Andy nodded, and they retracted the four staffs into their sleeves and grabbed the bridge officer's arms. The officer was delirious as they ran dragging him though the transport ship's hallways.

"I know this guy. We have seen him before—somewhere," George said as the hospital door slid open.

"Where?" Andy asked as they hurried across the hospital room to the stasis chambers along the far wall.

"Asteria station, when we were in the hospital," George said, staring at the bridge officer as they laid him in a stasis tube with the others. "He was one of the CORE officer hospital guards."

"The master will find you and destroy you. The master has destroyed all the teams of the prophecy that have threatened its existence," the bridge officer said, slurring his words.

"No, the evil that hunts us did not harm those teams. Beings from across the galaxy did out of fear and hatred. The evil itself cannot destroy. It must have others destroy for it. It is weak and cowardly as it hides behind the weak minds of others," George replied firmly.

"You do not know the rewards of the master. They are great and glorious," the bridge officer said, slurring his words again.

"I prefer to chose my own path and think for myself. The rewards I create are real and cannot be taken away because they belong to someone else," George replied.

"And your second, does he think the same?" the bridge officer asked slyly.

It was a diversion; the officer was regaining his strength. He flipped out of the stasis tube breaking free of Andy and George's grasp. With no time to think, the bridge officer pulled out a fiery red sphere and hurled it at George and Andy. They dropped to the floor as the red energy sphere zinged by, narrowly missing their heads and destroying a section of the hospital's inside hallway wall.

Andy rose up onto his knees and formed a red sphere before the lead officer could form another.

The officer laughed. "Child, put that away before I destroy you with it," the bridge officer yelled.

George laid his hand on Andy's shoulder and gave him every bit of strength he had. Andy threw his red-hot energy sphere with nearly all his might at the bridge officer. The impact was huge, yet it only knocked the officer out. He seemed to fall in slow motion, crumpling to the ground. Andy and George ran over and half lifted, half dragged the bridge officer back into the stasis tube in the hospital. They gave him more sleeping medicine and sealed him in the stasis tube away from the others worried he may be strong enough to wake the others.

"The energy sphere? What happened?" George asked cryptically.

"I don't know. It barely knocked him out. At first I was worried I had used too much energy. Something is really not right here, George," Andy replied, as cryptically. "It was a lot of energy. He should have been totally unconscious, not winded."

It was a mystery they would need to solve another day. In the hallway, they found a new problem. The red sphere energy explosion from the bridge officer caused a small pinhole fracture in the transport ship's hull. The squealing air echoed through the hallways as it escaped into the vacuum of space. They ran to the wall computer terminal to find the location of the leak.

George lifted Andy up into the ceiling vent system. He spun around and traced Andy's path through the ventilation system on the computer terminal. Quickly, he yelled out turns for Andy until he reached the leak. Andy let go of a small scrap of metal and it slammed hard against the outer shell of the transport ship. It was soft and would not last long. He pulled a bigger piece of metal from his sleeve. It was a piece of metal he had pulled off a chair leg in the hospital.

With the suction from the escaping air stopped for the moment, Andy positioned the new patch directly over the tiny hole. He made a small red sphere and used its energy to weld the chair leg patch into place. It wasn't pretty, but it would hold for a while. Andy climbed back out of the cramped ventilation system and lowered himself down into the hallway. After a quick high-five, they headed for the main command bridge.

"I really thought you were going to destroy the bridge officer," George said seriously, as they ran.

"I thought about it and then right at the very last second I remembered what grandfather said, 'their actions must be judged by their peers.' He is a Cal-shene, and I had no right to destroy him, but they might when we get to Asteria station," Andy replied cold and unfeeling, not looking at George. "Yet the energy sphere should have more than winded him," he added, still puzzled.

"Maybe they will ask him for information on the evil that hunts us," George said, trying to be positive turning another hallway corner.

"I think they will use him as bait for the evil the bridge officer called, master. Then, the good officers can find other evil officers, like him, that are infesting their ranks," Andy replied as coldly as before.

"I imagine the evil master, the bridge officer spoke of does not take kindly to failure," George said, looking down as they ran toward the command bridge.

"Nope, don't imagine a being like that does," Andy said. He had no sympathy for the officers.

They stopped at the kitchen on their way to the command bridge to pick up some rations, since Sara's virus would still be infecting the food supply for a few more hours. They had to eat or Gus would be, well, unhappy with them, to say the least. Rations were safe for now. You wouldn't say that if you had ever seen Anna eat a ration, but the rations didn't have Sara's virus right now so they were as OK to eat.

"Andy, about the whole red-glowing-sphere, defend-to-the-death thing. You seem so cold and calculated each time we, well you know…" George paused, hunting for the right word.

"It's OK, George. When I was very young my brothers, sisters, and I were nearly captured by some very bad people in my country. Our body guard died in front of us that day, saving our lives. He paid with his life so we could live. Nothing my father could do could ever repay him for his sacrifice that day. Oh, he took care of his family. He built them a new house on the ranch and put his children in school with us. But he never forgot the sacrifice, and I can't forget either. I saw death, fear, and hatred that day and what it does to a family. How it tore them apart. It is not something you can easily forget," Andy said, his voice sad.

Suddenly, he paused, stopping mid-step in the hallway. Turning, he stared at George with steely cold eyes.

"George, if there is ever a choice to be made, you must escape, you must let me buy you that time. I know why we are all together now, and I accept who I am for this team. We all have a part in history to play. You must not let your feelings be our downfall. I am sure it is what destroyed the other teams of the prophecy. Promise, George, here and now," Andy said firmly, raising his hand as a small red sphere glowed in the center of his palm. Andy offer his hand as an oath between them. George would have to accept Andy's decision to defend their team to the death if it was needed for their escape.

"No, Andy, no," George said, shaking his head, unwilling to accept Andy's words that he would die for them so the others and George could escape, whatever happened.

"George, what was it that Grandfather said? There is a defining moment in your life. Well, this is one for you. Don't let us die for nothing, George,"

Andy said. His voice was cold and harsh.

George stared back at Andy. Andy was so steadfast and confident in his decision. George straightened up. He was their leader, and they believed in him and in themselves. That was all that mattered. He grabbed Andy's hand. The red sphere burned for a moment and then disappeared. No red mark was left on the palm of their hands. George rubbed his hand from the sting, hoping he had made the right decision. They walked into the command bridge, tearing open their ration packs as they walked in silence.

Inside the command bridge, George and Andy entered the bridge officer's code from Emily's capture program to open the transport ship's main computer system. Their hands ran across the keys, replacing the old computer codes with their own passwords. Andy turned off Emily's internal programs and deleted them from the computer's main memory core.

With evil no longer in control of the transport, the ship returned to its normal operations and speed. George added one of Emily's engine programs to increase the transport ship's speed and left the comet disguise turned on. No unwanted contact, and no one would be looking for a comet.

For six days they practiced their Chen-Lo, read the ships database, ate, and slept on the command bridge on small short cots. The database had only the basics about the prophecy. There was more information about the energy of the universe, but it said nothing about how to control and use it. There was no mention of Max, a long-shot George thought when Andy ran the search on the computer system. All in all, the computer system on the transport ship had very little information, as if most of the information had already been erased.

"Odd that so much information is missing," George said after one of his searches.

"Maybe they needed the computer space for something else," Andy replied.

"Maybe, but then where is the something else?" George asked, puzzled.

Andy shook his head, he had no thoughts on the possibilities. Occasionally, they checked on the CORE officers in stasis in the hospital and on Andy's repair. They called no one and sent no coded messages, as they didn't know who they could trust. On the seventh day, they neared the asteroid field of the Calshene cadet station, Asteria.

"Are you sure there no other stations in this sector? I mean Anna's star charts have to show something else out here. Maybe a nice black hole to suck us into oblivion?" Andy asked, grinning, yet only half kidding.

"We are bringing them a present, so to speak, and maybe they will have the original prophecy documents," George said, trying to find a positive answer. "Then we'll know if we will live or die!"

Andy grinned, sarcastically rolling his eyes. "Great, just what I want- some old paper telling us what to do!" he said. "Like we don't have enough people telling us now!"

"Look passed where we are, Andy. We are missing something. Grandfather told us the truth when we asked him, and I'm pretty sure he was the only one who could. Now we need to figure out what he actually said," George said, trying to get Andy to focus on the opportunity in front of them instead of the problems behind them.

They entered the Calshene asteroid field and turned off Emily's comet and speed programs, deleting them from the computer's main memory. The transport ship was ready to enter the Calshene space. Two Calshene fighters immediately flew up next to the CORE transport ship. As Pete had done before, George answered the administrator's questions, quickly in rapid succession, until they had landing clearance.

"The administrator doesn't know who we are. We need to find the Viceroy quickly before we land," George said after the view screen turned off.

"We need quarantine level 10," Andy said, quoting protocol.

"Yes, yes we do," George replied matter-of-factly not really understanding Andy's words, but confident that Andy knew the right tactical protocols.

They strengthened their link and sent a message out to the local Viceroy. He was close and answered nearly immediately—it was Pete's dad, Viceroy Petrosky, who replied. His energy stabilized their link, and they had a conversation with him as if he was on the command bridge with them.

"Sir, we lied to the administrator. It's us, George and Andy, sir," George said honestly.

"We need a quarantine level 10 for ten minions of the evil we have captured, sir," Andy said formally.

"One of the bridge officers is more, though. The bridge officer with the—" George said when Andy cut him off. Andy completed the message, giving the Viceroy the information for the correct level of security they would need for the one specific bridge officer that the evil more than possessed, it controlled.

"It will be so," Pete's dad replied formally, and their link ended.

Nearly instantaneously, new landing instructions blinked on their control console. They changed course and landed in a nearly empty spaceport. In flashes of white light, the Asteria station CORE security officers, Andy requested, started appearing on the transport ship—even before the port doors rolled open.

The security officers entered the ship's cargo bay first and surrounded the two shipping crates. With their staffs raised, the crates disappeared in a flash of white light. Next, they went after the officers in the stasis tubes in the hospital room; and they, too, all disappeared. All the while, George and Andy stayed on the command bridge, waiting as George had watched Pete do the rotation before.

Finally, the command bridge doors slid open, and the Viceroy walked inside with two Inner Circle officers at his side. They both wanted to run to Pete's dad, but they were on the Calshene station, and protocol was everything here.

"Report, cadets," Viceroy Petrosky ordered firmly.

George stepped forward with Andy standing at his side. He told their story, starting with their abduction on Earth and the capture of the ten officers of evil. The Viceroy and Inner Circle officers were stunned, amazed that two third-rotation cadets could capture ten trained officers.

"Well done, cadets. Go with Inner Circle officer Shawne to the hospital. Dismissed," he said firmly.

"Yes, sir," George replied formally.

They wanted to ask him to call their parents, to find out if the rest of their team was safe, to tell everyone they were alive and well, but that would be a big protocol issue and they could not embarrass Pete and the other captains that way.

They thought only about food, hot steaming food, on their way to the CORE hospital. They knew the game—the Inner Circle officer walking with them wasn't your average officer. She was their escort, instructed to see if she could read their minds and find out if they had told the Viceroy everything there was anything else they had not told the Viceroy.

"So, you are alive?" Viceroy Shawne said, half taunting them as they walked through the CORE corridors.

"It's a trick," George signed, and Andy nodded.

"I'm sure it will disappoint some, sir," George replied, distracting the Inner Circle officer, while Andy tried to worm his way into the officer's mind.

"Two can play this game," Andy signed as George babbled on about nothing with the Inner Circle officer.

They walked on, taking only a few more turns through the CORE corridors before the Inner Circle officer stopped in front of a doorway. She nodded, and the hospital doors opened. Medics came running to their side. The Inner Circle officer glanced at the medics, and they stopped in their tracks, waiting. Next, she turned and faced Andy at the door.

"Keep practicing, cadet, you are getting better," she said with a little smile.

Then she left down the corridor, returning the way they had come. Andy was stunned. The Inner Circle officer not only knew what he had been trying to do, she complimented him.

The medics swarmed around George and Andy the moment the Inner Circle officer was gone, nearly carrying them to their beds. Changing screens appeared, and they put on new cadet uniforms with red stripes on the sleeves. They were sitting on their beds when the Viceroy appeared. The medics scattered as the Viceroy sat down on an old wooden chair between the two beds.

"Your parents have been notified that you have been found. Your team will be here in two days' time," he said formally.

"Thank you, sir," George replied formally.

"Rest now, regain your strength," his voice was calm as he patted George and Andy on their backs. They fell asleep.

Chapter 7

PROPHECY FOUND

George rolled over and opened his eyes two days later. Emily was sitting on the floor next to his bed at eye level. He swung back with surprise. Emily laughed and Gus, Sara, and Anna turned around to face George. They were smiling from ear to ear.

"Say nothing," Emily signed with a sweet smile on her face, her soft curls twisting over her rosy cheeks.

"All is calm and focused," Sara signed, holding Andy's arm as her head spun around to face George.

"Think less," Anna added, grinning as her hair swung forward over her shoulder.

"Tell us nothing," Gus signed, nodding his head and then resting it on Anna's shoulder.

George smiled, nodding his head. "Happy, happy, happy," he signed, lifting his hand only a little off his bed.

Andy rolled over and opened his eyes. George watched as the entire play unfolded before him again. Andy smiled.

"I'm hungry," Andy thought, and a medic suddenly appeared behind them with a tray of cereal bowls brimming with brown cereal.

"Thank you, Andy," Emily signed and smiled, gritting her teeth.

"Oh yes, it is my favorite," Sara added with a grin, rolling her eyes at Andy.

They each took a bowl and ate it down. George surprised himself and ate every bite. He didn't remember being hungry.

"Cadets!" said a loud voice from behind them.

Sara, Emily, Anna, and Gus jump up and came to attention. George and

Andy rolled over and twisted up a little in their beds. One of the cereal bowls flipped off the bed, rolling on its rim, circling and rolling to a stop under George's bed.

Pete walked across the room to the cadets. "Are you sufficiently rested to depart, cadet?" Pete asked formally, staring at George.

"Yes, sir. Ready, sir," George answered, twisting his body out of the bed and standing up next to Emily. Quickly, she reached behind her back and caught George's hand to keep him from tipping over as he leaned forward.

"Cadet, are you sufficiently rested to depart?" Pete asked formally, staring at Andy.

"Yes, sir. Ready, sir," Andy answered, also twisting his body out of bed and catching Sara's hand behind her back to steady his feet.

George stepped forward and Emily supported him from behind. Andy was between Sara and Anna. Gus caught the end. The team walked so close together it was hard to see Emily, Sara, and Anna supporting George and Andy. They followed Pete out the hospital door in close formation. They walked in silence down the corridor. Emily opened the doors, and Anna mapped their path. Pete stopped in the middle of a corridor and waited for the officers in the CORE hospital corridor to pass before having Emily and Anna make an archway and open a doorway. They walked out of the quiet CORE hospital into a noisy tunnel hog terminal.

They followed the small multicolored corridors until they felt a rumble in the walls. Pete reached over and opened a slit in the wall. The cadets climbed into the tunnel hog. Emily instantly hugged the tunnel hog.

"The tunnel hog's name is Sid," Emily whispered.

Sid glowed a bright red, and Pete smiled.

"Yes, Sid is my friend," Pete thought to the cadets as the tunnel hog's slit closed.

All of the sudden, they remembered that they could communicate through their minds clearly inside a tunnel hog and that you could not be scanned inside the tunnel hog—your thoughts belonged only to those traveling with you on the inside.

Emily, Sara, and Anna hugged everyone. Unlike George, Andy and Pete, they had not seen the others for the whole school year. Gus started a new link, and everyone joined in. In a short time, the events of the last month had been communicated to the whole team, including their thoughts about the Galactic council and the evil that was hunting them.

"We were so worried, George, when you and Andy went missing. No one would tell us anything," Emily said, hugging George.

"How did you get here so fast?" Andy asked.

"We were on Jupiter station when Grandfather suddenly appeared with three other old- looking dudes. Then in a flash of white light, we were in a classroom on Asteria station," Gus said, joking a little.

"Did Grandfather and the others look weak after you arrived?" George asked, suddenly interested in the story.

"Yes, like it drained their strength a lot," Sara replied, wondering how George knew to ask.

"It does. Moving on the raw energy of the universe is difficult. It requires tremendous focus and concentration," Pete added.

"Can you do it? Anna asked.

"No. It's way passed what we can do," Pete replied, laughing as if they had told a joke.

They stared at Pete, not really understanding what he had said or the control needed to do what the Senior Viceroys had done.

George turned to Pet and asked, "Is your whole team here, sir?"

"Yes, they are here; however, Frank and Toma's teams are at the second kitchen, gathering information," Pete said, telling them more information than he was supposed to. He was hoping it might be helpful somehow.

"That's where the minions of evil were taking us," George said, telling him more, too, hoping it would also be helpful.

"You're team would be there, too, if you did not have guard duty," Emily said kindly.

"Sorry about that—rather messes up your rotation," Anna added, apologizing.

"You are our first responsibility," Pete replied, hugging Emily, Anna, and Sara.

Of course, he and his team would rather be off on a terrific adventure instead of stuck on the cadet station they had grown up on, babysitting some cadets, George thought to himself. Gus walked everyone out of the link, and the cadets stood back and leaned against Sid's inner wall. Sid glowed a warm red color again, but did not take any of their energy.

"Odd, if any other cadets leaned against the inside of a tunnel hog, the hog would, by instinct, share the cadets' energy. Yet, for this team, the hogs only took the energy given to them freely," Pete thought.

Soon Sid started to slow.

"Remember where you are at all times. Guard your thoughts. Absolute protocol—nothing less will be tolerated here," Pete warned the cadets.

"Yes, sir," they replied together and then laughed.

The tunnel hog stopped. Emily hugged Sid and thanked him for the excellent ride. To their surprise, they reappeared in exactly the same corridor they had left an hour earlier. It was a joy ride so they could talk and greet each other after being apart for the whole school year. With their greetings and updates over, Pete led them to the red cadet sector on Asteria station. He got them settled into their sleeping room and left them in the red sector alcove.

"Dinner will be soon. I'll be back to get you—don't get lost," Pete said, shaking his head. "I don't know why I even say that. Just stay here," he added and hurried out the door.

The windows looking out over the spaceport were smaller than on Indus and Jupiter stations.

"Can they scan us in the alcove?" Andy asked.

"They can scan us anywhere on this station," Emily said seriously.

"You guys can't tell me anything. I can't seem to block anyone from reading my mind," Gus said, looking sad.

George glanced at Gus and smiled, then laughed. Emily, Sara, and Anna giggled, trying not to laugh out loud. Andy laughed so hard he had to sit down on one of the red leather chair arms to regain his balance.

"Gus, think about it, you walk in and out of anyone's link you choose. You can read anything anyone is thinking. You can make a link with us without even being near us; and unless you let us in, we can't read your thoughts, even in one of our own links you started, unless you let us," Sara answered.

"Don't you understand. If you make a link with me for example, I'm not strong enough to stop you from reading my entire set of thoughts. Whether I want you to read them or not," Anna added.

"I think George is the only one who can do that, and even he has to concentrate to do it. Your mind is the one mind that is already hard to read, like Rachael's is hard to read," Emily said, nearly exasperated.

Gus stood there in disbelief, leaning against one of the arms of an overstuffed red leather couch.

"Nooo," he said, shaking his head.

"Yesss!" they all replied in chorus, laughing as they all fell back into their chairs.

The door slid open, and another red team entered the alcove.

"Oh, we didn't know there was anyone one in here. Usually we are in here in the afternoons," the lead red cadet said.

"We can make room in the alcove, welcome," George said, holding his arm out to clasp the new lead cadet's arms.

"You must be the Earthers we heard were coming for this rotation," the team's second replied rudely.

"Since you're new, I'll explain it to you. This is our alcove, get out," the team leader said rudely.

He was big, imposing, and he tried to intimidate George and the others as he strutted into the small room.

"I thought the red cadets were a team," Emily replied, tilting her head.

Sara turned to Emily. "Apparently some non-Earther cadets are only in the "me, me" development stage. We should leave before they get to the temper tantrum stage," Sara answered Emily as if the Calshene red cadets weren't in the alcove.

"You calling me childish?" the lead cadet asked, raising his voice and staring at Sara.

"Oops, too late. You already proved it," Anna replied, laughing.

George stood up and signed to his team to stop. Quietly, they started to leave.

"You better watch your back, Earthers," the lead cadet said, threatening them.

"Too late for that too," Andy replied and laughed, exiting last.

They were all laughing in the corridor as the door closed.

"They are an Amusing team of cadets," George commented.

"Too bad they never learned what the word team really means," Emily added, shaking her head and grabbing George's arm.

"Some people are just like that," Sara said, putting her hand on Andy's shoulder to stop from falling over as she giggled more.

"They miss a lot of what life is all about," Anna added, holding Gus's arm as they walked toward the dining hall.

The girls had missed the boys over the school year, and they were happy their team was together again.

"We used a lot of your programs," George said kindly to Anna, Emily, and Sara as they walked.

"You would have been proud. A good sleeping medicine, a fake navigation array, and a computer system stopper with the comet disguise," Andy added.

"I cannot believe you two stopped ten officers all alone," Sara said softly.

"We weren't really ever alone, we had all of you with us," Andy replied, hugging Sara.

They all smiled. They had missed each other's company more than they had thought.

"We need to call Pete and tell him we're moving. We don't want him to think we're lost again," George said, nodding to Andy.

"True, he did specifically use non-cryptic words and say it this time," Andy said and sent the message on his pad.

"I wonder what new extra training we will get this rotation?" Gus asked curiously as they walked.

Andy stopped in the corridor and almost choked.

"Oh yes, that's right, Andy was promised some extra training last month. I'll have to ask about that so he doesn't forget," George replied, teasing Andy.

"No, no that's OK. It'll be OK," Andy said and winced.

"Inside joke?" Emily asked, turning another corner.

"Yes; however, I think we are all going to be getting specialized training for it this rotation," George added kindly.

The sound of running feet filled the air behind the cadets. George motioned everyone back against the corridor wall to let whoever was running pass easily. Nick, Rachael, Karmen, Han, and Jennifer came running by at full speed. At the next corridor, they split up with three captains going right and two captains going left. Then all of the sudden, George knew Nick had a realization—the sound of running feet stopped. They had run passed the very cadets they were looking for.

Nick recalled the team and headed back one corridor. Pete was standing with George and the others when they returned.

"Good afternoon, sirs," George said kindly.

"Good afternoon, cadets," they all replied, grinning.

"Good afternoon for a run, sir," Emily said, smiling.

"Yes, a good afternoon for a run, cadet," Nick replied, staring at her.

"Report, cadet. Why aren't you in the red alcove?" Pete said, using his captain's tone.

He was in no mood for any more humor. George and the others straightened up.

"Another red cadet team said the alcove was theirs, sir," George replied formally.

"They insisted we leave, sir," Emily added and the others nodded like a flock of geese.

"If you saw them again, would you recognize them, cadet?" Pete asked formally.

"Yes, sir. We can identify them, sir," Andy answered confidently.

"If we see them at dinner, you will identify them cadet," Pete pressed.

"No, sir. We can't do that, sir. They said they would watch our backs, in a manner of speaking, sir. I, we wouldn't want to miss an opportunity to have someone help us, sir," George explained as they entered the dining hall.

Pete understood George's answer, but he was still not happy with it. George and the others would not rat out the other cadets for such a minor issue. They sat down at a table near the front of the dining hall while Pete, Nick, and the others sat near the back with the other captains. The team from the red alcove entered and George, Andy, Emily, Anna, Gus, and Sara ignored them. As they sat down, their food appeared before them. George and Andy were hungrier than they had thought—the food on the table smelled good.

The team from the alcove walked passed George, Andy, and the others. As George bit into a spoon full of mashed potatoes and gravy, the lead cadet swung around and knocked into George's head with his elbow. The mashed potato spoon and its contents went flying across the table, landing squarely in the center of the back of another cadet. The cadet that was hit with the mashed potatoes swung around and flung his entire bowl of mashed potatoes back across the hall. George ducked, and slopped onto the neck of the lead cadet from the alcove as the bowl bounced across the floor. The lead cadet forgot about George and dove across the table at the other cadet. The food fight was on!

George slid under the table quickly, and the others followed. The tables had grown up out of the floor and as long as someone was near them, they would stay aloft. They pulled the chairs in close to the table to block the flinging food flying over the table and splatting on the floor and tables around them. George looked at Emily and Anna.

"Can you get us out of here?" he yelled, trying to be heard over the roar of cadets. Then he glanced at Andy. "Tell Pete we're leaving, be back soon."

Andy nodded and slid out his pad.

The commotion in the room was getting louder as officers started to arrive and shout commands over the roar of the wild cadets. Yet, the food fight did not die down; it only got worse as the officers were quickly covered in food.

Anna held out her pad and pointed to the floor. George and Gus touched Emily's shoulders as she reached out and touched the spot on the floor Anna was pointing at. A small hole opened in the floor. It looked like the hole in the ceiling of a dome as it spun open. Andy slid through first, followed closely by Anna, Sara, George, Emily, and then, Gus. On the other side, Andy pulled each cadet into the ceiling supports of a small dome. Emily closed the hole, and they climbed down the dome supports.

They had all tried to keep in shape over the school year, but they all felt stiff and awkward climbing down the dome supports. Emily reached down first and touched the floor of the dome before anyone could stop her.

"It's safe, it's like the caves on Jupiter and Indus stations" she said, smiling and playing with the whirling dust on the ground.

"Small dome," Gus commented, looking around.

"Everything seems smaller here. I suppose it's because it's an asteroid instead of a moon," Anna replied.

Everyone nodded as they spread out across the dome. Anna scanned for another archway and Emily talked with the dome walls as the dust swirled around her feet, wanting to play some more. In the quiet of the dome, Anna whistled. Everyone turned and ran to Anna.

"It's either a cave or a corridor. I can't tell," she said and created an archway. George grabbed Emily's hand before she could touch the door.

"Anna, are there any other archways or holes in the floor of this dome?" George asked, releasing Emily's hand.

"Hmm, I didn't think of another hole in the floor," Anna replied, smiling. The archway closed.

Emily and Anna stood in the middle of the dome while Anna waved her hand over the floor. Another circular door appeared. Emily waved her hand over the door; and it spun open, swirling the dust high into the air. George nodded and Gus went through first this time. George turned to Andy, send another message to Pete .

"We are OK, exploring caves, be back soon," George said to Andy.

"We are so dead," Andy said and the others agreed as Andy sent the message to Pete.

"We've been here for two days. How bad can it be?" George asked.

"We've only been awake for a couple of hours; so... I don't think it counts," Andy replied.

"They came running to find us when we were kicked out of the red alcove," Emily said, a little worried at what Pete would do to them.

George only smiled and slipped through the hole. Andy was last. This time they dropped into a larger dome. However, they did not come through in the center of the dome, but on the side of the dome, landing on a balcony, of sorts. Below them were rows and rows of wooden shelves filled with parchments and books. Officers, without colors on their sleeves, sat in dark blue easy chairs below them, reading the parchments. Others sat on the wooden chairs that ringed the long wooden bench tables scattered among the rows and rows of bookshelves.

Emily turned around and looked at the wall. More books and scrolls lined the small wall behind them. She forgot about Pete and being worried. Her fondest memories of home were in the London library with her favorite librarian. As Emily told the story, it was the one place she felt safe and free.

"Look! The wall has been carved out to fit each of the parchments," Emily whispered.

"Where are we, Anna?" George asked quietly.

She pulled up her pad and started typing as Emily turned and touched everyone's sleeves. Their red stripes disappeared; instantaneously, they were promoted to CORE office rank. George raised an eyebrow.

"I don't think this is a place that allows cadets," she signed, smiling sweetly, happy to have found a library on Asteria station.

"How old is this station?" Gus whispered, staring at the old scrolls in the walls.

"At least 5,000 years old, if the story is accurate," Emily answered, looking up from her pad.

"We're in a library, of sorts," Anna said, looking up from her pad and then looking down to read more.

"Yes, you are correct," said a pleasant voice from behind them.

The cadets spun around. A tall slender creature in shimmering silver clothing stood in front of them. The creature was nearly translucent with a long flowing, glistening robe that touched the floor.

"We are looking for the old prophecy scrolls. We thought they would be up here with the others, however, they seem to be misplaced, ma'am," Emily replied, saying the first thing that popped into her mind.

The translucent librarian smiled. "The scrolls you speak of were once stored here; however, they were transferred to the main archive long ago. I can direct you to a computer terminal if you wish to study them," the librarian said, her voice soft and soothing as she motioned toward the lower floor.

A computer copy here would be missing the same information missing on Earth, Emily thought.

"Do the original scrolls still exist, ma'am?" Emily asked, looking for another answer.

"Yes, of course. However, they are difficult to read as they have deteriorated over the millennia," the librarian answered kindly.

"May we still see the scrolls? We have come such a long way, it would be a shame to have come and then not even get to see them, ma'am," George said as graciously as he could, trying to find a compromise for Emily and the librarian.

Emily nodded and followed George's lead. "We would, of course, want to study the computer archive copies after seeing the original scrolls, ma'am," Emily added, smiling sweetly.

"Yes, that would be a good solution. Please follow me," she said kindly.

The translucent creature had a soft librarian voice. Her long flowing robe seemed to shimmer and change to a reddish color as she glided between the cadets, following the balcony around the upper ring of the library dome. Her strides were long and the cadets were nearly at a run just to keep up with her. She stopped at a wooden bookcase on the balcony level. It was the only wooden bookcase on the balcony level.

She touched the wood and then slid her hand over to an old scroll tied with a red ribbon and sealed with a ring of dark red wax. The bookcase creaked as the librarian pushed the bookcase inside an opening in the dome wall. It was a doorway into the caves that riddled the station. Emily held her hand on the wooden bookcase and touched the scroll as they walked into the cave behind the library dome. The door closed when they were all inside the cave.

The librarian opened a second door directly across from the first door and stepped into a small, brightly lit room. The cadets followed her inside, and again, the door closed behind them. A large wooden table was in the center of the room and eight wooden chairs were placed around the room.

"Reading room, sit down," Emily signed quickly before anyone could say anything.

The librarian moved her hand across the wall and a dozen scrolls appeared. "These are the prophecy scrolls you have requested. I will return when you are done," she said. Turning, she moved her hand over another section of wall, and a computer terminal appeared. "You can access the translation files from here," the librarian said softly.

"Thank you, you have been most kind and generous, ma'am," George said, dropping his head down low.

The others followed, lowering their heads and dropping their eyes. The librarian seemed to blush, then turned and opened the door with a nod, leaving the cadets alone.

George raised his hand immediately. "Focus, focus only on the task at hand," he signed. "No distractions."

They smiled and nodded. Emily went to the computer terminal and started her search. Gus, Anna, Sara, and Andy each took down three scrolls. One by one, they opened the scrolls and scanned the images into their pads.

"It is similar to ancient Egyptian hieroglyphics," Anna whispered.

"Can you translate any of it?" Andy asked.

"Not yet," Emily replied.

"The color is amazing. You would have thought really old scrolls would have less color and less picture words," Gus commented, scanning the second scroll.

"What do you mean, Gus?" Andy asked.

"Well, ah, ya know, the ancient scrolls of Egypt and China, I mean the really old ones, had very little color. Paper was difficult to make and few colors other than black could withstand the environment of the time; hot and cold, humid and dry. These scrolls have a lot of color, like when the monks wrote the original Bible copies by hand. They added color to highlight special passages and mark different sections in the Bible," Gus whispered, pointing to a colorful section on the scroll in front of Anna.

"A good observation, Gus. These must not be the original prophecy scrolls. Only a decoy to fool the unobservant reader," George whispered, nodding his head.

"I agree. These scrolls do have a lot of color," Anna said, nodding her head and hugging Gus.

Andy, Anna, and Sara returned the scrolls to their cubbyholes and everyone focused on Emily.

She was shaking her head. She was holding up her pad and pointing it at the computer and then accessing another computer informational portal. Each time, she came up without the files she was searching for. She had found a translator, a kind of Rosetta stone or matrix, that translated each character from one language to another. This was good; however, she really wanted the original prophecy file.

"Emily, can you find where the original scrolls are kept? The librarian gave us new scrolls, not the original old scrolls," Sara asked.

"The scroll is here in the room. The library database says the prophecy scroll is here in this reading room. We are in the right place," she whispered, not turning her head or removing her hands from the computer terminal.

The others spread out across the room, scanning for a hidden bookcase. George sat down at the table to think. He looked around the small white room. A single yellow sphere in the center of the ceiling lit the reading room brightly.

"Andy, where is the best place to hide something?" he asked.

Andy stopped and turned toward George, sitting down across the table from him.

"It's a trick question, right?" he answered with a puzzled look. He knew this answer, but he just could not think of the answer right then.

"In plain sight," Anna replied slowly, as if the words hurt to say.

"Yes, and where is plain sight?" George asked.

They all stared at George and then at the large wooden table in the middle of the room.

"It is an awfully thick wooden table. Now, isn't it," Sara said, sitting down next to George.

"It is, indeed," Anna said, touching the tabletop. A cabinet door appeared.

George ran his hands over the outline of the doors, but they did not open. Gus leaned back on two legs of his chair, touching Emily's elbow with one hand and the table with his other hand. The light in the room blinked and dimmed.

"That's it," Emily whispered.

The two flat cabinet panels embedded in the tabletop split in the center, curling back as if rolling up. Suddenly, the rolls dropped down below the tabletop, revealing a thin gray mist. Anna blew gently on the gray mist. As the mist cleared, a hidden compartment below the tabletop revealed a single parchment scroll tied with a red ribbon.

"Hidden in the table itself," Andy whispered.

"I have the real scroll on the computer," Emily whispered.

"So do we," Anna replied.

Emily was happy. George knew Emily would know the key for the translation of the prophecy scroll. He was sure it would not be written in English or any other known Earth language. George lifted the single large scroll out of the table and the cabinet panels lifted and closed, leaving a flat tabletop again.

The prophecy scroll was old, dusty, and dry to the touch. It reminded him of the ancient scrolls of the Egyptian architect he had seen when his school had gone to see an Egyptian exhibit at the museum in his city. It was a big exhibit with mummies, golden tombs, and all shapes and sizes of artifacts. There was a model of a temple to some god and the architects' scrolls were rolled out next to it.

George untied the red ribbon, and Andy separated the two wooden dowels. There was no color on this scroll, and the hieroglyphics were written tightly together. George glanced at Gus. He was right—no color, no wasted space.

Gus, Emily, and Sara scanned the scroll into their as George and Andy rolled the scroll open and closed over the table.

Before them was more than a 100,000 years of prophecy in a language they could not read, and somewhere buried inside was a chapter about them. Or at least they hoped there was. Was their future already determined for them? Who had written the prophecy so long ago? Could the prophecy be rewritten, and were they the ones to change it? A thousand questions ran through their heads. It seemed like only a few minutes had passed when they reached the end of the scroll. The last few turns were empty, as if there was room for more history or prophecy to be written.

George and Andy rolled the scroll back up in the reverse order, lifting it up off the table. The door panels slid open as if expecting the prophecy scroll to be replaced. Together, they carefully set the scroll inside the secret compartment, and the panels on the table rolled closed. Sara walked back to the scrolls on the wall and took out the last scroll as Anna loaded the file from her pad into George and Andy's pads.

Sara and Gus rolled it out across the tabletop.

"Are you done, Emily?" Anna asked quietly.

"Yes," she answered, closing her window then returning to the colorful scroll on the terminal.

"I cannot believe we made it through all twelve scrolls," Sara spoke loudly.

"Yes, the computer copy was much clearer than the twelve scrolls. Our librarian was correct," Emily stated boldly.

"I am pleased we could see the scrolls; they are so old," Anna said, adding to their deception.

Gus slipped the last scroll back into the cubbyhole, and the cadets all sat down to wait. Within a minute of the cadet's play, the librarian appeared at the door.

"You were all so quiet, did you find what you were looking for?" she asked kindly.

"Yes, ma'am. Thank you, ma'am," George replied generously.

"Are you done, or was there something else you were looking for?" she asked.

She seemed to glow with a multi-colored aura as she stood in the doorway.

"We are done for now. Thank you for your kind assistance, ma'am," George replied nearly mesmerized by her appearance.

"Please follow me. Which archway did you want to leave through?" she asked softly as she stepped out of the reading room and back into the cave.

The cadets shook their heads as panic raced through their minds. They had not planned on having an escort when they left the library reading room.

"The CORE hospital wing will do, if you please, ma'am," Anna piped in, saying the only place they knew other than the cadet sector.

"Our colleague is not feeling well, ma'am," Andy added, jostling Gus a little.

Gus did look a little pale, come to think of it. Actually, they all looked a little pale, even in the dim light of the cave, George thought.

"As you request," she replied, smiling and leading them through the cave.

Turning to the right at the first split, she stopped and opened an archway. Before she could open the door, Emily fell forward, pretending to trip and touched the door. It glided open. The librarian was a bit surprised; however, she quickly regained her composure and bowed her head to them.

"Thank you for your kind assistance, ma'am," George said, dipping his head and eyes while stepping through the doorway.

They all dipped their heads, and the librarian returned each gesture as they passed into the hospital corridor. Andy was the last, and the door glided closed as his second foot touched the floor of the CORE hospital corridor.

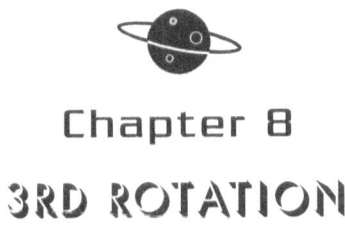

Chapter 8

3RD ROTATION

In the bright light of the corridor, they all looked pale and worn out.

"We need to eat," Gus signed.

"How long were we in the library?" Sara asked, whispering to Anna and Emily as they started through the CORE hospital corridors.

George nodded and the cadets lined up behind him as they walked. Anna held George's elbow and guided his turns. They were still officers, as far as anyone knew. One by one, Emily added the red color back to their sleeves.

She stopped at George's sleeve and turned him blue instead of red.

"Captain," she signed and rolled her eyes.

She knew he didn't like impersonating a captain, but she wanted to keep them out of trouble as cadets were not usually left to wonder around CORE hospital sectors alone. Again, he nodded reluctantly.

A group of non-color uniform officers came down the corridor and George spread out his arms and stopped the others, holding them back against the corridor wall as Pete had done to them dozens of times before.

He lowered his head and signed. "Clear your minds."

The officers passed without even a glance. A short distance further Anna stopped George and – with no officers in sight – she made an archway and a door. Emily opened it with a simple twist of her wrist. They walked out of the CORE hospital wing and into a tunnel hog terminal.

No joy ride this time – they needed food and water. Emily turned George's sleeve red as they passed through a crowd of cadets. Anna was still leading the way. Soon, only the thin red stripe of color was ,on the corridor wall. They were back in the red cadets' sector.

"We are so dead," Andy signed, thinking of Pete and wondering how long they had been missing.

"Yes, but not until after we eat," Gus signed, stopping in the middle of a corridor.

"Here, Anna, it's here," he said pointing to the wall.

"Are you sure, Gus? My map is pointing further down the corridor," Anna asked.

Gus shook his head and pointed to the wall again. Gus had never been wrong when it came to food and Anna was too hungry to argue. She made an archway and Gus opened the door himself. Andy glanced at George and smiled.

"Food talks," they laughed.

On the other side was a huge kitchen. Not the standard cadet sector kitchen, but a huge kitchen with every kind of food preparation machine you could think of. Gus went to work foraging for the foods he wanted in the large walk-in freezers and coolers, while the others gathered plates, cups and chairs. They turned a narrow silver service table into a dining table in only a few minutes. Gus handed Sara purple bottles of liquid for everyone to drink right away.

"What is it?" Andy asked casually, not thinking.

Gus turned his head and raised his eyebrow.

"Oh, I forgot, never mind, I really don't want to know, do I?" Andy answered grinning.

"Nope," Gus replied, starting a mixer. He poured a bag of this and a dash of that into the mixer, along with a bottle of red stuff and some green seaweed-looking stuff. "Nope, don't really want to know," he muttered to himself.

"We have to call Pete," Emily said, staring at George when the table was set.

"True. How about after dinner?" George said sweetly, staring into Emily's eyes.

"Ah, no, George," Emily said, shaking her head. "We have to call now," she said raising an eyebrow to George.

"Fine," George said, relenting and lowering his head to Emily.

She was right and he knew it. Andy was also right – they were going to be dead and it wasn't from the evil that now hunted them. It would be from Pete. George walked over to the archway and waved his hand. A computer terminal appeared. As it turned out, all permanent archways had computer terminals next to them. He sent a message to Pete telling him where they were and then returned to his seat next to Emily.

"Five minutes tops, and Pete comes bursting through the door," Sara said, smiling weakly – she knew they were about to be in big, big trouble for disappearing.

"Ten minutes, and it's all of them," Andy said, trying to make a game of when they would be in trouble.

"No way," Anna said as they continued their debate.

Emily turned to Gus, "Add six for dinner."

Gus smiled, nodding his head as if had been anticipating six more for dinner all along. Five minutes passed and Pete, Nick and the others burst through the archway doors out of breath.

"You all tied!" Sara said, laughing.

"Who would have guessed," Anna added.

"Please join us for dinner, sirs," George said graciously, motioning to the empty chairs around their makeshift table.

Pete would have yelled "report," of that George was sure, had he not been so out of breath. Sara and the others handed each of them one of Gus's purple liquid bottles to drink while Andy slid stools next to them to sit down on. Pete raised his hand, but George lifted his bottle in response to make a toast.

"To the ties that bind us and keep us safe," George said .

Pete smirked and took a sip of the purple liquid. It was good.

"What is this?" Nick asked.

"Don't ask, you really don't want to know," Andy signed.

Gus appeared with what looked like steaming hot biscuits and Anna jumped off her stool to help Gus carry a large pot over to their makeshift table.

"Stew, and it smells great," Andy said, inhaling the aroma.

"Yes, you could call it stew if you want," Gus said, dipping his head.

Having filled their plates with Gus's stew, Pete regained his breath and raised his glass of purple liquid.

"To the safe return of our lost cadets," he said seriously. "Eat now. Talk later," he added, staring at the cadets.

They looked weak and a little drained of strength. George and the others smiled. Andy dove in as if eating for three or four cadets. George was not sure Andy even tasted the food, based on how fast he was eating.

Nearing the end of the meal, Pete spoke up between bites. "Where were you? The last time we saw you, you were in the dining hall and a food fight had begun near your table," he asked seriously.

"We went to the Asteria library to read some books and scrolls instead of being involved in an unsightly food fight on a highly cultured station, sir,"

Emily replied sweetly.

"What library?" Pete asked, looking up.

"The officer's library here on Asteria station. The one through the floor, two domes down in the caves. The one with the silvery translucent librarians, sir," George replied.

Nick turned to Pete –his mouth was hanging open.

"How did you find out about the officers library?" Pete asked, stunned.

"We fell on it when we left the first dome, sir," George replied matter-of-factly.

"Cadet!" Pete's voice changed, thinking George was not telling the truth.

"Really, sir, we fell on it, right through the ceiling, sir," Emily answered quickly.

"You do not have high enough clearance to even enter the officer's library," Rachael said in disbelief.

"We do if we fall through the roof onto the upper balcony, sir," Sara added between bites.

Pete shook his head. "What did you read?" he asked firmly.

"The ancient prophecy scrolls, sir," Anna replied directly.

"They just brought the scroll out for you?" Nick asked with surprise.

"No questions, nothing?" Han asked, not believing what the cadets had said.

"Actually, they take you to a small reading room and open a panel on the wall. The scrolls are all lined up. There are twelve of them, sir," Anna said, speaking up quickly to keep George from being too flip and honest.

They had missed the point that Nick had only said the word scroll, not scrolls. He knew there was only one prophecy scroll.

"There's a computer terminal, too. It has a Calshene translated version, sir," Emily added quickly to hide the truth that they thought only they knew.

"What does it say?" Han asked between bites.

"We don't know yet, we got hungry before we could translate it so we came here, sir," Sara replied, munching on her roll.

"Not even I have ever been to the officer's library and you expect us to believe you happen to fall into the library while leaving a food fight on your second day at Asteria station, only hours after waking up in the hospital?" Pete said, not believing the cadets' story.

Pete and the others were in disbelief.

"Sorry, we didn't mean to upset anyone, sir," Anna added kindly.

"But it is the truth, honestly, sir," Sara added.

"Can you tell us about the caves on Asteria station, sir?" Emily asked Pete, changing the subject.

"They are very different from the caves on Jupiter station and Indus station, sir," Anna added.

"They are all sealed from the surface of the asteroid. Unlike the moon's, there is no rotation to hold even a thin atmosphere around the asteroids," Pete replied, finishing his last bite.

"This asteroid is the biggest piece that is left of the Calshene home world, right sir?" Emily said, looking down.

She was sorry she had asked; she had not meant to open up old wounds for Pete and his Calshene team.

"It is late, cadets, and your training begins early tomorrow," Pete said as he got up and placed some of the dishes and pans in a large silver barrel.

The others followed and Han started the machine.

"Dishwasher?" Anna asked as they turned heading for the door.

"No, more of a cleaner system," Rachael replied, stepping up next to Anna.

The cadets followed Pete to the right and Nick and the other captains went to the left as they left the kitchen. Pete had not yelled at the cadets and it made them worry. It didn't seem right. There was something they were missing.

"Pete, have you really never been to the officers library sir?" Emily asked as they walk though the cadet corridors.

"I have never been, very few are allowed inside," he said, oddly sad.

Emily described the library in great detail to Pete as they walked. She told him of the balcony and how the walls were carved to fit the various sizes of scrolls and books. She described the long wooden tables with hard wooden chairs, some soft leather-looking chairs nearby and rows and rows of wooden bookshelves on the main floor.

Emily talked about the librarian and her silvery translucent appearance and how easily she guided them around the balcony and out to the reading room in the caves. Pete actually felt like he was there with them on one of their adventures again. Pete dropped them in their sleeping room.

"Lock the door Emily and stay here until I come back in the morning," Pete spoke in his captain's voice.

Emily slid out her pad and loaded the locking code onto Pete's pad. The door closed and Emily locked the door and loaded another locking program into the computer system.

"Emily, what program did you give Pete's pad," George asked with a peculiar look on his face, thinking a simple locking program would have taken far less time to load on Pete's pad than what it had taken.

"A copy of the original 'locking program' just in case he needs it, of course," she said, smiling.

"Yes, he will need the original 'locking program', very thoughtful of you," George replied, nodding his approval.

Andy was beginning to understand cryptic now and he knew Emily had downloaded the original prophecy onto Pete's pad without him knowing. He nodded to himself as their beds rose from the floor and they all laid down to go to sleep.

George was calm that night, oddly calm. Someone was helping them sleep. In his mind's eye he knew it; yet he could not wake his conscious mind to see who it was.

Early the next morning, George rolled over and opened his eyes. Pete was sitting at the table with a stack of bowls and spoons and a box of brown cereal ready to pour. George was happy. His team was safe and for a few moments all seemed right with the universe. George rolled his legs around and stood up. He walked over to the table and sat across from Pete. He gazed into his cereal bowl of brown mush.

"So who is protecting us? I feel calm and at ease and I know that means someone is helping us block out others, sir," George whispered, trying not to wake the others.

"It's not my team; we have to be near you to do that. Any guesses?" Pete asked.

"Grandfather, of course, and maybe his triad, sir," George replied, then thought for a minute.

"Don't tell the others, Pete, they have been through more than they should and they need a little peace, sir," George whispered, and Pete nodded. "Someone was here last night, too, sir," George added pouring the cereal into his bowl.

"Didn't Emily lock the door?" Pete pressed, wanting to know who had been let inside.

"Yes, but someone was still here. Whoever it was, they calmed everyone's minds, sir," George added.

"Did you see who it was?" he pressed worried someone was trying to invade their minds.

"No, however, I know them, I have felt their presence before sir," he said, puzzled.

Andy yawned and their conversation stopped. First Andy, then Anna and then the others slid off their beds and came to the table to eat.

"Brown cereal, serves us right for having such a good meal last night," Andy said, bumping Gus in the shoulder.

Gus smiled. He would never be able to tell them what they had eaten last night or what the purple liquid really was. He had crammed as many nutrients into the 'stew' as he could and still have it be edible.

"You know, everyone, not all purple liquid is drinkable. You can't assume that because it looks like the purple liquid that we can drink it, right?" Gus said as they ate.

"We know, Gus, we would never eat anything but rations without you saying we can," Anna said, reassuring Gus. Everyone agreed.

"Besides, then I might actually know what I'm eating and that could ruin a perfectly good appetite," Andy added.

Gus smiled, taking a bite of his cereal.

"The Galactic council has decided you have a choice. Your team can stay here on Asteria station or return to Jupiter station for your third rotation," Pete said in his captain's voice.

George barely needed to glance around the table to know their answer, even Andy's.

"We would prefer to stay on Asteria station, sir," he replied.

"It will be significantly more difficult. This is not like the Earth or the Thorean cadet stations," Pete said.

"We need the practice, sir, or we will never learn to hide our thoughts," George said seriously.

"I will inform the Galactic council of your choice. As with your second rotation," Pete started as if he knew what their choice would be, "You will have three primary instructors: Major Ben Gatte, who teaches stellar navigation and map reading; Major Ruth Pennelo, she teaches basic flight; and Colonel Lukan Moawk, who teaches physical fitness and self defense training. Today you will have a half day with Major Gatte in the morning and Major Pennelo in the afternoon. You will need to get between classes and to lunch on your own. I will be back at dinner to take you to your additional training," he said, now in full captain mode.

Pete stood up and the cadets slipped their bowls into a small silver drawer on the end of the table. Emily slipped up next to Pete before he opened the door.

"Sir, I made an update to the locking program, can I add it to your pad, sir?" she asked kindly.

Emily had been quiet during their breakfast discussions. She had been busy on her pad searching for the prophecy files. They were all gone. Pete nodded and Emily added a slight change of the locking program to Pete's pad. More importantly, she copied the original prophecy files back onto her pad and the Rosetta stone file she had found while in the library file system. She finished, and Pete slid his pad up his sleeve. Emily copied the files to everyone else's pads while George distracted Pete as they walked through the corridors.

"Be careful George, things are never what they seem to be here," Pete signed, dropping the cadets at Major Gatte's classroom door, then disappearing quickly down the corridor.

Inside, the classroom was nearly full and George and the others sat near the back of the room. Major Gatte was a short, stout man with thin gray hair that was so short that it stood up like a brush on the top of his head. The last team to enter was the team that had kicked them out of the red alcove the day before and had started the food fight. Of course, they had to sit at the table next to George and his team.

"Look! It's the Earthers," the lead cadet said and pointed as they sat down.

"Where were you in the dining hall?" one of the cadets said, taunting the cadets.

"Elsewhere," Andy replied, turning his attention to the Major at the front of the room.

"Cadets, turn on your 3D holographic projectors and bring up the Calshene galaxy," the Major said to start the class.

"If the Major goes too fast, we can help you," a tall brown-haired cadet said tauntingly.

"Need help with the switch, Earther?" a fourth cadet said sarcastically.

"Thank you for your gracious offer of help. We will keep it in mind," Emily replied, starting the projector without touching any switches.

"It's a test," George signed to his team.

"A test? I hate tests," Gus signed, crinkling his nose.

"Yes, you're right, they are the test," Anna whispered, lowering her head.

"I want an easy test for a change," Sara added, whining a little.

"And not first thing in the morning on our first day of training," Emily signed, and sighed.

"Well, it's an annoying test. That's for sure," Andy whispered.

"Focus," George signed, and they all looked at the Major.

The Major had them bring up one navigational star cluster after the next. They plotted jump after jump until they could all do it in their heads without looking at their hands moving across the keypads on the tables.

"Sometimes you have to make course corrections as you are traveling at high rates of speed, and you cannot look at your hands to make those corrections as they are coming fast and you could crash if you miss one," the Major said.

"Can you sequence course corrections?" Anna asked.

Before the Major could answer, the classroom door burst open and an older looking CORE officer and two CORE guards hurried over to the Major and whispered in his ear.

"They want you, George," Andy signed, reading their lips. "They are looking for the copy of the prophecy scroll from the officer's library."

"Cadets Hawkins, you are needed in the corridor," Major Gatte said seriously and motioned for George to go with the officers.

Gus and Andy touched his shoulder and made the fastest link in cadet history – well, at least to them it was the fastest. He walked toward the door. Emily, Anna and Sara joined the link as the rest of the class sat in silence, glancing back and forth at the door and the remaining Earthers. Emily thought of their last galaxy jump from Earth to Calshene, and planted the distraction seed in their link.

"Pull out your pad, cadet," a second older looking CORE officers ordered as the door closed.

Outside in the corridor, the two CORE guards yelled at George, words that could be faintly heard through the door. In the bright light of the corridor, George knew they were not standard CORE guards. They looked like CORE officers! The third, older CORE officer scanned his pad for traces of the prophecy. A fourth officer who had not entered the classroom was waiting in the corridor for George. This officer's mind was strong, even Viceroy-like, and he invaded deep into George's mind as the two CORE officers yelled.

Unlike Pete and Frank's teams when they had taught George about mind invasion, this older officer was not stealthy. He was a brute on a search and destroy mission. George's mind burned as he worked hard to hide his thoughts. The fourth officer was ruthless, inflicting as much pain as he could to try and break George's concentration as he searched for information on the prophecy. George fell to his knees clutching his head.

"We know you were in the officers' library, cadet. Did you think we would not find out?" the first CORE officer yelled.

"Where is it? Where is your copy of the prophecy?" the second CORE officer yelled.

"Only the leader could be trusted with this important information. Tell me now!" the first CORE officer yelled.

The third CORE officer shook his head, "Nothing here, only a bunch of maps on space jumps, lists of edible food and the rules of Sport," he said, disgusted that he couldn't find what he wanted.

Inside, his team was straining to help George maintain his calm. The fourth officer was strong, and battered George's mind for information. After nearly thirty minutes, the officers stopped and the first older CORE officer and two CORE guards reentered the classroom with George. As the door opened, the cadets gasped. George's face was beat red and his hands were shaking. They held him up and pushed him into the classroom.

"He's all yours again," the CORE officer said, tossing George's body toward the Major as they left.

He took two steps, stumbled, and fell to the floor of the classroom. One of the cadets ran to the door and opened it to look and see if they had really left. They were nowhere in sight. Sara ran to the front of the room and lifted George into her arms, forming a small yellow sphere in her hand.

"No Sara, you are just as weak from helping me with my focus," he said .trying to push her hand back.

"Too bad, George, we're part of your team and we can't leave you like this. What little energy I have I freely share," she said out loud.

Gus, Andy, Emily and Anna sat down next to Sara at George's side and held each others' shoulders as they shared their energy. Sara's glowing yellow healing sphere barely glowed over George's body.

"Darn it!" came the voice of the team leader that had taunted them from the day before.

He pushed his way to the front of the class and placed his hand on Andy's shoulder. Soon the entire class was sharing their energy and Sara's little yellow sphere grew and grew, covering George, then their team, and then the whole classroom of cadets.

Slowly, he opened his eyes again, the flush faded from his face and he stopped shaking. Sara smiled and nodded to Gus. Gus stepped each cadet out of the energy link, releasing one cadet after the next. Soon only Sara and George were left. When that link was stopped, Andy helped George stand up and the class cheered.

"Thank you for your strength and energy. It is a generous gift, thank you all," he said looking directly at the team leader who had started the class sharing.

The lead cadet said nothing at first, then stared at George.

"What did the CORE officer want?" he asked.

"The CORE officers want documents that were copied from the main computer on Asteria station. When I did not have them in my possession, they were very disappointed and wanted me to know how disappointed they were," George replied weakly, fibbing a little about what the officers really wanted.

"They were CORE officers. They could have killed you, Earther," he said abruptly.

"Maybe, but there would have been too many witnesses and then there would be an inquiry, and it all gets very messy for a well-structured society. So they shared their disappointment with me instead," George replied, nodding to the lead cadet.

Andy helped George back to his seat.

"I am proud of all of you; you helped another without regard for your own safety. Few cadets would ever do that, and I have never seen it done at such a young level. I am very pleased. You may be dismissed early today," the Major said. He was actually grinning, as he held his arm out toward the door.

"Everyone!" Sara yelled over the commotion in the room, "You must not rest no matter how tired you are. Help each other, you must eat as much food as you can hold. We have all used up a lot of our strength and energy this morning."

The cadets nodded and started to leave the classroom, heading for the dining hall. The team leader walked up behind George and leaned over.

"We'll always have your back while you're with us," he whispered, oddly kind.

"We didn't forget," he replied.

George had a weak smile as the team leader and his team passed by to leave the classroom. Andy and Sara helped George as Gus helped Anna and Emily leave the classroom and head for the dining hall, too.

"Last night there was a great calm over all of us," George whispered to his team as they walked.

"Explains why I slept so good," Andy replied.

"Whoever it was wiped the prophecy from our pads. The officers could not find it on my pad. Not even a trace, it's all gone. Our answers are all gone, Andy," George said sadly.

Andy glanced at Emily quickly.

"Well, now here's the thing. Emily already retrieved it from Pete's pad this morning and put it on everyone's pad but yours. She was going to put it on yours, only she didn't have the opportunity yet," Andy said with a little grin.

"Perhaps in light of the most recent sharing experience, Emily shouldn't, at least not yet," George replied, smiling weakly.

"So they think only the leader could be trusted with such an important document. Weird," Gus said, shaking his head.

They turned the last corridor corner to enter the dining hall and all the cadets were lined up waiting at the doors. The doors would not open. Emily slipped forward. She looked at the leader of the team that had stepped forward and helped them.

"I can open the doors, however, I need your help and strength to do it," she said quietly.

He nodded and she placed her hand on his shoulder and the other on the door. It slid open. She thought of nutritious foods as tables and chairs rose from the floor of the dining hall. The smell of warm, delicious foods filled the air as dish after dish appeared on the tables. The cadets wanted to rush right in, but they waited for George and his team to enter and sit down before acting like crazed, starving animals. This time, not a drop of food was wasted. The room was quiet as the cadets ate bite after bite of food that appeared before them.

In time, they all beg to slow and then leaned back to rest. The chairs and benches were not the most stable of furniture, so the cadets leaned back and balanced on each other. They were beginning to trust each other; they were not in competition with each other anymore. A small transformation started to take place in the cadets in the oddest of places – on a station constrained by rules and mired in mistrust and competition. They saw past themselves and started to help each other.

The doors of the dining hall burst open suddenly and the team captains came running in, shouting orders. The thirty-six chairs and bench legs thundered to the floor at once. The captains stopped. The cadets stood up and George stepped forward.

"We were dismissed early, sirs. We were hungry, sirs. We came here where it would be safe, sirs," George said to the captains.

"Cadet, we heard there was some sort of trouble," a captain added, looking around the room.

The team leader that helped George earlier walked up next to George. "No trouble here, sir, only hungry cadets, sir," he said, wrapping his arm over George's shoulder and smiling.

"Carry on, cadets. Dismissed," the lead captain replied, and the others backed out and closed the doors.

"You stood up to the captains!" the lead cadet said, stepping back from George.

"Yes, so did you," George replied, nodding and walking back to his table.

"But you're an Earther!" the lead cadet replied.

George spun around. "And you are a Calshene. I guess it really doesn't matter when your team needs you," George said. holding his arm out.

The lead cadet clasped his arm and they all nodded. When George sat down, Gus pushed pie in front of him.

"Eat more, talk less," Gus said seriously.

George took a bite of berry pie and grinned at Gus. The other leader sat down and a low rumble of whispers filled the hall once more. The other red cadets entered the hall as their classes ended at the regular time and they came in to eat; however, the room was fairly quiet until the real lunch break was over.

Chapter 9

HIDDEN KNOWLEDGE

Everyone from Major Gatte's training was feeling better as they left for their next class with Major Ruth Pennelo. They looked forward to her basic flight training

George stared at Emily, Sara, and the rest of his team as they left the hall.

"Thanks, I would never have made it without your link," he whispered to his team as they walked through the corridors.

"Which CORE officer did the mind invasion?" Emily asked, slipping up next to George.

"You didn't see him. He stayed in the corridor when the others came in for me. He was older. I'd say he was a Viceroy we haven't met yet," George answered.

"And the yelling CORE officers?" Anna pressed as they walked.

"At first I thought they were CORE officers too, but I think they were really Viceroys or Inner Circle officers. They were too good to be anything else," George whispered, rubbing his head.

"About the locking program, Emily?" George asked, changing the topic to the prophecy.

"It's almost translated. Working on five pads is speeding the process along," Emily replied, smiling.

"We need to get it off our captain's pad. Since the officers believe that only the leaders can be trusted with important documents, Pete is now at risk. They didn't find it on mine. I'm sure they will go after Pete, Toma, and Frank next," George signed as they walked.

Emily frowned and thought. "He's not on the station right now or he would have been at the dining hall and he wouldn't have accepted your flimsy excuse," Emily whispered.

Emily was right. Pete would not have accepted his excuse, and they would pay for that later. Right now their captains had to be warned before they returned to the station that evening. They followed the other red cadets to Major Pennelo's training classroom and took seats near the back of the room. The Major came in and the cadets stood up.

"We will be in the flight simulators today. Cadets, gather your teams," she said and left the classroom, leading the cadets through the corridors. In the corridor they turned to the right, the left, and then walked straight ahead for a long time until the thin red lines on the walls joined with other thin colors striping the corridor walls. The Major stopped at an oversized archway and appeared to type in some sort of code. Gus gently lifted Anna up to his shoulder, and she signed the code behind her back to her team. The door opened after the seventh number was entered. The red cadets quietly followed the Major into the enormous cavern.

George, Andy, and the others stopped before entering the archway. The door closed. Emily stepped up and typed in the code Major Pennelo had just entered from her pad, and the door opened again. She touched the door as they went through, running quickly up to the other cadets who were looking up, all the while their mouths were hanging open. The cavern was enormous- certainly every bit the size of Jupiter city. In front of them were row after row of both single and team gliders. The single-person gliders were identical to the Thorean single-person gliders they had flown on their last rotation. They were sleek with a tail, like the gild on an arrow, and had short cupped wings. The team gliders were bigger, with the center of the glider bubbled out, but they had the same tail and short cupped wings. It looked like someone had blown up a balloon and stretched the middle of the glider around it.

"Why is this cavern so big?" Gus asked, still staring at the ceiling.

"Because you can't stay hidden with a bunch of gliders flying around an asteroid cluster," Anna whispered. The others nodded.

The cadets lined up across the cavern floor close to Major Pennelo.

"Today we will be training in the flight simulators. Once you pass your simulator program test, you will be allowed to ascend in one of the team training gliders. Are there any questions, cadets?" Major Pennelo asked.

The cadets looked too disappointed to ask any questions. George wanted some time to make a link, so he wasn't going to say anything about being the team that set the flight record on the last rotation.

"Leaders, assemble your teams at each of the simulators," she continued.

George and the others gathered around a rather beat-up looking simulator. It's hard to say how a simulator could be dented and scraped since it never actually flew; but there it was, banged and bumped. Its silver paint nearly all scraped off.

The team climbed in and Emily, Anna, and Sara took the lead. George knew better than to even suggest any other arrangement. Gus touched Anna, Sara, and Emily's shoulders and made a link for them. Anna started the simulator, and the small pod lifted off the ground.

"So I guess this is how the simulator got scraped," Anna said, giggling with Sara and Emily.

"Will you be all right?" George asked.

"We'll be fine, George," Anna said, moving the controls forward slowly.

George looked at Gus. "We need a link, you know the kind. Your first priority is Anna, Emily and Sara. OK, Gus?" he said. His voice was low and serious.

Gus smiled. "Preventing crashing to our death versus you two having a headache for breaking a link? Hmm, I think I got it," he replied with the 'duh' look.

"Sorry about that, I didn't mean to state the obvious," he said, apologizing.

"Concentrate now, George. If Emily is right, Pete is far away; and you have to get to him soon," Gus said as he sat down in the middle chair in the second row of the little simulator. Gus put his hands on George and Andy's shoulders.

"I will need your energy in the link, Andy," George said.

"Actually, only you and Pete will be in this link. Andy and I will share our energy; otherwise, we will slow you down this time," Gus said, correcting George and telling him exactly what was going to happen.

Andy nodded and Gus started the link. Gus first made a link with Andy and George. George reached out with his thoughts and Andy followed. They thought only of Pete, of finding Pete. A flash of thought and Pete answered George, and then Gus pulled Andy out of the link.

Andy concentrated on helping George focus and calm his mind. It worked. George found Pete more clearly.

"Danger, danger, destroy locking programs immediately, danger, danger!" George repeated over and over. He was cryptic, as he was afraid they could be overheard. Frank suddenly joined the link, and Pete walked out.

"What's wrong, George?" Frank asked, but George only repeated his warning.

"Danger, danger, must destroy locking programs, erase, erase, immediately!" George repeated frantically. A few moments later, Pete rejoined the link.

"Task completed, what happened?" he asked.

"No time!" George thought back. He knew their time was limited because each time they had tried to make a long-distance link, someone attacked them. Suddenly, George grabbed his head and Gus grabbed George's and Andy's shoulders again.

"Andy, stop whoever is trying to break into the link! Stop them now, they've got George!" Gus said, dropping the link with Frank and Pete instantly. They would have nasty headaches, but they would be OK. Now there was only George, Andy, and whoever was trying to break into their link. Andy made a small red sphere in his mind.

"Back away!" he said in his mind's eye, and the invader disappeared from the link.

Gus walked George and Andy out of the link. However, George still held his head. Andy and Gus looked up.

"Sara!" Gus yelled.

She spun around and seemed to glide off her chair, landing gently on the floor next to George's folded-over body.

"What did you do? Oh, never mind," she said, placing her hand on Gus's shoulder and Andy's hand on Gus's other shoulder.

"Gus, you need to regulate the flow of energy between us," she ordered firmly.

He was beginning to feel a bit like a conduit connecting everything together. Sara made a small yellow sphere and held it over George's forehead. Within a few minutes, George straightened up and opened his eyes. He grinned a little.

"Thanks, Sara," he whispered.

"The next time someone tries to suck the life out of you, would you blow them up first and ask questions later!" she said firmly, raising an eyebrow and then gliding back to her seat.

"Wicked," Andy whispered as he helped George back into his seat.

"If you're ready, we would like to pass our simulator test now," Anna asked, growing a little impatient.

"Yes. Thank you for your patience, Anna. Please pass away," George replied, smiling as he braced himself with Gus and Andy.

They hung on for dear life as Anna and Emily let loose and catapulted them into the last training program of the simulation test. A few moments later the controls console turned green and the autopilot landed the simulator pod gently on the cavern floor. The door opened and George was the first to step through. Major Pennelo was there to greet George and the others as they emerged.

"Congratulations, Cadet Hawkins, that was an impressive display of flying," the Major said.

"You need to be congratulating Cadet Jhang and her co-pilots, Cadets Millar and O'Conner, sir. I did not…," George said, but before he could finish his sentence the Major was pushing them over to another newer-looking team glider.

He shook his head and directed Anna, Emily, and Sara to the pilots' chairs. Turning around at the door, he whispered to Major Pennelo.

"I relinquish all team control to Cadet Jhang and her co-pilots, Cadets Millar and O'Conner, sir. I am redundant on this flight, ma'am," he said kindly. Smiling, he closed the door.

You could easily see the entire team inside the glider as it lifted off to fly around the cavern. The cadets smiled and swooshed off to make a lap around the cavern. Anna knew there was a flight course on Asteria station identical to the flight course on Indus station. Emily was working hard to find the code and open the hidden gates to the flight course.

"Shazam, I got it!" Emily exclaimed, keying in a code and watching the hidden gates spin open and the circle of white lights start blinking.

Anna dove and rolled as they entered the flight course tunnel. Sara and Emily plotted their course and speed, while Anna guided the small team glider in and out, over the hazards and traps in the tunnels.

"There is a shortcut up ahead," Emily said, showing Anna the coordinates.

"In we go," Anna said, rolling the tiny ship between the sharp, pointed rocky outcrops. Two dips under enormous stalagmites and a roll around a third before the ship popped out into the main cave again. They were making good time, but it wasn't about time or racing. The girls were enjoying the flight and didn't notice George, Andy, and Gus concentrating, focusing, and calming their minds. The flight was fun and challenging. The girls lost themselves in the moment of the flight. It was as if they were part of the little ship, feeling each stress, force, and load on the glider wings and engines.

"There is a second shortcut coming up. It looks tighter than the first," Emily said.

"It's a trap like on Indus station, remember," Anna said, rolling through a narrow section of cave.

"Yes, that's right," Sara replied smiling.

"And the third shortcut was good, but tricky," Emily added.

"So are we taking the third shortcut?" Sara asked.

"Not today, this ship is much too big if what Toma, Frank, and Pete have told us about the cadet stations all being alike is true," Anna said, reasoning the third shortcut would be as narrow on Asteria as it was on Indus.

Anna was a whiz at navigation, Sara a healer, and Emily a computer geek; nonetheless, at this moment, they were at peace. They had found an inner calm few ever recognize and immersed themselves in the flight. George, Andy, and Gus focused and concentrated. They could feel the happiness it brought to Anna, Emily, and Sara. They would do as much as they could to have some genuine fun on this rotation, even if it had to be one little bite at a time. The last twist in the tunnel opened up into the main cavern again and Anna circled around once before landing.

Major Pennelo came running up to the glider as they landed gently on the ground. This time George pushed Anna, Emily, and Sara out the door first. Although, it did no good. The minute George appeared, the Major congratulated him on his excellent flying. George swung his arms around Anna, Sara, and Emily and tried to convince Major Pennelo that they had flown the glider.

"Cadet Hawkins, you are too modest. I am sure they assisted you," she said. She was getting a little perturbed at his insistence that he had not flown the glider.

"Give it up, George," Anna, Emily, and Sara whispered and slipped back between Andy and Gus.

George smiled and nodded to everyone and Major Pennelo warmed and smiled, now that her cadet now accepted his role as flight leader, so to speak.

Eventually, the other cadets returned to their simulators. Some were able to make the glider trip around the cavern. Major Pennelo locked the tunnel gates to prevent the less experienced cadets from following George's lead through the tunnels.

"Where did you learn to fly like that? How did you know about the flight tunnels?" the Major asked.

"We were at Indus station on our second rotation, ma'am," George replied, grinning and thinking she would recognize them as the team that broke the record last year.

"Then you were there when the record was broken. Do you know the team that broke the flight record?" she pressed, getting excited to know someone who saw the flight record broken last rotation.

"Yes, ma'am, we do," George replied and smiled. However, before he could say another word, the Major cut him off.

"Did you know them well? I hear they were a fully integrated team. It must have been quite a treat for you to meet them," the Major said, carrying on and on.

"Yes, ma'am," he answered as the Major cut him off again and went on and on about the team that broke the record.

The cadets stood there with their mouths open. They were the team that had set the record on Indus station, yet the Major did not recognize them or listen to them.

"Listening is as much an art as speaking is," George signed to his team.

"Then we must be good listeners and find out what we did last rotation," Sara signed, teasing.

Andy and Gus lowered their heads to keep from laughing aloud.

"Yes, what did that incredible team do on the last rotation?" Anna and Emily signed between them.

Soon the class was over, and the cadets were headed back to the red cadet sector. George looked at Emily, her arm was blinking as they followed another group of cadets through the archway and into the red cadet sector corridor.

"Warning, warning," her pad repeated sending a message to Emily.

Emily stared at her pad not knowing it could send a message to her.

"Call Sid!" she signed quickly to her team.

The cadets fell against the corridor wall as CORE officers with no color on their sleeves ran passed them and into the flight cavern. George lowered his head and thought only of flight training. The wall behind him rumbled and a slit appeared. George and the others slipped into the tunnel hog. Sid took off like a bolt of lightening the instant his slit closed. The cadets tumbled to the back of Sid and Emily hugged Sid, thanking him for coming so quickly.

"What was wrong?" Emily asked Sid.

"Great danger in the corridor!" Sid replied to Emily.

Emily relayed the message to the others.

"How did Sid know there was danger, and how did he warn Emily on her pads?" George thought.

"Are we simply in the care of all the creatures we meet across the universe?" Andy wondered, staring at George and exchanging his thoughts too.

"It does seem like there are a lot of creatures watching out for us," George thought to Andy.

They all nodded. George turned to Emily as Sid took a hard left turn, and they slid into his warm, comforting side.

"Why is your pad now blinking green, Emily?" George thought.

Emily looked down and smiled. "The prophecy is translated," she replied.

The cadets forgot about Sid's danger warning and they all huddled around Emily and her pad. She expanded it to the size of a piece of paper and started to scroll through the prophecy.

"This is going to take some time," Gus said, rubbing his chin.

"Where are we going?" Sara asked.

"Sid said someplace safe," Emily answered, without taking her eyes off the prophecy.

George was reading fast, scrolling through the pages faster than even Emily could read. He needed to know if the answers to saving his team were hidden in the text of the prophecy. Sid bumped and came to a stop slower than usual. The cadets emerged from Sid to find themselves in an old, moderately sized cavern with a dozen sleeping tunnel hogs.

"Sid said we are all safe here. They know of our rescue of the tunnel hogs on Indus station, and they will take care of us on Asteria station," Emily replied, walking to the center of the room.

A light green moss on the walls glowed and created a dim light for the cadets to see by.

"We need to rest," George said, yawning.

"No, we need to eat first," Gus corrected.

He dipped his head to Gus. Gus was usually quiet, so when he insisted, they needed to listen.

"Gus, there are only rocks here," Andy muttered, shaking his head.

"Stone soup," Sara said, giggling thinking of the children's story she had been told many years ago.

Gus shook his head while slipping his backpack off his back and placing it on the ground in front of him. He pulled out two ration packs and slit them open. George and the others stared in disbelief. Gus sliced and diced the rations. Then he unzipped a small pocket on the side of the backpack and pulled out a little bottle. He carefully poured a few drops of purple liquid over each slice. Then he screwed the top back on the little bottle and slipped it back into its pocket.

"What's that purple stuff?" Sara asked.

Gus glanced at Sara and smiled.

"You remembered," Sara said filled with glee.

"Of course, I studied a lot over this last school year too," he replied kindly.

"Whaaat?" Andy asked. His head twisting back and forth between Gus and Sara.

"Vitamins and nutrients for energy, Andy," Sara replied.

She was happy; all the stuff they had talked about on the last rotation came flooding back. Sara looked down, she nearly cried. George looked at Sara as Gus handed everyone their ration.

"The purple liquid makes it taste better," Emily said, trying to distract everyone— well, everyone but George.

He focused on Sara as he ate; she was happy, yet somehow more emotional—not her usual calm self. He ate and leaned back, touching the rock wall. The green moss glowed brighter.

Emily reached back and held her hand over the moss. It was cold and seemed afraid.

"Gus, can I have a few drops of your purple vitamins for the moss?" she asked.

Gus glanced at George.

"Don't look at me," George said, raising his hands.

"Well, OK," he retrieved the little bottle.

"Right here, Gus, pour a few drops right here. It will do the most good here," Emily said, pointing to a brown spot on the floor of the cavern.

Gus dripped a dozen drops on the spot Emily had pointed at. The green moss behind them started to glow brighter.

"The ground is old and the moss exists on very little nutrients now," Emily said with sadness in her voice.

George stared at Emily. She was sad. How odd, he thought. Something in the cavern must be affecting them.

"We will need to rest on the tunnel hogs since the moss may not be able to resist us as energy sources even though they want to," Emily said, petting the moss softly.

"Then we must help the moss and find a new nutrient source for them," George said as he slid away from the wall and leaned on Sid.

Sid glowed a warm, reddish-brown color. The cadets yawned and huddled close to Sid. Mid slipped up next to them as the cadets curled up in the safety between the two bristly, dusty brown tunnel hogs. It was like cuddling up to two city buses covered in soil, but the cadets didn't mind. They felt safe and protected in the tunnel hog cave.

George rested, but he could not sleep. Emily rolled over and handed him her pad then rolled back over again. It was open to the prophecy translation. He started reading at a fast pace—much faster than he normally could have read. It was something about this cavern. However, it was a mystery to be solved another day. Right now he had to focus on the prophecy to save his team.

Similar to the Nostradamus prophecy on Earth, this prophecy talked of great cataclysmic events. Yet, George could not shake the thought that many of these events had happened on at least three planets that he knew of already.

The events written in the prophecy had occurred at different times in the development of each planet. They seemed to be more of a civilization or cultural type of development than a prophecy of the future. This was the information they had read on Earth—history, only history. George read on late into the night. First, a hundred pages and then somewhere in the 200s, he found the section he wanted. He struggled to keep his eyes open. His eyes blurred and his eyelids felt heavy. He fell asleep. In his sleep he saw Max. He was there talking with him. He felt calm and at peace.

"Max, how can you be here, sir?" George asked in his mind's eye.

"We are connected by the ties that bind us together," Max replied simply.

"Max, the prophecy. Every time I try to see and read the pages, I seem to fall asleep. I can't read the words even though they are translated, sir," he said, not awake and not asleep.

"Only he who is not of the prophecy can read the prophecy," Max answered cryptically.

George had no idea, at that moment, what Max's answer meant; however, he knew there was more he should ask—there always was. In that instant, there was only one thing he could think of to ask.

"Why, sir?" George pressed.

"If you knew the prophecy, then it would affect you and your decisions. Your free choice would be gone and your existence would be predestined," Max answered.

"What if we had someone else read the prophecy to us, sir?" George pressed, trying hard to concentrate and wake up from his dream.

"It is not allowed, a copy has never been taken from the officers' library, nor translated from its original language," Max said firmly.

"Who wrote the prophecy, sir?" George pressed.

"I cannot answer," Max said firmly.

"Then how do you know if what you have said is even true? Have you read the prophecy, sir?" George pressed in his mind.

"I cannot answer," Max said firmly.

"That means you have read some, but not all. Max, life is not predestined by a prophecy; we all have free will. The scroll is a history book and not a book of prophecy, sir," George argued, struggling to stay focused.

Max lowered his head. "You must delete your copies or return the copies, George. Your Galactic council knows. They will not let you keep it," Max said bluntly.

"You mean the twelve scrolls that were laid out for us in the library reading room, sir?" George pressed; he had to know if Max knew the difference.

"No, George! The copy in the desk—press me no further. Lock it out and tell me that you and the others will not read the scroll further. I will remove it from your pads when you return in the morning," Max said firmly, not pleased with George's question.

"Max, sir. You cannot come to Asteria station again, you have already risked too much on our behalf, sir," George said.

Lowering his head, he noticed Andy's hand on his shoulder. George's sleeping-dream transformed into a link.

"Max, stay where you are. Do not come here, sir. Emily will remove the files. We will read no further, sir," George said, lowering his head again as he realized what he had said.

"George, Andy do you really understand?" Max questioned George's words as if he did not understand what he had really said.

"Yes, sir. It will be done, sir. You cannot come, sir," George replied firmly.

"It will be harder than you think," Max said calmly.

"No, sir, it is not. It is only a thing, and we will not risk your life again. It is you we cannot do without, sir. We are sorry, sir," George said, determined to make Max believe him.

"Very well, I will speak with the Galactic council on your behalf," Max whispered, fading away as Andy and George fell asleep.

The next morning George and Andy awoke to find they were the last ones sleeping. Sid and Mid were gone and they were resting on a few rocks on the floor of the cavern. George and Andy whistled in Thorean to find their team. Four heads popped out across the cavern; Emily from inside a small crevice, Anna and Sara from around a corner leading into another cavern, and Gus from behind some large boulders that had been knocked loose from the cavern wall.

Everyone stared at George and Andy standing in the middle of the tunnel hog cavern.

"Look who's up!" Gus said, joking with them as he slid off the boulder below him and jumped to the ground. Sara and Anna laughed.

"What's going on?" Emily asked, walking over to the middle of the cavern.

George looked serious—not like his usual self. Sara hurried over to him and grabbed George's arm.

"Who did you link with? Did they suck out your energy again? Everyone, quick!" Sara said, starting to form a healing circle.

Gently he pulled her hand down off his forehead to stop her.

"The link was with Max," George said. looking down. His voice was low and somber.

He turned toward Emily and held her hand. "Emily, you must remove the prophecy, the translation, and the Rosetta file—all of it—from all of our pads; and the Galactic council will allow us to return," George said calmly.

Her head jerked up and she glanced around at her teammates. "No way, it's not fair! We got the prophecy fair and square. It's ready to read. You read it last night, George," she said, mortified, her face scrunched with hurt.

"True, I read the history of the prophecy, past events, things that we would expect in any civilization. However, when I tried to read the section on the team in the prophecy, I couldn't," George replied sadly. "I could only read what we found out about on Earth," he said, staring at Emily.

"What do you mean, George? You couldn't read it," Sara asked, stunned.

"Max said you cannot read the prophecy if you're in it," George said firmly.

"But you read it," Emily pleaded, holding onto George's hands.

"No, I read history. I could have said yes this section is talking about this historical event on Earth and that section is about another; however, I couldn't read the present or future events," he said, shaking his head.

"Did Max read the prophecy?" Anna asked further.

"I think it is about him, too, Anna, and he can only read the history like us," George added.

"Then we'll have someone else read it to us," Emily said, shaking her head to get George to agree.

"No. If we don't remove it, Max will come and you know what happened the last time he was on the Asteria station during our second rotation," he said with sadness in his voice.

"They tried to destroy him and he saved our lives," Emily said, lowering her head.

"I promised Max we would do it. There will be no originals, no copies, nothing left," he said, his arm wrapped gently over Emily's shoulder.

Gus, Sara, and Anna handed George their pads and walked into the next cavern. Andy handed George his pad last and went to sit on a large rock near the other cavern entrance, where he had a good view of all the cadets in both small caverns without leaving George's side in the first cavern. Emily started to cry, an emotion he had never seen nor felt from Emily before. George pulled her in close and gently wrapped his strong arms around her to comfort her.

"There is something in the cavern walls," he thought to himself.

"George, you have no idea what you are asking. I have worked on this decrypting program since we were on Earth, just waiting for the chance to use it. It is elegant and universal. It did in a few hours what the council took a hundred years to figure out," she said with tears, trickling over her rosy pink cheeks. George hugged Emily tighter as she began to wobble.

"Emily, you're brilliant like no one I have ever met before. Max trusts us to do the right thing. To do what was agreed to, even if we don't want to do it. How will he ever be able to trust us again if we don't keep our word to him now? At this moment, the prophecy is a big deal. But you have to decide which is more important, Max's trust in us or our wanting to read the prophecy. The others have made their decision. Now it is up to you. You worked the hardest and the longest on this, and you must make this decision. I can only offer you the choice. You have to choose the path you want to live your life by, a defining moment kind-of-thing," he whispered.

He leaned back and handed all of the pads to Emily. Slowly, he walked toward Andy and the cavern the others had walked into. He stopped at the entrance to the next cavern, not really wanting her to be alone.

Emily stood in the empty cavern with tears trickling down her dusty pink cheeks. In her heart, she wanted to know what the prophecy said so much that it was tearing her apart. She had worked on a translating program for more than a month. It was beautiful and elegant. Yet when she thought of Max, all she could see was him lying in the corner of the tiny starship, holding it together by shear will and strength of character until they could be rescued. He would have died for them—died to keep them safe. She may not have known Max the way George did, but she knew he was good and cared for their team.

Emily knew the right thing to do; she had to delete all of the files and walk away. She had to trust her team, and they had to be able to trust her. She sat down on the ground and a curl of moss circled her, as if protecting her. She erased the first pad and then the next and so on until only her pad was left.

A tear drop splatted on her arm as she looked down at the last pad.

"Max, I can't put your life in danger. I am so sorry I even hesitated. Please, Max, I'm so sorry," she whispered, her voice quivering and her hands shaking. "If nothing else, I want you to know you can always trust me," she added.

There was no answer as Emily erased the last file, wiping the sector clean on her pad. The files were all gone.

"It is done," she whispered into the air, a tiny single tear sliding down her cheek.

Emily linked all of the pads and stood up, brushing the dust off her suit. Max was standing in front of her. She saw him and rushed forward, wrapping her arms around him.

"It's gone, Max. It's all gone; you can trust me. Honest, you can," she whispered through her tears.

Max wrapped his arms around Emily to comfort her.

"I know, Emily. I did not come to check on the prophecy. I came to check on you. I know you can be trusted. I have never doubted any of you," he said, his voice kind and gentle. "Now you must help the others," Max whispered.

"Me? No, there is nothing I can do. They don't need me," she said.

Emily's heart hurt; she was sad and felt as if she had put all their lives in danger.

"Yes, they need you just as much as you need them. You are all linked on a great journey," Max said kindly, trying to get her to see passed the present moment and to look to the future and the adventures they were yet to have.

"Where are we going?" Emily pressed, wiping her tears and not understanding his words.

"I must leave you now. Go find the others," Max said softly.

She looked toward the other cavern and then back to see his body fading away from her arms. Emily turned and ran toward the cavern the others had walked into earlier. George and Andy were now standing in the middle of the second cavern, pointing at the walls when Emily entered. Gus, Anna, and Sara were perched on boulders and outcroppings of rocks, brushing away the dust covering the walls.

Emily ran into George, nearly knocking him to the ground. The others jumped from their rocks when they saw Emily and came running to her side. George looked at Emily. She looked straight back, handing everyone their pads without taking her eyes off of George's eyes.

"Max was here?" he asked gently.

"Yes, George," she whispered.

"Are you OK, Emily?" he asked softly.

"Yes, I am now. I let the prophecy cloud my judgment. I lost sight of our path, it nearly consumed me. Max didn't come to check if I had erased the prophecy, he came to make sure I was OK. He came for me. I'm sorry I lost track of what is really important. You're right, the prophecy is only a thing. The people you are with—your friends, family and those around you—are more important," Emily whispered to keep from crying again.

"Emily, if you tell George he's right, it'll go to his head and we'll never hear the end of it," Andy said, bear-hugging Emily's shoulder.

The cadets all crushed together, trying to hug Emily at the same time. They fell to the ground laughing as curls of dust rose from the ground around them.

"Look, Emily, look at the walls," George said, raising his arm and pointing at the walls from the ground.

Everyone leaned their backs together and looked at the cavern walls where they had uncovered the dust. Anna and Sara held up their pads and recorded the carvings on the walls.

"How old is this cavern?" Andy asked.

"It could be as old as Calshene itself," Emily answered, straightening herself up and leaning on George's shoulder.

Suddenly, the ground rumbled, like when a tunnel hog was close.

"Hurry, we need to get back to the other cavern. We don't want anyone to find this place," George said loudly over the rumble.

They locked arms helping each other up and ran to the other cavern, skidding to a stop near a small group of rocks on the far side of the cavern. Gus grabbed his little bottle of purple liquid and poured the liquid out on the ground as he ran.

"It's all I have, I hope it helps," he whispered, skidding up to the others.

"What?" Andy asked.

"Later," Gus signed to Andy, skidding up next to Anna.

Chapter 10

PROPHECY CONSEQUENCES

It seemed to George as if Sid was warning them of his approach and giving them time to change caverns. The rumbling became louder as Sid appeared crosswise in the cavern. He blocked the tunnel leading into the other cavern.

"Look what Sid did," Andy whispered to George.

"Clear your minds, focus, and think only of forgiveness for running away. Nothing else," George ordered.

"But I'm hungry—really," Gus whispered.

A slit formed in Sid's side, and Pete came running out with Nick and the other blue captains on Pete's team. Close behind them were four CORE officers. Pete looked really mad.

"Report, cadets!" Pete yelled.

Instantly, George and the others jumped up from their seats on the rocks stood at attention.

"Yes, sir," George replied as he stepped out in front of his team solemnly. However, Pete cut him off before George could say anything more.

"What are you cadets doing here in this cavern? We have been looking for you for two days. Stand at attention when I address you, cadets!" Pete yelled. His captain's voice was at full strength, echoing around the small cavern.

The CORE officers circled them casually. Suddenly George knew what was going on. Pete was the diversion, he was doing exactly what he had been ordered to do. The CORE officers were trying to read their minds while the cadets were focused on Pete. He slid his hands behind his back, signing "Diversion, focus on Pete."

He returned his hands to his sides. Pete yelled for nearly an hour before one of the CORE officers nodded and he stopped. Pete pointed to Sid.

"There will be consequences for your actions, cadets!" Pete was still yelling as they entered Sid.

Pete was trying hard to keep them focused on him. It was working. Inside Sid, all of their thoughts could become public if Sid forgot, even for an instant, not to share with them. Pete fumed and Nick, Rachael, and the others looked equally angry. George and the other cadets stood in fear.

Sara worried that Pete would pop an artery—or something worse. Gus was so hungry that he was having a hard time keeping his stomach from growling out loud. George and Andy were thinking of forgiveness and understanding. Emily and Anna thought only of having run away in fear. Quickly, Sid arrived at the tunnel hog terminal, and Pete continued yelling at them as they stepped out of Sid. One of the CORE officers pulled Pete aside.

"You did well, they are afraid and sorry for running away. We think something spooked these young cadets. You know they are only from Earth. Don't be too hard on them," the lead officer said, then turned and followed the other three CORE officers down the corridor.

The CORE officers had not been told why the cadets had really disappeared. Pete turned and yelled again at George and the others.

"They think I should be easy on you because you're from Earth and spook easily. Two days, cadets, missing for two days!" Pete continued yelling at them, only slightly quieter than before. "You have only been awake for three days!"

The other cadets in the corridor backed up as all of the captains yelled at George and his team. It was quite raucous on Asteria station. Rachael dragged her hand on the corridor wall as they walked and yelled. The wall rumbled and a slit appeared. Pete and Nick shoved everyone in so fast they all ended up in a heap on the inside of Mid. Mid moved away slowly. Pete, Nick, and the others bear-hugged George, Andy, and the rest of his team.

"Sorry for the show. I am pleased you all caught on so quickly. We knew you were safe. We didn't know where you were, but we knew you were safe. Next time tell us. The Galactic council is boiling mad, George. I don't know what happened, but Max and Senior Viceroy Petrosky fixed it, and the Galactic council agreed to let you return," Pete said seriously.

"I have never seen that happen before," Nick said, shaking his head and staring at the cadets.

Yet something looked very wrong, the cadets were solemn and quiet.

"Usually, you're banished to some awful outpost," Han added still, joking around until Nick bumped him.

George formed a small yellow sphere in the palm of his hand and the others joined the link. He told them the entire story about the library, the prophecy scroll, the CORE officers in the Major's classroom, finally reading the prophecy, Max coming to them, and then their deleting of the prophecy. He left out the part about their discovery of the other tunnel hog cavern.

Pete and the other captains couldn't believe that their cadets had stolen the prophecy scroll, deciphered it, and read it, all in the two days they had been gone. The captains were stunned.

"No wonder the Galactic council is so mad," Nick muttered still stunned.

"That's never been done before," Han said, shaking his head.

The cadets stood silent and still as Mid circled the station.

"This is bad, George. I have my orders directly from the Galactic council, and I have to follow them," Pete said, staring at the cadets.

"This isn't the end of it, Pete," Nick signed to Pete in their captains' sign language.

"Not even Max and Grandfather can totally fix this one," Han signed, knowing something worse would happen.

Pete nodded. The orders he and the other captains were given were harsh. Yet, he worried the Galactic council would be even more harsh and use George and his team as an example.

"I have to punish you ferociously for the next couple of weeks. It is going to be hard on you. It is protocol and I have to follow orders," Pete said seriously.

Yet, inside he had a bad feeling. He knew something else was wrong. George had left something out. They hadn't told the captains something, something important.

"No, it won't. We know what hard is and this isn't going to be hard at all," Emily replied somberly, still holding onto George's hand to hide her sadness as she buried her head into his strong shoulder.

George stared at Emily, trying hard to keep her focused. Pete turned his head and looked at Emily.

"What was in the locking program, Emily, really?" he asked, worried about his cadets and if they were going to make it through this next trial.

"Nothing, sir, it was only a program, nothing important. Something no one should have, sir," Emily replied, crying.

Pete stared at George and wrinkled his forehead, looking for further explanation.

"Nothing sir, as long as it is gone. It was nothing at all, sir," George said, answering for Emily as he wrapped his arm around her and he pulled her in closer to him.

"It is gone, as you requested," Pete replied, staring at his somber cadets.

"Are Frank, Toma, and the others OK, sir?" George asked quietly, still hugging Emily.

"Yes. They all asked I leave you in one piece," Pete said. His voice sounding concerned.

"Not going to happen, is it, sir?" Andy added somberly, holding Sara to keep her from crying too.

"No, Andy, the moment we step out of Mid, the grueling punishment will start again. We are on Asteria station, not Jupiter station," Pete said. His words trailed off.

What had really happened to them? Where had they been that had changed them so much? Pete needed answers, but he had to follow protocol. They were on Asteria station and he had few options available.

Jennifer squeezed Pete's hand. "They are already in so much pain, Pete, you can't do it," she signed in their captain's sign.

"We understand, sir," Gus said. "However, we need to eat, sir," Gus added, rubbing his stomach and hugging Anna.

The captains didn't smile. Pete and the others were worried about Emily and the others— something was very, very wrong. Mid slowed and came to a gentle stop. They all stepped out, and Pete started yelling again. As Sid had done before, Mid had made a circle and dropped them off in the same place they had started from. Nick and the others nodded and left them in the corridor.

Pete's yelling gave them focus and prevented anyone from listening to their thoughts. Pete brought them to the dining room for lunch. The room was crowded and noisy until they entered. It dropped into total silence as George and the others walked through to an empty table in the middle of the room.

"We thought you were dead," a cadet whispered.

"No, but we think it might be a better alternative," Andy whispered, staring at the floor.

They sat down and low murmurs and whispers turned into low talking for the rest of the lunch period. Pete stood up early and the cadets left before lunch was over.

"Good luck," another cadet whispered as George and the others walked back to Pete at the back of the hall and left the dining room.

The moment the door closed, Pete started yelling again. George and the others cringed as Pete picked up the pace, running through the red sector corridor. Gus wanted to ask where they were going, but it didn't seem like a wise choice to ask right then.

They passed the red sector physical training dome and Emily, Sara, and Anna sighed. They were happy Pete was not going to start out beating them physically, at least. They couldn't have been more wrong as they left their red sector and entered the blue captains' sector.

"You want to be older and have more responsibility, then you will be treated as such," he yelled, opening an archway and door. Inside, he was worried this was too much.

Behind the door was another training dome full of blue captains. Pete's team was standing on one end. Nick and the others did not even acknowledge them as they entered. Protocol was everything on Asteria station and the Galactic council was going to make the cadets pay dearly for entering the officers' library, taking the prophecy scroll, and disappearing for two days. Pete and his team would be the Galactic council's enforcer of the rules.

"This is bad," Andy signed to the team.

Nick turned, staring at Andy. If looks could kill, Andy would be dead. Andy dipped his head. Pete was ordered to make them pay for taking the prophecy. It was now his job to carry out the orders of the Galactic council. No mercy, so to speak. Yet, he had a nagging feeling that blindly following protocol was wrong. His only comforting thought was that the Galactic council didn't know they had actually read the prophecy, only that they had stolen a copy. He was sure the cadets would be banished and separated if the Galactic council ever found out!

George, Andy, Emily, Sara, Gus, and Anna lined up on one end of the columns of blue captains. Pete joined his team, and Nick stepped to the back of their team. Colonel Moawk appeared in the center of the dome. He did not speak a word. With a motion of his hands, the blue captains started running around the dome.

"Keep up!" Nick whistled in Thorean as he and the others left, following the last group of captains.

George nodded and they followed Nick, running around the dome. A wave of Colonel Moawk's hand, and the blue captains ran faster. They were nearly a blur as they ran, circling and circling ever faster. Before George knew it, they were running on the side of the dome walls, jumping over the support beams as they climbed higher.

The Colonel waved again, and the captains ran faster and higher again.

The Colonel wasn't waving his hands so much as he was changing the gravity controls on the computer projected in front of him on the dome wall. Up and up they climbed as if the training dome was somehow changing and rotating itself.

The Colonel spread his arms wide and the blue captains reached forward and backward, linking their arms and shoulders together. They slowed and locked their arms in place, weaving in and out, each captain supporting the others, three-quarters of the way up on the inside of the dome. George and the red cadets were breathing hard; however, the blue captains seemed hardly winded at all.

"How is that possible? Why aren't the captains tired?" he thought, then he caught Pete's eye.

"Stop now, concentrate on where you are," Pete thought back.

George lowered his head to Pete and cleared his mind. He wondered how Pete knew what he had thought or if he was able to send a message back even though they were not in a link.

The Colonel waved his hand over his head in a circle again and the blue captains started running again. In a few minutes their speed picked up and they let go of each other's arms. Faster and faster they ran. They circled the dome, running lower and lower down the walls with each rotation until they were back on the ground of the dome. The blue captains slowed and reformed their columns, not missing a step. George and his team formed a column next to Pete's team and slumped over, breathing hard.

The Colonel nodded and the blue captains left the dome in silence. George turned to leave with the others, but the Colonel shook his head. George and the red cadets reformed their column. Pete stepped forward to stand next to the Colonel.

"It is time you learned control," Colonel Moawk said firmly, forming two small red spheres in the palms of his hands.

Fear covered Gus's face. "I can't do this. I can't do this, sir," Gus gasped, backing up in the dome.

"Then you will die today or your team will as they try to protect you," the Colonel said, flinging a small red sphere at Gus.

George dove at Gus, knocking him to the ground as Andy flipped in front of him, catching the red sphere in his hand.

"I see you have mastered the catch, young cadet," the Colonel said, studying Andy's catch.

"And the throw, sir," Andy said, returning the red energy sphere. "Gus does not throw, sir," Andy added, stepping squarely in front of Gus and George as the Colonel caught Andy's throw.

"He will need to learn, young cadet, or you will all be at risk," the Colonel pressed, throwing another red sphere.

"No, we each have talents, sir. This talent is not for Gus. The end result will destroy him and I can't allow that, sir," Andy replied, firmly catching another of the Colonels throws.

They were having a cryptic conversation, and Andy was determined not to lose. The Colonel and Andy kept the conversation going as Pete and his team threw more small red energy spheres at Andy and George. Quickly, Emily, Sara, and Anna helped Gus back to his feet.

"What are they talking about, Gus?" Emily asked.

"Andy said the red spheres are used to destroy," Gus replied. "High energy kind of stuff."

"No, you mean to disable, Gus," Emily corrected.

"No, Emily. Destroy," Gus repeated. "Andy has thrown serious red energy spheres twice that I know of. He let one go with everything he had to protect George and himself on the warship last year. Andy said the control is huge and that once you have formed one you can't put it away, it has to go," Gus said, ducking as a red sphere zinged by Andy, barely missed them, and splatted onto the dome wall behind them.

"You don't have to throw it at someone, Gus, maybe you could aim at rocks and parts of structures instead of people," Emily said, encouraging him.

"I can't, I can't do it. Emily, you don't understand. I just can't," Gus replied. His voice was filled with desperation.

He could not explain that as a young child he and his father had been walking home from playing ball at a park when his father was suddenly gunned down in front of him by drive-by shooters aiming for someone else. It was too painful a memory, too much to share. Now he couldn't destroy, even to save his own life!

"Then you will need to help us regulate and balance our energy," Sara said, thinking of another way Gus could help.

"That I can do, Sara," Gus said, looking up from the ground.

Gus touched each of their shoulders as a red sphere spun passed them and splattered against the dome wall again.

"I think George and Andy need our help now," Anna replied, ducking as another red sphere flew passed.

They looked forward and Pete's entire team was there, tossing one red sphere after the other at George and Andy. Anna, Sara, and Emily slipped in between them as Gus touched each of their shoulders.

"Tell us. What do we do, Andy?" Emily, Sara, and Anna chorused.

"Treat the red spheres like hot potatoes. You can't hold them very long. When you catch them you have to go with the energy. Don't be a brick wall or it will hurt you. The red spheres they are sending over will not hurt you, but they will sting a lot," Andy whispered. "Where's Gus?"

"I am behind all of you. I will regulate the flow of energy," he whispered, his voice shaking.

"If they throw anything really hot, let it pass you. You can't catch a red energy sphere with a lot of energy in it. Those are meant to destroy and must not be touched. Focus your thoughts and energy on your hands. It will protect them from being burned," Andy said, teaching them the basics about red energy spheres.

Andy slipped a small red sphere into Anna and Sara's hands. George handed one to Emily.

"Concentrate. Focus on the energy in the sphere, and it will grow," George said, ducking.

Gus ducked with George as if moving as one, letting the zinging red energy sphere splat into the dome wall behind them. Emily, Sara, and Anna focused and threw their first wobbly red spheres at Pete's team.

"Child's play," Nick laughed, catching all three spheres at once.

He zinged them back at Emily, Sara, and Anna with a greater energy than they had originally sent. All three spheres hit their marks, and the cadets winced in pain. Gus watched as they learned how to form, throw, and catch the red spheres and when to let the ones that were too hot pass them by. After an hour, the red cadets were tiring and the blue captains and the Colonel looked fresh as daisies.

"Something is wrong. This isn't right. What am I missing?" Gus muttered to himself.

He studied Pete and Nick, then Han and Rachael, and finally Karmen and Jennifer. His head turned back to Rachael. She wasn't really throwing a lot of red spheres, but she did catch a lot.

"That's it. She's feeding them the energy of the red spheres. But how?" he muttered.

He stepped forward and took the red sphere from Andy that he had just caught before he could send it back. Gus focused on the energy, and the red sphere disappeared into his hand. He sent the energy to his team. They all turned and looked at him. The blue team took advantage of the distraction and hailed the red team with red spheres, hitting their targets and stinging them before they could turn and defend themselves.

The red team fell to the ground in pain. Gus raised his hands above them, catching the second wave of red spheres before they could hit his team again. He sent the energy to them, and they returned fire while lying on the floor of the dome.

"George, Rachael channels the energy in the red spheres back to her team," Gus whispered.

"He knows," Rachael thought to Pete.

"Then we are done for today," Pete thought back.

At that instant, Pete dropped his hands to his side and nodded to the Colonel. Nick and the others nodded to the Colonel and left without saying a word. The Colonel and Pete stepped outside the dome, leaving the red cadets on the floor, still stinging from the last volley of red spheres.

"Gus, how did you do that?" Andy asked spinning around in the dirt on the ground.

"Do what, Andy?" Gus asked, staring back at Andy.

"Catch the energy sphere and send it through the link for us to use?" George said, finishing Andy's thought.

"I don't know. It's something I saw Rachael doing, so I did it," Gus replied sheepishly.

George and Andy locked arms and helped each other up before helping the others up. Both were still amazed at what Gus had done.

"Where's Pete?" Gus asked, standing up. George looked around the dome. It was empty and they were alone again.

"Can't leave without Pete," Emily said, playing with the dirt on the dome floor. It was spinning in a mini whirlwind beneath her hand.

"We need to focus better or we'll never make it through the week with Pete yelling at us," Sara said sadly.

George glanced at Andy, motioning him to the center of the dome. Andy stepped forward and the others lined up in two rows behind him. Again, Andy was in the first row with Anna and Sara; behind them was George, then Emily, and Gus on the other outside.

"How long do you think the Galactic council will be mad?" Anna asked.

"Don't know, but this is only day one; and we are already in trouble," George replied, sighing.

They were tired. Only four hours of training with the blue captains, and they were nearly exhausted.

"Chen Lo, begin," Andy said, making the first motion with his arms and following with his leg.

Andy spun and stepped, stretched and rolled. Over and over they followed Andy's moves. Higher and higher they increased their level just as they had been taught the rotation before. They did not notice the Viceroy, Pete's dad, in the dome, watching them from a shadow. The door slid open and Pete walked inside to collect his red cadets. However, the Viceroy stepped forward and stopped him.

"Let them regain their focus. Come back in a few hours. They will be safe till then," he whispered.

Two of the Viceroy's Inner Circle officers stepped out of the shadows and then back. Pete nodded and left the dome. A few hours later, Andy slowed their team to a stop. They all felt better—not as tired, calmer, and more focused.

Pete appeared at the door as the cadets turned around. They left the dome without saying a word. Pete yelled at them for their poor performance as they walked down the corridor. He badgered them without mercy, stopping only when they reached dining hall again. They went inside and sat at their now customary table.

"What happened to you?" a cadet asked as they sat down again.

"Seems almost like a relief to sit," Anna whispered.

George leaned back on his chair close to the other cadet. "We are being taught a lesson for our disobedience," George whispered.

The cadet at the other table nodded and a whisper ran through the dining hall again. Pete stood up early.

"No dessert," Gus signed. "Everyone up."

The cadets stood and walked out of the hall, following Pete in silence as he told them how foolish they were and continued beating them with words until they reached another classroom.

"Protocol, begin!" Pete ordered before they even had a chance to sit. "Focus, you will be watched," Pete warned. Then he winked at the cadets and left the classroom.

The cadets smiled a little and focused on the 3D hologram in front of them. It was hard for them to have Pete beat them every time he saw them. However, it was equally hard on Pete to have to do it. The 3D holographic display droned on and on.

Their third rotation had started with their capture by CORE officers; and now, they were being yelled at every moment they were in training for having found and read the prophecy scroll. It was not the fun rotation they had all hoped for at all. George and Anna didn't actually think the protocol training was half bad. Sara and Andy fell asleep. Emily and Gus got bored with the protocol, so Emily brought up the images from the tunnel hog cave on her pad.

"We need to go back to the tunnel hog cave, Gus. These images are like the cave writings scattered across Earth," Emily whispered, her voice trailing off, lost in her own thoughts.

"I wonder how old the cave symbols are?" Gus asked, staring at a symbol that looked like the symbol for peace. "Emily, could this cadet station and all of the other rocks in this asteroid field really be all that is left of the Calshene home world?" Gus added.

Emily paused, thinking. "Anna will know for sure," she replied, turning to stare at Anna.

George looked up, raising his eyebrow. "We are probably being watched," he signed.

Emily shrunk her pad and slid it back up her sleeve. They started focusing on the protocol lesson again. Gus nudged Sara and Andy, and they too started watching the lesson with intent. An hour later, Pete reappeared right on schedule and took them back to their sleeping room. He left them alone, locked inside.

For nearly three weeks, their training hardly deviated from physical training with the blue captains to protocol lessons—over and over, no changes, no deviations, no fun. No flights around the tunnels of Asteria anymore and no lessons in stellar navigation—only grueling physical challenges. The blue captains never seemed to tire while the red cadets felt exhausted each day. Somehow, they were regulating energy and the cadets had to find out how, or they may never be released from training with the captains.

On the morning of their fourth week of training, Nick was in their room when the cadets woke up.

"Where's Pete?" George asked, sitting down and reaching for a bowl of brown cereal.

"Paying for your lack of obedience!" he replied loudly, angry inside that Pete had been taken by the Galactic council.

"What? Noooo!" Andy replied, jumping up from his bed.

"Who took him?" George asked.

"Who do you think?" Nick answered harshly.

"The Galactic council!" Emily replied, stepping up behind George.

"They can punish us, but they cannot take our actions out on Pete. It's not fair," George said, getting up from the table and stepping toward the door.

He was angry that Pete had been taken to be punished by the Galactic council for the team's actions. Nick jumped up and blocked his way to the door.

"What did you think was going to happen? You broke into the CORE officer' library and took the prophecy scroll. Did you really think the Galactic council wasn't going to find out? Did you think they would let you off with a slap on the wrist and say now be good little cadets and don't do that again? Pete is responsible for you and your actions. You knew this, and still you broke the rules! And here on Asteria station of all places, how could you be so inconsiderate and so uncaring, thinking only of yourselves?" Nick yelled, his anger boiling over.

"We will go see the Galactic council. This is wrong, Nick. This blind obedience to old protocols without thinking is wrong," Andy said, sliding up to Nick.

"Great, another huge breach of protocol," Nick replied in disgust. "Why can't you learn?"

"No one seemed to mind when we stopped the Zeleion invasion on Jupiter station or rescued the entire Thorean station from the Mahadean raiders. We broke a lot of rules then too. Seems like a big double standard to us, sir!" Andy said boldly, yelling back for the first time in three weeks.

"Maybe. However, even for the team of the prophecy, this is too much for the Galactic council," Nick replied.

"No, sir. For three weeks we have taken our beating in silence sir," Anna said boldly.

"This is wrong. Taking Pete to punish us is wrong; and you know it, sir," Sara said, trying to get Nick to see reason.

"Something is not right about this," George muttered to himself.

Emily stared at George. "Why now? Why didn't they do this right away?" Emily whispered as Nick and the others argued.

"What does taking Pete now do?" he whispered back to Emily.

"We have taken our beating and not complained," she whispered, thinking hard.

"We have not crumbled," he added, staring at Emily.

George knew the answer was right in front of him, but he could not yet put the pieces together. The Galactic council had made Pete yell at the cadets every waking moment. They had the red cadets reassigned to the blue captains' level training and still the red cadets had endured. After three weeks, the cadets had not broken down and begged for mercy. Their punishment had not had the effect the Galactic council had wanted so they changed the rules and went after the one thing they knew the cadets would not tolerate—the suffering of their triad for their actions.

Emily looked at Nick and then at George. "Is the Galactic council playing a game of chess with us?" she asked.

Nick spun around and faced Emily and George. "Maybe it took them time to find the punishment that fit!" he yelled.

"If we are the team of the prophecy, then maybe we should act like it, sir," Andy continued to argue to distract Nick and give George time to think. There had to be another way to get Pete back.

"How is arrogance going to help?" Nick replied, knocking Andy's comment squarely in the center.

Andy looked down, yet he smiled. Nick was focused on him again.

"How will further disobedience help Pete? Don't you all get it! The Galactic council will take Pete away, and you will have another captain and so will we. It's time to leave!" Nick yelled, opening the door and stepping out into the corridor.

Gus stumbled into Nick as the cadets followed him out into the busy corridor. In the bright light Nick looked bad, like he, too, had been beaten. Not physically beaten, but like when the CORE officers took George from Major Gatte's classroom to see if he had the prophecy scroll on his pad. His mind was beaten and searched.

Gus made a quick link, connecting George to Nick. George spoke with Nick in his mind as they walked along, weaving through the corridors to the captains sector. Nick was connected to Pete as Andy was connected to George and the images of Pete in Nick's mind's eye were bad.

"We can help him, sir," George whispered, confident they would think of something to free Pete.

"How? He will not let us help him," Nick thought back as sadness filled Nick's thoughts.

"We will find a way, sir," George thought to Nick.

Gus ended the link when they turned the last corridor corner, and Nick slowed down.

"When the time comes, help us, sir," George replied cryptically as they stood at the great cavern archway doors.

"Flight training today, sir?" Anna asked, staring at the cavern archway.

"Shouldn't we be in physical fitness or self defense training, sir?" Sara asked, thinking Nick had somehow lost his way.

Nick walked through the archway and joined his team without answering. George and the others lined up in a column next to them. They all looked like they had also been beaten.

"This is weird and wrong," George thought.

"Why would the Galactic council do this?" Emily whispered to George.

"Surely, they knew we would see the captain's condition and that we would react," George replied.

"That has to be it, George. They want us to break protocol so they can send us to isolation," Emily whispered when Nick spun around.

He shook his head and they stopped chattering, lowering their heads. Anna and Sara wanted to reach out and touch Pete's team. They could feel the sadness within them and the anger the rest of the blue captains felt toward the red cadets. For three weeks the blue captains had tolerated the red cadets in their training. Now, with Pete taken away and his team hurt, the blue captains were angry. They all knew the red cadets were the reason Pete was gone, and they wanted revenge.

Major Pennelo stood in front of the captains and started to shout out orders, sending the blue captains to the various small scout ships. There were a dozen small, silver scout ships, a little smaller than the transport ships they had been in, but bigger than the team training fighters they had flown before.

"This is a scouting mission captains, you each have your reconnaissance targets loaded into your navigational computers. Cadet Hawkins, your training scout ship will stay within the safety of the asteroid field, is that understood?" Major Pennelo said firmly.

"Yes, sir," George replied formally.

The captains loaded into their scout ships and quickly ascended to the top of the cavern, waiting to be released. The circle of lights around the gate door turned white and the enormous inner port door spun open. The scout ships hovering in the cavern carefully moved into position, filling the tunnel between the inner and outer gate port doors. Anna guided their scout ship in last and the inner gate port door spun closed. A dozen ships hovered in place, only a few feet from each other's wings as the atmosphere in the tunnel was removed.

"Who's staying behind to babysit?" one of the captains asked sharply on the communications system.

The chatter across the communications console from the blue captains was angry and cruel.

"They've probably never even been in space for real other than under transport," another captain said, taunting them.

Emily wanted to answer, but George raised his hand.

"We need to let the blue captains be angry and express themselves. It has to come out if they are ever going to understand that blindly following protocol rules is wrong," George whispered.

"We will be fine drifting close to the asteroids until your teams return, sirs," George replied over the communications console.

The outer port gate spun open, and the blue captains flashed their engines and left the tunnel. The thrust wake from the other scout ships washed over them and shook the scout ship, yet Anna held their position, still hovering in the tunnel.

"Anna, take us out," George said calmly, concentrating on keeping his team focused on the new task in front of them and not dwelling on the blue captains' anger.

As they left the tunnel, the port gate doors started to close. Anna and Emily guided the scout ship though the port gate, slowing the engines down just outside the sensor range of the main terminal.

Chapter 11

GALACTIC COUNCIL ASTEROID

Emily pointed out the front view screen and Anna landed the scout ship on a small asteroid.

"We're clear of their sensors here," Emily said and spun her chair around with Sara and Anna to face George.

"What's the plan, George?" Sara asked, hoping he had something in mind to rescue Pete.

"The images I saw of Pete within Nick's mind are bad. We can't allow this to continue. If they want us to break protocol, then we will break protocol. If that means they put us in isolation, then we will go willingly. We will release our triad from their oath to us. This is not the Zeleion, Mahadean or evil that we are fighting this time. It is our own structure, our own Galactic council. What they are doing is wrong. I do not care if the Viceroys say it has always been this way, it is still wrong. If obeying protocol means allowing this to continue, then we must change the protocol," George said strongly.

"The Galactic council will hide us away on a desolate rock somewhere or destroy us before they let us change protocol, George," Andy said seriously.

"Perhaps the evil that hunts us is also hidden within the Galactic council membership and it is afraid we are too close," Anna said, following George's lead.

"So now evil is using the Galactic council's own protocol against them," Emily added, thinking of a reason for all the rules being used to stop them and punish them for reading the prophecy scroll.

They stood silently staring out the front view screen, thinking and wondering.

"I can't ask you all to do this," he said.

Emily lifted her hand and stopped him.

"You can ask us, even order us not to help, but we will not leave, just as our triad will not abandon us no matter what we say," Emily said firmly.

Slowly, he lowered his head in acceptance.

"Then let's begin. Anna, we need to know where, in this entire asteroid field, the starships never seem to go near. Andy, we are going to need staff weapons or something. Gus, I need a solid link with Toma and Frank. They will need to know what has happened on Asteria station. Sara, we need energy and nutrients. Emily, we need to look like a drifting rock," he said, giving orders to his team.

Sara went to check on the food stores, while Emily and Anna started writing programs and mapping the courses of the other starships through the asteroid field. Andy placed his hand on George's shoulder.

"What are you doing Andy?" he asked.

"I know you're going to make a link. You're not going to do it without me, George. You're a lousy aim with a red sphere. I said I would not leave you, not even for a moment, and I'm not leaving you now," Andy replied firmly.

"The Galactic council will destroy you, too, if they find out," George replied somberly.

"I think that was already made clear in our last discussion. Now are we going to do this or what?" Andy said, chuckling manically.

The three stood in the little command bridge arm over arm. Gus linked them together and George reached out across the universe to find Frank and Toma to report what had happened. The three cadets gasped. Frank and Toma were with Pete! The images the cadets saw in the minds of the three captains were not good. The captains' minds were being beaten by strong CORE mind scanners. The scanners were brutes, trying to inflict as much pain as they could as they searched for information within the three lead captains' minds.

Gus made the link with the captains. Andy formed a red sphere in the palm of his hand and handed it to Gus. Gus absorbed the energy and put it in their link. Then George sent the energy through the link to the three unconscious captains. Over and over they sent energy to the three captains until they were conscious again. Gus ended the link. George never spoke or said who they were; they only sent energy to help them.

"Call Max, George," Andy whispered.

"We have the coordinates we need to navigate our ship to the Galactic council station in the asteroid field," Anna said confidently.

"We will look like a rock. A little rock with determination," Emily said quickly, before George even asked.

"How long until we are there?" he asked.

"Ten or fifteen minutes—it's very close," Anna said, smiling. She was pleased they had found it so quickly.

"Do it," George replied seriously.

Inside he was a little afraid, he had just doomed his team. He wasn't sure the Galactic council would even listen, or if they were strong enough to stand up to the power of the Galactic council. Yet despite the odds, he had to try. They could not stand by and do nothing, hiding behind a millennia of protocols and regulations.

Anna disengaged the holding clamps from the asteroid. They clanked as they settled into their hatches and the thrusters engaged. Gus thought George was talking to him and made a link reaching out for Max. George looked up suddenly, surprised when Max appeared in their link as if he was next to them.

"What is your plan?" he asked firmly.

Oddly, George wasn't that surprised by Max's question.

"We are going to stop the Galactic council and have them release our captains," George replied, equally seriously.

"What do you offer them in return?" Max pressed, playing the part of the Galactic council members.

"Our lives," George replied flippantly.

"It is too high a price. Remember, they think you're the team of the prophecy," Max said. He was concerned they were letting their feelings overrun their focus.

"Too bad, then they just lost another team of the prophecy and this time they didn't have to wait for the evil that hunts us to destroy us. They did it themselves—more efficient this way," George replied harshly.

"They will try to stop you, George," Max replied serious.

"Sir, there have been teams before us and there will be teams after us that fit the story of the prophecy. We are not special, and we will not sit idly by while others are hurt in our name. If they want to punish a team, then they can punish us. We knew the risk and we took it. Pete, Frank, Toma, and the others were not involved; and to make them involved because they were tricked into a triad not of their own free will but by some misguided sense of duty and honor is wrong. What is it you said? Duty and honor must be freely given, knowing the risks, done because it is the right thing to do at that moment in time," George said as firmly as he could.

"Well stated, George," Max replied, knowing their compassion was their greatest strength.

"Are you here, sir?" George pressed, looking for help if they needed it.

"Not here, but I will be close if you need me," he replied.

George grinned a little and rubbed his chin. Gus closed the link. Max had agreed with their plan.

Sara pushed food in front of them. "Eat, it will taste bad, but it has the best nutrients I could find quickly on this little scout ship," she said. Gus nodded.

It had been too long since they had last eaten and they would need the energy when they arrived at the Galactic council station. Fifteen minutes passed quickly as the cadets finished their rations.

"Look!" Anna said, pointing out the front of the scout ship's front viewer.

"Look at the defenses on that asteroid," Gus said in awe.

"Considering no one is there!" Andy added, laughing.

"If they are not expecting us, then who are they expecting," Gus said, taking the last bite of his ration.

"George, this scout ship is too big to just drift by unnoticed. Their sensors may say rock, but their eyes will say ship," Emily said, worried.

"We need to get in without being noticed," George said, thinking of disguises they could try.

"Too bad we can't ride on the energy of the universe like Max and grandfather," Sara whispered.

"Well, maybe if we had enough energy, we could," he said, wondering how it could be done.

Suddenly, his thought was interrupted by an energy blast across the front of their little rock ship. An enormous galaxy-class starship appeared out of nowhere, firing energy blasts over their scout ship at the asteroid in front of them. It was focused solely on the asteroid. A wake of rubble following the huge starship flipped the tiny scout ship over and over as the enormous starship flew over them. Anna launched the grappling clamps at the enormous starship, trying to stop their rotation. One clamp caught and twisted tightly, slowing the tiny ship's rotation and whipping them back against the underside of the hull of the starship. The sound of crushing metal from the ship's hull echoed through the small scout ship. The cadets fell silent, listening for the squeal of leaking air while Emily checked the sensors.

The galaxy-class starship continued to fire energy blast after energy blast at the asteroid. The energy cannons of the asteroid fired back; however, the asteroid's cannons had little effect on stopping the enormous starship. The enormous starship landed smoothly on the asteroid. A rumble shook the scout ship and the cadets bounced around on the floor as the rumble vibrated through the galaxy-class starship.

"What are they doing?" Anna asked her voice vibrating as she spoke.

"Look at the rubble and the rock," Gus said, waving his hands across their view screen.

"They're boring into the center of the asteroid. They must be after the Galactic council, someone on the Galactic council, or someone held there," Andy answered, stunned at the sheer power required to tear apart an asteroid.

"Call Nick, we need them now," Emily said to George as she bounced across the command bridge, grabbing onto the computer console to stop.

Gus made the link with George and Andy. George reached out and found Nick.

"The Galactic council is under attack. Must return, help." Was the message George sent before his head started to burn.

Gus broke the link with Nick as Andy launched a fiery red sphere into the invader's link. Andy and George grabbed their heads when the link snapped closed.

"Man that hurts. We really need to find out who that is and stop them," Andy said, wincing.

"It would hurt more if they sent your present back, Andy," George replied, grinning a little and squeezing his head.

"Call Pete, Frank, and Toma, George, you need to warn them now," Anna added.

"I can't," George whispered before he wobbled and fell to the floor of the ship, passing out.

"Andy, can you call Max?" Emily pressed.

"I can try," he said as Gus linked Andy to Emily. Andy reached out with his thoughts. There was no answer.

"Now what?" Anna asked.

"Anna, can you unhook our clamps from this enormous starship?" Andy asked next.

"If you can't then we are going along for the ride, right?" Gus said a little worried.

"I'll try," Anna said, her hands flying over the control panel.

"Sara, can you help George?" Andy said as he took command of the tiny scout ship.

Soon everyone was busy with a job again. Sara made a small yellow sphere and held it over George while Gus regulated the flow of energy. George slowly regained consciousness.

"Report," he whispered weakly.

"We are locked onto the hull of the galaxy-class starship. We cannot release the clamps and we can't communicate with anyone," Andy replied with a half grin.

The ship rumbled hard, and the standing cadets fell to the floor of the ship.

George grabbed onto Andy and Gus the moment he was free of Sara.

"Link now," he ordered firmly. Gus linked them and George reached out for Nick.

"Nick, we are clamped onto the galaxy starship, attacking the council asteroid. We need you now!" George's message was intense. George grabbed his head and Gus broke the link again. George crumpled to the floor.

Four hours later, the galaxy-class starship lifted off the Galactic council asteroid. As it turned, they could see the destruction. The entire center of the asteroid was hollowed out. An enormous crater sat where the center of the asteroid had once been. The galaxy-class starship lumbered slowly away from the asteroid. It carefully maneuvered between the large rolling asteroids and passed by Asteria station as if it wasn't even there. Fighters from Asteria station pelted the enormous ship's hull with rockets. However, its thick armor didn't break or weaken. The starship had what it had come for and didn't even bother firing back.

Anna caught a glimpse of a small ship rising from the surface of another asteroid as the huge starship passed over it. Without seeing the markings on the small ship, Anna assumed it was one of the invaders' scout ships, returning from their mission. Thinking the scout ship had seen their ship attached to the galactic-star ship, the scout ship was now after them.

One clamp from the small scout ship passed over their ship and secured itself to an exhaust manifold of the galaxy-class starship. A second clamp attached itself around the cadets' scout ship. Gus ran to the back of the ship to stop the invaders from entering their scout ship through the docking port.

"Go, Andy. Defend," George whispered as his head rolled back. His limp body was lying over Sara's lap.

Her forehead crinkled, and the veins on her neck seemed to grow as she strained to push energy into George. Emily and Anna ran to the back of the ship to help Andy and Gus defend. Andy flicked out two staff weapons and threw one each to Emily and Anna.

"Sorry my friend, you're more of the pick-them-up-and-toss-them kind of guy," Andy said to Gus.

Gus nodded as the cadets prepared to be boarded. The hatch rolled open in a swirling fashion like when the floor had opened in the labyrinth. A burst of air filled the tiny ship. Nick, Han, Rachael, Jennifer, and Karmen came running in through the port. Andy jumped out with Emily and Anna, staffs and glowing red spheres drawn.

"Whoa!" Nick yelled, jumping back. "We come in peace!" he yelled quickly.

Andy pulled back his huge red sphere of energy. Gus grabbed his hand and absorbed the energy, running back to Sara with the energy for George. Andy collapsed and Anna rushed to catch him with Karmen.

"Report, cadet!" Nick yelled as the others ran to the command bridge of the scout ship.

Emily stood alone, facing Nick. She started shaking.

"George, he... George... Andy... we need help. The Galactic council is gone. Pete, Toma, and Frank are all gone. Can't, can't call anyone. Need help, stuck. Can't unhook," Emily stammered, her body shaking hard as fear flooded her thoughts.

Nick grabbed her with one arm and pulled her in tight to his side. He focused on her thoughts. She was filled with fear and rage as her emotions ran wild.

"Emily, listen to me, we're here now. We are here to help," Nick said, his voice softening as he worked hard to calm her fear.

Emily started to cry. It was all she had left. Three weeks of being yelled at by her triad was too much. Without George helping to calm their fears, the cadets' focus was falling apart and fear was overtaking their thoughts and minds—good judgment was gone.

"You. You hate us. Why? Why would you help us? You blame us for everything bad that has happened. We are on our own without our triad in a place that hates us," she said as her voice cracked and fell into a whisper. She pushed against his strong muscular shoulders to break free as tears ran down her rosy checks.

Yet, Nick would not let her go. They had been wrong and now their cadets needed them more than ever.

"We were wrong, Emily. We followed protocol blindly when you tried to show us we needed to think for ourselves and see if the protocol and rules still applied today. We did not listen, we were wrong. And yet again, we find your team that has been so badly mistreated trying to rescue the ones who have hurt you the most. We will always be your triad, it is we who are sorry for hurting you," he answered, picking up Emily in his arms and carrying her into the command bridge of the tiny ship.

In Sara's hand a small yellow sphere glowed dimly over George's forehead. Slowly, she was feeding energy into George's unconscious body.

"Nick, sir. Can you make red energy spheres like Andy?" Sara whispered as Nick set Emily gently on the floor next to George.

"Yes, of course," he said kindly, trying to reassure her and calm her fears.

"Please make them and give them to Gus as fast as you can. He knows what to do, sir," she said as a tear slipped down her check too.

The cadets were an emotional wreck and Nick knew it was his team's fault. They had not realized how much George had been supporting his team over the last three weeks, preventing them from feeling the anger and fear the Galactic council had put on them. Nick wondered how a third rotation cadet could have protected them so well. He sat down next to Emily and began forming two red spheres in his hands. Gus took the first one and converted it into energy for Sara. Her yellow sphere grew. Nick handed him another and then another. Hours passed, and Nick continued feeding Gus energy until he was getting weak. George was breathing better, although not yet awake.

The scout ship the captains had arrived in was only slightly larger than the training scout ship the red cadets were in. Their stores were as meager as the red cadets' stores. The scout ships were meant for one to two week reconnaissance trips, not flights across the open galaxies. Jennifer and Karmen stood at the controls for each scout ship and prepared the ships as best they could for the trip they were now going to take.

Rachael and Han rolled out small cots from the storage lockers. They laid the weary cadets out on the cots and covered them as the enormous galaxy-class starship cleared the asteroid field. The invaders kicked in the starships after burners increasing their speed. The tiny scout ships jolted.

"We live or die now," Karmen whispered to Jennifer in their link.

"We live."

Chapter 12

OPEN SPACE

Two days passed and the invading galaxy-class starship did not slow or change course. There was no need to hide their trail, they were not being pursued—there was no one left to mount such a quest. The sector Galactic council was gone. The individual Viceroys left behind had to guide the raw energy of the universe in their sector alone—a task they had not been trained to do. An uneasy calm filled the spaces in the known galaxies. A new Galactic council would need to be chosen soon and the power transfer accepted willingly by the new members.

In a thousand years not one of the sector Galactic councils had ever been disrupted. The succession of Viceroys was planned for many years, and Viceroys destined for the council are trained until the day they are needed. Now there was no protocol to direct their actions. They had become complacent, blindly following rules and protocol written a thousand years ago, not keeping up with the changes in the universe.

The Samurai of ancient Japan on Earth disappeared when the culture of their country changed around them. With the ruling sector of the Galactic council gone, the protocol structure was falling apart. The rules and protocol so far out of date, that the Viceroys left behind were having difficulty thinking for themselves. They started to argue, and the raw energy of the universe ran wild across the galaxies. Without the focused concentration of the Senior Viceroys, the systems on the stations slowed to minimal power. They were defenseless and vulnerable to attack. Fear ran wild through the cadet stations as the young Viceroys and Inner Circle officers tried desperately to control the raw power of the universe.

Nick knew there would be no one coming or mounting a rescue as they raced across the galaxies. They were on their own again. George, Andy, and the others had been on their own before, they had rescued the Thorean cadets, officers, and Viceroys, but right now, they would need to rescue themselves. George woke up after two days and rolled off his cot in the morning of the third day landing on the floor with a thud. Nick slid over to him and lifted him back onto his cot.

"Rest, George," he said kindly.

"Nick, you heard us. You came, sir," George whispered, happy he was there.

Nick smiled weakly. "George, we are sorry for the way we treated you and the others. You were right, about the Galactic council, the protocol, all of it. You are the team in the prophecy," he whispered. "We are sorry for not listening." He apologized.

"No, we're not, there is no team in the prophecy. It is all a lie, sir," George whispered bluntly.

"What are you talking about?" Nick asked. "You read the scroll of the prophecy. It is real."

George smiled and leaned up on his elbows. "If you give the people a place to focus, a place to be looking all of the time, then you give them false hope for the future. Hope that it will get better without them having to do anything. Yet things really never change and improve because you can't improve without work and focus, without caring and compassion, without knowledge and strength of will. Look around, what do you see in these little scout ships, sir?" George asked, lying back down to rest.

Nick stared at George, his thoughts wandering to memories of his great-grandfather. When Nick was twelve-years old, he left the city and traveled to the foot hills of South Dakota with his dad. He had always known he was Calshene, but there was more he didn't know. When he and his dad had arrived in South Dakota, his great-grandfather was waiting for him on an Indian reservation. Until that moment in time, Nick had never known he was part Native American Indian, only that he, like many of the old immigrant families, had Native American blood in him.

Nick's dad left him with his great-grandfather for the summer. Nick was face-to-face with a great-grandfather and a heritage he knew nothing about. He listened to the stories of the Native American people that summer and learned to hear with more than his ears and see with more than his eyes. Nick's great-grandfather was nearly blind, yet Nick had not noticed all summer. His great-grandfather moved seamlessly through nature and the challenges of everyday life.

He died the following year. It was as if he had been waiting for Nick to come of age, and once he had been taught the ways of the people and the land, his grandfather could become a spirit of the sky. Odd that Nick should think of that while they were hurling through space in tiny ships clamped onto the tail of another enormous starship, running low on supplies, air, and energy.

"Sometimes I think Max is a spirit of the sky," George whispered, somehow having heard Nick's thoughts.

Nick smiled a little. He had to agree with George, it was only with work and focus that things could change.

"We have to save the Galactic council and Toma, Pete, and Frank," George whispered somberly.

"First, we need some energy and some food," Nick whispered, worried.

Rolling off his cot, George crawled across the floor to Emily and Anna's cots.

"We need your expertise," he whispered, explaining the energy crunch and food shortage to Anna and Emily.

"And the bad air, George?" Emily asked, holding his hand as she slipped off her cot.

"Oh, that seems to go without saying, Emily. After all, we're in space in a tiny ship again, low on energy with little food and even less water. The bad air is a bonus," he said, smiling.

"Happy to see we are starting where we always do," Emily replied as Anna dipped her head so George would not see her smile too.

George returned to Nick as Emily and Anna slid across the floor to the command bridge of the ship.

"Thank you, sir," he said.

"For what, George?" Nick puzzled.

"For helping Emily when she was afraid, I did not have the strength to calm her mind and help stop her fear. It has been hard on them," George replied, staring across the room at his team.

"George, it was not me. I do not have that kind of strength. Only Pete, Frank, and Toma can calm someone's mind without a link. Emily was barely able to speak when we got to her and the others. All I could do was hold her, help her feel safe and try to focus her thoughts," Nick replied and paused. "They were nearly consumed by fear when we got here, George. We are linked with them now and will do our best. But when we first arrived, it wasn't us. I tried, but we couldn't stop them from feeling the fear."

"Then it was Max. He is the only one strong enough to have helped us from such a long distance," George said, wondering where Max was and how he knew.

Nick was surprised at George. For the last three weeks, he had been calming his team's minds and preventing the fear from the Galactic council overtaking their thoughts. Only Pete, Frank, and Toma could do that, and they were much older and more experienced than George. Nick wondered how he could have learned this skill at such a young age and how he possessed the strength to do it.

The lights blinked and brightened and the blowers started blowing better air through the ventilation system.

"Emily and Anna—can't do without them," George said, crawling to the command bridge of the tiny ship with Nick.

"We are draining power from their backup systems and pulling in air from their main air supply. Our ship's systems should have fresh water from the air in about an hour and, in a couple of hours our own air supply system will restart when our energy cells are fully charged. As for food, well, you'll have to wake up Gus for that," Emily said and slid back onto her cot to sleep a little longer.

George leaned out the command bridge door and laid on his back staring at Gus.

"Gus, we need you," George mumbled.

"You're hungry, aren't you?" Gus grumbled, rolling off his cot and crawling to the small alcove he called a galley.

"About an hour if we have power," Gus said, yawning.

"Yes, Emily and Anna got us power," George replied. "Come to think of it, where is Anna?"

He rolled over again and crawled up to the small command bridge in the ship. Anna was sitting on the floor, typing with her hands over her head on the control console. He stared at her, not wanting to disturb her typing. She touch-typed like Emily, unlike the hunt-and-peck method that George used.

"Emily said we can't stand until the blinking red light on the console turns green," she said, without stopping her hands.

"Anna, what are you doing?" George asked, teasing her a little.

"Well, I thought it would be nice to know where we are being dragged off to as we hurl through space at a phenomenal rate of speed," Anna replied, pulling her hands down and rolling over. "That should do it."

"Do what?" he pressed.

"Oh, the program will figure out where we are going so I can get some rest. Is Gus cooking?" she asked.

"Yes, Gus is cooking. He thinks everything will be ready in about an hour," he answered.

"OK, I'm tired now. Please wake me in an hour," she said softly, lying her head down on the floor, not bothering to return to her cot. George rolled over to crawl toward the back of the ship.

"Max!" he whispered, sliding to the floor. No one answered.

In the center of the ship, George felt suddenly tired and laid his head down. The cadets and the captains slept without dreaming, no thoughts, only a deep sleep.

Weeks later, Nick and Andy were the first to wake. The air was clean and they could breathe easier. Andy pushed George and he rolled over.

"Where are we?" George asked.

"I don't know. But we are still attached to the other ship," Andy replied with a smirk.

"Wake the others," George said quietly.

Andy left and George woke Anna and asked where they were. Again she sat on the floor and pulled up the data from the console over her head.

"The air is good now, the blinking light is green," George said encouragingly.

"True, the air may be good, but I am not," she replied with a little half smile.

"So where are we?" George asked kindly.

"We are almost to the Mahadean home world! How did we get here so fast?" Anna gasped. "We'll never fit in!" she said, worried because they didn't have any holographic projectors.

"Actually, we will fit in just fine," Nick replied as he slid into the small command bridge. "Long ago the Mahadean home world became more of a trading post. There are many off-worlders living there, as well as many slaves to do their labor," Nick said seriously.

"How far away are we, Anna?" George asked.

"Twenty-four, maybe twenty-five hours, depending on whether or not they can keep their speed up," Anna whispered.

"What day is it? How long did we sleep?" George asked, stunned they could be nearly to Mahadean so soon.

Anna scanned the computer and read the date. "Twenty-one days, George, we have been asleep for twenty-one days," she replied, stunned. "Why aren't we dead from dehydration?" she asked, puzzled.

The captains and cadets were surprised. "Someone has been helping us sleep and stay healthy for the long journey across the galaxy," Nick said, wondering who it was.

"We will need to call for Max and any other Viceroys. We will need their energy," George said, hatching a plan in his mind.

"No, you need to come and eat first before Gus blows a gasket," Andy called sliding into the command bridge on the floor.

"You too, Andy?" he asked.

"Yes, a little hard to stand right now," Andy said, sliding back to Gus's makeshift galley on his belly.

Nick followed Andy's lead with Anna and slid to the back of the ship.

"Max, where are you? We are alone, and I fear our parents and Viceroys are captured by the Mahadean," George whispered sadly.

"I am always with you, I will come when you need me most," Max answered in George's mind.

He smiled and slid to the back of the ship with the others. Gus and Han were sliding white bowls of what looked like brown cereal to everyone as they all lay about on the ship's floor near the makeshift galley.

"Gus, Han, this looks like brown cereal," Andy said, rolling the white bowl in his hand.

"That's good, because it is," Gus said, grinning and high-fiving Han.

"And you thought the white bowls would fool them," Han replied, laughing.

"OK, everyone vote. What do you dislike the most, rations or brown cereal?" Emily asked as she slid over next to George and Anna. The cadets and captains voted. It was a tie! They all laughed.

"Who didn't vote?" Sara asked, staring everyone in the eye with her eyebrow raised.

She got to George and he looked away.

"It was you George, wasn't it? OK, now you're the monkey in the middle, you have to vote to break the tie," Sara said, trying to stare him down.

All eyes turned toward George.

"Now we will see what he has really learned," Nick whispered to Andy.

Andy thought Nick's words were a little cryptic, yet he understood most of his thought. Nick wanted to see if George was becoming a leader, a diplomat of sorts.

George nodded, smiled and took a bite of his cereal. Raising his eyebrows, he made the yummy, happy face all children see their parents make when they are trying hard to get their children to eat food that is good for them.

"Stop stalling and vote," Anna said impatiently, leaning around Emily to try to stare down George.

"Well?" Sara asked, her voice pushing for an answer.

"Gus, Han, your abilities make even the most tasteless foods edible," he replied, dipping his head.

"That's not an answer, George!" Sara said, staring squarely at George as he took another bite.

The captains all laughed—it was a Pete-type answer.

"It may not be an answer, but I think it's the closest we're going to get to one," Andy said, laughing and hugging Sara's shoulder.

"Awww," they all replied, pretending to throw things at George.

They finished their meal and George started to talk.

"Excellent, Gus, Han, thank you, it really was edible," he said, coughing. "Now on to business, we need to have a plan before we get to the Mahadean home world. We need options for unhooking the scout ships, holographic ship disguises, energy and food resources, armaments, navigation, and escape routes. I will need reports starting in about four hours from now, any questions? OK, everyone knows their assignments, help each other," George said and slid off toward the smaller scout ship's command bridge area.

"Sounds a bit like Pete," Nick muttered as the others nodded and slid to complete their assignments. No one asked what their tasks were; they simply took a task to accomplish and helped each other when they got stuck.

George sat up in the little command bridge as he thought of the Viceroys, their parents, grandfather, Frank, Pete and Toma. He recalled sitting in the Thorean galaxy-class starship's command bridge with Pete and Frank the day before they started their rescue of the Thorean cadets, officers and Viceroys from the Mahadean slave ships. At that moment, he wished he had Pete and Frank's help now. Before, they had enormous galaxy-class ships with food supplies and weapons to help them rescue the Thoreans. Now, they had few weapons and limited food and water. This rescue would be harder, George worried.

When they rescued the Thoreans, Pete had used protocol to impart the seriousness of their mission and he had his team help George's team keep calm and focused. He would need to do the same on this mission too. Focused and calm, somehow their plan would take shape and the rescue would occur. Flipping his head around the corner of the command area, he called for Andy and Nick.

The two came sliding down the little hallway from the back of the ship. Nick caught George's face and stopped Andy at the corner of the wall before entering the little command area. Nick knew the look from when Pete was serious and the time to lead began. Patiently they waited. Andy smiled, he understood why Nick had stopped him.

George glanced back at Andy and Nick and nodded. They finished their slide and sat next to George facing him with their legs crossed like pretzels.

"Nick, it will help us if your team can help keep us focused and calm. We are a year older, but we have not had the practice in staying focused that we need, sir," George said seriously.

When the team leader was absent, the second was the next team member in command. Nick was now the leader of the captain's team.

"You have learned well. It will be done, sir," Nick replied formally, nodding.

Quickly, he sent the message to the other captains through their link. George and his team were not the only ones who were almost always connected in a link now.

"Andy, Nick, I need your help now. We need to find out who is alive on the Mahadean ship," George added.

Andy looked down, sadness filling his thoughts. "Yes, it is time for that, isn't it," he whispered.

"It'll be OK, Andy," Nick replied, slipping his arm over Andy's shoulder to help calm his fears and strengthen his focus.

George was still weak, and while he had been helping his team and blocking out the Galactic council before, he was having difficulty helping them stay focused now. Little did George or the others know that for the past three weeks Viceroy Petrosky had been helping George focus on Asteria station so he could learn how to focus and help his team. Now he was on his own.

"We need Gus or he'll, well, he won't be happy with us," George said, making an odd face.

"I'll slide," Andy replied, flipping over one shoulder and sliding back to get Gus.

"Thanks, sir," George whispered. "I think this rescue will be harder than when we freed the Thorean cadet station from the Mahadean starships."

Nick smiled. "Yes, it will be harder because we have no one specific to attack. We will need to out-think the Mahadean officials and use their system to free the Galactic council," Nick whispered, not sugar-coating the difficulty of the rescue ahead of them.

Gus and Andy slid back to the command area. Andy stopped Gus at the corner just as Nick had stopped him. Patiently they waited.

"Like before?" Gus asked, staring at George.

"Like before," Andy answered seriously, watching George.

"This isn't good," Gus replied cryptically.

"Nope," Andy replied as George nodded and they slid forward to George and Nick.

"Gus, we need a link with the Mahadean ship, the Viceroys and whoever else is there or is at least is conscious," George said seriously.

Gus looked down at the floor, fear and worry clouding his thoughts. A moment later, Han came running into the little command area and skidded to stop as he crashed into Gus, Andy, George, and Nick, toppling them over.

"Sorry about that, sir," Han said, slipping his arm over Gus's shoulder and concentrating as they all straightened up.

The group laughed, it was funny in a weird way. Gus's mind started to refocus and fear left his thoughts. He lifted his head confidently.

"See, Gus, I even asked this time," George said, smiling.

"Humph! A first, I'm sure," he replied dryly, yet inside he was happy George had remembered to ask.

They sat in a circle on the floor, arm over arm. Gus started making a, small-glowing yellow sphere in the palm of his hand. George, Andy, and Nick joined the link and then Gus walked out. Andy and Nick held George's shoulders as George reached out to find their triad, as it was their most powerful connection.

George could feel Pete, Frank, and Toma's conscious thoughts; however, he could not make the connection.

"Max, I need to find them, help me," George thought.

Nick and Han's mouths dropped open. They did not know George could call Max so easily.

"Focus, I need help!" George thought back to them, and they cleared their minds.

"It is within you, George, you can find it. Try again," was the thought Max sent back to George.

Nick was astonished, hardly able to believe the message. How did George communicate so easily with Max? Not even Toma, Pete, or Frank could do that. He would need to tell Pete, Frank, and Toma when they were freed.

Nick had never heard that the beings of white light could be called before. George may not have understood who the beings of white light really were, but Nick did, and they commanded great respect across the universe.

George focused harder on finding their triad. If it is within him, then where was he to look for them to make a link?

"The link that connects us is energy, George, it is always around us. However, we can only focus the energy for a short time. Look at the energy in the link," Nick thought in their link.

"The energy of the universe is boundless. It only has those limitations we choose to put on it," George replied, reaching out again and using Nick's thought. He opened his mind to all the possible places they could be in their known galaxies focusing in on them and the energy within their triad.

"George, we have them," Nick thought, seeing their thoughts in the link.

"Yes, they are alive but barely. I need the energy in your red spheres, Andy and Nick, they are very weak," George said and reached out with his arm to pull Gus back into the link. "We need to convert Andy and Nick's energy spheres again, Gus," he thought in their link.

George motioned to Nick and Andy's glowing red spheres dancing above their palms. Gus picked up the energy spheres and changed that into a form George could send into their triad. Slowly, one by one, the energy spheres were sent over the link to Toma, Frank, and Pete until they regained full consciousness and replied.

"Stop. Report," Pete said weakly in his message.

George told the triad where they were and where the Mahadean ship was heading. George asked for a count of how many of the Galactic council had been captured and what their status was.

"Nearly the entire Galactic council is here," Frank replied, looking around at the cages.

"And a few of the local Viceroys as well," Toma added.

"They are all being prevented from making a link and drawing energy from the universe somehow. They all look weak," Pete said with sadness in his voice.

"Can you touch them? I mean physically touch them, sir?" George pressed.

"Yes, yes, we can," they answered together, making physical links with the Viceroys closest to them.

Nick and Andy started making red spheres again, Gus converted the energy and George sent it through the link. One by one, the Viceroys nearest the captains started to join their physical link until they could hold it and understood how to form and control the red spheres of energy themselves. They were using the energy of the universe through the red spheres. An unusual idea, yet it was working. Viceroys were getting stronger as they were now able to make their own red energy spheres and absorb the raw energy. The block was still in place, but they now had a way to slowly collect energy to sustain their lives.

As the Viceroys' strength grew, George explained where they were and how close to Mahadean they were.

"We have a plan," George said. However, the Galactic council members started to disagree before even hearing the cadet's plan.

Eventually, George asked Pete to stop the link with the Viceroys, who were now able to gain their energy from their own red spheres, since they weren't listening anymore.

"Pete, our plan will work," George said firmly in their triad's link.

"We know," Toma replied seriously, trying to reassure George and build his confidence.

Suddenly, Frank broke their link. They all crumpled down on the floor of the scout ship holding their heads as the link ended abruptly. Gus grabbed George and Andy's shoulders and walked them out of what was left of the link. Then he grabbed Nick's and Han's shoulders and walked them out too. George, Andy, Han, and Nick shook their heads.

"Man, that smarts," George said, rubbing his head.

"That was weirdly abrupt," Andy said, shaking his head to stop it from smarting.

"Someone, a scanner maybe, must have found our link and Frank broke it to protect us, that's all," Han replied, trying to keep them calm.

Nick sat staring at Andy and George. He was stunned, not by the ending of the link, but by the arrogance of the Galactic council.

"We taught the Viceroys and Galactic council how to use the red sphere energy to regain strength and communicate, and it will probably save their lives. Then when their strength started to return, they dismissed us and would not listen to our plan," Nick said, disgusted.

"Welcome to our world," Andy laughed, still rubbing his head as his laughing made it hurt again.

As Nick and Andy talked, George turned to Han. "Andy and Nick need energy, and Gus will need his hands mended," he whispered.

Han stood up and grabbed Gus by his collar, dragging him to the back of the ship to Sara and Rachael's hallway hospital. Han then slipped back to the galley to start their next meal while Rachael and Sara stayed with Gus, holding their glowing yellow spheres over his hands.

Gus's hands were beet red. Pain shot up his arms as he tried to bend his fingers. Anna and Karmen slid in next to Sara and Rachael to share their energy with them. Soon, Gus's hands were better. The pain stopped and the bright red color was gone. They were sore, yet he could move them easily again.

"You need to tell George. It was too much this time, Gus," Sara whispered as the others retreated back to their stations to continue their assignments. She stopped her yellow healing sphere and stared at Gus as firmly as she could. "You need to tell him," she repeated firmly.

"You know I can't. They needed me and, well, I can't. Like, you can't stop healing someone. It's like that. I can't, but thanks," he said, sliding to the galley to help make the next meal with Han.

Anna slipped up to the ship's control console with Emily and started typing in commands. Emily loaded program after program into the main computer system on the two scout ships and into the main computer of the Mahadean slave ship.

Rachael was walking around injecting everyone with one of her vitamin concoctions when Gus called. Everyone stopped their assignments to go and eat the food Gus and Han had fixed. This time the food-like substances were rations with large white cups of water carefully poured and measured to be equal for each cadet and captain.

"Gus, you and Han are amazing," were the compliments they made as they bit off parts of their rations.

The cadets and captains all thought Han and Gus secretly manufactured rations at night when they all slept. They all laughed and joked about the food, yet they were all grateful to have something to eat and drink.

"OK, so we missed our meeting. Can we have it now?" George asked the teams as they munched through their rations.

Andy smiled and said, "We have eight staff weapons and four minor rockets, mainly for use in a planet's atmosphere or up really, really close to another starship."

Emily spoke next. "The energy sources in both scout ships are now fully charged. The air supply and auxiliary oxygen storage cells are also fully charged. Each system can sustain us for 14 days in space once we disconnect from the Mahadean ship. To their sensors, we look like a part of the ship and to a passerby we look like an extra engine on their ship. These little scout ships have more speed than the trainers on Indus station; however, they have very limited range. We are currently draining less than ½ percent of 1 percent of their energy," Emily said, smiling.

"And?" Andy asked.

"And what?" Emily replied.

"And you always have something extra," Andy pressed.

Nick and the other captains stared at each other and then at the cadets, not fully understanding Andy's odd question.

"Well, I have some special viruses loaded into the Mahadean's main computer systems if we ever need them," Emily added with a devilish grin.

"Similar to our last encounter with the Mahadean slave ships?" George asked, a little worried by Emily's devilish grin.

"With enhancements!" Emily replied gleefully.

The cadets and captains all laughed. Devilishly good computer programs designed to bring the Mahadean to their knees with enhancements—it was really funny if you thought about it.

"She is on our side, right?" Nick asked, nudging Andy.

"Oh ya, she's as wicked as the rest of us, sir," Andy whispered, grinning. "She just looks all sweet and nice, that's all, sir." He laughed.

"Anna, where are we?" George asked, drinking his water.

"We have about eight hours until we reach the Mahadean home world. I've plotted several escape routes. However, unless we get a bigger ship, we'll be trapped on Mahadean as these scout ships are too small to make it to any trader's outpost from the Mahadean home world even at our maximum speed," she reported.

"Then we will need to get a bigger ship," George said rather matter-of-factly, not worried about how they would get a bigger ship.

Nick wondered what made George so confident that they would succeed when most third year cadets would have crumbled under the stress. Perhaps that is why the Galactic council started to punish Pete, Frank, and Toma when they saw George and his team handling the punishment they were given so well. The Galactic council must have figured out that George's team's weakness was their connection to the members of their triad—the care and respect they all had for each other. The other captains heard Nick's thoughts in their link, and like him, they were also stunned.

"By Emily's sensor count, there are 92 members of the Galactic council, including associated CORE officers and Viceroys," Sara added and Emily nodded.

"Pete, Frank, and Toma are on the Mahadean slave ship and need to be rescued too," Anna said.

"Yes, we will need a bigger ship," George repeated, nodding in agreement with Anna and Emily again. "Did anyone find a map of the Mahadean home world? Is it a big place?" he asked, smiling.

"Yes, it is loaded into everyone's pad already," Anna replied with a gotcha kind of look, done-before-you-asked kind of thing.

Everyone laughed.

"Gus, how much food do we have?" Gus smiled. "We have enough rations for 28 days."

Andy coughed. He almost choked on his ration. Nick hit him on his back.

"Are you OK?" Nick asked.

"Yes," Andy squeaked, not looking forward to rations for 28 days.

"We may need other food to keep Andy alive," George said, joking as everyone chuckled.

"We will have the same in water supplies once we disconnect from the other ship," Gus added, sliding his hands behind his back and trying to casually lean against the wall. George knew what Gus was hiding; however, he said nothing and turned toward Sara next.

"Sara, how are we doing?" he asked, drinking more water.

"We have only basic medicines and maybe five or six days of vitamins left," she said, staring at Andy as she spoke to make sure he was OK.

"I'm fine, stop staring at me!" he said, grousing.

Everyone laughed again. It was weird, funny humor.

George looked at Nick last. "Do you have anything to add or does anyone else?" George asked.

"We need to get some rest before we land," Nick replied as he reached around and opened a console on the wall.

He flipped some switches and dimmed the lights. Everyone finished their meal, sliding the cups back to Gus and Han as they all spread out to rest. George slid over to Gus and picked up some cups to hand to him for the cleaner. He looked at Gus's hands as Gus set the cups in the cleaner.

"Why didn't you say something?" he asked, worried about Gus converting too much energy and getting hurt.

"Nothing to say, you know," Gus replied, looking down and sliding more cups into the cleaner.

George grabbed Gus's shoulder. "Gus, don't you get it? You're the glue. Without you we can't break a link. We certainly would starve, and you join our energy. You may not value these gifts, but the rest of us do. We can't do it without you. You gave the mighty Galactic council a way to regain their strength that even they did not think of, and now they will live. Gus, we cannot transfer energy again if it is going to hurt you. I can't have a member of our team hurt," George whispered in his most serious voice.

Gus looked down. It seemed so important when George said what he did that way.

"Gus, we need you. You have to tell us when it is too much. We don't always pay attention. Remember, we forget to eat," George added with a little grin.

Gus lowered his head, he really had not thought of it that way.

"No more blood, Gus. No more," he said and rolled over, sliding to the front of the scout ship to rest.

Gus's mouth fell open. George knew, Gus didn't know how he knew, but he knew. Gus set the last cup in the cleaner and shut the door, sliding back to rest against the wall.

Chapter 13

MAHADEAN SLAVES

The cadets and captains rested as the hours passed. Emily set up a warning program to alert them if their speed changed. A kind of an alarm clock for them, she thought to herself as she fell asleep. Again they did not dream, only a silent deep sleep. A few hours later, a quiet buzz filled the small ships—Emily's alarm. The Mahadean ship was slowing down. They had arrived at the Mahadean home world.

Emily walked into the command bridge, stood at the control console, and called out the readings. Anna stepped up next to her, scanning the planet as they made a full pass before the enormous slave ship started its decent through the atmosphere. Jennifer and Karmen were helping, their hands speeding across the computer consoles together.

The heat shields of the enormous galaxy-class starship covered the two smaller scout ships still clamped to its side. As they descended into the planet's atmosphere, Emily called the port administrator, asking for clearance to land. She then transferred the old trader's code they had used a year earlier at the second kitchen to pay the port fees. The code was good, and they were granted a landing port space. The administrator disconnected the communication.

"What was that for?" Andy asked, stepping up next to George.

"After we free our ships from the slave ship, we will need a port. Now we have our space reserved," Emily replied and Jennifer nodded.

"We will need tribute on this planet," Nick added seriously. "It is the form of money here."

"Nick, do you know how the slave system works on Mahadean?" George asked, staring intently at Nick.

"I know the new slaves will all be sorted by age, strength and gender. Then they will be sent to medical for inspection and then to holding for the final sort. The Galactic council is quite the prize, so there will be a big auction. It will take time for the Magistrate to make all of the arrangements. Buyers will want to see the slaves before they buy, so maybe five or six days before the big auction begins. The Galactic council really is an enormous prize. The Magistrate will be greatly honored," he said coldly.

It seemed to George that Nick knew more than he was saying about Mahadean. He would have to remember to ask for more details later.

"Then we have five days to free them or we will have to buy their freedom. When we land, we will need to split up into three groups: one group to acquire food, one group to free the scout ships from the side of the slave ship, and one group to follow the Galactic council prisoners," George said, giving orders like a captain.

"They are slaves now, George, not prisoners. There is a difference," Nick corrected coldly.

George nodded, yet he wondered why Nick had made the distinction. Then he continued his assignments.

"Gus, Sara, and Rachael will find food; Nick, Andy, Anna, and I will follow the captives; Han, Emily, Karmen, and Jennifer will free the ship. Nick, is there anything else we need to know?" George asked.

From a cabinet behind them, Nick started, throwing robes, sandals, cloaks and wraps to all of the captains and cadets.

"When you are out on the planet surface in the city, say nothing; and I mean nothing. Empty your mind of any thoughts. There are freelance scanners here that will turn you in as a traitor for only a few pieces of tribute. If someone asks you anything, say nothing, look down. Never look them in the eye and never push back or they will hurt you for being in their way. Consider yourself less than the dirt you walk on and you may be alive at the end of the day," Nick ordered firmly.

"Why? Aren't these beings like us?" Gus asked, not understanding Nick's harsh words.

"No. There are some free people on Mahadean; however, most are servants and slaves. The servants are bound to their masters by legal contract. Often a poor family will trade a family member to pay a debt. If the servant can gain enough tribute, they can buy their freedom. Slaves are different, they can never buy their freedom and disobedience is punished by death," Nick replied coldly as if he knew too much about life on Mahadean.

Everyone nodded. The ships jolted and the cadets tipped over a bit as the ships descended through the planet's lower atmosphere on the thrusters from the enormous starship. Out the front viewer, the cadets and captains saw a dry and dusty world.

"It's like the surface of the cadet station moons," Emily said, staring at the land.

"Your home world is a jewel, Earthling. It's too bad your people don't treat it like one," Han said, shaking his head.

"Most worlds are like this one, Emily. Water is a precious commodity, that's all Han meant," Jennifer said, patting Emily on the back.

Nick glanced at Han, Rachael, Jennifer, and Karmen and shook his head. The look on his face said, no upsetting the cadets; this was going to be hard enough as it was. They nodded and Han dipped his head, apologizing.

The solid brown land mass gave way to an enormous city before their eyes as they descended lower and lower toward the planet's surface. Circles of green crops dotted the land outside the city walls. Soon they could see steady streams of carts and wagons filled with goods for the people, entering the city gates. Quickly, the city overtook their view and the traders' space ports appeared before them. Every size of starship was resting on the ground in large circular ports beneath them. Some ports had many small ships, and some ports only had one enormous galaxy-class starship in it.

Soon there was a final jolt from the enormous starship as it settled to rest on the dusty ground. A swirl of dust rose up and filled the port as the thrusters blew out excess gases. They had landed in one of the enormous circular walled ports. The inside walls were a dusty gray with large two-story arches that opened the port up to other ports and to, what looked like, a main road on one side. The galaxy-class ship took up the entire port.

"We look like a part of their ship," Emily said, jumping in with an answer before anyone asked.

The Mahadean starship's port hatches opened as the dust settled, and Mahadean guards came streaming out. Standing shoulder to shoulder, the guards formed a solid double row of bodies outside the enormous ship. George and the others slipped out of their scout ships and joined the crowd that was forming behind the two rows of guards.

"I know where we are," Anna signed to George.

She had been studying the Mahadean maps as soon as she knew which city they were landing in. He nodded.

Above the arches were intricate carvings of animals and other creatures.

Some of the carvings seemed alive and changed perspective as the viewer moved around the port. As a young child, George's parents had traveled to Rome in the south of Italy. A guide had taken George and his family through the Vatican and they had seen the great tapestries of the ancient world. There was one tapestry in particular that had held George's interest. As he had walked by the tapestry, the man sitting on the end of the table become the man sitting on the side of the table and the man on the side of the table become the man on the end of the table.

Now the figures in the carvings above the arches followed them as they walked around the crowd, trying to get a closer look. The port was old and the stone work from an era long since past. Swirls of dirt coated everything, making the city and port look old and worn—as if nothing had changed in a thousand years.

With rows and rows of guards in place around the starship and out through the enormous port archway, the first slaves were led down the gangplanks out of the starship. The crowd cheered. Some of the new slaves were carried on stretchers with their hands and legs bound. Many more were chained together in one long, continuous stream of slaves.

A cold chill came over George, and the hairs on the back of his neck stood up. He looked around the port, scanning for someone new, for someone who was not there before. Across the port in the shadows of the great arch stood four tall figures covered in long black robes, their face covered by their hoods. They looked like they were, scanning each prisoner for something as the guards led the new slaves in front of them before the slaves left the port.

Andy walked up next to George with a small yellow sphere in his hand. George slipped his hand out of his brown robe and next to Andy's. Their link was made.

"Do you see them?" Andy signed, nodding in the direction of the large archway.

"I felt them come," George replied, rubbing his head.

"Who are they?" Andy asked quitely.

"Scanners. They work for the highest pay. Their minds are strong and can rip your thoughts from you, leaving you a heap of nothing. Contact with them must be avoided," Nick whispered.

"But who are they really?" Andy pressed.

Nick looked down, he really didn't want to answer this question and scare the cadets. "Well, some of the scanners are captured Viceroys from other sectors; however, there is a race of beings that have mastered the art of scanning.

They are the most ruthless and must be avoided," Nick whispered.

"Look," Anna signed.

It was Pete and Frank. Like the other new slaves, they had been badly beaten. Behind them was Toma. He towered over the Mahadean guards. He had chains on his legs and arms and wings. The guards hit him with their staffs as if he was a wild beast and the crowd cheered. Next were the Viceroys and a few of the CORE and Inner Circle officers.

George nodded, and they moved forward into an archway closer to the figures in the long black robes. From their new vantage point, they could see the figures more clearly. A bad feeling started growing in George's mind. Soon he was having difficulty focusing his thoughts. One of the figures in black looked up from the line of new slaves, flinging a fiery red energy sphere from his hand in their direction. Instantly, the crowd dropped to the ground to avoid being hit. The cadets and captains dove with the crowd. The energy sphere hit the wall behind them and the rock wall blasted apart. The people screamed in terror and started to frantically run across the port, crashing into the rows of guards, and breaking their straight columns.

A dozen prisoners fell from their cots and quickly disappeared into the crowd. Pete and Frank were gone, but Toma and the other Thorean Viceroys were too big to escape. The guards went wild, flinging red sphere after red sphere into the crowd. George, Andy, Nick, and Anna ran from the port and hid behind an archway wall.

"Are the others safe?" Anna signed.

George thought for a minute then signed, "Yes, they are all in the ships again."

The blasting stopped and the cloud of dust slowly cleared from the air. The enormous port area was empty. The guards reformed their double column lines and the crowds now peered around the archways at the guards to see the new slaves. They saw Pete's grandfather on one of the stretchers. Then George saw his parents and Pete's parents on other stretchers. He turned, looking away and slid down the outside wall as sadness filled his mind.

"We have to follow them, George," Nick signed. "Now! Get up!" he yelled in sign.

Nick couldn't let George fall into fear and sadness, not here, not on Mahadean.

He got up, and they took off, hurrying along the wall of another port. Again they came to the column of guards. This time the guards' path led across a busy road. The growing crowd on the main crossroad was getting impatient at having to wait for the new slaves to be carried across. On the other side of the dusty road was a huge gray fortress with three-story-high-walls and an enormous archway.

"The auction house," Nick signed.

"The prison, you mean," Andy replied.

"No, not a prison, auction house," Nick replied with an odd look on his face.

Inside, George knew Nick was not telling them something. He knew too much about this place and how it worked.

Again George felt fear and darkness overtaking him. He could not let himself be drawn in and let fear overtake him again. He focused his mind and thought only of the gray walls of the fortress and the small shops that filled the street between the port and the fortress.

The hairs on the back of his neck calmed, and his mind and thoughts opened to the people around him. Before them in the narrow streets were the poorest people of Mahadean. They were the merchants, shopkeepers, laborers, and farmers that sold their goods for a meager living.

Finally, the last of the new slaves were carried into the auction house and the columns of guards followed them inside, allowing the crowds to pass through the busy road again. Nick motioned and George, Andy, and Anna followed him into the open-air market. George caught a glimpse of Gus and they walked over to him. He had three dark brown canvas bags filled with roots, vegetables and berries. He handed each of them a canvas bag to carry before picking up a fourth canvas bag in front of him, paying the merchant with two tribute coins.

George wanted to ask where the tribute came from as they walked through the market; nevertheless, he stopped his thought when they came around the corner of the next street. Sara sat on the ground with her legs crossed, like a pretzel, on a bright yellow mat. A yellow scarf veiled her head and face. Rachael was sitting next to her with a little brown leather sack. In front of Sara, Rachael, had scrawled on the ground, 'healer, one tribute.'

There was a line of half a dozen people waiting to sit on the ground in front of Sara to be healed. Each time a person sat down, Rachael collected one tribute and then wrapped a yellow scarf around Sara's hand and the arm of the person she was to heal to hide her glowing yellow sphere. Rachael placed her hand on Sara's shoulder, and Sara healed the person in front of them.

Gus came up and stood in line. George, Andy, Nick, and Anna followed his lead. When it was Gus's turn, he handed Nick and George his sacks of vegetables and lifted Sara up and over his shoulder. It was midday and she was already too weak from healing to walk and he knew it. Rachael picked up the yellow mat and carried Sara's veil. Together they left the market. Anna led them back to the Mahadean galaxy-class starship port where they had landed earlier in the day.

Emily stood in the main archway and stopped them before they entered the port. Instead she led them two ports to the south. It was a port with a dozen smaller scout and transport ships like theirs sitting on the ground.

"This is our new port," Emily signed, smiling.

Han, Emily, Jennifer, and Karmen had freed their two ships. As they entered the new port, Han lay on a mat next to the underside of one of the scout ships. He was fixing the grappling hooks that had been damaged back at Asteria station. Next to him laid a roll of shiny new tools Jennifer had bought with some of Sara and Rachael's tribute.

George and the others brought the sacks of food over to the scout ship's gangplank and dropped the heavy canvas bags to greet the others.

"It's amazing what you have all done in only a few hours," George said, tipping his head in respect to acknowledge their hard work.

Jennifer and Karmen smiled and went to tend a small camp fire they had made near the front of the scout ship. A few large empty kettles and pitchers filled with water were lined up along the outside of the other scout ship, waiting for Gus to return and start cooking. Han stood up and carefully lifted Sara from Gus's arms. He carried her inside the larger scout ship and Anna and Rachael went in with him. Nick moved some wood they had bought next to the small fire and built the fire larger.

"We need to peel the roots, cut off the top of the vegetables, and clean the berries. Then, place them in the boiling water," Gus said, giving orders for the cooking.

Han came out of the ship and sat down on the ground to help peel the vegetables and clean the berries Gus had brought back with George and the others. Andy helped Gus set up a tripod and hang one of the large empty black kettles over the fire. Soon they were filling it with water and roots, vegetables and red berries.

Emily sat on the ground, removing the green vegetables' flowery tops and stacking the bottoms in a neat pile next to the fire. The ground swirled around her as if wanting to play. She was talking with the soil of Mahadean. She seemed happy talking with the soil, yet sad too, George thought as he watched her.

George sat down with Nick, peeling a mound of roots, and dropping them into an empty black pot before their mound started to topple over. When he was done helping Gus, Andy walked over to Han to help him work on the grappling hook; all the while, never taking his eyes off George.

"Nick, were you a slave, here on Mahadean?" George asked, peeling a root with a small knife that Gus had bought.

"No, my great-great-great, well many more great-grandparents were Calshene pilots. They were captured by the Mahadean and sold as slaves to the mighty Magistrate of this region. The story of their capture and enslavement has been passed down for more than ten generations in my family. Nothing has changed in all that time. I know nearly every detail about this place. From the time I was old enough to talk, I was told the story in the greatest detail over and over, until it became a part of my life," Nick said somberly.

"How did they escape?" George asked, wanting more details.

"They didn't, they were killed flying in the Turns. Their children were thought to have been killed with them in the Turns; however, they weren't. With no one looking for them, the children grew up to become merchants and bought their way off the planet as galaxy pilots. Once in space, they made it to a trading outpost like the second kitchen and then to the Calshene home world," Nick said, telling George the whole truth.

He was hoping it would help George and his plan to rescue the Galactic council.

"Calshene was once as beautiful as Earth, wasn't it? A place filled with water and life?" George asked, slicing open a root and peeling away the heavy yellow skin.

"Yes, it was. A beautiful blue sphere in the Galactic sea. It teamed with life. It was an amazing place. Well, so I have been told," Nick said, grinning weakly. "My family was sent to Earth to live after, well, you know," he added.

"The Calshene people, like the people of Earth, did not see the planet for the gift it was until it was too late; and it was destroyed. And now, that is why Han and the other Calshene dislike the Earthers so much," George said bluntly.

"Yes, George, you are observant. They are nearly as angry at the Earthers as they are at themselves for not seeing the gift they had. Now it is gone forever," Nick said as Gus walked over to them.

"The cost of a meal is two tribute per bowl tonight," Gus said, walking up to them rolling another empty black kettle.

"How do you know they will come?" Nick asked.

Gus did not even look up. "They will come," he muttered, rolling away with their nearly full kettle of roots.

Gus started mixing and George went inside the small ship to check on Sara. Andy left Han and sat inside the small ships door waiting for George, watching all the people coming and going in their little port. By mid-afternoon the sweet smell of Gus's food filled the air of the port and wafted over the archways into the main streets and other ports. As with Sara, people now lined up for a taste of Gus's food. As he emptied one pot, the next pot was ready.

Gus would not let any of the cadets and captains on their team even taste the food he prepared. They could only eat rations and the brown cereal, he said. Andy asked for a taste from one of the kettles, and Gus nearly bit his head off. He muttered something about microorganisms and Sara not having enough medicine to counteract the food enzymes. It seemed like a riddle to Andy. But he had learned if the answer was a riddle or cryptic, then whatever had been said was only part of the truth.

Andy watched the people in the lines waiting for Gus's food. They were a pushy group, not concerned with each other, only wanting food for themselves. Andy didn't like so many people knowing where their ships were and where they were sleeping.

Nick sat down next to Andy on the gangplank in the late afternoon.

"Gus cannot keep cooking here. There are too many of them now and they know who we are and where we are staying," Andy whispered, scanning the crowd of people who had lined up for Gus's food.

"We will help Gus move the cooking fires in the early morning," Nick replied, watching the wild group of people as the lines grew.

"We should never have let Gus cook so close to the ships. I thought he was going to be cooking for us," Andy said, worried they would be discovered and turned into the Magistrate as escaped slaves.

"Patience, Andy. Gus couldn't have known his food would be this successful. He is doing the best he can to earn us tribute," Nick said, counseling Andy.

Andy nodded. However, patience was not one of his virtues.

That evening, after all the pots were emptied and cleaned, Han and Gus entered the larger scout ship and cut up two rations for their evening meal. The captains and cadets were all hungry and wanted to taste the delicious food they had served the local people. However, no one wanted to cross Gus or Han and so they ate their meager ration pieces in silence.

"Gus, you and Han need to move the feeding line away from our port in the morning," George said when he finished his cup of water.

Nick had spoken to George. Gus and Han nodded. That night they all slept together in the main command bridge, not an arm's length away from each other.

Early the next morning Gus and Han left the ship to buy more food with the profits from the day before. A local merchant around the corner from their port offered space in his market stand to Gus and Han for them to cook. Andy, George, and Nick came to help move the kettles, pitchers and tripods while Gus and Han filled more pitchers with water from a merchant's faucets. Emily and Jennifer started the cooking fires, while Karmen and Anna moved the wood. The cooking fires were warm in the cool morning air. Sara and Rachael were on their corner healing while the others cooked.

With new bags of roots and berries to prepare, the team sat down on a black bench behind the merchant's stand and began peeling the thick roots and topping the vegetables for the kettles. It wasn't as far from the scout ships as Nick and Andy would have liked. On the other hand, at least it wasn't at the end of their gangplank anymore.

"Nick, tell me more about the Mahadeans and the auction," George said, peeling more roots for Gus's kettles.

"The Mahadean auctions are legendary across the galaxies. Somehow they always end up with the most prized slaves. The slaves are conditioned or beaten by the scanners until they obey their new masters without question. If you buy a slave from the Mahadean and they don't work out, you can get a replacement for no tribute," he said, dropping another root in their empty kettle.

"But then if all the slaves misbehaved and escaped, wouldn't the Mahadean go broke?" George asked, not understanding the hold the Mahadean had over the slaves.

Nick smiled. "No, George, any slaves returned are beaten in public by the scanners to scare the other slaves into behaving," Nick said, looking down.

"What do you mean the scanners beat the slaves?" George pressed, not understanding.

"The scanners can destroy the slaves mind and then they die. No one ever escapes once they are…," Nick replied coldly, his words trailing off.

Nick reminded George of Andy when Andy used the red energy to defend them, cold and unfeeling. George paused and stared at Nick.

"But your great -great, you know, grandparents escaped," he said.

"No, George, they died. Their children escaped because the Magistrate thought their children had died with them. Otherwise, our family would still be slaves," Nick replied sadly.

"And the auction, what about that?" George pressed, trying to keep Nick talking.

Nick was sad, and the planet seemed to be sucking the joy out of their lives. Yet, George had to know what Nick knew. They needed a plan if they were going to rescue the Galactic council and the others, and right now George was still grasping at straws for an idea.

"Dignitaries and wealthy merchants from across the galaxy will come here to the main auction house on Mahadean to view the Magistrate's latest prize. The new slaves will be conditioned and then put on display. The Viceroys will most likely be made into scanners, as their minds are the strongest. The others will be sold as pilots and workers. The auction usually lasts a few days. There are a lot of new slaves to process, so it might take longer this time to get all the arrangements made," Nick replied.

"I imagine the Viceroys will put up a good fight against the scanners," George said, trying to think of something good.

"Not really. Do you remember the scanners we saw yesterday?" Nick asked, forgetting for a moment that they were only third-year cadets.

"Sure, they really hurt, and they didn't even focus on us," George said, rubbing his head.

"Well, they are nothing. Just freelance scanners, peasants on the city streets compared to the scanners in the auction house, George. They are nothing by comparison," Nick replied seriously.

Nick was becoming a little too spooky, and George was getting more worried about the Viceroys and his mom and dad. Nick stopped suddenly and stared at George.

"I'm sure they are fighting back," he added, bumping George's shoulder to help calm his mind and keep his focus. Yet Nick worried he had said too much.

"Ah, sure," George replied.

Nick pulled over another canvas bag of roots, and they started peeling again.

"What about the Turns? What is it really? It sounds like a race. When is the Turns run and how do we enter?" George asked, picking up another root.

"It is one wicked race, George. The race is held once a year, and it covers the entire Mahadean planet. The racers start and end here in this city. They race across the land as fast as they can and then dive into the great gorge in the planet's surface. Some racers then circle the planet in the gorge and then reappear on the other side of the city to claim the prize. However, few win this way, I mean, by playing it safe," Nick answered.

"So, what do the other racers do that's so different that they win?" George pressed, curious as to how else you could circle the planet.

"When the racers get to the great gorge in the planet's surface, they dive in and race through the molten center of the planet. Then they emerge on the other side of the planet sooner than those ships that circled the planet and they win the race," he said calmly.

"Then why do the pilots circle the planet at all?" he asked.

"The pilots fly around the planet to try and win the race because so few make it through the center of the planet. From time to time, the circling pilots do win the race when no one returns from the core of the planet," Nick replied honestly, yet worried he had told George too much about a very dangerous race.

George thought the story that he had heard in the market about going through the center of the planet was only a story to impress people; yet, it wasn't a story at all. It was true. George stared at Nick, a little stunned by his words.

"What is the prize for winning the Turns, Nick?" George asked as Gus set another empty kettle in front of them and rolled the kettle full of roots toward a second fire.

"Anything, George. Anything at all," Nick replied, dropping more peeled roots into the empty kettle.

His hands hurt from peeling and he wiggled his fingers as George thought.

"Anything, anything?" George asked again.

"Really, anything at all. Whatever the winner wants, the winner gets," Nick said and chuckled.

"That would be a prize worth having," George said, beginning to make a plan in his mind. "So what do we need to do to enter the Turns?" George asked, peeling another root.

Nick stared at George. "We will need a lot of tribute, maybe four or five thousand tribute, and a good ship that can take the heat in the core of the planet. Then we can buy our way in, enter the Turns, fly through the center of the planet and win the race," he said, laughing and slicing open a large root, thinking it was an insane idea for a bunch of captains and cadets to even consider.

However, George didn't laugh. He was making a plan.

"No, George, seriously now," Nick said, staring at George in disbelief, suddenly knowing he had made a plan.

George smiled. "So tribute talks on this planet," he said deviously.

"So, that's the plan," Nick said, sighing shaking his head.

"Yup, that's the plan," George replied with a grin, looking out over the market.

Nick shook his head. "OK, but we will need to find out more about the competitors if we are going to enter the Turns and fix our ships," Nick said, knowing there was no talking George out of the new plan.

The customers from the market had been a wild group the first day. Now, on the afternoon of the second day, the people were calmer, aside from one or two people now and then. All day Gus taught the merchant how to cook the roots and feed the people.

That night, after their evening meal of rations, George, Andy, and Nick slipped out into the shadows of the city, learning and listening to the conversations they overheard from the people on the streets and in the shops. They sat in the dirt and on the curbs of the streets outside the open-air restaurants listening to conversations. However, Andy leaned against a light pole to get a better view of the people having conversations inside the buildings, watching through the windows and open doors. At an early age, he had learned to lip-read his parent's secret conversations. Now, it was paying off.

To enter the auction house and buy the prisoners, they would need a great deal of tribute, and the only way to get it was to win the Turns, the race through the molten core of the Mahadean planet.

In their evening outings over the next few days, they had learned that the conditioning of the Galactic council was not going as well as the Magistrate had hoped. The Viceroys were difficult to handle and had somehow managed to maintain their strength and energy. The Magistrate had been counting on weak Viceroys that would be easily conditioned by the scanners. To add to the Magistrate's problems, more and more buyers poured into the city each day, all wanting a Galactic Viceroy as a slave. The city was packed and squabbles among the buyers and traders were disrupting the Magistrate's plans.

Finally, on the fourth day after their arrival, the Magistrate declared the auction would begin after the Turns, in order to give the scanners a few more days to condition their new slaves.

For four days, Sara had healed and Gus had fed thousands of people. The rumors of the healer spread like wildfire, and Sara's line got longer and longer each day. Most people had simple ailments, some a little more serious; however, nothing she could not easily fix. Each afternoon Andy and Nick made red spheres to help Sara recover from the energy drain of healing.

Gus was feeding thousands of people each day now. With the cooking pots moved to the main street outside their port after the first day, the feeding lines now wrapped through the narrow streets and open-air markets. He had the local people helping him cook and prepare the vegetables, freeing up the cadets and captains from having to peel and top the roots and vegetables. Gus taught the local people how to feed the others of Mahadean for little money with good tasting vegetables. On the fourth evening, he sent several merchants out to the other cities across Mahadean to feed more people and teach them how to cook and feed even more people.

On the fifth day, they had earned the 5,000 tributes required to enter the Turns. That evening, George, Nick, and Andy posed as serving slaves for a fancy party that had been hastily thrown together for dignitaries and wealthy merchants who had come to the city for the auction.

The hall was small and crowded, with many minor merchants and traders. Listening to the conversations in the small hall, they learned about the competitors in the Turns this year. Two competitors were new and three competitors were from last year's Turns. Their ships had been destroyed, but they had escaped alive.

As they served dinner and dessert, they learned more and more about the Turns and the competitors who would be competing for the top prize. The Turns was a race, all right, and just as dangerous as Nick had said. Small fighter ships ran the course through the center of the planet. As the Turns was run only once a year, the competitors were treated like kings because they could die, never making it to the end of the race to claim the prize. The winner could name their price, and whatever it was, it would be granted.

There was a lot of lore about the Turns. Some years, no one finished the Turns and the farmer's crops had done poorly. The Mahadean had made the Turns a matter of life and death for their planet and this year was no different. The race was in four more days. The people and merchants of the city seemed to get more tense and uneasy as the day of the Turns approached. The failure of a pilot to win could mean the starvation of many of the poor on their planet.

George and the others could feel the people's stress increase in the market place; however, they did not understand how strong the people's belief was that there had to be a winner for them to prosper the next year.

The competitors had been paraded around the city like kings for nearly a week. They were a demanding group of pilots who compromised on nothing, reeking havoc if their every want was not meant.

By the end of the evening, they had learned there would be a larger, more extravagant costume ball held at the Magistrate's personal residence the next night. It was the ball they wanted to be at. It was when and where they would enter the Turns. With servants and slaves in short supply in the city, George, Andy, and Nick were ordered to be at the Magistrate's residence before they left the ball in the small hall that evening.

The morning of the sixth day on Mahadean was quiet. Gus and Han were up early helping to get the merchant set up for cooking. Six feeding areas had been set up across the city now, and Gus and Han visited each one to make sure the cooking was going as planned. The people in the streets were beginning to look better to Gus and Han as they made their way through the markets. Each evening the tribute collected was put into the local bank and then distributed to the farmers and workers. Life on Mahadean was harsh, with little hope for escape or change for the people. Yet Gus, Han, Sara, and the others had made a difference in the lives of the people of Mahadean.

The team was quiet, all working, planning, feeding, and healing. Nick and Andy worked on the small scout ship, adding reinforcements to the outside hull and engine covers. Anna, Rachael, and Jennifer hauled the reinforcement plating around and positioned it so Nick and Andy could weld the pieces into place. Emily had more plates delivered each time Andy and Nick ran out of the reinforcement plating.

At mid-afternoon, George, Andy, and Nick walked quietly through the streets to the Magistrate's residence. They stood at the back gate waiting to be let inside with the other servants and slaves standing in line. Once properly dressed in brown and white serving costumes, they were loaded with heavy silver trays filled with foods of every kind to carry into the grand ballroom. Serving tables lined the walls of the grand ballroom where other servants unloaded the trays of food from George, Andy, and Nick. Then, they were sent back for more food and desserts.

The grand ballroom and hallways were covered in sparkling gemstones and twinkling lights. Golden tablecloths glistened and sparkled, reflecting the twinkling lights. The guests were dressed in fancy costumes of every type. Some had flowing, floor-length robes that swirled and sparkled as the guests danced around the floor of the grand ballroom. Others had costumes that glowed and changed color as the guests talked with the different dignitaries from Mahadean and the regional Magistrate in the grand ballroom. The five competitors sat at tables on raised platforms covered with glittering blue and red carpets. They all acted like spoiled kings with servants running to and from their tables with glorious foods and flowing drinks. A fountain of shimmering water sparkled in the center of the grand ballroom, reflecting the lights.

Around and around George, Andy, and Nick travelled, carrying heavy trays of food, never being noticed by the dignitaries and guests. They lingered near the tables, listening to the conversations of the competitors as they carried the heavy trays from table to table to refill the serving tables lining the grand ballroom.

On one of their rounds, George and Andy emptied their silver trays quickly and slipped them under Nick's tray behind a large golden table covered in a tower of flowers and food. Nick waited behind the table as George and Andy casually wandered through a smaller servant's archway over to a small table setup on the far side of the grand ballroom. The band played and the people danced as George quietly took the 5,000 tributes that Sara and Gus had earned out of his pockets and set it on the table in front of the two servants.

The Magistrate's servants gasped. "How can you enter the Turns, you are servants like us?" the head servant asked in a whisper, afraid of being caught speaking.

"I only dress as a servant to know my competitors," George replied with an evil looking grin.

The servants smiled and nodded their heads.

"A good disguise, sir," the lead servant whispered.

Andy stared across the crowded ballroom, watching and blocking anyone's view of George.

"Where can we find you, good sir?" the lead servant asked, filling out the papers for George.

"Where the people are fed and healed, my friend. However, there must be no fanfare, we are a simple people and require none of this extravagance in our name," George whispered, motioning to the fancy ballroom and music.

In reality, he was insisting on their secrecy. The servants nodded. Quickly, he and Andy left the servants to finish their paperwork with great care.

Silently, they walked around the outside of the ballroom unnoticed. They stopped at the edge of the flower-covered table and Nick slipped them their empty trays. Walking quickly around the outside of the grand ballroom behind the fancy dressed serving tables, George suddenly doubled over, dropping his empty silver tray. Andy dove and caught the heavy tray inches above the ground. Doing a perfect somersault, he rolled and stood up holding both trays, having made no sound.

However, Andy's somersault with large glistening silver trays caught the attention of several guests and a crowd started to gather. Across the room, four figures dressed in black robes turned and stared at the gathering crowd. Quickly, they glided across the ballroom to investigate the commotion. The crowd split instantly, not wanting to be in the way of the Magistrate's scanners.

"Run, Andy. Take George! Hurry! Run fast before they get here," Nick signed, dropping to one knee with his tray at his side. Andy grabbed George with one arm and added his tray to George's tray with his other arm. Swiftly, Andy dragged George out of the grand ballroom, through the kitchen, and away from the scanners. Nick was about to sacrifice himself so George and Andy could escape, and Andy knew it!

"We have to go back, Andy. We can't leave Nick," George said, struggling to free himself from Andy's grasp as they hurried out of the back entrance of the Magistrate's residence.

"No, George. We need to wait out here, away from the scanners. This is what I was talking about, George. You have to let Nick and I protect you and our team," Andy said quietly as he released George from his grasp. He held a small red sphere in the palm of his hand to stop George from going back inside as they stood on the curb by the back gate.

"No!" George signed, his face showing his irritation as he stared at Andy's red sphere.

"Yes!" Andy signed back, his face straining. "This is what I meant. You have to listen to me, George."

Inside the ballroom, the four scanners surrounded Nick. Their minds were strong and Nick dropped down to the ground on both knees, lowering his head to the floor as they approached.

"Forgive me, master. I did not know," he whispered over and over. It was the words of a slave, begging for his life; words that he had been taught since he was a small child.

The Magistrate hurried over to see the commotion. He nodded and his scanners backed away. Quickly, he motioned for two guards to come and throw Nick out.

"It is so difficult to get good help," he said loudly, and all the guests laughed as the guards roughly dragged Nick out to the back entrance of the residence.

The guards dropped him in the dirt on the side of the street, then returned to their posts inside the ballroom. Andy and George rushed over to Nick when the guards left.

"What happened?" Andy whispered, staring at Nick.

"They were strong scanners. They must have sensed something in George and gone after his mind from across the ballroom," Nick replied as Andy and George helped him stand up.

"They were a lot stronger than the ones in the port when we landed," George whispered.

"They were the Magistrate's scanners. I warned you they would be stronger," Nick replied firmly.

"Why did we have to leave? What happened after we left?" George pressed as they hurried across the main street, away from the grand party.

The further away they walked, the stronger George and Nick became.

"The scanners are very powerful, George. They can easily destroy your mind," Nick said, resting on a curb outside a café.

"But they didn't destroy you. Why?" Andy asked, staring at Nick.

"I begged for my life, and the Magistrate dismissed me to stop the disruption of his grand party. If it hadn't been for all of the guests staring, he would have had the scanners destroy me," Nick said harshly, snapping his fingers.

"No," George replied shocked.

"Yes, George. Life isn't worth much here," Nick said bluntly.

"We will need a defense against the scanners," George whispered, resting on a curb at the edge of a street with Nick and Andy.

Yet Nick knew of no defense. He worried that George's confidence would give them away.

Despite the appearance of the scanners, their trip that night had been good. They had found out that the auction was taking longer than expected. The prisoners were difficult to manage and many more merchants and traders than expected wanted to bid on the Galactic council slaves from old Calshene. The auction was now definitely delayed until after the Turns, regardless of the wealthy merchants and traders' complaints.

At each place they visited on their trip back to the port, George and Andy felt the cold shiver of the figures in black robes. Scanners working for evil were here. Evil was listening through them and waiting for an opportunity. The control of the Galactic council and its large number of Viceroys and Senior Viceroys would add greatly to the power of evil in this sector of the universe. George and the others were also waiting patiently for an opportunity. The opportunity to free the Galactic council and return peace and calm to this sector of the universe.

As they entered the scout ship, Nick pulled Andy back and George entered alone to check on the others.

"Andy, you need to talk to George. He needs to understand that you and I are the defenders. There is no defense against the Magistrate's scanners. The Senior Viceroys are barely able to defend against them, and I am sure in the end they will lose the battle they are now fighting. George must understand. He cannot fight the scanners. He is not strong enough and they will destroy him. He must understand we are his and the team's defenders," Nick said seriously.

"I have tried to tell him, but he will not listen. I worry he will sacrifice himself for us and all will be lost," Andy replied sadly.

"You must try again, Andy. George has to understand," Nick said seriously, and Andy nodded as they walked inside the ship.

They would need to make a plan.

Chapter 14

HELP ARRIVES AGAIN

After entering the 'Turns' race the night before, Nick, Han, Anna, and Emily were now working feverishly on the smaller of the two scout ships during the day to improve its speed and energy supply. George and Andy spent most of their days focusing and concentrating, calming the team's fears as the evil around them grew stronger.

On the seventh night as George, Andy, and Nick returned to the port, three figures came out of the shadows and approached them. One held a glowing yellow sphere in the palm of his hand as he walked forward. George reached forward, and Andy stepped in front of him, blocking his way. Nick slipped in behind George, covering his back.

"You should be more careful, George, as Andy and Nick are. They protect you well," a muffled voice said.

"How do you know who we are?" George whispered.

"As the wind knows the sand, so I know Pete and Frank," the cloaked figure whispered.

"Are they safe? Can we see them?" George asked, looking around.

"They are safe and well," the figure answered, stepping further out of the shadows.

It was Max!

"Sir, what are you doing here?" Nick asked, clasping his arm and scanning the port.

"Bringing you help," he replied, opening his arm.

He motioned to the shadows and Pete and Frank stepped forward. They looked bad, even in the dim light from the two moons overhead; they looked really bad.

"And the others, sir?" George asked hopefully as they began to walk so as not to look suspicious.

"Still in hiding. They are safe, George. What is your plan?" Max asked. However, he knew only Pete and Frank had not been recaptured.

"To win the Turns and free the slaves sir," George whispered.

"Risky, George," Max replied, frowning.

"It's always risky, sir," Andy replied, grinning as if it were easy; only a task they needed to complete.

"Evil will be there, trying to stop you; and if it cannot stop you, it will try to destroy you," Max said ominously.

"It is to be expected, sir," Nick added, grinning a little.

"Nick, this is so different for you," Max said, patting him on the back.

"True, at first I thought we were coming to save them, then I found out it was really us who needed to be saved, sir," Nick said nodding.

"So they are the ones of the prophecy?" Max signed, smiling as they walked.

"No, sir, they are not, the prophecy does not speak of a team to save the universe. It is a myth created to control the galaxies," Nick replied in common sign, knowing George and Andy could read his answer.

Pete and Frank nodded. Nick and the captains knew what they could not say. They had figured it out a while ago and were sworn to secrecy from that time on. They came to the port where the two small ships were docked, and Max disappeared into the shadows. George, Andy, and Nick made a link with Pete and Frank, standing in the shadows of the arches. They watched Gus's fire cast flickering shadows across the silhouettes of the two ships.

"You flew here in training scouts?" Frank said stunned.

"You are all nuts!" Pete said, shaking his head with Frank.

"Well actually, we were stuck on the tail of the Mahadean galaxy-class starship and dragged here. So since we came, we thought we should rescue everyone. Nothing much else to do, you know," Nick said, laughing.

In the last few weeks, he had changed and grown. Now he better understood this young cadet team he had sworn to protect.

True to form, Pete said only one thing. "Report."

They smiled, it was like home. George made their report and explained all they had been doing and that they were now entered in the Turns in two days.

"Who else knows you have entered the Turns, he asked.

"Only the servants who filled out the paperwork for us, and they can't say anything, sir," George said confidently.

"Good," Pete replied, ending the link.

He no longer needed Rachael, how odd was that!

"What did they do to you in the starship? We could barely make a link, sir," George asked Frank as they walked up to the ship.

"They scanned us and beat us. The Mahadean scanners are very strong. They made what the Galactic council did to us seem like nothing at all," Frank replied with a painful look on his face. "Their scanners are not from here. They're from…," Frank said, and Pete waved him off. "Well, they're unbelievably strong," he said, nodding to Pete.

Pete turned to Nick and started signing quickly in their captain's language while Frank stared at George.

"George, something bad is going to happen. I don't know what. But you must follow Pete's lead on this one, no matter what happens. You will know when to step up. We have only one chance. You must promise—focus and calm are your allies. The evil here will do anything to prevent you from keeping your wits about you. Do you understand, George?" Frank said quickly before they entered the ship.

His voice was not mournful or stern, it was direct and focused as if it was the only thing he had left that had not been stripped away.

"Yes, Frank, I understand," George said, tired and a little sarcastic in his reply.

"And if they destroy Pete and I in front of you and your team, will you still understand?" Frank pressed.

"There is no prophecy, Frank. Each day we make our own decisions and determine our life's path, sir," George signed with his hands at his side as they walked into the scout ship.

Frank nodded, listening to George; yet, he worried that his little brother could make a good decision if he and Pete were destroyed. Jennifer and Rachael nearly tackled Frank and Pete when they saw them. Inside the small scout ships, Sara healed Pete and Frank's visible wounds as Han locked down the ships for the night.

"Did you see the Viceroys, grandfather, mom and dad, and…?" George asked once inside.

"Tell us how everyone is, sirs," Emily asked, followed by Anna and Sara.

Pete raised his hand and laughed. "I missed your speed and your ability to all talk at once and not miss a beat. Yes, they are all here, our parents escaped during the commotion; and they are recovering well enough. We have not heard from Grandfather and the other council members. However, the energy you sent did them a world of good. They would have died during the space voyage without it," he replied seriously.

"Can they keep it up, sir?" Gus pressed.

"Yes, Gus, it is hard for them, but they keep trying. I think it is the only thing keeping them alive," Frank added.

"Well, that and confounding the scanners to prevent them from being controlled," Pete replied with a nod.

"Can we speak with them, sir?" George asked.

"No, and you must not try. They have blocked all outside contact. They do not want the scanners to find any more of our people," Pete said firmly. "What is your plan, George? I know you have one," Pete said, changing the topic and trying to be his captain-like self even though he was still weak.

"Sir, we will win the Turns and ask for the freedom of all of the slaves, sir," George replied matter-of-factly.

"Then what?" Pete pressed, stunned that they thought they could win the Turns.

"Then we all go home, sir," he replied as if he was stating the obvious.

"George, the 90 plus officers, Viceroys, and Galactic Council will not squeeze into these two tiny scout ships," Pete said.

The cadets and Pete's team burst into laughter.

"Yes, even we knew that, sir," Anna said giggling.

"Remember the Thoreans? They all fit into three galaxy-class cruisers—we counted this time too, sir," Emily replied, trying not to laugh again.

"Well then?" Pete insisted.

"We bought one old but functional galaxy-class cruiser sir," Andy said, nodding to Emily. She blushed.

"No, it's more of a frigate of sorts, Pete," Nick answered.

"It's not pretty, but it can get us all home," Han added.

"We have quite a lot of weapons now and supplies, too, sir," Emily added.

"And where did you get all the tribute to buy a galaxy-class cruiser frigate and enter the Turns race?" Frank asked directly, raising an eyebrow.

"Gus's cooking and Sara's healing, sir," Andy replied, stretching his fingers.

Pete stared at Sara, thinking for a moment. "Sara, are your healing cases getting more difficult?" he asked.

"Yes, sir. How did you know?" Sara said, puzzling.

"You are being intentionally drained now. These next two days before the Turns, you cannot heal. You have to regain your strength. Do you understand?" he ordered.

"Yes, sir, sure," she replied, hesitantly.

"If they bring you a child that was beaten and mortally bleeding and you know that the child will die without your help, will you still obey and do nothing?" Pete asked, pressing hard.

Pete knew something, she was sure of it.

"There will be a test for each of us and it will be, well, let's say it will be aimed at each of our weaknesses, and you want to know how strong we are. Can we do what has to be done to save the galaxies from the great evil that is now among us? Can we see it for what it is? Your question is in error, sir. We made that decision long ago, before we knew of the great evil around us, before we ever heard of the prophecy and the Galactic council. It is a part of our very existence, who we are inside. Sometimes we do what appears to be great works of good, and yet inside, we are simply too stupid or too naive not to help others. We cannot always help, but we do our best, sir," Sara answered and the cadets nodded.

"As long as we strive to make where we are better, than our efforts do not die with us, they live on in the lives of those we have fed and healed, sir," Anna added confidently.

"This will be hard for you," Pete said as if he was preparing them for the worst.

"No, sir. No, it will not be, sir," Emily replied, remembering having to delete the prophecy from their pads.

She turned away as George held her hand tightly.

Pete stared, pausing for a moment, then he pressed harder. "If you have to choose between freedom for the Galactic council and Frank's and my life, what do you chose?" Pete asked firmly.

"Both, as our fortunes have yet to be written, sir," George replied seriously.

Pete nodded, dipping his head to them; however, like Frank, he was not convinced they could make the choice.

"Rest now, I want to see this heap of junk you spent your tribute on in the morning," he said, patting them on their backs, pleased with their work.

The cadets slid over to their cots and laid down to sleep. George and Andy slid up to the small command bridge and made a link. George cleared his mind and focused on calm and peace. Pete and Frank followed them and watched, then joined their link. Calm filled the air as they opened their minds to the galaxy and focused on calm and peace.

Many times in the night, the evil outside their little link tried to break their concentration, to consume them with fear. Each time George and Andy answered with peace and calm, no longer falling into the trap of fear and distrust. In the morning, the cadets were rested; and George, Andy, Pete, and Frank ended the link. They slid back to the corridor where Gus and Han were slicing and dicing rations for the cadets and captains.

"I thought you were cooking, Gus?" Frank asked, staring at the meager rations.

"I am. You can't eat it. It's not meant for you, sir," Gus said firmly.

"We eat rations, only rations, sir," Anna said with a grin.

"We love rations, sir," Emily added.

"We want to live," Nick said.

"Gus and Han will be disappointed in us if we eat the mounds of food we prepare for the people of this city each day, sir," Andy said half smiling.

"Why?" Pete questioned.

"Because it is what I have requested. It is what you will eat, sir," Gus replied firmly, sliding a white bowl to Pete and then another to Frank.

"We trust each other, without question or reservation. Gus has said this is what we eat, so this is what we eat. We do not have time to make sure everyone is doing their duties, we simply trust that they are. Then we can focus on our duties and accomplish more efficiently the tasks we have been given, sir," George said firmly.

Captains or not, they would eat only rations as Gus and Han had said.

"Eat every bite. We won't eat again till dinner this evening, sir," Gus said firmly.

"Aren't you hungry?" Frank asked, biting into his ration.

"We all are; however, we have to think about each other. We can survive for a long time this way, sir," Andy answered this time.

"We will be all right, Pete, Frank. It is what needs to be done. Now eat, sirs. Sara, as you will not be healing today, can you and Han take Pete and Frank to our other place?" George asked.

"Yes," she answered, smiling in a perky way.

"Remember to…," George said cryptically.

"Yes, yes, we will avoid the main streets today," Sara replied, cutting George off.

The meal was over quickly with such meager fare; yet, they were happy to be working toward a goal.

Pete and Frank could hardly believe the transformation that had taken place in them as they walked out into the marketplace on their way to the other ship. Weaving in and out through the side streets, Pete wondered what had been said to them to cause such a change. He knew they were different from the day he had first met them, but this level of concentration in cadets so young was startling.

"Scanners!" Han signed, and their group stopped suddenly in the market, concentrating on Sara and helping her shop for the right thing.

Sara picked up first one scarf and then another. She held the second scarf up into the sky and then shook her head. She had a perplexed look on her face. She spun it around and the scarf slipped in front of the two scanners, breaking their concentration as she dropped her head, hiding her face and distracting them further as the scarf fell toward the ground.

With elegance and grace she wove the scarf back up high into the air. It swirled in a circle in an elegant dance, mesmerizing the scanners and the crowd for a few moments longer. Pete, Frank, and Han scanned the scanners and had what they needed. Han reached out toward Sara with his hand. She gracefully swung the scarf around, refolding it in midair and set it back on the merchant's table. Gently grasping Han's hand, she stepped to the side.

The crowd went wild, wanting to buy the scarf, crushing the scanners as Sara and the captains slipped away, out of the market to another port.

"Did you have enough time, sir?" she asked cryptically.

"Yes, thank you," Pete said, smiling.

"Where did you learn to do that, that scarf thing?" Frank asked, waving his hands in the air.

"My grandmother, she is much better than I am, sir," she said, looking down with sadness creeping into her thoughts.

"She would be very proud of you. You were flawless, Sara," Pete said, slipping his arm over her shoulder and helping her confidence return.

One more turn and they entered another port. Before them was a galaxy-class or frigate or cruiser starship. It rather leaned to one side, as the landing struts were not even. It was not shiny and new—it was old with, what looked like laser cannon burn marks on the hull.

Pete and Frank looked around the port, hoping to find a better looking starship. Yet every other ship in the port was smaller. This battle-scarred starship was it!

"Can we go inside?" Pete asked, looking for words of encouragement.

Frank and Pete glanced at each other and hoped the starship looked better inside than it did on the outside.

"Only as servants," Sara replied quietly.

They walked over to a stack of boxes and each picked up something to carry that was well beyond their ability. Now they were properly loaded. Other servants and slaves joined them as the ship's gangplank opened and the servants started loading the cargo.

They carried the cargo into the main cargo hold and then looked around on their trip out to get more cargo. On one of their outbound trips, a man in a clean blue uniform walked up to them.

"What are you doing here? This is not your place," he said, raising his hand to strike Sara.

She lowered her head and dropped to the ground on one knee to beg. A few of the slaves jostled against the walls to distract the man.

"Be off with you, pray your master does not hear of your poor work," he said as Sara hurried out the ship's port and down the gangplank.

She smiled and nodded to the servants and slaves that had saved her.

"We must leave now," she whispered, motioning for the others to follow her out of the port.

They slipped out one of the archways and back into the busy street. Han led them down a smaller side street filled with cloth shops and back to the two scout ships, avoiding the corner Sara sat on when healing people in the main market. It was late afternoon when they returned, weaving around other small ships in the port. Gus was outside in the main market, feeding the people with other local merchants, peeling the roots and starting another cooking fire when they walked through their port to the other archway near Gus's cooking fires.

Han, Pete, and Frank laid down wood near their ships for the little fire at the night. Gus was feeding people earlier and earlier each day. He now had three dozen local people helping him with cooking and feeding the people. A servant carved Gus's recipe in the wall between two arches. Pete watched in amazement as Gus taught as many as would listen how to spice and cook the roots and berries.

Soon, Gus left the people and joined the teams in the spaceport for their meal. He and Han sliced and diced and set out thirteen bowls of rations and a small white cup of water for each person. Everyone slipped into the larger scout ship and ate their meal together. Soon, Gus left to pay the workers as they were cleaned the kettles. Not a drop of food was left. Quickly, he returned to the ship to finish his ration.

"Gus, why can't the food be kept overnight?" Frank asked.

"The roots and berries make a chemical reaction when they cook. However, it is not so stable out in the air. If eaten within the time written, all is well and it will nourish you. If not, it will make you very sick. It will not kill you, but you might prefer it to the stomachache you'll have. These are a good people trapped in a bad system. We are trying to offer them a way to change, a place to start, to get out, that's all, sir," Gus answered, biting into his ration.

"Who is this young cadet who a mere two summers before could only smell out food from behind walls and is now feeding thousands of people and teaching them a different way of life in the process?" Pete signed to Frank.

That night when George and Andy slipped into the little command bridge, Pete and Frank watched from the corridor. Nick walked up behind them.

"They will need all of our concentration to keep them focused for their flight in the Turns," Nick whispered.

"You and Rachael will need to help them; Frank and I are needed elsewhere," Pete replied.

Nick curled his lip and placed his hands firmly on Pete and Franks shoulders. They bent down in pain, spinning free of Nick's grasp. Pete stopped Nick and held out his hand. A glowing yellow sphere danced above his palm. Quickly, they made a link and Pete and Frank shared the truth about the Galactic council.

"The Viceroys are nearly dead. They are holding on by sheer will. George, Andy, and Gus's little energy trick is the only thing keeping them alive and preventing them from being totally controlled by the scanners," Frank whispered.

"All of the Viceroys that had escaped were recaptured—only Frank and I made it to safety. Max is equally weak as he is now guiding all the cosmic energy alone, whatever that really means. It doesn't really matter because he cannot help. If the Viceroys die, Max will die, the galaxies will fall into chaos, and evil will win this time. George and the others will need every advantage. We have only one course of action," Pete said firmly, thinking they would sacrifice themselves so the others could remain free.

"The price is too high, Pete, and you know it," Nick thought in their link.

"There is no other way, Nick," Frank said firmly.

"We are still being hunted. We can distract the Magistrate and officials. There is nothing left. They must escape with or without the Galactic council. They must live," Pete said firmly. "And it is your job to see that they do."

Nick narrowed his eyes. "You sit among a team of third rotation cadets that are about to save the entire Galactic council because their grappling hook got caught on an invader's starship. And they ended up on a slave trader's home world, feeding and healing thousands of people two days before they start a race through the molten center of the Mahadean planet; and you say there is no other way. Look around you! Look at what they have done! There is always another way. Look past the protocol and see them for who they are. Pete, Frank! I know what the prophecy scroll says, the team is real and like it or not, it is them!" Nick said abruptly.

Frank and Pete stepped back and stared at Nick.

"How do you know they are the team of the prophecy? You are like us. How could you have read the scroll?" Pete pressed.

"Whose family do you think brought the prophecy scroll to the Calshene officers' library in the first place?" Nick replied firmly.

"But you grew up on Earth" Frank said.

"My great-great-great-, well, many greats grandparents were galactic pilots and brought the prophecy scroll to the Calshene home world long before its destruction. And just as the stories of your forefathers were passed down to each of you, so too, were the visions and stories of the prophecy scroll passed down in my family," Nick added.

"But you're in the prophecy scroll, how could your family have read the scroll?" Frank asked.

"We are all in the prophecy scroll. Anyone can read the scroll, Max must have made George and the others fall asleep or something every time they got too close to the truth. I don't know how, but I know he did," Nick said seriously.

This was serious business and Nick had now told them more than anyone outside his family had ever been told.

"Nick, you agreed with George about the prophecy earlier," Pete pressed.

"Like you, I told young cadets what they have to believe," Nick said and flipped his hand over, revealing a red-yellow sphere glowing in his palm. "Now you know the truth, a truth that can never be repeated," Nick said firmly.

Like the oath George and his team had taken to each other, so too, Pete, Frank and Nick were going to join in an oath of energy. They joined hands, arm over arm. The energy was intense, yet they did not break their grip until the pain subsided. Only a small red dot remained on their palms, and then, it was gone.

"Find another way. They will need you again another day; of that, I can promise you," Nick said cryptically.

Rachael walked Nick, Frank, and Pete out of the link from her cot down the hallway. Nick left the two leaders leaning on the wall of the small ship and returned to his cot to sleep.

"We will need to find another way," Pete signed to Frank, nodding.

They were amazed at what Nick had told them. They stared at George and Andy and started to see them through new eyes, without the eons of protocol and rules. They were changing everything and breaking all of the old rules in the process.

They walked forward and joined George and Andy's link. Peace and calm again filled the space around them and their teams. Pete blocked them from reaching Max, as Max had requested. Out into the galaxy their minds went, with calm and peace surrounding them. The freelance mind invaders tried to read their thoughts from time to time. George and Andy now brushed them off with little effort. What a change the young cadets had made. Their control was astonishing to Pete and Frank.

In the morning, the link was ended and their small part of the universe was at peace. Gus and Han were laughing and measuring out bowls of brown cereal in the galley when there was a knock on the outside of the ship's hull. Frank and Pete stepped back into the shadows. Nick, Andy and George opened the door and looked down before sliding out the gangplank. The two servants from the grand ball were standing outside the little ship. With Andy behind him and Nick in the port door, George walked down the short gangplank and met the two men near the fire.

"Sir, our master wants to see your ship. However, we fear it is to do damage before the night begins," the taller of the two servants said in a voice barely above a whisper, staring at the ground.

"You have risked much to warn us, thank you for your great kindness. Tell your master we are two spaceports to the south. Say it is near the end of the food line. It will be that long if you come in the late afternoon. It will look like you have good information and he will be pleased," George said kindly.

"Whose ship is in the southern port sir?" the servant asked quietly.

"One ship in the port belongs to the Magistrate and the other ship belongs to one of the other competitor's. I heard him say he has three ships hidden in the city," George replied honestly.

"Ahhh, this will be good, sir," the taller servant whispered and the two servants nodded.

"Now, tell me what I can do to repay you for your great risk," George asked kindly, dipping his head to show respect.

The second servant gasped. No master had ever shown them or any other servant respect.

"Win, sir, just win, sir," the tall servant said hopefully as he smiled a weak smile.

"Do you not have a family member who could be freed today?" he pressed, reaching into his pockets.

"Well, yes, yes, we do, sir, but…," the other servant spoke softly, his mouth hanging open.

"But nothing, you will need enough tribute to free them," George said and set a hundred tribute in each of their hands. "Go quickly now and free them, before you are caught and your tribute is taken from you unjustly," he said, closing their hands around the tribute.

The servants nodded and hurried off to free their families from servitude. George turned around and Pete was sitting on the gangplank at Nick's feet. Andy was moving a few pieces of wood around the fire, scanning the port to make sure the two servants had not been followed. He and Nick were always watching.

"How did you know they had family members who were slaves or servants?" Pete asked.

"I didn't, but everyone has someone they care about, so I guessed they did too, sir," George replied, helping Pete up. Pete slipped back inside the ship with Andy right behind them.

"We had better go eat or Gus will be disappointed, sir," George whispered as Nick and Pete headed for the galley in the little ship.

"I'm glad they are with us," Andy whispered, stepping close to George as they entered the galley.

"Me too," George said, grinning.

The cereal bowls and cups of water were all lined up on the floor when they walked inside.

"Will the servants be OK?" Sara asked kindly, taking a bowl from Gus and passing it to the others.

"Yes. But I think one of our competitors is about to lose one of his spare ships," George said with a grin.

"And the servants' families?" Anna added, passing another bowl.

"Well taken care of, thank you for asking," George replied, taking a bite of his cereal.

The dry flakes were as bad as flakes with milk, yet no one complained.

Frank and Pete never even asked how the cadets knew what George and Andy were doing. They had grown up so much. They simply assumed they were nearly always connected in a team link, sharing their thoughts and plans.

"We will have something special for tomorrow, the day of the Turns," Gus said, teasing the teams as he took the last bowl of cereal.

Andy choked on his cereal and Nick hit him on the back. Sara stared at him. It was like watching a replay of a few weeks earlier when they were hurling through space.

"I'm alright, stop staring at me," Andy said, grousing.

"Yes, it was a replay," George muttered and grinned to himself.

The day passed without incident in their part of the world, except for the small explosion and black smoke coming from the spaceport two ports to the south in the late afternoon that is.

Han, Emily, and Anna had souped-up the scout ship's engines and shielded everything they could think of over the last five days. Emily, Han, and the others finished all of the modifications to the smaller scout ship by mid afternoon. Every fuel tank and air tank was filled. Extra tanks of fuel and air filled the entire back of the second ship. Only a small path to the command bridge was left open.

By late afternoon, Gus had all of the workers set up to feed the people without him. The tribute collected went into the Mahadean's main bank and would be distributed to all who worked. There would be money to send more groups of merchants and new cooks across the planet to feed others in other cities and more money to buy food, pans, pots and wood for the fires. Gus had a good system set up for the people trapped in the Mahadean system.

That night they were quiet at dinner. Hardly a word was spoken—they were ready. George, Andy, Pete and Frank slid to the command space of the scout ship and made a link. Calm and focused, they filled the air with peace.

Chapter 15

THE 'TURNS' RACE

Gus and Han had promised something special for them for breakfast, and special it was. Instead of rations in a bowl, it was more dry brown cereal in a bowl. Andy turned and beat his head into the wall.

"You have one wicked sense of humor, Gus," Andy said, moaning.

Gus and Han beamed. It was very nearly a compliment and they were going to take it as such.

The teams reviewed the plan for the race at breakfast. George and his team, with Pete and Frank would fly the reinforced, smaller of the two scout ships to the staging arena for the Turns race. At the staging arena, Pete would act as the leader with Frank as his second.

They would be taken hostage by the Magistrate and be the distraction while George and his team flew the Turns alone. Emily and Anna had gathered as much information on the Turns as they could and had devised several strategies. All the while Han, Nick, Rachael, Jennifer, and Karmen would load the other ship into their galaxy-class frigate ship. The team would assemble near the council slave chambers, just off the main Turns gallery, and focus on George and the others, helping them focus. The plan was complete.

Nick, Rachael, Karmen, Jennifer, and Han formed a link and invited George, Andy, and the others in.

"Keep this link close and focus on the ship and the course, only on the ship and the course. We will send you energy and focus," Nick said encouragingly.

"There will be strong scanners trying to invade your thoughts. Do not let any fear enter your minds, or the scanners will find you," Karmen added softly.

"What about Pete and Frank again?" Gus asked, staring a Jennifer.

"Gus, they are the distraction, to keep the Magistrate, officials, and honored guests off balance," Jennifer replied patiently.

"They will be our yelling officers so the Magistrate and his scanners don't find our link," Rachael added.

"So the Magistrate cannot do anything to influence the outcome of the Turns," Karmen added.

"Frank and Pete will keep them busy," Rachael added with a devilish grin, and the captains all chuckled.

The cadets smiled—the art of misdirection was one of their favorites. Gus lowered their link without breaking it.

Han, Nick, Rachael, Jennifer, and Karmen slid back into the larger scout ship and lifted off. The others slid forward and George, Anna, and Emily lifted off, following Nick and the others. Quickly, they were over their galaxy-class frigate starship and watched as Rachael and Jennifer landed the larger scout ship. Nick and the others started preparing to leave.

George stared back at the port as Anna and Emily flew low over the city to the Turns gallery.

"Andy, have you noticed how much our captains' teams are like our team? Pete and Frank don't really fly. Rachael and Jennifer do. Like Anna and Emily," George whispered.

Andy stared at George. "Ya, I guess they do. I never noticed before, weird," he replied.

Now both of them stood silently staring at Pete and Frank. Frank's hairs on the back of his neck stood up and he slowly turned his head around and stared back at George and Andy.

"Nothing, all is good," George signed quickly, and Frank turned back around and signed something to Pete in their captains' sign language.

Pete just smiled, not answering Frank or turning around. Frank had told Pete that George had just figured out how similar their teams really were. Pete mused at how long it had taken the cadets to figure out the obvious while they so easily understood the complex and obscure.

As they entered the gallery, Pete and Frank stepped forward toward the two control consoles and took over the ship's controls from Anna and Emily. The ship wobbled, teetered and tipped as Pete and Frank guided the scout ship around the gallery. Gus touched Pete's shoulder and linked with Anna,

Emily and the others to help smooth out their flying abilities. The two captains' link was strong, nearly overpowering for George and the others.

Hastily, Gus separated Pete, Frank and Anna from the new link. With Anna helping Pete and Frank fly, the ship stopped wobbling and bouncing on the air currents over the gallery. Soon their flight around the gallery smoothed out.

George wondered why the captains' link was so strong. Usually when they were joined in a link with their captains, they only felt a calm and focus add to their link. He wondered if the captains were really sheltering the cadets from the true strength of the link. It was a question he would need to ask later. For now, the team would stay focused only on the ship and the race and Anna would help the two captains fly. They were sure there would be strong scanners in the arena, and they didn't want to take any chances on being discovered.

The gallery was more of a corridor with spectator stands on opposite sides. There were several enormous video screens on opposite sides of the gallery with scanning views of the planet outside the city. Like many buildings in the city, the gallery was made of a gray granite stone covered in a light coating of sandy brown and gray dust. The gallery was enormous in size, covering nearly five city blocks in length and climbing to five stories in some sections of the gallery.

The dignitary's box seats were high in the upper levels with servants running in and out serving their masters. The lower sections were covered with carved wooden chairs and benches for the next group of wealthy people. The lowest level was standing room only on large flat stone steps.

Carefully, Anna had Pete and Frank land the scout ship on a small gray circular platform next to a large silver ship. The silver ship reflected the gallery. The effect made it nearly invisible in the morning light. It had a giant engine in the middle that appeared to take up most of the central body of the ship. The small circular platform could hardly be seen beneath the ship's engine.

Behind the silver ship on another circular platform was a ship that looked like a large, flat, green dinner plate. The only visible engines looked like yellow soup can thrusters that dotted the bottom of the ship. A small clear dome covered the top of the green plate. The whole dome was barely two feet tall.

On their other side was a gleaming golden ship that glistened in the morning sunlight. The ship's front command bridge view screen looked like their little scout bridge, except it was clean, shiny and gold on the inside.

Two large engines protruded from the back of the ship. The fourth ship was flat and shaped like a black belt with joints connecting each section. It couldn't have been more than 4-feet thick by 6-feet wide; however, it was at least 25-feet long and waved in the light morning breeze like a fluttering flag above the platform. The cadets couldn't see any engine ports, engines or thrusters, and they wondered how it flew.

The fifth ship looked like a heap of rusty orange steel plates someone had thrown high up into the air. When the rusty orange plates landed on top of the ship, someone welded all of the plates to the ship underneath and declared it ready to race. The ship beneath the wild stack of rusty plates was only a little bigger than their scout ship. How oddly different the six ships were for the Turns.

"How can the engines lift that much weight?" Anna puzzled, staring at the fifth ship.

George signed "focus," and they all cleared their minds again, thinking only of the race.

Pete and Frank opened the port door and stepped out of their little scout ship. Casually they strutted down the short gangplank as if they owned the place. As Pete's feet touched the platform, he turned toward the ship's hatch as George and Andy peeked out for a look around.

"Get back to work before I beat you!" he yelled and turned toward Frank. "They're all lazy, you can't get good help anymore," he added.

The game was on! George and Andy lowered their heads, looked down, nodded, and backed up into the scout ship out of sight.

The regional Magistrate was dressed in flowing gold and red robes and his four sub-administrators, who were overseeing the Turns for the Magistrate, were dressed in green and gold robes. They all stood at the edge of the gallery waiting for their guests' arrival. Servants rolled long blue carpets out in front of the Magistrate and other officials as they came strolling over to the platform where Pete and Frank stood. Hidden behind the group were two scanners dressed in black robes with long hoods, obscuring their faces.

George grabbed his head as the two scanners dressed in black got closer. Andy grabbed George and shook his shoulders.

"Concentrate, George. Think only of the Turns, focus, focus, we are so close. You can do it, George," Andy whispered as the others added their hands to his shoulders, strengthening their link.

He stared back at Andy, then Emily, Sara, and Gus.

"We are all here, George. They will try and do this to us again—you have to focus," Emily said. Her voice was soft and calm as she squeezed his hand hard.

He focused on her voice and concentrated on his team. He thought only of the Turns and the pain in his head lessened.

"You're right. They will try again. Excellent, thanks," he whispered.

A bit cryptic for Andy; however, he would take it as a good sign.

"Psst, psst," Anna said as if she had sprung a leak.

She was waving them to the front console. She had the outside hull inspection camera turned on and aimed at the regional Magistrate who was now standing next to Pete and Frank.

"What's he saying, Andy? He's too fast for me," she asked.

Andy stared at the viewer repeating as many of the regional Magistrate words as he could.

"Your entry into the Turns is late," the Magistrate said rudely.

"We have all the correct paperwork filed and have paid the appropriate tribute," Pete replied arrogantly as the scanners circled the two captains, trying to read their thoughts.

"We know nothing of you, where is your ship registered?" the Magistrate pressed flippantly, staring at Pete.

"Why, here in your great city, Magistrate," Frank replied, playing tag team with Pete.

"I do not remember a new ship being built recently," the Magistrate pressed again now staring at Frank and the dented silver ship in front of him.

"This is our second ship. It is small and old. We came with the other racers," Pete said, motioning toward the scout ship's damage, dings and dents.

"We had a better ship, it was much newer and faster. However, it was somehow accidentally destroyed," Frank said, staring at the Magistrate.

"Most unfortunate," the Magistrate mumbled slyly.

"Have your guards found the ones responsible yet?" Pete asked, changing the subject.

"No, not yet," the Magistrate replied abruptly, knowing it was his men who had destroyed the ship. "Nonetheless, as we do not know you and our prize is absolute, you will not be allowed to race," the Magistrate said as he grinned, thinking he had them trapped.

"I protest! We have done what is needed!" Pete said, raising his voice as he signed to Frank.

"We have met your requirements! Do you now change the rules of the Turns?" Frank yelled.

"What will your masters say?" Pete yelled angrily, pressing the Magistrate.

The Magistrate stepped back and shook his head. He knew he could not change the rules . Yet he didn't want to let them fly the race. Thinking for a moment, he grinned an evil grin and leaned toward Frank and Pete.

"Your ship may compete in the Turns. However, you both will be my guests in my box for the race. Your servants will race your ship for you," the Magistrate pronounced with a 'gotcha' smirk on his face.

Pete and Frank tried to protest again, waving their arms wildly as the Magistrate's guards closed in around them, thinking they were going to attack the Magistrate.

"Be happy this is all I have done to you," the Magistrate replied, flicking his hand in the air and thinking he had won. He turned, hurried off the platform, and across the blue carpet toward the gallery steps.

Frank and Pete burst through the guards, stepping in front of the Magistrate and stopping him at the edge of the gallery wall before the steps leading to the Magistrate's box.

"We need to instruct our fool servants!" Frank said gruffly.

"They are foolish and frighten easily. We need to tell them what to do!" Pete added loudly.

The Magistrate stopped. He was distracted and focused on them. It was what the two captains wanted.

"You may instruct them from here," the Magistrate replied, pointing to the ground.

With an evil grin, he stepped around Frank and Pete, leaving the gallery ground level for his box seat high in the stands.

They nodded and spun around, facing the tiny scout ship with the guards standing next to them. Frank and Pete waved their hands wildly in meaningless motions, while Pete mouthed words he knew Andy could read.

"You are on your own now. Fly well and focus," Pete instructed in a very captain kind-of- way.

"Odd that he can do that so captain like without actually saying a word," Anna whispered.

The cadets laughed as they retracted the last foot of the gangplank and closed the scout ship's port door. Anna, Emily, and Sara took their positions, standing right behind George, Andy, and Gus at the command console.

"First, they will scan us to see how many servants are inside the ship and where each of us is standing inside the ship. When all of the ships have been scanned, the first rock will fall from the center pillar," Emily said, pointing to the far side of the gallery as she continued telling everyone what was about to happen.

"We need to start the engines when the first rock hits the ground. Soon after, a second rock will be dropped. The Turns starts when the second rock hits the ground. That's when we take off as fast as we can—well, kind of," Emily said, twisting her hand in the air, wobbling like Pete and Franks' flying as they all laughed.

"Remember to hesitate on your start—after all, you're only a servant, and your masters are not here," Sara added, and they all laughed again.

"When we clear the gallery, we will switch positions," George added, grinning with Gus and Andy.

Soon they felt the scanners' strong minds and thought only of the race. A few minutes later, the first rock was pushed off its pillar and fell to the ground on the Magistrate's side of the gallery. The crowds roared, cheering, and chanting for the next rock to fall.

"Rock, rock, rock," they chanted.

The six ships all started their engines, lifting off their pads, hovering, waiting for the second rock to fall.

The second rock was huge, more of a bolder than a rock. A long silver rod expanded out from the gallery wall. The end of the rod was crushed from years of use. It groaned and creaked as it pushed on the side of the second stone. Soon, the boulder started to teeter. Another slight nudge from the long silver rod and the second boulder tipped off of the center column. Moments later the boulder hit the ground hard with a loud thud, sending a shudder through the ground and gallery. A huge plume of dust rose up, wafting high into the air and spreading out quickly across the gallery in the light breeze.

The crowd jumped to its feet in fright, first coughing then screaming and yelling as the plume of dust overtook them. Suddenly, their screams became cheers as the golden ship and green saucer ship appeared, flying out of the cloud of dust and racing around the gallery once before leaving the gallery. George sent their ship straight up out of the cloud of dust to start their lap around the gallery.

The shiny silver ship tried to go through the dust like the green saucer ship and the golden ship. However, it's engines sputtered and misfired, dropping the ship onto the platform with a loud crunch of metal echoing throughout the gallery. The rusty orange steel-plated ship went up with the scout ship, above the dust cloud. The belt ship seemed unaffected by the dust and bolted through the cloud into the clean air for its lap around the gallery.

Quickly, the golden ship and the green saucer ship became the two lead ships to catch. They left the gallery and raced across the city toward the great crevice in the crust of the planet's surface as George and the others finished their gallery lap. By the end of their gallery lap, the cadets were in third place. The scout ship raced across the city, skimming over the building tops, leaving torrents of swirling dust and wind whipping through the city streets. George and the others switched positions at the city limits as they passed the last of the main scanning stations. Anna, Emily, and Sara stepped forward and sat in the command seats George had raised from the floor.

George, Andy, and Gus sat behind them on the floor of the ship, calmly concentrating and focusing only on the race. Gus smoothed out their flow of energy and George calmed and focused everyone's thoughts.

Andy was the power, the energy, the spare battery one might say. Yes, that was what he wanted to be, the battery, Andy thought until he caught George's glance and stopped.

Passed the city limits there was nothing. The land had only a few desolate farms growing the vegetables Gus had been cooking to feed the city. In between the farms, the land was brown and dry—no lush forests and flowing rivers or vast lakes—only windswept dunes and rocky outcrops. The crevice in the planet's surface soon appeared on their front view screen.

"How far are we from it?" Gus asked, more in awe than as a question.

"It is enormous. Almost as if someone tried to cut the planet in half and stopped," Sara said, gasping.

"They settled with the evil and the evil stopped destroying their planet," Anna replied somberly.

"Now they all have masters," George said, sighing.

They all nodded as Emily and Anna guided the tiny scout ship around the rocks mounded up in the middle of the planet. Soon they reached the edge of the crevice. Anna flew over the crevice's rim and dove into one of the large canyons below.

"Look there, where the dust is swirling. One of the ships ahead of us must have gone down that canyon. See over there," Gus said staring out the front view screen, mesmerized by the sheer size of the canyons.

"Yes, Gus, I think you're right. However, they are wrong," Emily answered, smiling calmly.

"Novice mistake," Anna said, chuckling with Emily and Sara.

With a swoosh of its wing, the silver ship passed the little scout ship. The wake from the larger ship's exhaust port sent the tiny scout ship spinning out of control. Emily and Sara fought to regain control as they hurled toward the planet's surface. Their hands were a blur over the consoles.

"He did that on purpose!" Gus yelled.

"Focus!" George thought hard through their link.

Emily and Sara turned the ship into the spin and then pulled hard to the right, shearing the air over the short wings. The air across the short wings popped and crackled. It was nearly deafening inside the tiny ship as it leveled out a few feet above the canyon floor.

"That was close!" Sara whispered as the girls high-fived each other.

"There, that's the canyon crevice we want," Anna said, regaining her focus.

Emily and Sara swerved, stirring the dust over the canyon floor as they went in the wrong direction. They climbed straight up the canyon wall as if doing a dead man's stall, flipping the scout ship over in a loop and diving into the smaller canyon at the bottom of the enormous crevice that Anna had pointed out. The new canyon was nearly the size of the canyon they had been racing through. A cloud of dust flipped up behind their ship as they cruised a few feet over the smaller canyon floor.

"Look, there's a dust cloud over there," Emily said, motioning to the far right.

"Yes, it must be the golden ship," Sara answered, thinking about the other pilot's choice.

Quickly, they approached a group of caves on the far canyon wall.

"Right!" Anna thought as Emily and Sara veered right, guiding the tiny ship around an outcrop of jagged rocks that had fallen onto the canyon floor.

Flying low over the canyon floor, they rolled right and dove into the mouth of a large cave. Anna flipped on the ship's landing lights and illuminated the cave ahead of them for a moment. She turned them off when she felt Gus not feeling so well.

"We'll do this one by sensors," she said, sensing Gus was regaining his focus.

Turn after turn the scout ship sped toward the molten center of the Mahadean planet.

"Can the shielding withstand the molten part of the planet's core?" Gus asked.

"No," Emily replied coldly.

"We will have to help with the shielding. Gus, I need you to transfer a lot of energy to me when Emily tells you. You must keep sending me energy until Emily tells you to stop," George thought in their link.

"Why?" Gus asked, wondering what was really going on. If the shielding couldn't protect the scout ship from the molten core, then what was going to protect them, he wondered.

This time Andy shook his head and Gus backed off. George was going to attempt Max's old traders' trick when he held their ship together on their escape from the Calshene station on their second rotation. Andy knew it, and he didn't like it. He also knew there was nothing he could do to stop George.

The trip so far had been nearly uneventful, not at all what they had been expecting. Emily and Sara were skilled pilots; however, Anna was brilliant. She was an exceptionally skilled navigator and pilot. Gus, Andy, and George sat quietly, calming and focusing their energy. No fear would enter their link. To win they had to work together as equals, using the strengths of each team member.

The deeper they raced into the center of the planet's core, the higher the ship's hull temperature rose. The shielding was holding; however, the cadets were sweating inside the scout ship. Like steaming clams in a pot, the heat was beginning to slow their minds and reaction time. The wing touched a rocky outcrop in the cave, sending sparks flying and igniting the volatile gases in the cave. The front wave of the exploding gases caused a massive fireball, which propelled the tiny ship faster and deeper toward the planet's molten core. The girls smiled at the burst of speed, working hard to ride the wave of fire.

Soon, the walls of the cave glowed red hot; and they could see the cave walls in motion—barely above their molten state.

"Now, Gus, now!" Emily yelled, sweat trickling down her back.

Gus kept a small stream of energy flowing to Emily, Sara, and Anna, although not as much as before. For the moment, they would have to sustain themselves. Andy started making red energy spheres and handing them to Gus. Gus converted the energy and sent one after another into the link with George. George slid back from Andy and Gus, resting against the ship's inner hull as he had seen Max do the year before. He remembered the feeling he had gotten from Max as he had fed him a ration and shared their water with him. He thought only of the ship and the shields and the energy needed to strengthen the shielding.

He focused hard, concentrating on the ship's hull and its shielding. Beads of sweat formed on his forehead and ran down his neck. The tiny command bridge got hotter, and Andy's energy spheres became stronger. Gus could barely hold them and convert them; yet, they continued—one red hot energy sphere after another. The cave was gone now and they were flying through a sea of molten rock. Anna kept them on course as Emily and Sara guided the ship around thermal pockets and cooler vertices in the molten sea.

Within twelve hours, the molten cave walls reappeared; and the rocks started to solidify again. Higher and higher they climbed out of the molten magma. The cave walls turned a burnt orange and then a solid, blackened gray. Sharp outcrops of rock formed the lining of the cave with pointy squires.

"We're clear, Gus, the shielding will hold again," Emily said, without turning around as she wiped the sweat from her face.

Andy slowed, making his fiery-red energy spheres as Gus focused the energy back on Emily, Sara, and Anna. Their speed increased as Gus redirected the energy. George did not move from the hull where he was leaning. He resumed his concentration on the calm, focused flying of the ship. A few more hours passed, and the team was getting tired of staring at the gray cave walls.

"What's that?" Andy asked, pointing out the front viewer.

"We caught one of the other competitor's ships," Emily answered.

"What's he doing?" Gus asked.

"He's trying to start off a fire storm!" Anna yelled.

"He must know about the gases in the caves!" Emily yelled.

"We need more shielding now!" Sara yelled as the golden ship ahead of them clipped an outcropping of rock, creating a shower of sparks. Andy handed Gus a red energy sphere; and almost instantaneously, Gus sent the energy to George, their shielding strengthened as the gases around them burst into flames.

"We need to get on the front side of the burning gas wave!" Anna yelled over the roar of the flames outside their ship.

Sara accelerated the ship to its maximum speed. Emily's hands were racing over the controls, adjusting their course as each new obstacle in the cave came into their sensor range. Emily, Sara, and Anna moved in fluid motion together. Behind them Andy was now feeding Gus more red energy spheres to keep up their energy and focus. They burst into a larger cave and overtook the golden ship, leaving it behind in swirls of dust and gas.

Higher and higher they climbed in the cave. The cave ended, and a narrow lower canyon opened up in front of them. The shiny silver ship burst into the same canyon from a cave above them, sending a shower of rocks down on top of them. George maintained the ship's shielding; and Emily, Sara, and Anna never even blinked. Sara spun the ship and passed through the exhaust trail of the silver ship, narrowly missing the engine shielding. The wake from their exhaust trail sucked the silver ship's engine dry, and the ship's engine sputtered as it failed. The shiny silver ship's pilot threw on the maneuvering thrusters to keep from crashing into the canyon wall or landing on the golden ship below.

Up, up, and out of the small canyon the little scout ship rose, nearly vertical in their ascent. The lower canyon opened up into a larger, wider canyon. Cresting the ledge, they saw the flat, green plate ship ahead of them. It was accelerating up out of the larger canyon, leaving them in a dusty fog. The flat green ship ascended into the largest canyon and swooped across the canyon floor to the last canyon wall. Energy weapons suddenly rained down on the flat green ship from another cave, as the long belt-like ship flew out over their scout ship, chasing the green ship.

Emily turned hard to avoid crashing into the tail end of the belt ship as it crossed their path. The green plate ship returned fire, narrowly missing the belt ship; however, striking the canyon wall. The blast showered more rocks down on the tiny scout ship as the silver ship and the golden ship emerged from the canyon below.

The ship with the mound of rusty orange plates was nowhere in sight. The flat green ship and the belt ship were now in a furious battle. Since they had almost no weapons, it was a battle the tiny scout ship could not enter. Anna changed their course, and they slipped quietly passed the fighting ships as the silver ship launched a barrage of torpedoes at the belt ship.

The smaller golden ship followed the tiny scout ship around the canyon and around another enormous outcropping of weather-worn boulders, before emerging into the larger canyon. The canyon opened up to the crevice that encircled nearly the entire planet. The tiny scout ship crested the rim of the enormous crevice with such speed that an entire section of the wall gave way and enormous boulders went crashing to the canyon wall below.

The missing rusty orange plated ship suddenly appeared and shot a few torpedoes at the tiny scout ship and the golden ship. The golden ship dipped its wing into the sandy surface of the planet's vast wasteland and raised a huge dust cloud. Emily dropped her thruster and blew more dust high into the air behind them as Anna plotted their course correction from having to exit the crevice in a different place.

Emily flew the scout ship close to the surface to prevent anyone from hitting the bottom of the ship with a blaster. An enormous dust cloud followed their ship, obscuring it from sight. Emily and Sara wove in and out of the rock pillars that covered the planet's desolate landscape. The golden ship was close on their tail and the rusty, plated ship right behind the golden ship.

With the three larger ships locked in a furious battle, it was a race of pure speed between the three smaller ships, and the golden ship was gaining on them again.

"We need more speed!" Emily yelled, having pushed the controls as high as they could go.

George nodded from the wall of the ship, and Andy started making larger and larger red energy spheres again. Where Andy was taking the energy from, no one knew. However, in the galactic sea, Max felt Andy's pull and guided the raw energy of the universe so he could use it.

Gus's hands and arms were burned from Andy's high energy spheres. Each sphere of energy sent pain shooting through his arms and shoulders; yet, he continued converting the energy, never letting on that he was in pain. Soon George's skin was nearly translucent as he forced the energy into the ship's engines. The golden ship stopped its slow overtake of the tiny scout ship. If only they could hang onto their lead for a little while longer; and if the larger ships kept up their battle, they could win—a lot of ifs.

Soon, they could see the farms surrounding the city again. Suddenly, a sonic cannon shot at the racing ships from the ground. The vibration shook the tiny ship, sending it into another spiral. However, this time they were dangerously close to the land and there was little time to react. Emily stopped their twisting spiral inches above impact with the planet surface, scraping the belly of the ship on a rock formation as they rose into the air again. The golden ship hit the ground on its tail and was not as fortunate, skidding to a stop in a vegetable field and igniting the crop in its efforts to regain control. Seconds later the golden ship burst into flames as the crew escaped.

The rusty, plated ship lost visibility and clipped a rock tower, shearing off a part of their wing and sending it spinning to the ground in a cloud of dust and flying rocks. The tiny scout ship raced on alone, dodging the sonic cannon fire from the ground.

At the city's edge, Emily called to George to take over. He didn't move. She left her seat and knelt down next to George.

"We survived the night, George. We've made it back to the city, and you'll have to fly now. I'll be right behind you," she said softly as she dragged him from the back wall of the ship.

As she lifted George up into her arms, the ship quaked and shuddered. Somehow, it was still in one piece. Emily sat George in her seat and the scout ship's shuddering stopped. Gently, she set George's hands on the controls, holding him up between her arms. In the bright sunlight, Emily could see

George's blood-soaked cloak.

Anna lifted Gus up next, setting him in her seat. His hands and arms bleeding as he continued converting Andy's fiery, red energy spheres. Oddly, they were simply appearing in Gus's hands now without Andy having to hand him the spheres.

Andy's face and skin looked as translucent as the librarian in the Calshene library in the bright light. Gently, Sara lifted Andy into her seat next to George and Gus. Still he formed more and more energy spheres for Gus and George. George kept sending the energy into the ship and into their link. George may have been sitting in Emily's chair; however, he was still holding the tiny scout ship together and feeding the ship's engines—like Max had done a year ago.

Sara, Emily, and Anna slid their hands beneath George, Andy, and Gus's arms and controlled the ship from behind them. Their arms and cloaks were soon stained red. Emily's shirt was soaked with George's blood. Sara wanted to stop and heal George, Gus, and Andy.

"Focus!" Was the only word coming through their link loud and clear. Yet they all knew George had not sent the message. It had to have been Nick and the other captains.

As they made their approach to the gallery, a hail of torpedoes rained down on them. The shiny silver ship had won the battle with the other large ships and was now racing to claim their prize. George leaned into the control console as another hail of torpedoes raced toward them. The burst of speed from the tiny scout ship disrupted the torpedoes' flight path and the torpedoes crashed into each other above the city.

"Almost there, almost there, speed, speed!" George thought, as if willing them to win.

Beneath them, Emily and Anna's hands were moving so fast that Gus could no longer see their hands. It was all a blur as Gus sent more and more energy into their link. They swooshed through the gallery passed the Magistrate's box an instant ahead of the larger silver ship, winning the race!

The crowd went wild, cheering as a cloud of dust rose swirled in the air from their victory lap around the gallery. Suddenly, the silver ship sent a barrage of torpedoes at the tiny scout ship, trying to destroy them and claim the victory. However, the Turns had been won and what was acceptable moments before the finish line was not acceptable after the finish line.

A stream of massive energy bursts were launched from the gallery towers, exploding the torpedoes in mid-air above the crowd in what looked like a brilliant light display. A second focused energy burst brought the silver ship crashing to the ground and bursting into flames in the middle of the gallery. The pilots narrowly escaped the burning ship and were quickly captured by the guards. The crowd cheered wildly in the gallery. They had seen energy bursts, a flaming crash and the guards capture the escaping pilots, all in one Turns!

The smoke cleared, and the tiny scout ship landed carefully on the victory pad as the crowd screamed and cheered again. A few minutes passed before the port hatch opened and the small gangplank slid out. Emily, Anna, and Sara were having difficulty lifting George, Andy, and Gus off the seats inside the scout ship. They were all exhausted from the race. Without the extra energy from the boys, the girls were slowing down.

Pete and Frank had spent their time well in the Magistrate's box. They had sat quietly concentrating, planting many seeds of deception and trickery in the minds of the honored guests, officials, and the Magistrate. The Magistrate stood up and looked suspiciously around at his guests before leaving his box suite. Frank and Pete followed him with the other officials down the steep stairs to the winner's platform.

Inside the scout ship, Emily locked her hands together under George's arms and across his chest under his cloak. Carefully, she lifted him from his seat. Slowly she walked him to the port and down the gangplank to the platform below. Sara lifted Andy from his seat and Anna lifted Gus from his seat in the same way. The girls were exhausted; yet, they could not stop. Victory was so close.

Sara and Anna followed Emily out of the scout ship into the bright sunlight, pushing the boys' feet along in front of theirs. They stopped at the end of the gangplank. The girls held the boys in front of them with their arms wrapped around their middles under their cloaks, holding them up. Silently, they stood on the platform waiting for the Magistrate, the officials, and their masters, Pete and Frank, to arrive.

The blue carpets were rolled out to the winner's platform and the Magistrate, his guards, and two cloaked scanners walked out to meet the six servants who had won the Turns. Slowly, the Magistrate walked closer to them with his guards at his side. The two scanners in black cloaks stood silently by, waiting for the Magistrate's signal.

The girls helped George, Andy, and Gus kneel down before the Magistrate.

"I give you your champions!" the Magistrate shouted into his microphone, and the crowd roared. Pete and Frank stepped forward, waving their hands.

"So to our prize," Pete said, rubbing his hands together.

The Magistrate turned to Pete. "You, sir, did not win the Turns, they did! The prize belongs to them!" the Magistrate said, pointing to George and the others.

"Noooo!" yelled Frank, jumping forward toward the Magistrate.

"They are our servants!" Pete yelled as he made wild gestures in the air with his arms.

Frank and Pete protested well. However, if Frank and Pete had known how exhausted the cadets really were, they would have protested even more. Instead they stepped back behind the Magistrate's guards, waiting. The Magistrate flicked his hand in the air and the guards restrained Pete and Frank.

Carefully, the Magistrate stepped closer to the cadets, thinking they truly were Pete and Frank's servants. He wanted to manipulate their thoughts. Snapping his fingers, the two scanners in black robes approached the kneeling servants, following the Magistrate's lead. Little did they know that George, Andy and Gus were nearly unconscious. Emily, Sara, and Anna were the only reason they were even upright. Standing behind them with their heads lowered, the girls weren't even sure they could lift the boys to their feet again.

"So young men, what shall you claim as your prize? Do you want to set some family members free? Perhaps, you want riches beyond your wildest dreams or an elegant home and servants of your own. What shall it be?" the Magistrate yelled into the large circular microphone for all in the gallery to hear.

Quickly, the Magistrate's two visible scanners started to concentrate and focus on the three boys and their thoughts. Within a minute they shook their heads, they had nothing to hang onto in the boys' minds. The Magistrate snapped his fingers and two new, even stronger scanners hiding in the shadows closed in to manipulate the boys' answers.

Too bad, they were concentrating on the wrong people! If they found out, all would be lost. If they had only known, they may have won. Their arrogance blinded them and they were about to lose. Emily, Sara, and Anna struggled to get George, Andy, and Gus straightened up enough to look the Magistrate directly in the eyes and answered the question. The Magistrate's scanners and the figures in black robes probed and probed; and yet, there was nothing for them to hold onto in George, Andy, and Gus's minds.

Emily pulled on the back of George's hair, and his head lifted toward the Magistrate. The Magistrate lowered the microphone so all could hear his choice for a Turns winning prize. Emily whispered in their link to George.

"All servants, slaves, and guests held against their will on Mahadean are freed today!" George yelled into the Magistrate's microphone.

Then his head fell forward as Emily struggled to keep him upright.

The gallery crowds exploded in excitement, running wild, and starting to riot. The slaves and servants of Mahadean were free! The Magistrate fainted and fell to the ground. His guards, who were themselves slaves, cheered and ran from the gallery.

Pete and Frank rushed forward, pushing the four scanners off the platform. Pete flipped George and Andy over his shoulders. Frank flipped Gus over his shoulder and spun quickly around, pulling Emily, Anna, and Sara together with his free arm. Frank wanted to gasp when he saw them up close. They looked weak, with blood soaked through their clothes. Together, holding each other, Frank, Emily, Sara, and Anna ran out of the gallery following Pete, George, and Andy.

The slaves were rioting in the streets and the guards were opening the auction house cells, one after another, releasing the unconditioned slaves. The news spread like wild fire across the Mahadean planet. Riots broke out in all of the cities as families raced to rejoin their loved ones taken from them. The officials and honored guests ran for their lives, afraid their newly freed servants and slaves would harm them.

Han and Nick had paid servants to help them free the Calshene slaves from the auction house cells and carry them to their waiting frigate starship. The servants lifted Viceroy after Viceroy onto their shoulders and carried them like sacks of coffee and rice out of the auction house, not knowing or caring who they were. They ran on foot through the crowded streets with the Viceroys bouncing over their shoulders, weaving in and out to avoid the rioting slaves and servants, racing to the frigate starship.

During the race, Max had stumbled into the port. Rachael and Jennifer carried him from the port and placed him in a separate section of the starship before the first Viceroys started to arrive. The freed servants now ran quickly back and forth making ten times their standard wage for every Viceroy they brought to the starship.

Within two hours, the starship was loaded with the entire Galactic council. Four servants carried Toma from the auction house to the starship last. Jennifer gasped when she saw him and had him carried to the hospital room on the ship. He had been badly beaten and could not lift his head. Nick returned from helping get Toma into the frigate's hospital and stood anxiously by the gangplank, waiting and watching for Pete and the others. Han gave all of the tribute they had away to the servants who had helped them and paid the others with some of the tribute in the city bank.

The cadets were in serious trouble, yet Pete and Frank had had to weave through the city streets and take the back alleys to keep from being identified by the freed slaves. They were splattered with the cadets' blood by the time they reached the frigate's port. They arrived at the port archway with George and the others a few minutes after Toma was carried inside. Quickly, Frank and Pete ran across the port and up the frigate's gangplank, slipping into the starship. It had taken two and a half hours to travel through the rioting city from the Turns gallery to the starship unnoticed.

Pete bumped Nick as he came through the port door and joined his team's link.

"Everyone accounted for?" Pete asked in their link, hurrying into the main hallway.

Nick nodded as Rachael and Han helped Emily, Sara, and Anna inside. Jennifer watched them enter on the computer monitor and spun the port hatch closed, retracting the gangplank from the command bridge the moment the last one stepped through the port door.

"Lift off," Pete thought in their link.

Nick lifted Andy from Pete's shoulder and led the way through the crowded hallways toward the hospital. Gently, Jennifer and Karmen guided the old frigate starship up and out of the atmosphere of the Mahadean planet, sending tribute with their old code to the sector administrator.

"What is our heading, sir?" Karmen asked in their link.

"Calshene," Pete replied in their link, hurrying to the hospital room with George and the others.

"Can we cloak?" Nick asked in the link.

"Yes. But it will slow us down," Rachael replied.

"We need to be cloaked until we are free of Mahadean space," Pete said through their link, entering the hospital.

Without the constant drain of energy from the evil that inhabited the Mahadean planet, the Viceroys could recover their strength and energy. The captains had filled every room and hallway on the frigate ship with officers. All of the officers were now resting and slowly regaining their strength, as they entered the hospital with the cadets.

Chapter 16

THE PRICE OF FREEDOM

In the hospital, the cadets and Tomas' condition was another matter. Rachael had each of the cadets laid out on beds and under yellow healing light beams within a few minutes of arriving in the hospital room. Yet, she was worried.

Emily, Anna, and Sara had used a tremendous amount of energy guiding the tiny scout ship during the Turns race; and their bodies were shaking uncontrollably with exhaustion. Gus's hands, arms, and chest were bleeding, badly burned from converting Andy's huge red spheres into energy for his team. The captains were nearly as weak from having focused on the cadets to keep the calm during their race. Now, Rachael couldn't make any yellow healing spheres in her hands. So instead she wrapped Gus's arms in gauze with a healing salve.

Andy was so drained of energy that his skin was as translucent as the Calshene librarian's. Where Andy had found all of the energy to send into their link, no one knew. The captains and the Viceroys were all too weak to make a healing circle, and Max was on the verge of collapse from guiding the raw energy of the universe alone.

Then there was George. Rachael placed her hand over him and a tear slipped gently down her cheek. She was afraid he would die. His skin was a pale white and his body shuddered on and off. He and Gus had lost a lot of blood, and she had no way of bandaging George's back. When Max had held their tiny ship together in space, it had drained his energy immensely. However, he was able to summon vast amounts of raw energy from the universe to hold the ship and himself together.

The price for George was much higher. He did not really know how to keep himself separate from the ship without being absorbed into the energy. His entire back, arms, hands, and legs were bleeding through his uniform—all badly burned from contact with the ship's hull when they passed through the molten core of the Mahadean home world.

In the bright lights of the hospital, Pete, Frank, and Nick shook their heads. The cadets were nearly destroyed by the Turns race, and now there was little the captains could do to save their lives.

"This is not how it is supposed to be, Pete," Nick said frustrated, staring at the cadets.

"Has the prophecy ever been wrong before?" Pete asked in a whisper.

"No," he replied, shaking his head.

"Well, it won't be now either, Nick. We can't let them die," Frank said, staring in disbelief.

"This cannot be," Nick repeated, not knowing what else to say.

Never before had the prophecy been wrong. He was stunned. In thousands of years, the prophecy had never been wrong.

"How is this possible? They are supposed to live, not die in space," Nick muttered when Pete cut him off.

Pete, Han, and Frank walked over between Gus, Andy, and George. Nick stepped in with Rachael between Sara, Emily, and Anna and they concentrated on healing. They did not have Sara's gift; hopefully, they had enough energy left to save them. At that moment, Pete wondered if they had made the right choice.

"It was the right choice, Pete," Frank thought back in their link. "The Viceroys and Galactic council of elders are free."

"Yes, but at what cost," Pete replied.

He wondered if the Viceroys would change and grow from the experience. Would they even recognize George and his team for saving their lives, or would they continue to punish the team for breaking old, out-of-date protocol rules? Pete was filled with so much anger. How could they have so blindly stuck to their protocol and standard operating procedures and not see what was before them?

Change was hard and difficult, and often outside of the things they were comfortable doing. Yet, if it had not been for change, they would have all died. The Galactic council Viceroys would have been slaves across the universe, and the galaxies would have been thrown into chaos. Evil would have triumphed.

Pete recalled Nick's words back on the Mahadean planet, 'this team was the team of the prophecy, and they were special because of it.' The cadets only knew they had to do what was right, not because they were special; since they had already outright rejected that idea. They did what was right because that was who they were; it had become their very nature.

They used their skills to improve the lives of the people they came into contact with because it was simply the right thing to do. Their only reward was in knowing they had made good choices and helped in the fight against an ever-present evil. Pete felt small standing there that day, slowly feeding energy to his cadets to keep them alive until they could get more help.

Two days passed and Rachael, Han, Nick, Frank, and Pete never left the cadets' sides. Pete was now relying on Nick's red energy spheres to feed them energy. From the command bridge, Jennifer and Karmen had joined their link, feeding them energy too. By the third day they had all passed into a near-coma state. The ship was now guided solely by the auto pilot, headed for Asteria station. It was a journey that would take at least eight weeks while cloaked at their maximum speed.

They had escaped; however, there was little energy left to keep any of them alive for the long journey home. As the last captain drifted away, a flash of white light appeared on the command bridge. A glowing human form took over, guiding the ship and keeping it on its course. Another flash of light appeared in Max's room.

"Max, is that what they call you? What have you done?" the glowing white light figure questioned, solidifying into a human form.

"Nothing," Max replied with a weak grin, looking up.

"You have interfered in the natural order and existence of these races," said the glowing white figure, accusing him of meddling.

"You know I have not, or you would not be here now," Max replied with a little smile.

"I will never understand why you have chosen them," the glowing white figure said, sitting down and helping Max channel the cosmic energy of the universe. Another glowing white figure appeared and then another until there were six glowing figures in the small room. Calm filled the universe again, and Max dipped his head to the elder being of white light.

"You must go, Max. There are several who need you greatly and one young child in particular who tried one of your old tricks and is now about to pay with his life," the elder white light being whispered.

Max jerked his head up. "George, what have you done?" he muttered, running through the door of the little room into the hallway and down to the hospital room on the starship. Max ran through the hospital room doors, solidifying next to Pete.

"George, what have you done? Don't you know you cannot do my tricks?" he said, holding his hand over George's forehead.

A bright white light glowed beneath his palm. Soon it was covering George, Andy, Gus, and the other captains and cadets. The healing energy flowed through George, hiding Max's true identity to all except George. It had taken four Senior Viceroys to strip most of the evil from George on their second rotation. However, all of the evil was stripped away when Max joined the Calshene Senior Viceroy. Max and the beings of white light could use more of the vast, raw energy of the universe than any of the Senior Viceroys. They were beings of pure energy.

With help on board the starship, Max now focused solely on healing George, the cadets, and captains in the hospital room. The cadets stirred and George saw Max's face for a brief instant and then Max was gone. He returned to the small room as the other white light figures disappeared one by one.

"They are a remarkable team," said the elder glowing white light being.

"Yes, however, they are very young," Max replied worried. "They are reckless and do not seem to listen as well as they should."

The elder being smiled. "It is not an issue reserved for only the young," he said, vanishing from the starship.

George and Gus had stopped bleeding. Emily, Sara, and Anna were no longer shaking and Andy had color returning to his skin and face. The cadets were all unconscious. At least, now they would not die.

Pete, Frank, and the others woke up as Karmen called into the hospital for Pete to come to the command bridge for landing instructions at the Asteria station asteroid field.

"Somehow we made it home to Asteria station in only three days!" Karmen said to Pete in their link as he ran through the hallways to the command bridge.

Jennifer's and Karmen's hands raced over the consoles as they replied to the Calshene administrator's questions as fast as they could. Pete ran through the door and signed them out. Without missing a step, Karmen and Jennifer spun on their heels and raced from the room as Pete ran up to the control console. Pete sent only one message.

"Quarantine, level ten, all Viceroys and Galactic council contained within the space," he typed.

The station administrator turned white. His hands were now racing across the console in front of him. He never lifted his head or looked at Pete again. He nodded and the viewer turned off, sending new landing coordinates to the ship computers. Pete ran back through the doors signing "land," to Jennifer and Karmen as he raced back to the hospital room.

He passed Max's room on his way. Skidding to a stop, he sat down outside the door, concentrating. "Max, we are about to land at the Calshene station. We will protect you," Pete thought firmly.

"It will be OK, Peter. Don't worry," Max thought back.

Pete grinned weakly, shaking his head. "You will not be hurt again," he muttered as he stood up at nearly a run again, skidding around the corner and sliding into the hospital room. "They all look so weak," he thought, resuming his place between George and Andy.

Jennifer and Karmen landed the ship at the new coordinates without turning the viewer on again. They didn't have the intuition of Emily and Anna, yet they were talented in their own right and well trained so making a blind landing was not a problem for them. The ship landed softly and the engines started to slow as the side and rear gangplanks on the ship opened and the port latches released, spinning open the doors.

Chapter 17

RETURN TO ASTERIA

Jennifer and Karmen were gone by the time the CORE officers entered the ship with the doctors and medics. They had heard Pete's message in their link and took up their guard posts on either side of Max's door. Each captain held two small, glowing red spheres in the palms of their hands. They knew Max would need to be protected, and they would not leave their posts until Max or their triad released them.

The medics ran into the cargo bay three by three, surrounding the council Viceroys and Senior Viceroys and whisking them away in flash after flash of white light. Three medics approached Jennifer and Karmen. They increased the size of their red spheres and the medics retreated. CORE guards approached next and Jennifer and Karmen lifted their hands and shook their heads. The guards backed down and posted two CORE guards down one corridor and two more CORE guards down the opposite corridor. The captains lowered their hands, although they did not lessen the strength of their glowing red spheres.

Other medics entered the hospital room on the ship and saw the cadets and captains inside. They called for more and more help. They would have to take the entire group off the ship as one unit. The lead doctor worried that separating them might kill them. The small room was soon packed tight with doctors and medics. In one enormous flash of white light, they were all gone. They reappeared in a CORE hospital classroom. The CORE hospital rooms were overflowing into the corridors with officers and Viceroys laying on cots and beds. The group was carried together on stretchers into a small conference room that had been converted into a makeshift hospital room.

"Do you know who these cadets and captains are?" a medic asked, staring at the young cadets.

"Why were they on the starship carrying the Viceroys and the Galactic council?" another asked, lifting Han from a cot to a wooden bed.

"They are the team of the prophecy. They rescued the whole Galactic council, all the Viceroys, and set all of the slaves of Mahadean free," Han whispered, laying his head back down with a thump.

"They saved the Galactic council, the Viceroys, and freed all the slaves on Mahadean," the medic whispered, repeating Han's words as he slipped off to sleep.

The medics' mouths dropped open, stunned by what Han had said. They could hardly believe what they had been told. Soon the whisper ran through the CORE hospital and all of Asteria station. The team of the prophecy was there on Asteria station. Carefully, the doctors slid the cadets and captains into glowing yellow healing tubes, all except Karmen and Jennifer, who maintained their vigil, guarding over Max.

On the second day after their return to Asteria station, Senior Viceroy Petrosky, Pete's grandfather, was carried to Max's room in the Frigate. He was weak and looked thin. His face and hands were bruised. They gasped when they saw him.

"Worry not, I will heal. However, you must rest," he said, his voice warm and comforting.

"No, sir. We cannot leave our posts until the one within requests us to," Jennifer whispered.

"We know what happened the last time he was on Asteria station, sir; and he is currently holding the raw energy in this sector of the universe together until the Galactic council is ready to receive it again, sir," Karmen added softly.

"May I pass?" he asked kindly.

Karmen and Jennifer stepped to the sides of the door, and the Senior Viceroy slipped off his cot and entered alone. The Senior Viceroy sat down on the floor next to Max.

"The council grows stronger each day, Max," the Senior Viceroy whispered.

"So they do, old man," Max replied, not looking up.

"Soon, you can be released from your burden," the Senior Viceroy added.

"Fortunate for you, I was here to hold it until your Galactic council could be reassembled," Max whispered back.

"Can you release Karmen and Jennifer?" he asked quietly.

"I have tried; however, until the Galactic council can once again guide this sectors energy of the universe and I can leave Asteria station, they will not leave my side. I have tried," Max said with great sadness in his voice.

"They are so weak," the Senior Viceroy added.

"I know; however, their triad is strong. They will find another way of supporting their team," Max said, closing his eyes.

The Senior Viceroy backed out of the room, leaving Max and the captains alone.

Three more days passed, and Jennifer and Karmen were still standing outside Max's door. They were weak, yet they had not gotten weaker. From within the yellow healing tubes George, Pete, Frank, but the others had somehow maintained their link. The stronger they became, the more energy they were able to give to Karmen and Jennifer.

On the sixth day, the council was strong enough to hold and guide the energy of the universe in their sector again. The Senior Viceroy returned to the room on the frigate where Max sat, with Pete and George's dads, as they were Viceroys in his triad and part of his Inner Circle. Karmen and Jennifer let them enter without saying a word—they only stepped aside.

Max sat alone on the floor, not recognizing them as they entered the room. He looked weaker.

"It is time," the Senior Viceroy said softly.

However, Max did not reply this time. He slumped over more. The Senior Viceroy called Karmen and Jennifer into the room. The glowing red spheres they held in their palms faded away when they saw Max.

With a tear in her eye Jennifer looked up at the Senior Viceroy. "We need Pete, Frank, Toma, and George, sir," she whispered.

Pete's dad turned and left the room quickly. In a flash of white light, he was gone. A few moments later he returned in another flash of white light. Pete, Frank, Toma, and George were standing in the corridor with him. They rushed into the small room with the others. George knelt down next to Max.

"It is time, sir. Time to release the energy of the universe, sir," George whispered, kneeling down and placing his hand on Max's shoulder. He placed his other hand on Pete's shoulder as he stepped closer.

Pete's dad stepped forward and shook his head. He lifted Max to his feet and placed George's hand back on Max's shoulder. Up close, Max looked very, very old to George, not the strong middle-aged man that had pulled him from the cool spring stream only two months ago. A million thoughts ran through his mind.

What were the beings of white light? Why did Max always seem to be so close by? How could controlling the energy of the universe weaken Max so much? Did that mean that the beings of white light were not all powerful? Where did they live? Was it on a different plain of existence? George wondered as Pete's dad moved Pete, Toma, and Frank into a tight circle around Max and George.

George held Max under his arm as Pete, Frank, and Toma placed their hands on George's shoulders. The Viceroys placed their hands on their son's shoulders and the Senior Viceroy place his hands on Pete's and George's dad's shoulders.

"We are ready, sir," George whispered.

Max straightened up a little and sent the energy he guided slowly through George to the captains and Viceroys. Soon Max and the others were all gaining strength and George stepped back, releasing Max as small streams of white light glided through the air to the Viceroys. A stream hit George's dad and another hit the Senior Viceroy. Another stream of light went off in space through the wall and another and another until the room was filled with a multitude of streams of white light. The cadets and captains backed up, closing their eyes, yet still focused on healing Max.

In the center of the blaze of white light, George opened his eyes and stared at Max. He understood; Max was not a being like them. He truly was a being of pure energy and only assumed human form to communicate with them.

So why was Max here, why was he helping them? What did Max know that would cause him to take such a great interest in them, in his team and in their triad? Why did the Senior Viceroy and Max not get along, and yet, they were always helping each other? George's understanding of what kind of being Max was only seemed to create more questions than it answered.

As Max released more and more energy, he became more aware of his surroundings. It was as if guiding the energy in this sector of the universe took all of his concentration. He seemed to grow stronger and no longer looked old and worn. Slowly, the rays of light dimmed. Max reached out and touched George's shoulder. In a flash of white light, he was gone, as was George's memory of who Max truly was. The Viceroys touched the shoulders of the captains and George again. This time they slipped gently to the floor, asleep.

A day later the captains and cadets woke up in the CORE hospital room on Asteria station. The Viceroys and Galactic council members were gone. A medic came to George's side when he rolled over.

"Are you hungry?" she thought to him.

He nodded and she left to get nourishment for him. Looking around, he saw his team; however, Pete, Toma, Frank and the others were missing. George sat up on his elbows in his bed to look around as his team started to rollover and wake up. Oddly, after all they had been through, their team link was still connected. George was sure it should have ended when they fell asleep. The medics brought six white bowls of brown cereal to the cadets.

"Only thing missing is Pete to make our morning start off right," Andy signed, eating his cereal.

"Who said I was missing, cadet," Pete answered as he entered their hospital room. The startled cadets looked up and smiled. Nick, Rachael, Jennifer, Karmen, and Han followed Pete into the room. Everyone was all smiles, the medics were even whispering—not really something done on the Calshene station ever before.

The cadets set their cereal bowls on the little white table between their beds and stood up to greet Pete's team as Frank and his team stepped into the hospital room following Pete's team.

"I see you are all better," Pete said, smiling kindly.

"Yes, sir. We need more training, sir," Emily said, teasing Pete.

"Happy to hear that, cadet," Pete replied, winking at Frank and the other captains.

"No, no come on, you're not serious are you, I mean, no sir," Andy said nearly in a panic. Gus groaned.

Nick, Niels, and the others broke out into laughter, nearly falling down. Even the medics giggled and laughed under their breath.

"You should see your faces!" Nick said, laughing.

"Funny, very funny, sir," Andy replied sarcastically.

"No, actually there will be more training, but for now you all have a day off," Pete replied kindly.

"Where are we going today, sir?" Anna asked eagerly. "I mean if we are released from the hospital, sir," she added, looking down at her foot, her voice waffling a little.

"We!" Pete replied, motioning to Frank and their teams. "Have amazing places to be. However, Colonel Moawk said he would take you for the morning. Then I'll be back at lunch and we'll make further plans," Pete said, speaking in his usual cryptic way.

He motioned them all to come over. The cadets stepped forward and wobbled a little. Frank and Pete's teams rushed to their sides and steadied them. Two captains supported each cadet. The lead doctor nodded to Pete and released the cadets into the captains' care. Together they all filed out of the hospital room and headed down the CORE hospital corridor.

"It is odd that we are all feeling better in only six days," Anna whispered.

"It doesn't seem like enough healing time," Sara whispered back.

"Eight days and we agree," Karmen replied, motioning to the others as Jennifer and Rachael nodded.

"And we have gained back all of the weight we lost on Mahadean eating only rations," Gus added quietly, patting his stomach.

"Someone has to be helping our triad," Han replied. nodding.

"It isn't the Viceroys this time. They are still weak, and now controlling the energy of the universe in this sector," Nick whispered, joining in the conversation.

"Perhaps it is Max?" Jennifer added.

Yet Sara and the others all wondered if Max was still weak from controlling the energy on his own.

"I wonder if someone will help Max regain his strength," Anna said.

George smiled to himself as they walked quietly through the CORE hospital corridors, listening to their team's conversation. It was weirdly odd that they would even be able to have the conversation on Asteria station and in the CORE hospital corridors at that. Around the next corner, a group of no color officers approached and Pete and Frank lowered their heads and pushed George and the others back against the wall.

"Think wall," George signed, and Andy and the others thought only wall.

The officers passed and the group continued on.

Some things have changed, but not all, George thought to himself.

Andy bumped his arm and signed, "I agree."

They approached another bend in the corridor, and Anna thought archway and one appeared before them. As if it was a game, Emily smiled and thought open, and the door easily glided open, letting them through. No one said a word, even so Anna and Emily were pleased that their little game had worked.

Pete, Frank and the other captains were stunned and all shook their heads together, looking like a group of geese, as they walked through as if nothing was wrong. They knew many CORE officers could not do what these third year cadets had just done by only thinking. They came out of the CORE hospital near one of the main Sport arenas and walked down the multi-color striped corridors in silence, guarding their thoughts and thinking only of Sport.

Soon Frank, Nick, and the others had to leave and walked down the blue and green captains' corridors after a few more turns.

"Is all of Toma's team here on Asteria station, sir?" George asked Pete as they walked on.

"You tell me," Pete cryptically answered.

He was still a little tired, and George did not actually want to work at anything right then. He never answered.

At Colonel Moawk's space dome, Pete stopped. "I'll see you at lunch. Stay here. Do not leave. Do not fall through anything. Do not open any odd doors. Do not go anywhere, got it?" he said in his captain's voice.

"Yes, sir," they replied weakly.

Then he turned, hugged them all in public—a very non-Calshene thing to do—and ran off back down the corridor they had just come down. The weirded-out cadets stared after Pete and then at each other. Emily rolled her hand and opened the door. Quietly, they walked into the training dome, not knowing what day it was or what teams would be inside.

"He didn't say anything about the caves," Emily half said, slipping up next to George and Andy.

"It was implied," Andy whispered, not wanting to bother George.

Inside the dome, the red cadets they had started their third rotation with were swinging from the long Sport vines hanging down from the center of the dome ceiling. Colonel Moawk yelled and the swinging red cadets picked up the pace. He was standing next to Major Pennelo when George and the others entered the dome. Quickly, he walked over to them and motioned them to the small room off the side of the training dome. He waved his hand at the dome wall and a small archway and door appeared and opened. He stood inside, facing the cadets until the last one entered and the door closed.

"Welcome back, cadets," the Colonel said with nicely, again a most un-characteristic greeting for a Calshene.

"Thank you, sir," they chorused cheerfully.

"I heard you are all still tired from your travels. We will do Chen Lo today for training. You can swing with the others in two days," the Colonel said. He turned around and stood in the start position, waiting for the cadets to get ready.

As was their standard now, Andy stood in the first row in the middle between Anna and Sara. They would follow Andy, and he would follow the Colonel. George, Emily, Anna, Sara, and Gus followed Andy's lead without hesitation. They started slowly with basic moves, stretching and bending, loosening their muscles and joints, breathing calmly as one. The Colonel took them through level after level until they reached the tenth level. They were now jumping, ducking, diving, rolling, and spinning with speed and precision.

Their focus was intense, and as before, they found a great calmness overtake their spirits. The Colonel stepped out of the motions, standing off to the side of the room as Andy stepped forward to take the lead. On and on they practiced, as if they were one with the universe again and all was well. They had made it to the eleventh level when the door slid open and Pete and Major Pennelo stood in the archway, shaking their heads.

The Colonel stepped back into the motions as if he had never left and slowed the cadets down to a resting position. The cadets were not tired like the first time. This time they felt calm and rested, at peace with the universe.

"Can we have them back?" Major Pennelo asked, teasing Colonel Moawk.

"Yes, Major," Colonel Moawk replied with a smile.

Pete motioned and the cadets bowed and left with Pete and the Major. As the door closed, Senior Viceroy Petrosky appeared in a flash of white light in the little room behind the Colonel.

"How are they doing?" he asked.

"Sir?" the Colonel answered, a little startled.

"The cadets?" he asked again.

The Colonel smiled. "Sir, they are unbelievably focused and calm. They are fluid, strong, and unified. They may have thought they were tired; however, from what I saw in here today, they could have given any CORE officer a workout. They are ready for the next level, sir," the Colonel said smiling, pleased with the cadet's progress.

"Will you teach them?" the Senior Viceroy asked.

"No, sir. I have taught them all I can. They are ready for a true master level, sir. I am only a poor substitute, sir," Colonel Moawk replied humbly.

"I will arrange it as you request," he replied. "Good work, Colonel."

Colonel Moawk turned around to thank him, but the Senior Viceroy was gone.

The cadets followed Pete out of the dome and down the corridor.

"I thought you would be done at lunch. Called that one wrong," Pete said, muttering and grinning a little.

"What do you mean, sir?" Andy replied, his mouth dropping open, moaning a little.

"We're going to dinner," Pete answered and smiled.

Andy shoved Gus's shoulder.

"We missed lunch again," Gus whined, wondering why he hadn't been hungry.

They turned another corridor and entered the dining hall. The other red cadets were still entering the hall as they made their way to an open table near the front of the room. Pete sat in the back with the other captains. Delicious foods appeared, filling the table as the cadets sat down. There were hamburgers, hotdogs, steak, fish, and chicken in front of them. There were potatoes, yams, beans, peas, carrots, corn, and broccoli-vegetables of every kind. There were breads, salads, milk, and bottles of water. The cadets knew if wasn't real food, only synthesized to look and taste like real food. But the cadets were in heaven after the weeks they had spent on Gus's diet of rations and brown cereal.

"Hey, Gus, you never said why we couldn't eat the food on Mahadean," Emily said as she scooped some yams and vegetables onto her plate with her hamburger.

"It is like eating poison to us. There is a chemical in the soil on Mahadean that creates a second chemical in all the food grown on the planet. It will kill us if we eat too much of it. A small taste will make you very sick. Some races take a kind of antidote so they can eat on the planet, but we didn't have any so we couldn't eat any of the food," Gus replied, biting into a steaming hot roll as the melted butter dripped onto his plate.

"OK," Emily replied slowly as the others stared at Gus in disbelief.

"Why didn't you tell us on Mahadean?" Anna asked, biting into her steaming mashed potatoes.

"You never actually asked, and you were all busy with other things," he said between chomps.

They all smiled. He had them there; they never actually asked. They accepted his answer and knew he would have a good reason.

"So how many days of ration food did we have left, and what would we have done if we ran out?" Sara pressed, scooping rice onto her plate and covering it with little colorful vegetables.

Gus stopped chewing and looked up for a minute. "It is not a question you really want answered," he replied solemnly.

"So what would have happened to us?" Emily pressed, staring at Gus.

"We would have died or starved. No, we would have starved then died. Yes, that's it," he answered seriously, scooping up another pile of green beans onto his plate.

The cadets were stunned. Gus wasn't going to tell them how many days of rations were left. Only Han and Gus knew that it wasn't enough to get them back to Asteria station, even if they hadn't had the Galactic council with them. There was no need to scare them. The team needed a rest.

Andy scooped up another helping of mashed potatoes onto his plate and gulped down his milk. He was happy he had followed Gus's directions back on the planet. There had been a couple of times he had thought of taking just one little bite of the local food, for a taste, that's all. Now he was pleased he had listened to Gus.

"So, George, is Toma's team here?" Emily asked, changing the subject.

"Don't know, hadn't really thought about it. I'm so tired of thinking. I can't bear the thought of having to look," he said, stuffing a small potato into his mouth.

George was staring at his plate and began to eat more of his green peas piled high on the edge of his plate before they slipped off onto the table. Emily had to agree, she was tired too, more in her brain than her body. Pete stood up in the back of the hall and George nodded to his team. They set down their forks and stood up, stretching and yawing.

"I wonder what lessons Pete has arranged for us tonight," Gus said.

The others groaned as they walked to Pete. In the bright light of the dining hall Pete looked tired too. They left the hall and walked down the corridor, stopping at their sleeping room.

"What's up, sir?" George asked as they walked inside.

"The doctors said you need to rest. Lock your room, remember? Stay put, do not leave. Don't go anywhere," he said, glancing at Anna and Emily.

"Yes, sir," they replied quietly.

Pete left and their beds rose from the floor. Emily and Anna locked the doors and laid down on their soft silvery beds.

"I missed you, bed," Emily whispered, hugging her bed as it curled around her.

"Only Emily would talk to a bed," George thought as he, too, drifted off to sleep.

The next morning Pete was in their room with bowls of brown cereal all ready poured when the cadets woke up. Everything seemed back to normal, even a little dull, at least by their standards. One whole day had past and nothing had exploded or tried to capture them.

Soon three weeks passed and the cadets went between training with Colonel Moawk and Major Gatte with no problems or extra training, only the peace and rest the doctors had ordered.

As was now common, Pete led them to stellar navigation training with Major Gatte in the morning. Today when they entered the classroom, Major Gatte was not in the room. They sat near the back of the class at an open table and waited with the other red cadets. Anna brought up the 3D holographic projector of the galaxy as they waited. She signed their path to Mahadean and then opened up the Mahadean home world so they could see the path they had taken through the center of the planet in the Turns race. The door started to open and Andy flicked off their holographic display as Major Gatte rushed in.

"Today we will be working on energy consumption. Everyone pull out your pads and expand them to tablet size. Your team of six will be in one of the team training fighters. You will be traveling to a nearby star cluster to take gamma radiation readings. First, who can tell me what stores are on the training fighters you have been training on this rotation? What is the fuel consumption rate, air supply rating and maximum speed?" Major Gatte asked politely.

A few of the cadets raised their hands to answer the question. George and his team didn't move. They knew everything about the little individual fighters from firsthand experience last year and the team training fighters were only a little smaller than the team scout ship they had just flown. The other cadets in the room guessed, hopelessly trying to find answers on their pads.

"Don't bother looking," Emily whispered, "he's blocked them all."

"Cadet Hawkins, your team has been quiet, please answer the questions," he said, staring at George and then Gus, wanting him to start.

"Yes, sir," George replied, motioning his team to their feet one by one. He nodded to Gus to start.

"There are 90 ration packs on a standard team training fighter. It is assumed that six cadets will eat three ration packs each day. This will give you enough food for five days. However, if you limit your team to three ration packs per day, dividing each ration pack into six equal parts and doing the same with the water supply, you can sustain your team for 30 days," Gus said, sitting down.

Emily was next to speak. "The engines on the team training fighters are sub-light, and the fuel consumption is measured in dynes. There is sufficient fuel to sustain the fighter at maximum sub-light speed for five days. However, if you decrease your speed to 85 percent maximum, you can reroute the superheated plasma exhaust back into the plasma reaction chamber and regenerate the fuel. This will extend your fuel supply to nine days," she said, sitting back down next to Gus.

Anna was not comfortable with speaking to a crowd of people. George slid his hand over her shoulder and whispered in her ear. "Teach them, it may save their lives someday."

Her confidence returned as George helped focus her thoughts. Slowly, Anna stood up.

"Well, ah, using the nine days Emily has given us, that means' we can travel for four and a half days in any direction. At under sub-light speed, that can get us to the nearest trading outpost and back without refueling. If on our way, we plot a course that is not a direct path, but one that takes advantage of the gravitational pull from the fixed orbit asteroids and planetoids. We can effectively use that energy to help pull us along and our speed will increase by one light speed while our engines are running at 85 percent capacity. At that speed we can travel out 7 days and back 7 days for a total of a 14 day trip," Anna said, sitting down.

Gus slid his arm over Anna's shoulder as George slipped his hand off her arm. Sara stood up next.

"The hospital and vitamin supplies are limited on the team training fighters. Basic wounds and plasma burns can be mended. There are no toxin medicines, only a few motion sickness medicines. The vitamin supply is set up the same as the ration supplies. As Gus said earlier, the rations can be cut back and the vitamins can be cut back as well. By adding the vitamins directly to the rations, the body can more readily absorb them," she said and sat down next to Andy.

George glanced at Andy next and nodded in Emily's direction, making a split sign with his hands. Andy smiled and stood up.

"The team training fighter has four low-yield cannons. They are used mainly to confuse an invading ship, since they will do little damage to even the most basic of shielded starships," Andy said, motioning Emily up.

"The computer can be reconfigured to emit an external holographic picture of a comet, and the sensors can reflect a similar image back to any starship scanning the sector of space you are in. Slight modifications to the plasma ports can make the exhaust appear similar to a comet's signature tail to all but the best sensors arrays," Emily added.

"This allows you to fire your cannons into an invader's exhaust ports, igniting their plasma. It will look like your ship is destroyed and there is only a sensor signature of a comet on their viewers," Andy added, and they sat down together.

"And what do you do?" one of the Calshene cadets asked George in a sarcastic manner.

"Sit around and let everyone else work?" another cadet jabbed and laughed.

"Yes, yes I do. I let them each do their work the best they can. I do not tell them how to do the tasks that need to be accomplished, only what the tasks are that need to be done. I formulate the plan on the command bridge of the training fighter and listen to the advice of my team. I remain calm and focused on our mission and share the information through sub-space communications with the officers on the primary station," he replied and sat down next to Emily.

The cadets in the room sat with their mouths hanging open like cod fish.

"How do you know all of this, Earther, if you're a third rotation cadet?" the pushy cadet pressed.

George glanced at his team for anyone to answer.

Emily replied, "We read a lot, training is not only when we are in this classroom. The manuals for all of the equipment we use are loaded on our pads. As are all of the star charts we have studied and the equations to use them," Emily replied kindly.

"Thank you, cadets," Major Gatte interrupted before any more questions could be asked. He pressed a few buttons on a wall console, and the information on the training fighter appeared on everyone's pads. "I expect everyone to read this evening. Dismissed," the Major said with a grin.

The red cadets groaned and started heading for the door. Major Gatte walked back to George and the others.

"Thank you for your general report on the team training fighter's capabilities. They are not ready for the more, shall we say, specific details," he said, smiling and shaking their hands.

"Thank you for the opportunity, sir," George replied formally, knowing the Major's exceptional kindness had to be hard on an officer who had grown up in a very strict environment.

The Major turned and left the classroom. The cadets stood alone in the room, rather surprised.

"He thanked us!" Andy said, dumbfounded.

"Anna are you sure we are on Asteria station?" Gus asked. "I mean I know it looks like Asteria station, but are you sure?"

He laughed and Andy laughed, grabbing a table to keep from tipping over. Anna shook her head and stared at Emily and Sara who were also shaking their heads and laughing.

"Gus, we are on Asteria station," Anna replied, smiling and chuckling.

"We may be on Asteria station, but all this niceness must be really hard on the Calshene, especially the officers. They have lived their entire lives by the strictest of rules and protocol. We must try and maintain protocol to make them feel comfortable with the changes," George said as they walked out of the classroom.

Chapter 18

TUNNEL HOG MYSTERY

In the corridor, two of the red cadet teams from Major Gatte's training class ambushed George and the others, knocking them to the ground. Instantly, George glanced at Andy and shook his head. One of the lead cadets stepped up, leaning over George's face.

"You look at me. You don't need him," the lead red cadet yelled gruffly, coming nose-to-nose with George.

"Actually, you do need me to look at him and stop him, or he'll hurt you," George replied as the lead cadet lifted George up from the floor and shoved him hard against the corridor wall.

"Who do you think you are, Earther, the team of the prophecy or something? Next time the Major asks you a question, you don't know nothing. You got it?" the leader yelled, inches from George's face as he poked him in the chest.

George smiled. "Apologize now, and we'll let you go," George replied politely.

"Remember, we read," Emily added, rolling up from the floor.

"There are 12 of us and only 6 of you. We are smarter, stronger, and faster than you, Earther," the lead second said, taunting the Earthers.

"Yes, you are stronger as twelve; however, I don't personally know about faster and smarter," Anna replied as Emily pulled her up from the floor.

The lead cadet swung his fist at George's face. George ducked, and the lead cadet hit one of his team members in the face, instead of George, sending him to the ground with his nose bleeding.

"Hold still, you worm," the lead cadet yelled, swinging at George's stomach this time. George rolled to his right and pulled the other red cadet, holding him forward and into the lead cadet's swinging fist. The lead cadet's fist crashed into another cadet's ribs. Sara cringed as the cadets ribs cracked from the impact. The second cadet fell to the floor in pain from his newly cracked ribs. Andy seized the opportunity and flipped up and over, grabbing George's arm and rolling both of them free from the lead cadet's grasp.

Quickly, George, and Andy spun in opposite directions, leaning back and knocking over three more cadets. Emily, Anna, and Gus were now free. Gus dropped to his knees as two cadets rushed in to tackle him. The instant they touched him, he grabbed their arms and swung around, lifting them off their feet as he stood up. He let go as Anna and Emily dove to the corridor floor, knocking over two of the Calshene cadets and trapping them on the ground. Sara was free. Emily and Anna released the Calshene cadets, and they jumped to their feet. Gus released the spinning cadets, and they sailed through the air, hitting the two standing cadets. Their thuds echoed through the corridor as the four cadets hit the walls and slid down to the ground into a moaning heap with the others.

Four more cadets rushed in toward Andy and George. George and Andy pushed off of each other, flipping through the air and landing just behind the cadets and tripping them with a simple Chen Lo step. The four cadets fell and skidded across the floor, landing on the heap of moaning cadets. The lead cadet and his second were now the only two cadets left standing. The lead cadet looked at his second and nodded. The second cadet lifted his hands—Andy knew the motion and dove on the second cadet, pinning him to the ground.

"You never create a red energy sphere unless you're willing to destroy with it," he yelled, lifting his hand and forming a red energy sphere inches from the second cadet's head and firing it into the corridor wall. "Do you understand?" Andy said, his eyes glowing red.

The wall shook and trembled from the blast. Andy left the stunned second and rolled over, knocking the lead cadet to the ground with his legs.

Leaning over the lead cadet and crushing his shoulder into the floor, he whispered. "I could have destroyed all of you the instant you attacked us. As my lead cadet said, his look is the only thing that spared all of your lives. Don't ever try this again. Don't even think about it."

Andy looked around at the other cadets on the floor, making sure no one was getting up. He turned back to the lead cadet and leaned in close to his ear so only the cadet could hear his words.

"Cause you see, without my lead cadet, you're all gone. I have no problem with it. Asteria station or not. You get it?" Andy whispered, his eyes burning with a reddish glow.

He shook the lead cadet and rolled over, jumping to his feet as security guards came racing up to the cadets in the corridor. The guards grabbed the twelve cadets, surrounding them until the medics arrived. Then the medics whisked them away. A cadet sector officer and three guards stayed behind.

"What happened here? Are you cadets alright?" the cadet sector officer with three stripes on his sleeve asked, turning toward George.

It was the station cadet Commander! George lowered his head and his team followed.

"There was a tactical disagreement, sir. We are all fine, sir," George answered formally.

"Guards, make sure these cadets get safely to the dining hall," the station Commander said, and the guards nodded.

"Sir, what will happen to the other cadets?" George asked, his head still lowered.

"They will be punished for their lack of good judgment," the Commander replied.

"Sir, it was merely a misunderstanding, sir," George added, trying to soften the Commander's pending harsh punishment.

"As you wish, cadet. Guards, follow me," he said, his voice not as formal.

"Thank you, sir," George answered.

The Commander motioned, and he and the guards left the cadets in the corridor. The instant they were out of sight, Andy spun around and hugged the corridor wall.

"Andy, you OK?" Gus asked.

"Emily, tell the wall how sorry I am. I never meant to hurt the wall, I was only trying to scare them," Andy said with sorrow and sadness in his eyes.

Emily smiled.

"Tell him," Sara said, giggling.

"What? Tell me what?" Andy asked, twisting his head to look at Emily.

"Well, we may have helped you a bit on that. Gus and I braced the wall. Gus converted the energy. I had the wall shutter for effect, and Sara made your eyes glow red," Emily said, grinning.

"Man, you guys are the greatest. So, the wall's OK?" Andy asked again.

"Yes, the wall is fine. Gus is not--one heck of an energy burst, Andy," Sara said, holding her hand over Gus's palm to heal his burns.

George made a link to share the energy with Sara. The others joined the link and Gus's hands mended quickly. The sound of running footsteps echoed in the corridor.

"Pete's coming," Emily whispered.

"They are all coming," George replied.

They dropped their link as Pete, Frank, and both of their teams came running up the corridor.

"Report!" was the only word out of Pete's mouth.

George and the others broke their circle and stood up straight as Gus slipped his hands behind his back. George stepped forward and explained what had happened in class and in the corridor after class.

"You didn't hurt anyone?" Niels asked Andy.

"No, sir," he replied as Nick and Niels slid their arms over his shoulders.

Andy had made a large intense red energy sphere, hence the burns on Gus's hand from only one sphere. Andy was still wired from letting it fly. They needed him to focus and calm down before the CORE guards came. They would not be as forgiving as the cadet sector guards for launching a red energy sphere. Pete and Frank thought of Sid and Mid, two of the tunnel hogs on Asteria station.

A rumble in the wall told Pete they were there. Pete pointed and Anna and Emily made an archway and opened the door. The cadets all slipped through and squeezed into Sid. The door closed and the archway disappeared as CORE guards rounded the corner of the corridor in front of Major Gatte's classroom.

"You are all a sight, again!" Niels said as he and Nick slipped their arms over Andy's shoulder.

Pete and Frank's teams were all working on calming the cadets' minds and refocusing their thoughts.

"Why are you here, sir?" George asked inside of Sid.

"Andy is wired, George. He let go of one huge red energy sphere," Frank replied, hugging his little brother.

"We don't know how he was able to control it. It is way passed his years, George," Pete said, and shook his head with a worried look on his face.

"It's how we found you so quickly, George," Jennifer added kindly.

The cadets stared at the captains, not understanding what they were talking about.

"Every energy burst leaves a signature. We know your signature; we can feel it," Nick added, still focusing on Andy's mind.

"I can't feel it," George thought back.

"You will be able to in time," Pete said.

"Right now, we need to walk Andy out of this one," Rachael said.

"What do you mean, walk him out? Out of what?" George pressed.

"George, you have never seen what happens to Andy when he lets go of one of his real energy spheres, have you?" Pete said, staring at George. "No, of course not, you would have been concentrating or using the energy," Pete continued, muttering to Frank and himself.

"George, look at Andy, look at Nick and Niels, what do you see? Concentrate," Frank whispered.

He turned around and stared at Andy. It was as if it was the first time in a long time he looked. Inside Sid he could feel the torment inside Andy. The oath to defend and protect and the conflict of having a weapon so powerful at your finger tips, it was both comforting and terrifying.

He knew Andy's anguish was hiding inside him and the terrible toll it was taking on him. He looked at each of his team members and started to understand the conflicts that raged within each of them.

"George, focus," Pete and Frank said, calling him back from his thoughts.

"George, Andy can barely control his red energy spheres anymore. His spheres have grown faster than his ability to control them. He needs to go for specialized training. Nick and Niels can take him. He needs to go now. Do you understand?" Pete whispered.

"No, we will all go together or not at all, sirs," George replied formally.

Pete's face crinkled and his head twisted not happy with his answer.

"Sir, Andy is bound by the orders of the Galactic council. He cannot leave my side. We cannot break our oath to the Galactic council, grandfather, or Max. He will not do it, even if it means he will die. So we will go together, sir," George said firmly.

"The Galactic council will not permit that answer," Pete replied firmly, yet stunned by George words.

"They cannot have it both ways. We gave our word, sirs," George replied firmly again.

"Certainly the Galactic council will make an exception for your earlier commitment?" Frank questioned.

"No, they will not, not on this one, sir," George replied, looking somber.

Pete stared at Frank.

"We were there this spring. When could the Galactic council have made them make a commitment so strong that they would rather die than break it?" he whispered to Frank.

They shook their heads, thinking back to the spring as Sid slowed. Emily thanked Sid for the transport to safety as they all squeezed out the narrow slit. Sid let them out in a corridor near the main spaceport on Asteria station.

There were only a few cadets in the corridor they entered. Pete started running down one of the corridors and the others followed. Niels signed guards, and Pete ducked into one of the empty classrooms. Pete ran to the back of the classroom and searched for a door. Anna slipped up and made an archway, and Emily opened the door without even touching the classroom wall. Pete and Frank shoved George and his team through the door and closed it without making a sound.

Jennifer brought up a 3D holographic image of the main Sport area as Kate added last year's final match teams. Nick, Niels and the others quickly sat down in the classroom chairs, staring at the display as CORE guards burst into the room.

"Where are they, captains?" one of the CORE guards yelled.

"Who are you looking for, sir?" Pete answered, standing up at attention.

"We traced them here. Don't lie to me captain," the lead CORE guard said, threatening the captains. "Where are they?" he pressed, standing inches from Pete's face.

"Sir, only our two teams are in this classroom, sir," Pete replied, choosing his words very carefully.

They knew intimidation and these CORE guards were not even on their scale, yet they would have to play along to give George and the others time to escape. Once Andy's mind could calm down and his energy rebalanced, they could return to the cadets' sector and the CORE guards wouldn't be able to trace them anymore.

"Then what are your two teams doing in this classroom, captain?" the second CORE guard pressed.

Suddenly, four older CORE officers burst into the classroom before Pete could answer. Instantly, all of the captains jumped to their feet, lowering their heads and lining up behind Pete and Frank. The original CORE guards backed up and the older CORE officers began circling the captains. True to form, one of the older CORE officers started yelling at the captains, trying to distract them while the other three tried to worm their way in to read their thoughts. Pete, Frank, and the others thought only of Sport and how much strategy time they were losing as it was hard to get everyone together. Now the teams had CORE officers, interrupting their free time. It was all they kept thinking for the officers' benefit, over and over.

The CORE officers were wolves in sheep's clothing. They weren't regular CORE officers, they were too well trained. They had to be Inner Circle officers in disguise. They wormed and wormed as the older lead CORE officer yelled. The captains fought for control of their thoughts. The older lead CORE officer was a brute, but the three other officers were not. They were smooth as silk. The captain's minds burned as they focused only on Sport— no stray thoughts for the invading older CORE officers to hang onto.

After an hour, the older lead CORE officer nodded; and they left, taking the real CORE guards with them.

Nick shook his head slowly after the CORE officers left the classroom. Slowly he signed, "Outside door, not gone, trap," then he fell to the ground, his mind on fire.

Niels reached down and lifted Nick up from the floor, helping him into a seat. The captains followed his lead and sat down on the classroom chairs, holding their heads. Pete and Frank restarted the 3D Sport finals hologram from last year and sat next to each other to discuss strategies for the others to focus on while they waited for the officers to leave. They held each other's arms, making a physical link and sharing their strength. Their minds were on fire, fighting the CORE officers as they continued mind invasions. The captains kept their focus on Sport for hours, buying the cadets time to escape, not knowing where they would go to hide.

George, Andy, and the others rolled into the cave behind the classroom wall. They hardly stopped to brush themselves off as they took off, running through the narrow dusty caves. There was no breeze to stir the dust and guide them on Asteria station. Emily was still surprised there was any atmosphere in the caves, considering the station was what was left of the Calshene home world.

The deep crevice on the Mahadean home world was not caused by environmental erosion. Instead, something had cut the planet apart and had stopped when it reached nearly halfway around the planet. Calshene was not so lucky. It was cut apart and sometime during the process, the planet violently imploded on itself and then exploded, leaving behind an asteroid field and no home world for the Calshene people—only lifeless hunks of rock. Emily's mind raced as they ran through the caves away from the classroom.

The cave wall rumbled and Mid appeared. George and the others slid into Mid and the tunnel hog took off like lightning. The cadets flew to the back of Mid.

"She's scared," Emily whispered.

"Tell her to go to safety," George whispered.

"Already done," Emily thought back.

"Can you call Pete and Frank?" Andy asked.

"No, they're blocking us, like before," George replied.

Within a few minutes, Mid slowed and stopped. The cadets stepped out of Mid into the tunnel hog cavern again. Emily hugged Mid, thanking her for helping them.

Chapter 19

GALACTIC COUNCIL CHAMBER

The last time they were in the tunnel hog cavern, they were hiding from the Galactic council after acquiring the prophecy. Now, Pete, Frank, and the others were protecting Andy from the CORE officers for creating and launching a red energy sphere in the cadet sector.

"What is really going on?" George muttered to himself.

"Don't know," Andy replied, staring at George.

"Start of our third week since our escape from Mahadean, and we are attacked," George whispered.

"Someone must have put the idea in their minds," Andy whispered. He was as puzzled as George.

"But why?" George asked, thinking hard.

"Whoever did it must have known we wouldn't be scared," Andy said quietly.

"So why did they do it?" George replied.

It was getting late and they had not had any food since before lunch. They did not know if it was safe to go back or if they should stay. In the tunnel hog cave, doubt and fear were taking over their thoughts.

"George, Andy come here. Look at this," Anna called from the second cave.

George and Andy hurried over to Anna, Gus, Sara, and Emily standing at the entrance to the second small cave. Anna pointed inside at the bright green glow coming from the walls.

"It's the fungi we fed when we were here the last time," Gus said, smiling. Pleased the purple liquid had helped the fungi.

"Yes, but look at the cave walls behind the glowing fungi," Sara replied, pointing to the walls.

The fungi's glow illuminated the cave walls that were covered with symbols and writing.

"How old is Calshene?" George asked Emily, staring at the symbols.

"I'd say 5,000 or 10,000 years of evolution ahead of us," she said. Anna nodded in agreement.

"Yet, it's like somewhere along the way, they stopped evolving," Anna said puzzled as to why.

"You could say that about all of the races we have met on our rotations," Sara added, walking over to the far cavern wall.

"It's like we, Earthers, somehow caught up to them," Gus added, runing his hands in the lower grooves of the symbols on the cavern wall.

"Why? Why would so many civilizations stand still for so long?" George half asked, staring at the walls.

"Look at Rome and the kings, Caesars, emperors and czars of Earth. They became complacent and turned inward. They stopped exploring and became civilized and structured with rules. With no new challenges left to overcome, they stopped evolving," Emily said, quoting Earth's history.

"Mired in their own bureaucracy with no escape," Gus replied, nodding his head and rubbing his chin.

"What?" Andy and the others spun around and stared at Gus.

"What? I studied, too, ya know," Gus answered.

They laughed, but they understood his words. It was as if becoming civilized with no challenges had slowed their evolution and development. Without challenges, the Calshene society had stalled. Then when they were faced with a great challenge, their planet was destroyed because their society could not fight back against the attackers.

"So, any thoughts on what these symbols are? Or what they might mean?" George asked his team.

"In the American Southwest there are drawings similar to these," Emily said, squinting.

"The Egyptians have similar hieroglyphs too," Anna added, twisting her head.

"The ruins of Ireland and England have similar drawings," Sara piped in, lining up a symbol between her fingers.

"And the ancient South American civilizations too?" George asked Andy.

"Yes, I have seen this one in the museum before. It means courage and this one next to it means honor," Andy replied, rubbing his chin thinking back to his youth.

His mom had dragged him and his brothers and sisters off to nearly every museum in South America and had even thrown in a few of the old churches and sacred city sites along the way. The sites had seemed old, run down and dumb at the time. Now, he wished he had paid better attention to what he had seen.

"One more, Andy—do any others look similar to what you remember?" Emily pressed, making a map on her pad.

"Kinda, that one is similar to the symbol for war, but it is missing a line here," Andy said, climbing on a rock and motioning with his hands.

"Could it be peace?" Gus asked as he helped Anna off some rocks.

Andy shook his head and spun around, scanning the walls. "No, no. Stand here and look. That's war," Andy said, correcting himself and pointing across the room.

George stood in the center of the small cavern with Emily, pointing to two symbols on opposite walls.

"If that's war, then peace is this one," he said, pointing 180 degrees apart with his arms wide open.

"It's yin and yang, night and day," Emily said, adding the symbols to her map.

"Good and evil," George whispered, stopping on evil, lingering long over the word as if it would not leave his mind.

Andy raced across the small cavern, tackling George and knocking him to the ground.

"George, are you OK?" Andy yelled, shaking his shoulders as the dust rose up around them.

"Ya, how'd I get down here?" George asked, bewildered as to why Andy knocked him to the ground.

Andy stood up and grabbed his arm. "You were staring at the symbol for evil and fuzzed out," Andy answered, lifting him to his feet.

Gus wanted to say, "George was non-responsive;" however, after the reaction he got from his last comments, he decided to say nothing at all.

"I've seen that symbol before," George said, thinking hard.

"Where?" Emily asked, staring at George and her pad, looking for more information to add.

"In the Zeleion warship, when we went inside to rescue the Viceroys," Andy answered, solemnly finishing George's thought.

"Emily, do you have enough?" George asked cryptically.

"Yes, I think I can do this," she answered with hesitation in her voice.

"We need to leave this cavern. Scan it, and we'll build an image in the other cavern," George said, shaking his head.

They quickly scanned all of the symbols on the walls and left the cavern for the first cavern where Mid had dropped them off.

"There is something about that little cavern," Andy said, swinging his arm over Sara's shoulder.

"Maybe it's something in the rocks that makes things seem weird," Sara said thoughtfully.

"I've heard of that. There are places on Earth where there is a lot of iron ore near the Earth's crust, and it can mess up compasses and make people and vehicles do funny things," Emily added, smiling as she studied the map on her pad with Anna.

Sitting on large rocks that had collapsed onto the cavern floor, the cadets placed all of their pads together, and Emily and Anna brought up a 3D image of the other small cavern. Meanwhile, Gus slipped out two ration packs and sliced and diced dinner for the cadets. Again, he added a few drops of purple liquid to the rations before distributing them to his team.

"Gus, if it wasn't for your rations, we would all starve to death," George said, dipping his head toward Gus.

Gus grinned a little. "You're only saying that because you're hungry," he replied.

"Well, ya," Andy teased, grinning.

They laughed and stared at the image on their pads while eating their rations as Emily and Anna connected the opposite words with red lines on the 3D image in front of them. Sara rotated the map as they added more and more lines.

"That looks so familiar, like we should know this one," Sara said thoughtfully.

"We have seen this before," Anna added, crinkling her forehead.

"Yes, but where? It's like we know this, but can't find it," Emily said, straining to think, trying to remember.

Andy was staring at George. He didn't like George fuzzing out, and him fuzzing out on the symbol for evil wasn't a good sign.

"Emily, where were you when you saw yin and yang?" Anna asked, pointing at the crisscrossing red lines.

"About the middle of the cavern next to George, why?" she answered.

"I don't know, maybe it's something you can only see from inside," Anna surmised.

They pulled their pads back away from each other, and the 3D images dimmed and then expanded to fill the cavern. The cadets stood inside the 3D image and saw the same lines crisscrossing the space from symbol to symbol.

"This isn't working and we need to get back. Gus, what time is it?" George said, shaking his head.

"It's late, all the cadets will be sleeping soon. There may be some cadets still in the alcove," Gus replied.

"Close the projection down, Emily. It is a mystery we will solve another day. Think of Sid and Mid, everyone," George said, looking around the cavern. "The tunnel hogs should be back soon to sleep themselves."

A small rumble appeared and two tiny baby tunnel hogs appeared. They made tiny slits in their sides, and Emily placed her hand in each one to talk with them.

"They are Sid and Mid's twin boys, Bid and Kid, and they will take us where we need to go. Sid, Mid, and the others are being held for questioning by the Galactic council," Emily whispered.

George gritted his teeth. He knew the Galactic council had taken Sid and Mid for helping them escape.

"Thank them for their bravery and kind hearts," he whispered kindly.

Gus poured out all of his purple liquid into the fungi and then petted it softly.

"I will bring more. I hope this helps," he whispered.

He knew it could nibble on him, yet he thought it was so sad and lonely. Feeding it was all he could think of to do.

Emily hugged the tiny tunnel hogs, and three of the cadets squeezed into each of the two tiny hogs. The cadets shared their energy with the hogs since the young hogs were not accustomed to the energy draw and their passengers' weight. The ride was slow and bumpy, not the smooth ride from Mid and Sid. Kid and Bid dropped them off outside the red sector corridors. Emily thanked them and told them never to come this close again—it wasn't safe. The twins sped off to safety.

One corridor down and the cadets saw guards posted outside their sleeping quarters.

"We need another way in," George signed to Anna.

Almost instantly, Anna's archway appeared, and Emily opened the door into the cave with a twist of her wrist. Anna guided them a short distance through the cave and made another archway and door. The cadets laid against the wall and Emily opened the door.

Andy slipped in first. Their sleeping room was empty. The cadets stepped inside and raised their beds to sleep. Emily closed the door and the archway disappeared as the cadets laid down. They slept in shifts that night, not wanting to break their link and give away their location while they slept. In the morning, Pete was not in their room. Gus and Sara retrieved the cereal and bowls and the cadets ate. Gus restocked his backpack and Sara added a few things to Gus's backpack. When everyone was nearly done eating, George had Gus break their link.

"Think about Pete missing. We will need to send a message to his team to find out where he is," George signed as Gus broke their link.

Within seconds, the guards were in the sleeping room, screaming orders at the cadets.

"Where's our captain sir?" George asked as fearfully as he could.

"Where is our captain, sirs?" the cadets all asked at the same time.

It was the only answer the cadets would give to the guards. Shortly, two older CORE officers appeared and threw the cadets out into the corridor.

"Where have you been, cadets? You have been missing for two days!" a third CORE officer said, yelling at the cadets in the corridor.

"Sleeping sir, where is our captain, sir?" George answered.

The others stared at each other. How could they have been in the tunnel hog cave for two days? They thought it had only been a few hours!

For every question the officers asked, George's answer was the same, "Where's Pete?"

A crowd of cadets gathered in the corridor and the two CORE officers couldn't get them to disperse. The CORE officers directed George and his team down the corridor and away from the growing crowd of cadets.

In the commotion of moving them, the cadets made another link. Sara jumped and pretended to hurt her ankle. Andy bumped another as he knelt down to help Sara. George, Gus, Emily, and Anna bumped their shoulders to see if there were holographic bars on their arms or shoulders. Nothing appeared, other than the CORE officers becoming angrier than before and yelling even louder. They started pushing the cadets down the corridor.

"Where's captain Petrosky?" Emily whined.

"Focus," George signed, trying hard to block their mind invasions.

They needed to keep the CORE officers off balance and thinking that the cadets were weak and needed their captain to take care of them. The CORE officers laughed, thinking the cadets' minds were weak and afraid. Two corridor turns and Pete appeared in front of them, or at least someone copying his image appeared before them. He reached out to hug each of them as they were pushed into him in the corridor.

Emily hugged him back and ran her hand over his shoulders. "Holographic bar," she signed as he released her.

"Where have you been?" the imposter asked kindly.

"Oh ya, this was not Pete," Andy signed in their newer sign language.

George picked a new thought and sent it to the others—Colonel Moawk's training dome. They each received their hug and the fake Pete officer tried to make a link with them.

"We were in our sleeping room, sir," Sara answered, nearly in tears. She let her emotions fill the CORE officer's thoughts.

"You were not there when we woke up, sir," Anna added, a few tears running down her rosy cheeks.

"These CORE officers came and took us away, sir," Emily added, looking lost as her emotions overflowing.

Following Anna and Emily's lead, Sara started in on the fake Pete.

"What's going on, sir? Please help us, sir," Sara whined, hugging the fake Pete again and filling him with extreme emotions.

They all asked nonsensical questions all at once in their most worried voices. The cadets thought of training and being worried. It was working. Gus and Andy wormed their way into one of the CORE officer's minds. Tears ran from Anna and Emily's eyes as they hugged the imposter. They filled his mind and the CORE officers' minds with strong emotions they were not accustomed to sensing. Gus nodded and they released them. He and Andy had what they needed.

They started to walk down the corridor again. George kept the CORE officers busy with ridiculous questions and thoughts, while the rest of his team made a plan. There was really only one place George wanted to go after Bid and Kid had risked their lives to save them, and Andy and the others knew it. However, they would have to ditch the CORE officers and the fake Pete to get there.

The Galactic council asteroid in this sector of space had been destroyed. The Galactic council had to go somewhere until a new asteroid could be hollowed out for offices and living structures. Asteria station was their only place to go for temporary housing and offices. It was a small asteroid already, compared to Indus station and Jupiter station; and now it was even smaller, as they were sure the Galactic council had locked off some of the sections for use as temporary council chambers.

That is where George wanted to go today. He did not care about protocol anymore. The Galactic council punishing George and his team was one thing, but punishing their triad for their actions was another. However, detaining the tunnel hogs and hurting their families was seriously one step too far. The sector Galactic council was about to be taught a lesson in appropriate behavior, and George and the others were going to send them to the timeout chairs if they didn't shape up. All these things ran through Andy's mind as they walked.

"Where are we going?" George pressed the fake Pete, keeping him concentrating on his continuous stream of silly questions.

"To training, of course," fake Pete answered kindly, straining against the cadets' emotions.

Another turn and the CORE officers and cadets stopped in front of an archway.

"Go on inside, and I'll be back after training," he said, pointing to the archway as the door slipped open.

"How dumb does this officer think we are?" Andy thought to all in the link except George.

Anna and Emily had already told everyone, except George, that they were in the brig and this was not a training dome. Instead, it was a holding cell with holographic projectors used to make it look like a training dome. Slowly, George raised his head and looked up at the fake Pete officer with fear of the unknown. It was the performance of a lifetime!

"Can't you all just come in with us for a moment? I mean, you know how frightening all this is for us so far away from home, and you not being there this morning," George whined, looking down and sliding his foot back and forth across the floor in front of the brig door.

"Yes, yes, of course, we will go in with you," the imposter replied and motioned the CORE officers inside as he stepped back into the corridor with the cadets.

The CORE officers and guards passed through the archway and into the room. Andy signed to George and he dropped like a rock to the ground as Andy, Gus, Sara, and Anna barreled into the fake Pete, shoving him through the archway. He landed squarely on the four CORE officers and guards in the cell. The CORE officers slid to the back wall, thumping to a stop as the cadets scrambled to their feet. Quickly, Emily closed and locked the door. Andy swung around and grabbed George's arm, yanking him off the ground. They took off on the run with Anna in the lead. Gus touched George's shoulder, told him everything that had happened on their trip to the brig, and what they had read in the minds of the CORE officers.

They knew where the Galactic council chambers were on Asteria station. It was the one place the officers had not been recently in the CORE offices. They were going there now! As they ran, they communicated in sign language, fearing someone may be scanning or listening. They would not have much time before the CORE officers and imposter were discovered and set free.

"I need a terminal," Emily signed, and Anna slid to a stop in front of a classroom.

They ducked inside, and Emily pulled up the Asteria station sensor matrix on the main computer.

"We need to disappear, and tell them we are in our sleeping room with the door locked," she whispered.

Emily's hands flew across the keys in mid-air. George and the others smiled; a good diversion. They were amazed at Emily's abilities and the ease at which she was able to hack into the station's main computer system. In a few moments, she sent her sensor modifications into the station's main computer. George turned toward the door, and Andy reached out and stopped him.

"Think wall!" he signed, and the cadets pressed against the inside wall of the classroom.

The door slid open, and they could hear two guards talking.

"Wait, they found them, they're back in their sleeping room," the guard said in the corridor, his voice echoing around the room.

The guard standing in the doorway turned around without going inside, and the door closed behind him. They waited until Andy nodded that the guards had left before they opened the door and left. George led with Anna, sending directions from behind. Soon the corridor walls were covered with many striped colors. There were only a few cadets in the corridors as George and the others ran by the Sport arena.

At high speed, Anna created an archway in the middle of a corridor wall in front of the running cadets. Emily opened the doors just before George ran into it. Behind the multi-colored, brightly lit corridor was a dimly lit smaller corridor. George slowed to a walk inside the smaller corridor, and Emily touched everyone's arm, making their red stripe disappear. They walked in single file through the small corridors. Again, Anna directed George from behind.

Several Inner Circle officers passed them without stopping their conversations. Ahead of them, Anna made another small archway, and Emily opened the door. George walked through as if he owned the place. Inside he was angry, yet he had to use his anger for good because yelling and hollering at the sector Galactic council would change nothing.

George concentrated and focused as he followed Anna's directions. The corridor was gone now, and they were walking in a narrow cave. The walls were carved, with different symbols etched into them.

Emily shook her head. "They are not that old—mostly they are for effect or as a distraction," she signed.

"What was it grandfather had said?" George mumbled as they walked on.

Calm and focus filled the cadets' minds as they walked closer and closer to the sector Galactic council chambers. Anna was about to make one more archway when George turned and stopped her. He looked at each of them directly in their eyes.

"The Galactic council of Senior Viceroys is very strong—even after their capture by the Mahadean, they are strong. Andy and I have felt only a small part of their strength and power. Yet knowing this, I still cannot stand by, watching others get hurt in our name. Grandfather said there would be those moments in your life that define who you are by the decisions you make. Sometimes there would be time to think clearly and sometimes the decisions would be nearly instantaneous. Those decisions say a lot about who you are and how you have chosen to live your life. This is one of those times for us," he said unafraid of being overheard.

Emily reached forward and uncovered the award on their uniform they had received on their first rotation.

"The award is for outstanding courage and compassion in the face of great danger and personal risk. The field of red symbolizes courage when confronted with a relentless enemy. The white star laid over the field of red symbolizes compassion to share what you have to save the lives of others," she said, repeating Colonel Hawk's words from their first rotation.

George laid his hand out to his team. A small yellow sphere glowed, dancing above his palm. "Peace is our path, it unites all beings," he said.

Andy placed his hand next to Georges. "Courage is our character, it joins us as one," Andy added.

Emily added her hand to the bottom with her palm up. "Harmony is our nature, it connects us to the universe," she replied.

Anna added her hand over the yellow sphere. "Strength is our will, it protects us all," Anna said, nodding.

Sara placed her hand next to Anna's. "Four parts come together to heal the fear of the past and present," Sara whispered.

"To start anew with peace, courage, harmony and strength," Gus said, completing their circle with his hand.

For a moment, they could feel Pete, Frank, Toma, and the others in their triad. They were weak; nevertheless, they were alive. They pulled back their hands as a group of Inner Circle officers came walking down the cave corridor. The team pretended to be talking to each other as the officers walked by and disappeared down the corridor.

"I cannot help you with this, George. Remember you are stronger together. Forget not your compassion," was the thought George heard from Max as the officers passed by.

George had a funny look about him. Andy spun around and stared at him. Every time George seemed to fuzz out he had been attacked by a stealthy mind invader. Andy needed to figure out what was going on with George, now!

Andy signed to George, "What's up?"

George replied in sign, "All good. Later." He nodded to Andy. "It is time to break another rule," George said, grinning.

"Yes, and we are getting quite good at it," Emily said, jokingly yet feeling a little uneasy.

"I think they make new rules just to see how fast we can break them," Gus added, yet he, too, was uneasy.

With their link as strong as they could make it, George nodded and the team focused its thoughts. Anna made an archway, and Emily lifted her hand. The door shook and then slid open. George led his team into the Galactic council chamber. Before them were the most powerful Senior Viceroys, Inner Circle officers, and Viceroys in their sector of space.

The room was as George and Andy had remembered it, with a single circle of white light shining down in the center of the room. The single white light was surrounded by three white circles of light. The three circles of white light were surrounded by nine circles of white light and they were surrounded by more circles. Pete's grandfather stood on one of the three inner circles of white lights. Pete's dad, George's dad and Toma's dad stood on three of the nine circles. The cadets had never seen the Senior Viceroy in the center.

Hardly three weeks had passed since they had rescued the Galactic council from the Mahadean. They knew the Galactic council was tired, yet in the Galactic council chamber they looked strong and intimidating.

The cadets stepped forward toward the center of the room. The Galactic council members did not even acknowledge their presence. Andy was annoyed, but George glanced and shook his head. Andy nodded and cleared his thoughts. George was determined. They had to work together. He motioned for the cadets to step through the outer rings of Viceroys, encircling the nine Viceroys. Once in place, George nodded again, together they stepped through the nine Viceroys, encircled the three Senior Viceroys, and the Senior Viceroy in the center.

A third nod and Gus joined the cadets into the Senior Viceroy's link. Up until then, the cadets had been only an annoyance to the center Senior Viceroys. Now, they were downright insolent, stepping into their link. The Senior Viceroy in the center opened his eyes and stared directly at George.

"I can destroy you this instant for your behavior, and no one will blink an eye to stop me," he said firmly, threatening them.

"You could have destroyed us at any time, when we entered the council corridors or the council chamber, sir. Your threat is thinly veiled, sir," George replied as firmly, not falling into the center Senior Viceroys simple trap.

"Your team is well controlled," he said, taunting the cadets.

"They are not controlled, sir. We are a team sir," George replied, dipping his head.

"Have you come to beg for mercy for your triad? It is too late for that. You and your team have tried our patience once too often," the center Senior Viceroy said firmly, being cruel and arrogant with his words.

"No, sir. We have not come to beg for mercy, unless you require that of us, sir." George said, turning the center Senior Viceroy's words around.

"Your thoughts betray you cadet, your fear is great," he said wickedly, trying to trick the cadets again.

"Sir, you know we come before you without fear, yet again you test us, sir. Why, sir?" George answered calmly with a question.

The Senior Viceroy lifted his hands, and the other three Senior Viceroys stepped back from him. George and the others could see him more clearly now. He was old, as old as any one they had ever seen. Yet he looked strong.

"Come here, Cadet Hawkins," the center Senior Viceroy said, inviting George to the center of the white circle of light with him.

"No, sir," George replied firmly, staring down the center Senior Viceroy.

"What?" the Senior Viceroy said, agitated as no one ever refused his requests.

"Sir, you know we are strong only because we are together. If I step forward, I will no longer be connected to Andy; and he and I will break our word to the Galactic council. That will not be done by us," George replied, nodding to Andy.

"You are most clever, Cadet Hawkins. Still, it will not spare your lives or the lives of your triad," the center Senior Viceroy threatened them again.

"Again you taunt us with death, sir. It is a sign of weakness. We all know—full well—the price of entering the council corridors uninvited, to say nothing of the council chambers, is death. We have been taught of the great power and wisdom of the Galactic council, sir. Yet with absolute power there comes great responsibility. While our team could boast many great accomplishments," George replied.

"Oh, here it comes. Now you will tell me how you saved us and therefore deserve great rewards and special treatment," the center Senior Viceroy said, snapping at George and cutting his words off mid-sentence.

George smiled. "Yes, sir. I will continue, our greatest accomplishment is our smallest, our most unnoticed of all accomplishments. While what you say is true, it is obvious and expected. It is the small and unseen that is the true treasure, sir," George said, leading the center Senior Viceroy down a new path, not falling for his treachery.

"So, speak and tell us what task have you done that we have not seen," the center Senior Viceroy taunted again.

"Hope and change, sir. A people can lose their way, becoming mired under the weight of their own bureaucracy. We bring hope and change to life in its many and varied forms. It is one of the most precious of gifts. Just as with each generation, the Galactic council grows and learns from the successes and mistakes of past generations. Courage and compassion in the face of great danger, sir," George said, lowering his head.

"You will all be separated and your triad destroyed," the center Senior Viceroy said, threatening the cadets a third time.

Nearly instantaneously their team thought the same words. "It's a test."

George smiled and continued with his thought unstopped by the center Senior Viceroy's threats. "We posses neither the power of the galaxies nor the wisdom of the ages; however, to every question we know there is an answer, to every problem, a solution. At times, we do not like the answer and work hard to find an alternate solution. Our existence is defined by the choices we make along our path. Now is a defining moment in time, sir," George replied, lowering his head again.

Together his team stepped back behind the ring of the three Senior Viceroys.

"And the choices have you made today, what do your choices say to you, Cadet Hawkins?" the center Senior Viceroy questioned. He was still trying to threaten George and his team.

"This defining moment in time is not for us, sir. It is for you, sir," George replied, finally understanding what Max had said and why he had used the word compassion as the team repeated their oath.

"Peace is our path, it unites all beings. Courage is our character, it joins us as one. Harmony is our nature, it connects us to the universe. Strength is our will, it protects us all. Four parts come together to heal the fear of the past and present, to start anew with peace, courage, harmony and strength," they whispered, yet they all knew the Galactic council members heard the words.

George and the others stepped backwards together, again and again, until they were at the back wall again. Anna made an archway, and Emily opened the door with ease. The cadets walked out into the council caves and then to the council corridors in silence as Anna and Emily opened the door and archways again. As they left the last council corridor behind them, they stopped in the blue cadet sector corridor and rested.

"What did Max say, George? I know he said something to you," Andy pressed, having figured out why George looked so odd before and not caring who was listening anymore.

"Before we entered the council chamber, he said he could not help us, but to remember we are stronger together and not to forget our compassion," George replied seriously.

"You didn't ask the Viceroy to stop hurting the others, why?" Gus asked, knowing he had to understand all that had just happened in the Galactic council chamber.

"Yes, he did Gus," Emily answered kindly.

"How, I don't see it?" Gus pressed harder, this time knowing it was important to understand the cryptic language.

"When I saw the center Senior Viceroy, Gus, I knew asking him for anything was the wrong thing to do. People ask him for things every day, it was what he was expecting us to do," George answered.

"Three times he threatened us with death," Andy added.

"They were tests, weren't they?" Gus said, beginning to understand.

"Yes, they were tests, Gus," George replied, nodding his head. "The center Senior Viceroy has lost his way, he only needed to be reminded of the path and his choices," he added.

"That was why we left, wasn't it? We reminded him of his choices, his chosen path, and compassion made us leave so as not to rub his face in it. That we had noticed something and now he had work to do." With each word Gus said, his mind was opening to the true understanding of the word compassion.

He was happy he had asked. This time he didn't feel foolish, only happy he understood.

"I couldn't have said it better myself," Andy added, grinning.

Chapter 20

TO LEARN SPORT

The cadets placed their hands together and reached out to Pete, Frank, Toma, and the others. They found them in the CORE hospital; how odd, since they were not there before they had entered the council chamber.

"We are coming," George replied, and Gus lowered their link.

Anna called up a map and figured out where they were using her triangulation method.

"I need to learn that," Andy whispered.

"Andy, you need to stay awake in training class," Emily said, grinning. Andy blushed as they walked quickly through the cadet sector corridors.

"We cannot ever tell anyone we were there," Gus signed as they picked up speed now, running through the captain corridors.

"You are right, Gus, it would be wrong," Emily agreed.

"Sometimes people do the right thing and tell no one. They save a life or they call for help and do not need their fifteen minutes of fame," Anna whispered.

"They act simply because it is the right thing to do at the time," Sara said, adding to the thought.

They all nodded and Anna opened an archway in front of them. Emily opened the door and they slowed down and walked through the doorway and into the CORE hospital again.

"It's been three weeks since we were here," Andy muttered, thinking they should sleep in the CORE hospital to save time.

"At least we are not patients this time," Anna whispered, adding to his words.

In the bright lights of the hospital corridor, his team did not look that well. They were thinner and paler than before their rotation had started. How was that possible, when only three weeks earlier they had been healed and looking good? George wondered as they hurried along.

The other officers they met in the corridors lowered their heads to them or stopped and waited for them to pass as they hurried through the CORE hospital corridors quickly.

George led them into the hospital room that Anna had pointed out and stopped. Before them were eighteen glowing yellow tubes. Even though Pete, Frank, Toma, and the others were returned, they were nearly dead. The medics came up to the cadets and then immediately left the room as if in fear. George and the others hardly noticed.

They walked up to the first tube and Sara made a small yellow healing sphere. George reached out with his mind and touched the cadet that had first kicked them out of the alcove on Asteria station. Somehow, he reached out again and touched the Thorean cadets on Indus station and the Earth cadets of Jupiter station. George did not know that Pete's dad was helping him again, teaching him how to use the resources around him.

"We need you to share your energy, it will be long and hard. You will need to eat immediately after our link is ended. Will you share?" he asked in their minds. Without knowing, he had formed an enormous link across the galaxy.

Without hesitation, energy started to come to George and his team. Gus, Anna, Sara, Emily, and Andy started to regulate the flow to George and Sara. Sara's yellow sphere turned white and encompassed one yellow tube at a time and their team. One by one, George opened the tubes as their triad regained consciousness. The hours passed, and finally, they were all conscious and sleeping, although not fully healed.

George thanked the cadets of the link and told them to eat immediately. They were not to rest until they could eat no more. Gus closed the link out in huge groups. An amazing feat, George thought. The control was enormous, yet he made it appear easy—like a skilled acrobat in a circus. Until you see a common person up on a platform with them, you forget how good the performers really are.

How George had learned to reach out to so many cadets across the galaxy was a mystery to Andy. It is a question Andy would need to ask another day. Pete looked up and saw only Inner Circle officers and bowed his head a little. George crinkled his forehead.

"Pete it's us, Andy, Emily, Anna, Sara, and Gus," George signed.

Pete smiled and fell back asleep.

Gus and Andy closed all of the yellow healing tubes as George concentrated and chairs rose from the floor of the hospital room. They sat down to stay with their triad. A medic appeared at the door, and George motioned her in. She carried bowls of medium-brown cereal for the now sleeping captains. At first, George thought the food was for them, but she gave him the oddest look and left with the food.

Minutes later she returned with an even darker shade of brown cereal and gave it to the cadets who looked like Inner Circle officers. Gus was the first to bite into the cereal when the medic left. It was bitter, not sweet like the cereal the cadets ate—even more bitter than the CORE officers' cereal they had tasted on their second rotation. Yet this time, they felt their energy and strength grow with each bite.

"You were right, Emily, the cereal does connect everyone. This cereal must have a lot of the enzyme that helps us all connect to each other," George signed.

Emily nodded.

"And the bitter taste?" Andy asked, choking down another bite.

"Bonus land," Gus said, cracking a joke. The cadets all laughed.

They slept in shifts for the next five days, not leaving Pete and the others' sides. On the fifth day, Pete and Frank were the first to stir and wake. CORE doctors and medics rushed in and slid the captains out of the yellow tubes and laid them on the standard white hospital beds. By then the story of Inner Circle officers taking care of captains was running rampant across Asteria station.

Pete opened his eyes, "Sir?" he whispered, his voice weak and raspy.

"No, Pete, it's us—Andy, Emily, Anna, Sara, and Gus," George signed.

"They will punish you if they find out," Pete signed.

"Maybe, but it was an accident, and now we have to play it through until it is done," George signed.

"Why are we alive?" Pete signed.

"We were left for dead," Frank added.

"Because all the cadets on Asteria, Indus, and Jupiter stations shared their strength and energy and you lived," George replied in sign.

"We will be OK now, you must leave. Do not return, not even as red cadets. Go back to training. Change out of sight, that's an order," Pete signed, laying his head back down.

George signed to the others and they all stood up, leaving Pete, Frank,

Toma, and their teams. George nodded to the CORE doctors and medics in the room and led his team into the small room off the side of the main hospital room. As the door closed, Anna made an archway and door, and Emily opened it.

The cadets slipped through into the cave behind the wall. Andy set off a flash of white light for effect, and they disappeared like Inner Circle officers did. Well, at least it looked like they did. Andy slipped out a staff and made a yellow sphere to illuminate the cave. It was the first time they had been alone.

"Why did they think we were Inner Circle officers?" Andy asked.

"I can see CORE officers since we were without our red stripes—maybe, but where did they get Inner Circle officers from?" Sara said.

Emily slid her hand over George's chest and a second award appeared next to the red and white star award. It was a yellow circle with a white star centered over the circle. Like the previous award, it was no bigger than 1 inch or 25 mm in diameter. Emily slid her hand over everyone and the award appeared on all of them.

"Anna, what is it?" George asked.

Anna was searching her pad the instant she saw the first new symbol on George. They started to walk on in silence. Emily started searching with Anna as Sara led the way.

"Got it," they chorused together and stopped in the cave at the same time. Anna and Emily laughed.

"Go ahead," they each said at the same time and then laughed even harder.

"Yes?" George said, smiling, and both cadets laughed again. "Will one of you please start?" George said, motioning to one and then the other.

They were all waiting for them to start again at the same time. Anna giggled, motioning to Emily.

"The award is one of the highest commendations in the CORE. The field of yellow symbolizes honor, the giving of your life to save others. As before, the white star, now laid over the field of yellow, symbolizes compassion to share with others all that you have," Emily said as they walked along the cave.

They stopped and stood in the cave in silence, hardly believing what Emily had read. Time passed slowly as the words sunk in to their minds. George nodded and Emily slid her hand back over everyone's chests and arms, hiding the awards and revealing their red stripes again.

"We are at our sleeping room. It should be about time to leave and go to our first training class," Sara said, pointing to the cave wall.

Anna made an archway and door in the cave wall. George raised his hand and motioned for Andy to go first.

Andy concentrated. "Empty."

Emily opened the door, and the cadets slipped into their sleeping room. Andy went to the door and listened again to the corridor that was alive with cadets on their way to training. George and the others stepped out, not knowing what day it was. They saw a team they had been in all of their training classes with and followed them through the corridor to Colonel Moawk's training dome. They followed the other red cadets into the dome and lined up in columns.

The dome was filled with the vines of Sport. The girls sighed. It was not their favorite activity. Over the last five days, the cadets had regained their strength, and the boys were smiling, wanting to swing on the vines today. Colonel Moawk slid down one of the center vines to the dome floor.

"You have all trained hard, and today we will have a real tournament. The rules of Sport apply. Any team intentionally inflicting harm to another team will be disqualified from the tournament. Let us begin. Cadets, ascend!" Colonel Moawk yelled.

The cadets ran to the dome walls and climbed the dome structure as the floor of the dome turned to Slugamie. George and the others started to run. Emily tripped, flipped, and rolled, standing up again and touching the Slugamie in the process, asking it to follow them instead of overtake them. They reached the dome structure one step ahead of the Slugamie, and the other red cadets cheered.

The cadets did not know Emily had asked the Slugamie to slow down. Still the cheer was a very un-Calshene thing to do; yet it was good of the cadets, they thought. The other cadets may not have noticed George's team had not been in training for the last week; however, Colonel Moawk did, and he was not pleased by their week of absences. George was sure there would be some sort of grueling work they would have to do to get back on the Colonel's good side. Andy wondered if the Colonel had a good side, really.

The Colonel called two teams to the center of the training dome. They climbed across the vines and hung on them, all at the same level, facing each other team's cadets. Colonel Moawk threw the Sport ball high into the air, and the cadets dove wildly for the ball, crashing into each other. The team on the right caught the ball and flailed it wildly towards the opposing team's goal. It hit one of their team members in the head, knocking him off his vine and sending him crashing into the Slugamie below. The Slugamie softly caught the cadet as the ball ricocheted off the edge of the goal, spinning and then falling to the floor of the dome. The remaining cadets hung on their vines, not even chasing the ball as it fell.

Andy and Gus looked at each other with surprise.

"It was a free ball, why didn't they go after it?" Gus whispered.

George glanced and their whispering stopped.

Colonel Moawk reappeared in the ceiling of the dome and dropped the Sport ball again. With one team short a member, the opposing team made a quick goal and the match was over. The tournament was not a timed match, it was sudden death; the team that scored first won the right to move forward in the tournament. Two new teams climbed out onto the vines and faced each other as before.

"Why are they all at the same level?" Sara asked.

Sport was not Sara's favorite activity; however, she understood the advantages of the different levels and the disadvantage of all starting on one level.

One of the teams that played in the second match was one of the teams that had jumped George and the others in the corridor outside Major Gatte's stellar navigation training two weeks before. They made quick work of the opposing team and sent two of the cadets hurling into the soft Slugamie below.

Andy was sure it was a cheap shot that had done it. He wanted to see their move again so he could plan a counter move. The next two teams moved into place. The second team that had ambushed them was now hanging across from a team that looked terrified.

"They're scared," Emily whispered.

"Probably should be, if their opponent plays anything like the last team," Gus whispered.

"I hope so, I need to see that move again," Andy answered, without looking away from the field of vines.

George leaned back and concentrated, helping focus his team's thoughts. Sure enough, the second team made the same move. They were not as slick and Colonel Moawk saw the illegal move as two of the opposing team members crashed into the Slugamie, and the other team scored. Andy had what he needed; George smiled, he knew.

The Colonel disqualified the team for their conduct, and they started running laps around the edge of the dome floor. The Colonel called George's team, and the last team up for the last match of the first round of play.

George signed "start level" as they swung into position.

Colonel Moawk threw the Sport ball into the air and Andy leapt into the air, landing on a new vine and catching the ball, then intentionally swinging out of the way so as not to collide with one of the opposing team members. He threw the ball to George as he rolled down a vine. He passed the ball to Sara, and she spun, flipping the ball to Emily.

Emily seemed to fly through the air, tossing the ball to Anna. She spun gracefully around her vine, sliding down to Gus's level before she handed him the ball. Gus stared at Anna and set the ball in the goal behind his back for the score. Quick and easy work, all six cadets touched the ball.

"Five points," Andy whispered as they returned to their perches on the side of the dome.

Remember the first time we saw Colonel Hawks swing down from the dome structure?" Emily signed.

"It was amazing," George signed back.

"Now it is so commonplace," Sara thought.

The winners of the first two games faced off in the middle of the dome. The team that had jumped them in the corridor was tough. This time when they ran their plays against the other team, Andy ran the counter moves in his head. He had their team swing up and across, depending on which side the other team would attacked from. Andy glanced at George and Gus. Gus raised their link, and the cadets listened to Andy's plan. Twice in the match, the team that had jumped them knocked players to the ground.

With their link raised, they followed Andy's plans. The expected team won. Colonel Moawk called up George's team and the other team that had won earlier.

Again George signed "start level" as they took their positions on the vines.

The Sport ball was dropped from the ceiling, and the opposing team caught and threw the ball directly for the goal. They did not hand off the ball to each other, they only threw the ball for the goal. Anna easily caught the ball and flipped over backwards, tossing the ball to Emily. Emily twisted on the vine, sliding down to George's level and nearly handing him the ball.

George threw the ball up to Sara and she bounced it off to Andy. Andy leaned back and then pulled forward as one of the opposing team members leapt at him, missing him and missing the vine to stop his fall. George dove and caught the cadet a few feet above the Slugamie. Andy handed the ball to Gus as all eyes were on George. Gus set the ball into the goal for the win again.

The final match was set. It was George's team against the team that had ambushed them in the corridor. The Colonel gave George and his team a five

minute rest before starting the final Sport match. The opposing team swung
out onto the vines all at the same level positions, waiting for the five minutes
to pass and wasting precious strength and energy.

The Colonel whistled in Thorean to George and his team when the five
minutes was up. Quickly, they left their perches on the dome walls. George
glanced and shook his head as they swung into place on the vines, then nodded toward Andy. This was Andy's game now, and he was to call the plays.
George's team took their positions on the vines. This time they were high
and low on the vines. The leader of the other team snarled at their new tac-
tic. George smiled, nodding in response.

Colonel Moawk dropped the Sport ball from the ceiling, and the opposing team dove for the ball. Their second tried to knock into Emily as all eyes
were on the ball; nonetheless, Emily was ready and rolled back with her legs
firmly wrapped around her vine. Quickly, she jumped over to the next vine.
flipping past the other team's second. Missing his hit, he missed his next vine
and grasped wildly in the air for a new vine. By the time he got a firm hold
on another vine, he was falling too fast and slid nearly to the floor of the
dome, blistering his hands to stop his fall.

George was low and caught the ball. He swung up and released the ball almost immediately. The leader of the opposing team made a late hit on George,
hoping to knock him out of play. Instead, George grabbed onto their leader,
and they both fell into the Slugamie and out of play.

The opposing team was now without a leader and George's team still had
theirs. Andy caught the throw and tossed the ball to Anna. She knew where
to swing and flipped off the vine, landing next to Sara and literally handing the
ball to her. One of the opposing team members dove on the two cadets and the
ball. Anna and Sara pushed off each other's feet and they flew apart as the
other cadet came sailing through between them. She was going at too fast to
catch another vine. Nearly at the top of the dome supports, Gus flipped end
over end and grabbed her by the collar of her uniform her suit neck edge and
pulled her back from the dome support, spinning her over to another vine.

"Get your hand off of me, Earther!" she yelled.

"You're most kindly welcome," Gus said, smiling as he shinnied back up his
vine.

Sara threw the ball to Gus as she spun around her vine and climbed up to
his level. Gus glanced at Andy. Andy nodded, and Gus rocketed the ball into
the opposing team's goal. Their second dove forward to stop the goal and
ended up stuck in the goal with the ball, scoring the point.

On the ground, the leader of the opposing team gasped then spun around, taking a wild swing at George with his fist. George leaned back, and the cadet's swing sailed him into the dome wall.

"Are you OK?" George asked kindly.

The lead cadet snarled and spun around again, launching another fist at George. George ducked, and the cadet stumbled forward into the Slugamie. It curled around him, holding him in place. George glanced up at Emily, shaking his head. She smiled and placed her hand on the dome wall. Kindly, she asked the Slugamie to release the lead cadet as she slid down her vine, dragging her hand on the dome wall to the waiting Slugamie below. Slowly, it slipped off the cadet's struggling body. When he broke free, he ran at George. Easily, George flipped up and over him. The team slid down their vines to help George, although he didn't look like he needed much help. The lead cadet missed George again and ran headlong into Gus.

Gus braced for the impact and grabbed the cadet's head with one hand and his shoulder with the other, using his own weight against him. Gus flipped the lead cadet over onto his back and pinned him to the ground with his hand. Gus leaned forward.

"Andy would destroy you if George would let him. But there will be inquiries, documentation to fill out, depositions and all kinds of other paperwork that has to be done, very messy for a Calshene cadet station. Me, I'm more subtle, no one will ever know," Gus whispered coldly.

"Get off me, Earther," the leader said meanly.

"And I was so hoping you would apologize," Gus said politely as he wiped his hand off on his own backpack and then lightly tapped the lead cadet's collar before releasing him.

"What's going on, cadets?" Colonel Moawk yelled, walking up to the cadets as the lead cadet got himself up off the ground.

"Nothing, sir, only a slight disagreement on tactics, sir," George replied formally, straightening up.

"Well?" the Colonel pressed.

"Nothing," the lead cadet replied, brushing off his suit.

"What!" the Colonel yelled, shaking dust off the dome walls.

"Nothing is going on, sir. It is like he said, a disagreement on tactics, sir," the other lead cadet replied weakly, straightening up.

The Colonel knew they were both lying. He and everyone else in the dome had seen what had really happened.

"Class dismissed, except you two. You both owe me an hour's worth of laps, starting now!" the Colonel said firmly.

The other cadets and the team of the opposing leader started to leave the dome. George and his team started to run around the dome.

"What's with them, sir?" the lead cadet said snidely, motioning toward George and his team.

"They are a team, they stick together," the Colonel said, motioning him to start running.

He turned and yelled for his team. They waved back and blew him off as they walked out the door. The cadet leader ran up next to George.

"You're going to pay for this, Earther," he threatened, snarling.

"All things are possible; however, some are more probable than others," George answered cryptically.

Andy overheard George's reply and smiled. He understood what George had said. He related George's words to Gus and food, although there are infinite possibilities of things to do in a kitchen, the highest probability is that you are there to eat or make something to eat and while it is possible, it is less likely you are there to play Sport.

Anna saw Andy's smile and picked up the pace.

"No, no, that wasn't why I smiled," he muttered, yet it was too late.

Soon the cadets were nearly a blur, running to be free. Colonel Moawk whistled loudly, and the cadets slowed and came to a stop.

"Dismissed," he said, leaving the dome.

"Who are you? Mutants?" the other cadet leader asked, breathing hard as he left the dome.

"Well that's a new one, mutants!" Andy said, laughing.

"Funny," Gus added, shaking his head and high-fiving Andy.

Even Emily, Sara, and Anna had to laugh.

Chapter 21

SILENT EVIL

No one was waiting for them in the corridor when they left the training dome. They had half hoped to see Pete or Nick out of the hospital; they were a little sad. The team wanted to tell them what had been going on since they had left the hospital and before.

"We need to call," Sara signed as they walked through the red cadet corridors.

Emily opened an empty classroom and the others followed her inside. Emily sent a message on the computer system, and Gus made the link for George and Andy to reach out for their triad. There was no answer, only empty space. The cadets were confused.

"They are always there," Gus said, confused and a little concerned.

"Maybe they are not out of the hospital yet. Try Grandfather or Max, George," Emily said confidently as she quickly added them to her list for her computer message.

The cadets stood in a close circle, arm over arm and concentrated on finding the Senior Viceroy or Max. Yet there was only silence.

"Can you reach out to anyone?" Anna asked surprised they were not close by.

On Mahadean, George and Andy had found peace in the universe, yet now they found only emptiness.

"Is someone messing with us?" Andy asked, trying to make a cryptic connection.

"I don't know, we are never alone," George answered as puzzled as the others.

"What could we have done now that we are being punished for?" Sara asked, a little infuriated.

"You would have thought saving the entire Galactic council from the Mahadean would have made up for any rules we broke recently," Emily said, yet she wondered what rules they had broken.

"Maybe the Galactic council found out about us being mistaken as Inner Circle officers in the CORE hospital," Gus said, looking for a reason.

"No, this is something else. Someone who has been trying to stop us from the very beginning," George said, saying his thoughts out loud to see if his team had any ideas.

They sat in the classroom for hours, trying to make a link with anyone. Was this to be the rest of their existence, this awful emptiness? Was this what Grandfather meant when he said the Galactic council would put them in isolation? George and the others stared at each other, as if lost and without focus. Their triad had been with them for two years, and they were never alone. Gus lowered their link, and the cadets left the classroom.

They ended up at the dining hall and sat at their regular table. A cadet from the next table over leaned back in his chair.

"Hey ah, thanks for beating them today, they have been bullying us all rotation," the lead cadet said.

"You can learn to stop them too. We can teach you how," George replied, offering to help.

"Ah no, no we can't, but thanks anyway," he said, shaking his head and going back to his table.

On and off during the whole meal other cadets sent notes thanking them. Each time George offered to help them stand up to the bullying team, but no one would. They had convinced themselves they were too weak and couldn't do it. They were afraid they would fail and so they had failed before they had even started.

Somberly, the team left the hall and headed down the corridor to their evening training. Their team was sad and lonely. George could not focus his thoughts or help calm the team's fears and loneliness. They entered a classroom and brought up their three training holographic displays. Emily sent another message through the computer system to Pete, Frank, and Toma.

George and Sara were listening to protocol lessons and Emily and Anna were studying star charts. Gus and Andy were studying the Thorean language. George, Sara, Andy, and Gus fell asleep. Emily and Anna lasted a little longer. There was something familiar about the star charts, something they were missing and could not yet see.

In his dreams, George reached out and again found only empty space. Sadness filled their hearts and minds. The next morning they awoke in the same classroom with their lessons still running. George turned them off and woke everyone up to go and get breakfast. Emily sent a third computer message. This time she spammed their entire triad and every Viceroy and Senior Viceroy they knew. She didn't understand, someone had to be out there.

For seven days, the cadets went from training to lunch to training to dinner to more training. No words or ideas crossed their minds. They were sad and losing focus, the fun and adventure was gone. Message after message was sent and not answered. After studying on the seventh night, they went back to their sleeping room and laid down instead of eating. It was a mistake. It weakened their link with each other.

The center Senior Viceroy of the Galactic council may have thought he was teaching the cadets a lesson for breaking the rules and protocols that had stood for a millennium; however, it was the mistake evil was waiting for. With their connection to the outside blocked and their internal link weakening, the cadets were vulnerable to be influenced. The Galactic council's center Senior Viceroy would not listen to the change that was happening around him. Even the Galactic council's capture by the Mahadean and rescue by the very cadets he was now punishing would not open his mind to change. In his arrogance, he had made a serious mistake by separating the cadets from the others and isolating them from all those supporting them. George and his team would soon be ripe for the picking and evil was ready.

A few hours later they woke up, still in their sleeping room. For some reason George's only thoughts were of the prophecy scroll; a seed planted by evil itself. He wanted to finish reading it, and he no longer had any respect for the Galactic council or their old obsolete rules and protocol.

"Who's up for the library?" George asked, rolling over on his bed in mid-afternoon.

The others nodded. Emily touched their sleeves and their stripes disappeared. Anna made an archway and door in the floor, and Emily opened it with a look. The cadets jumped down three levels. The fall was oddly slow, and they landed softly on the balcony of the library again. The three story fall should have injured them, yet it didn't. The cadets didn't even notice. With the others gone, evil now protected them.

"Can you call Max?" Andy asked George, looking around the library.

"Nope," George said, shaking his head, not actually caring anymore.

The cadets walked around the balcony and slid down the long spiral staircase railing to the main reading floor. They walked through the rows and rows of wooden book shelves, scanning the titles of the books and scrolls on each shelf before them. Each cadet pulled out scrolls and books that fit their fields of interest. Their librarian came around the corner after helping another officer, and George waved her off. She stared at them oddly and then turned and left quickly, leaving the cadets alone. She sent a message for help to the CORE officers, yet no one came; evil didn't want any interference now.

Sara chose some old scrolls on medicines and poisons, while Gus chose several books on chemical combination in food and more poisons. Anna gathered old scrolls on navigation, first contact and annihilation of entire races and civilizations. Emily found books on computer viruses and ways to devastate entire civilizations based on technology-driven systems. Andy found ancient scrolls on the control and use of red spheres, Chen Lo, and the destruction of planets using their own energy against them. George waved his hand and the prophecy scroll appeared before him.

They all sat down on the old leather couches and soft leather chairs to read their new treasures of destruction. Without any Rosetta stones or translations, the cadets were reading texts and symbols they had never seen before—slipping ever further from their chosen path. They stayed all afternoon and then late into the night—never eating or renewing their energy. Evil needed them weak and vulnerable or they could not be easily separated from their triad.

Without Max to prevent him, George read the whole prophecy scroll. It was as if their entire lives had been laid out for them. Regardless of the circumstances, what had happened was in the prophecy scroll. The saving of a Jupiter cadet station, their rescue of the Thorean cadets far from home, the saving of the sector Galactic council, and the freeing of the multitudes of Mahadean slaves.

Ahead of the team of the prophecy lay many more trials, difficulties, and finally death at the hands of evil. Further into the scroll George stopped and stared. There was some sort of faint split in the path written onto the edge of the scroll. The new split showed great comfort and sharing. The trials were easier and the team of the prophecy did not die. The path looked inviting to George, something he should consider for his team.

Their whole team could share in the good fortune. The path was peaceful, and they did not have to make any decisions. Everything was laid out for them. How excellent that would be, not having to choose anymore. The thoughts enticed George as he lost himself in each new section of the scroll.

With every hour they stayed in the library reading, their connection to each other slowly faded away. They were truly alone, connected to no one. The translucent librarian came back from time to time to check on them. George waved her away each time. She sent message after message to the CORE officers for help, but no one ever came. The cadets read on and on late into the night. Their bodies and spirits were growing weaker and weaker as they slipped further and further from their chosen paths.

Emily and Anna downloaded a hundred scrolls and texts into their pads. Andy practiced crushing objects around the library with a single look. George's mind raced out of control to the outer reaches of the universe, to the place of darkness that he had never been able to see into before. It was warm and comforting. It seemed to be calling them each of them by name. Gus and Sara read poison recipe after recipe, planning the destruction of all who would keep them from their new path.

After a week in the hospital, Pete, Frank, Toma, and the others could no longer take it. They were now captives of the CORE doctors and escape was their only option. They had been held against their will long enough. On the eighth morning, with the medics out of the room, Jennifer and Rachael opened an archway into the caves. Quickly, they ran from the CORE hospital room. Pete, Frank, and the others knew they had very little time before the doctors called the CORE guards to find the escaped captains.

They ran though the caves and left the CORE hospital far behind. Jennifer and Rachael opened an archway into a classroom in the captains sector and they all hurried inside. Karmen locked the doors as Pete and Frank reached out to find George and his team. They were gone. They made another link and reached out—nothing, only emptiness and despair. They were never alone, yet they were now!

"Max, where are you?" Frank yelled, yet there was only silence.

"Grandfather where are you?" Pete yelled, yet again only silence.

"No cadets, no Viceroys, no Max. What has been done?" Pete yelled out loud.

"I have more than a hundred messages from Emily," Jennifer said, shocked as the captains spun around and stared at her.

"They have been looking for us for the last seven days," Darri said and then gasped.

"They are alone, cut off from all of us," Sheta added, worried that they were even safe.

"Look, they have sent messages to everyone and no one has answered. How is this possible?" Lucita said, staring at the messages with Jennifer and Darri.

"Who would do this to cadets?" Kate said, stunned by their messages.

The three seconds stared at each other.

"I know who has this much arrogance!" Nick said angrily.

"Who?" Karmen asked, spinning around and facing the three seconds.

"The Galactic council, that's who!" Niels yelled.

"I know how to get to the Galactic council chambers," Cal whistled, looking at Toma. With the holographic bars on, the Thorean's looked human.

"How do you know?" Tillie asked, staring at Cal.

"I just do!" Cal repeated angrily. Cal was fearless and the Galactic council had messed with their triad for the last time.

"Then we go now!" Frank said, holding his arm out for Cal to lead; his calm and even temper was gone.

"Where are we going?" Maria asked as Jennifer opened the door to the corridor, and they began to run at speed through the corridors.

"To die," Han replied half-heartedly.

"Not again," Darri said, shaking her head.

"The last time was no fun at all," Lucita said, joking and yet equally angry inside.

"Well, this time should be worse," Niels replied seriously.

"The Galactic council has made their last mistake!" Nick yelled as they ran.

Toma glanced back and their chatter ceased. Ahead of them, Cal whistled and Marie made an archway and door. Kate opened the door as Cal got to the wall. They slid into the narrow, dimly lit corridor and never slowed their speed.

Another archway, another door and they were suddenly in front of the Galactic council chamber door. Sheta, Jennifer, and Kate touched the chamber door like Emily had; however, it did not move. Toma frowned and Cal, Niels, and Nick grabbed onto the edges of the door frame beneath the arch and ripped the sliding doors from the cave wall. They threw the doors down the corridor. The thunderous crash caught the Viceroys in the Galactic council chamber off guard. It was not as elegant an opening option as Emily's, yet it was equally effective.

The stunned Viceroys stared at the triad as they marched quickly into the Galactic council chamber. Toma, Pete, and Frank led the way to the center of the small chamber. They moved the stunned Inner Circle officers out of their way as they stepped passed the Viceroys, standing on the nine white light circles with their fathers standing on three of the nine glowing white circles. The teams stopped behind the center three white circles glowing on the ground, encircling the four Senior Viceroys.

"Step out, Senior Viceroy Petrosky!" Pete said firmly, ordering his grandfather off of one of the three glowing white circles.

"Step out, Senior Viceroy Heto!" Toma said firmly, ordering his grandfather off the second of the three glowing white circles.

"Step out, Senior Viceroy Margo!" Frank said firmly, ordering the last Senior Viceroy off the last of the three glowing white circles.

The two grandfathers and Senior Viceroy Margo were stunned by the captains' actions. Abruptly, Rachael joined them into the Galactic council's link. Instantly, the Inner Circle officers and the other Viceroys in the council chamber broke their link to the four Senior Viceroys. The captains were a blaze in a fiery red glow. Their frustration with the council's actions over the rotation was boiling to the surface. Nick, Niels and Cal physically lifted their grandfathers and Senior Viceroy Margo gently off of the three glowing white circles. Pete, Toma, and Frank took their place on the three white circles, surrounding the center Senior Viceroy. They knew the only Senior Viceroy strong enough to block everyone's thoughts of their triad was the center Senior Viceroy.

"Who do you think you are?" yelled the elder Senior Viceroy on the center glowing white circle.

"Step down!" Toma ordered firmly, staring the center Senior Viceroy directly in the eyes.

"You have deceived the Galactic council for the last time!"Frank yelled, staring at the Senior Viceroy as well.

"No! You will leave or you will die now!" the center Senior Viceroy yelled, threatening the triad.

"It is you who will leave. It is you who has tried to stop the team of the prophecy at every step along their journey!" Nick yelled, as he knew what was written in the prophecy.

"No! You will leave or you will die now!" the center Senior Viceroy yelled, repeating his threat.

"No! George and his team nearly died to save your lives from the Mahadean and then again to save ours. Where are they?" Toma yelled, demanding answers.

"They are here!" the Senior Viceroy replied flippantly, waving his hand and looking away.

"Where are they?" Frank and Pete repeated as abruptly as Toma.

The three other Senior Viceroys were stunned. What did the captains mean? Weren't the cadets in training on the station?

With his mind the center Senior Viceroy superficially reached out into the Galactic sea of thought and energy to find George and the other cadets. Yet, all he found was the emptiness he expected. The cadets thoughts were hidden from the council

"You are infected with the evil that hunts them!" Toma yelled, and the others gasped.

Without warning, Max suddenly appeared in the council chamber's inner circle with Pete, Frank, and Toma, glowing a bright white. This time he didn't solidify into a human form but stayed as a shimmering cloud of glowing white light. Most of the Viceroys and Inner Circle officers had never seen a being of white light before. They gasped, fell to one knee and lowered their heads in respect.

"What have you done?" Max yelled, his voice booming around the council chamber. His face glowed as blazing red as the captains'. Max knew what the center Senior Viceroy had done; however, he had to wait until the captains had discovered it before he could help.

"I was simply teaching them a lesson, that's all, for their disobedience!" the center Senior Viceroy replied indignantly, not dipping his head in respect or moving from the center glowing white light circle.

"Disobedience! I will never understand why the cadets saved your life or why you have chosen to treat them with such great disrespect!" Max yelled. "In your arrogance, you have condemned all the planets and galaxies to destruction. What evil could not succeed in doing, you have done for it, you fool!" he yelled, his voice shaking the walls of the council chamber.

Max knew the triad was not strong enough to stop the center Senior Viceroy. His mind was strong and well trained. They would need his help to show his deception. Max's white light cloud swirled high into the air above the council chamber filled with Senior Viceroys, Viceroys, and Inner Circle officers. As the cloud descended, it swirled around the Senior Viceroys and Viceroys weaving in and out. Slowly, the center Senior Viceroy's deception was revealed to all in the council chamber. They knew the truth of what the center Senior Viceroy had been blocking from their thoughts. How he had set up the cadet team each time for evil to attack, and finally, how he had isolated George and his team from their triad. Pete's grandfather, Toma's grandfather, and Senior Viceroy Margo reentered the link. The stepped onto the three white spots again.

"Max, if you would?" Pete's grandfather said, glancing at him and then twisting to face the center Senior Viceroy.

In an instant, the three Senior Viceroys and the center Senior Viceroy were gone in a flash of white light. Max solidified into human form and started to crumble to the ground. Pete's father lifted him up, placing him in the center of a single white light circle. Toma's dad, Pete's dad, and George's dad took the three empty white lights circles, as more and more Viceroys and Inner Circle officers moved in to support them. Max was still weak from the last time he had guided the energy of the universe in their sector. Now, he had to do it again, and he was not yet fully recovered.

"Pete, Frank, and Toma, go to the officers' library of Calshene—you will find your missing cadets there. The evil that hunts them, possesses them once again. The strength of your triad is their only hope," Max thought through the crush of raw Galactic energy.

The Senior Viceroys made it look easy to maintain the flow of energy throughout their Galactic sector. It was anything but easy. However, the Inner Circle Viceroys, Viceroys, and Max would maintain order until the Senior Viceroys returned. Pete and the others ran from the Galactic council chamber as more Viceroys entered to help balance the flow of energy.

"Karmen, path to the Calshene officers' library," Pete yelled as they ran down the corridor.

Karmen's face went white. "Pete, it's not. I can't," she stammered.

All of her life it had been a forbidden place, she couldn't do it.

"It is OK, right now we have full access," Pete said, cutting her off.

"Left, then right and the following turn," Maria piped in.

Maria was not Calshene and the fear of the officers' library did not bother her.

"Kate, ahead!" Maria yelled as the captains raced through the council caves, nearly knocking down every officer they met.

Nick, Cal and Niels carried small red spheres in the palms of their hands to intimidate anyone in their way. The archway and door appeared and opened as the captains ran through into the Calshene officers' library. The captains skidded to a stop on the upper balcony, catching the wooden railing.

Pete looked around in awe. The officers' library was exactly as Emily had described it to Pete two months earlier at the start of the rotation. Pete, Frank, and the others ran for the spiral staircase, while Toma and the other Thoreans spread their wings wide and jumped off the balcony, gliding down to George and the others who were sitting in the brown leather chairs on the floor of the main reading room. Toma approached George first and then backed away, motioning the others back with him.

Pete and the others ran up to Toma; however, Cal and the other Thoreans held them back until they could see what Cal and his team had seen in the cadets a few moments earlier.

"Are they lost?" Gabe asked, staring at the cadets.

"They look so weak," Tillie said, kneeling down in front of Emily.

She did not look up from her scroll to even acknowledge Tillie's presence.

"We need help," Sven said, his voice trailing off, not believing his own eyes.

"It's only us, there will be no help coming," Toma replied sadly.

"We are on our own," Pete added somberly, kneeling down in front of George with Frank.

"Can you and your team come with us, George?" Toma whispered.

George looked up, his eyes were black as coal and his face was pale. He looked weak.

"We can help you, brother," Frank added, holding his hand out to George.

"We have always come for you. We have rescued many races, yet when we called out for you in our loneliness, you did not answer. Now another has taken your place," he replied casually, returning to the scroll in his hands.

"We are here now. It is safer with us," Toma whispered calmly.

"You know us well. The other does not know you as we do," Pete said, trying to keep George talking and distracted.

Somehow they had to break the connection George and the others now had with evil. It was as if last year's rotation when George and Andy met evil on the battle cruiser was happening all over again. The captains were worried as they all tried to get the cadets to look up and talk with them.

"We were kept from you," Kate said softly.

"We could not see you," Sheta whispered.

"But we are here now," Frank said, nearly pleading with his little brother.

"Then you did not try hard enough to see us," George said angrily.

"We were there right in front of you," Anna said.

"Yet you did not see us or answer us when we called," Emily add, her eyes narrow slits.

"Now your sacred scroll tells us the truth and we have changed paths. It is easier now and we can rest," George said, his words fading away as his eyes returned to the scroll in his hands again.

Pete was frantic. He had to keep George talking. "Then we will make a link with you and rest too," he offered, reaching forward towards George.

"No!" George yelled firmly. The bookcases shook.

"The master does not want you," Andy said, his voice low and threatening.

"The master only wants us," Emily said harshly.

"We are the chosen ones," Sara added, boasting.

"The great team of the prophecy," George replied wickedly, chuckling with the other cadets.

With a simple flick of George's hand, Pete, Frank, Toma, and the others were thrown across the library's main reading room. Nick, Niels, and Cal flew through the air, landing on the large wooden bookcases and dragging the manuscripts and scrolls down on top of themselves.

Andy laughed a deep and ghoulish laugh as Karmen, Rachael, Jennifer, and Lucita landed on a large wooden reading table, shattering it under their weight. They tumbled to the ground among the pieces of broken wood as Gus and the others laughed cruelly. The other captains were scattered through the library as the bookcases teetered back and forth. The translucent librarians and officers rushed around, trying to stop the shelves from toppling over and helping the captains up. Emily flicked her wrist, and the scrolls flew from the shelves, burying Sheta, Kate, Darri, and Tillie again. They fell to the floor and the cadets laughed at the chaos.

"Will this team of the prophecy die, not fighting for their lives, but by slowly fading away into oblivion?" Nick whispered, as he straightened up and lifted a bookcase off of his back. "No. I will not allow it," he muttered, pausing for a moment to think.

"I have read the scroll of your great, all-seeing prophecy with my own eyes. Now the master knows the words in your precious scroll too," George yelled tauntingly, his eyes returning to the scroll again.

"Then evil has read a lie!" Nick yelled loudly, pushing aside a large leather chair that had landed between him and George. Boldly he strode across the library toward George, stopping only few feet in front of him.

George's head jerked up and his gaze met Nick's eyes. "How can you know this? You are nothing!" George yelled back, the room shaking with his words.

Nick held his ground. "I know the scroll of the prophecy you have in your hand is a fake. It is what you are supposed to read," Nick said, jabbing back equally hard. Nick was taking an enormous risk ,yelling at George. At any moment the evil within George could make him destroy Nick with only a thought. Evil was strong and getting stronger as George and the others became weaker.

"It is the scroll from the reading room desk. It is the real prophecy scroll!" George yelled, gritting his teeth, his coal-black eyes narrowing.

"No! It is not! The scroll in your hands looks exactly as you think it should look. It actually looks a little different to each of us, as there are holographic projectors in the Calshene officers' library," Nick replied, strong and forcefully. He was now edging forward, getting closer and closer to George.

"Now you lie! Do not take me for a fool, child!" George yelled.

However, this time his voice changed as he spoke. It was now raspy and cold as if another being was speaking through George's body. Suddenly Nick dropped to one knee.

"Master, forgive me. I did not know you were here. Please, master, please," Nick whispered, begging for his life and yet still moving ever closer to George as he sat in the chair.

Nick would say anything to free George from the evil with in him. His mind raced.

"Please, master, do not take my word for it, look at the scroll in your hands. Study it well. Do not the images appear to change as you look at them, master? It should be easy for someone of your skill, master," Nick said begging, carefully manipulating the evil being within George's body.

Nick was trying to get George to doubt what he had read and what the evil within him had told him. "Does not the scroll seem to be fitting more and more of the events in your lives the longer you read it?" Nick said, pressing harder, slowly sliding closer to George with his head lowered.

Evil was the master hiding within George, and Nick had to get evil to blink. Nick had never lied so much in his life. Behind him, out of George's view, Pete, Frank, and Toma were working hard at blocking Nick's true thoughts. Beads of sweat trickled off their foreheads as yellow spheres glowed between their palms, keeping their link strong and helping Nick hide his true thoughts.

Slowly, George looked down at the scroll again. He was so weak he could barely focus. His eyes played tricks on him—the scroll seemed to wave and change length in front of his eyes. The words blurred on the scroll, and he snarled. George threw the scroll down and it rolled a few feet across the floor, coming to a rest at Nick's feet.

"Where is the real scroll?" he yelled, leaping forward out of his chair and attacking Nick.

It was what Nick had been waiting for, a moment of doubt. Nick jumped up and George missed him, falling to the floor at Nick's feet. Nick grabbed George's shoulder as he struggled to get up off the ground. George suddenly stopped struggling and slumped back down on the ground. He was asleep.

Andy leapt up from his chair to defend George. However, Niels jumped out from behind him, quickly grabbing his shoulder from behind. His body thumped on the floor, asleep.

Gus, Anna, Sara, and Emily bolted from their chairs and rushed toward George and Andy to rescue them. With amazing speed, Sheta, Darri, Maria, and Tillie sprang up from behind the bookshelves and landed on the cadets backs, knocking them to the floor. Instantly, they, too, were asleep by a simple grasp on their shoulders.

Toma, Cal and the other Thoreans rushed in, flipping George, Andy, Gus, Anna, Sara, and Emily up over their shoulders. Pete's team led the way, racing up the spiral staircase of the officers' library to the balcony. Rachael and Karmen had archways and doors open into the hospital corridor, and the council caves before they reached the top of the stairs.

"Where to?" Toma whistled, rounding the last step onto the balcony.

"CORE hospital!" Pete whistled as the Thoreans passed Pete and the others before they even reached the door.

The Thoreans were faster and stronger than the humans and the Calshene. Now they needed their speed to save the cadets' lives. Pete called the CORE hospital on his pad and told them Toma and his team were coming. Pete turned his and Frank's teams toward the council chamber and Max. They ran at top speed to the council chamber. Frank and Pete feared what they might see—Max dying, crushed by the energy of the universe. By the time they entered the council chamber, it was crammed with nearly 50 Viceroys from across the galaxies.

"How is this possible?" Pete thought in their link.

"How long have we been in the library with George and his team?" Frank asked.

Max was crumpled over, barely standing on the center white light. He was dying and the Viceroys all knew it! The Viceroys thought there was nothing they could do. In that instance, Pete looked at Frank, they all knew what had to be done. Oddly, they all smiled; George and his team had rubbed off on them.

"It is a good day to die!" Niels said, repeating an old Earth phase.

They knew they had to add their strength to the Viceroys'. Just as George, Andy and Gus had sent energy to the captured Galactic council on the Mahadean starship and taught them how to make the energy themselves to keep them alive, now Pete, Frank, and the others knew they had to show the Viceroys another way. Together they would not control the energy of the universe in their sector of the galaxy but guide the energy and save Max's life.

Threading their way forward, Pete, Frank, and the other captains stepped passed the rings of white circles on the floor. Nick, Niels and the others stopped at the ring of three glowing white circles on the floor. Pete and Frank stepped into the center light and lifted Max up. The others surrounded Pete, Frank and Toma's fathers, holding their sons' shoulders—concentrating, calm and focused.

The energy of the universe was random and wild, not the calm and focused patterns they were accustomed to. The Viceroys were struggling, trying to control the energy of the universe. The captains saw the new way through Max's eyes and turned the Viceroys' path from controlling the energy to guiding the energy. A few hours passed, and Max looked up and grinned.

"You understand now. The energy is for all of us. It is only guided, not controlled," he whispered to their minds.

"We are learning from a most unusual group of young cadets," Pete answered, dipping his head.

Max straightened up, his strength returning as the flow of galactic energy calmed.

"How is this possible?" Frank asked in their link, not totally understanding Max's answer.

However, Max only smiled a broader smile. "Help has arrived."

It was a mystery they would need to solve for themselves. The captains had learned to open their minds to the possibilities of what they could do if they worked together, instead of being stuck in the past with old ways and old protocol.

"Go now, you have young cadets who need you more," Max whispered, pleased they were learning and changing.

The captains stepped out of the center white lights and Pete and Frank's dads took their place as they, too, now understood. Together they could guide the energy of the universe, at least in their sector of space.

Quickly, the captains backed out of the council's link and wove their way out of the council chamber. As each captain reached the door, they took off like a bolt of lightning, headed for the CORE hospital.

Toma had made a new link, and his team now surrounded George, Andy, Emily, Anna, Sara, and Gus in the glowing yellow healing tubes. Toma was reaching out to the cadets on Indus station, Jupiter station, and Asteria station. They needed energy, and the cadets had it. Toma followed the path George had used before when they were weak and their minds were beaten.

Pete, Frank and the others came skidding into the hospital room to join their triad's new link. Toma tilted his head and stared at Pete as he and the others entered the room. They seemed to glow with a white aura as they walked into the link without any help, an odd occurrence, even now. Pete and Frank glanced at each other and smiled.

"Help has arrived," Pete thought in the link.

"Who?" Toma asked, puzzled as to whom they were talking about.

"Don't know. Max only said help had arrived," Frank replied.

Toma nodded and the captains calmed their minds, following his lead. Toma was their leader when the triad was all together. Pete and Frank started to regulate the flow of energy for Toma and the others. Soon the cadets and the captains were glowing with a brilliant white light.

Only twice before had Frank, Pete, and Cal seen a light so bright. The first time, the Viceroys had removed the evil from George, Andy, and Cal on their last rotation. The second time, Max released the control of the energy of the universe on this rotation. The captains were focused only on the cadets in front of them and did not see the glowing beings of white light behind them in the hospital room—just like the last time their strength was needed. The captains were all concentrating on connecting all things together and sharing the energy of the galaxies.

The other beings of white light had been the help Max spoke of in the council chamber. They felt a great calm overtake their world, spreading out through the galaxies. Their connection was greater than the three cadet stations they had started with. Quickly, it spread to other cadet stations they had yet to visit. All across the galaxies the energy flowed and peace returned as evil was driven far away.

"Perhaps peace, hope, and a connection to all things was what the prophecy was really all about," Nick thought.

Toma, Pete, and Frank found one section of the galaxies they could not see into, and something seemed to guide them away, to another group of planets and another group of cadets. Quietly, the day passed into night.

Early the next morning, loud cracking sounds pierced the air as the yellow healing tubes broke apart, crashing to the ground in pieces. George, Andy, and the others stretched and sat up slowly from the healing tube cots. They looked strong and healthy again, no longer thin and weak. Evil was gone from them, fleeing the light.

"It is time to release the cadets," Sheta thought to Toma.

"Remind them not to sleep, they must all eat," Tillie thought kindly.

Toma smiled and nodded his head. Slowly, the energy in the room lowered and the bright white light faded away as the glowing beings in the back of the room disappeared. This time Rachael, Karmen, Maria, and Sheta rushed forward, hugging the stuffin' out of Emily, Sara, Anna, and the others. Pete, Frank, and Toma walked over to George.

"Report," Pete said kindly.

George glanced at Andy. Yes, this was their Pete, not the imposter from before.

"You all disappeared from us, sirs. We thought you were summoned to the Galactic council chamber, and they took you away to punish you for our actions again. Yet, we don't know what rules we broke this time. After you were gone, we broke into the Galactic council chamber to stop them from destroying you. Then you appeared here in the CORE hospital, and we found the energy of the cadets to save you, sir," George reported.

"You told us to leave and then we were alone—all alone. We couldn't make a link with anyone, sir," Emily added, looking down.

"We think now, the Galactic council or the center Senior Viceroy did this to punish us after we saved you, sirs," Anna added, piecing the events together.

"Then we were lost, sir," Gus said looking sad.

"When Max said 'we are never alone' we didn't understand how important our connection to everyone was out here in space, sir," Andy said, thinking.

"Now we know how important it is to stay connected," Anna whispered.

"We didn't know how much we were depending on all of you," Emily added sheepishly.

"We took you for granted until you were gone, sirs," Sara said, dipping her head.

"Without your help, without your strength and guidance, we slipped ever closer to evil, sir," George said, his heart heavy and sad.

Jennifer hugged Emily and Anna as Sheta and Darri wrapped their arms around the others. A huge hug followed as the whole triad crashed to the floor, laughing, happy to be together again.

George smiled and rolled his hand over, revealing a small glowing yellow sphere. The cadets and captains shared their thoughts and other events of the last few weeks. A few hours later, they got up from the floor and headed to the door to leave the CORE hospital room and return to the captain and cadet sectors.

"This will not happen again," Toma said firmly.

"We understand now," Pete said seriously.

"It will not happen again," Frank added confidently.

George stopped at the hospital room door and caught Pete's arm.

"We need Max, sir, and soon, sir," George whispered, his forehead crinkling.

"He will come, for now we will be here to help," Pete replied, wrapping his arm over George's shoulder and thinking he needed help focusing his thoughts after their ordeal in the Calshene library with pure evil.

"No, you don't understand, sir," George said cryptically, shaking free of Pete's arm.

"Maybe Nick can help," Pete said, staring at Nick and smiling trying to be helpful.

Nick overheard Pete and shook his head.

"I knew this little family secret would cause trouble one day. I asked not to be told, but no, my parents loved me and cared about me and wanted me to be educated and happy and healthy and…," Nick muttered on until Toma cut him off with a glance.

Nick paused. "Oh, yes, I'll help, I understand. I only thought I should whine for a few minutes. You know, take the opportunity when it's presented and all," Nick added, muttering some more.

"Nick!" they all said out loud, laughed and then laughed again.

Pete had misunderstood the urgency of George's request!

Chapter 22

TOO MUCH KNOWLEDGE

The station felt different the next day when they woke up in their sleeping room. All seemed calm and in harmony with the universe. It was as if good had washed over the station and their world was at peace. Pete was sitting at the silver table with six bowls of medium-dark brown cereal when George and Andy walked over to the table.

"What's this? Oh no! Why are we getting CORE officer cereal?" Andy asked, staring at the medium-dark brown cereal and rolling it around in the bowl.

"How did you know that this was CORE officer's cereal?" Pete asked, stunned that the cadets knew the difference.

"We have had CORE officer cereal before," Andy replied rather matter-of-factly.

"We have had the Inner Circle officer cereal too," Emily replied, sitting on the bench seat next to George and staring at George's cereal.

"The Inner Circle office cereal is wicked bad, though," Andy added, shaking his head.

"I suppose it's the amount of enzyme that is added to it that makes it taste so bitter," Sara said, sitting next to Andy.

"I just wish Gus had some of his purple liquid to make the CORE officer cereal taste better right now," Andy said with a giant grin, staring at Gus as he sat down on the end of the bench.

"Too bad. No purple liquid today unless we stop at a kitchen. My supplies are a little low after returning from Mahadean and all that has gone on for the last couple of weeks," Gus replied, reaching over to pick up his backpack.

Pete was always amused by his cadets. Just when he thought he knew something they didn't, they'd surprise him.

"Well tasty or not, it is what we are all eating now," Pete answered with a weak grin.

"You can't tell me you, Frank, Niels, Nick, Toma, Cal, and the others like this stuff. It's worse than the cadet brown cereal, and we could barely eat that," Andy grimaced, taking a bite.

"Who ordered this?" George asked, taking a bite too.

"Grandfather," Pete replied seriously.

"No more pie for him!" Andy said, joking as he took another bite and made happy yummy sounds as George pushed Andy for being goofy.

Pete slid a bowl to Emily and her face changed instantly from happy to grumpy. George and Andy laughed out loud.

"You should see your face, Emily," Andy said, teasing.

Pete looked down to hide his smile.

"It's just fine," Emily said, taking a bite and swallowing hard with a smiled glued to her face.

"What'd I miss?" Gus asked, looking up from his backpack.

Pete slid a bowl of cereal over to him. Gus looked down at the cereal and reached back into his backpack. He found a small pocket and pulled out a small bottle of orange liquid. By now, everyone was staring at Gus. With great flourish he poured a few drops of the orange liquid over his cereal and took a bite. Sara looked at Gus and then at the little bottle with orange liquid but said nothing. Anna sat down last and Pete slid a bowl of cereal over to her. She swallowed hard.

"Two or three drops should do it," Gus said encouragingly.

Anna added two drops to the cereal as Gus made the yummy sounds and ate his cereal.

Sara followed Gus's lead. "Yum, this is better, Gus," Sara said, choking down her cereal and making the yummy sounds.

"Ah, can I try that orange stuff?" Andy asked, raising his eyebrows.

"Sure Andy, but not more than three drops, OK?" Gus warned.

"Sure, anything to make this taste better," Andy replied, eager to try anything to make it taste edible.

"I wouldn't say it tastes better, let's go with more nutritious," Gus said, correcting Andy and trying to not totally lie to his team.

"Where are we going today, sir?" Emily asked, choking down another bite of cereal.

"You have stellar navigation this morning and flight training this afternoon," Pete replied.

"Will we see you at lunch, sir?" Anna asked, wanting to know how closely they were going to be watched.

Pete didn't answer. He only stood up and walked to the door. Quickly, they finished their cereal and put the bowls in the cleaner. The table and benches melted back into the floor as they followed Pete to the door of their sleeping room.

"I will be waiting for you when you are done with your flight training. While much has changed, some things have not, and the Galactic council is still watching you closely. They want to make sure evil is really gone from you," Pete said, stopping at the door.

The Galactic council may have been watching them; but Pete, Frank, and Toma were also worried. Their third-year cadets had been through too much this rotation. Coming face-to-face with evil and surviving was something no one else had ever done before. Now George and Andy had done it twice!

He waved his hand, and the door didn't open. He spun around and looked at the cadets as the cadets stepped forward. Shaking his head, he pointed to the cadets' sleeves.

"Emily, please," he said, his forehead wrinkled as he motioned at their sleeves.

Emily slid her hands over everyone's sleeves and their red stripes returned and their awards disappeared.

"And the door?" Pete asked kindly, pointing over his shoulder. It was locked with one of Emily's new special programs, and she would need to unlock it as Nick, Cal, and Niels were not there to rip the door from its frame.

"Yes, sir," Emily said, blushing as the door slid silently open. She held out her pad and loaded her latest locking program on Pete's pad. Pete nodded and the cadets left the room.

Sara slipped up next to Gus as they walked. "Gus?" she whispered when he stopped her.

"I know, I know, the orange liquid was vitamins, but if they think it makes it taste better and it's healthier, then is it really wrong?" Gus whispered, hoping she would agree.

"No, Gus. It's still wrong even if your intentions are good," Sara replied quietly.

Pete stopped at Major Gatte's classroom. The door opened, and he left the cadets standing in the corridor. The cadets looked inside and half expected the blue captains to be inside watching them. However, only red cadets sat in the classroom. George and the others entered and took their seats in the back of the room around a small round table.

The team they had beaten in Sport training a few weeks earlier entered the classroom after George and his team and sat down at an empty table next to them. They had not forgotten about losing to George's team in Sport training, and they wanted revenge.

"Where have you been, Earther?" their second said, whining.

"You can hide, Earthers, but we have not forgotten," another of the cadets said.

"You think you're hot stuff," their leader sniped.

"Not for the reasons you think," Gus replied quietly.

"You got lucky. You beat us once, it won't happen again," their second threatened.

"We have no desire to argue with you, please leave us alone," Sara said as warmly and kindly as she could.

George was concentrating hard. Under the table his hands were shaking trying to maintain their focus. Evil no longer possessed them; however, his team still possessed the knowledge from the scrolls they had read in the Cal-shene officers' library when they were with the evil entity. He knew Andy could destroy the other cadets simply by thinking it, and he was sure the others could inflict pain with a mere flick of a hand. George had to keep his team focused and calm. A single bead of sweat trickled down his temple. His concentration was amazing for a cadet so young.

"Your very presence on this station annoys us," said another of the cadets.

"You should never have been allowed to even come here," their leader said coarsely.

"You are so weak, Earthers," their second added with disdain.

"You have no idea what you are saying," Andy said, his eyes turning red as he stared at the cadets.

George shook his head, and Emily, Gus, and Sara turned back around.

"Don't you turn your back on me, Earther," the lead cadet said angrily.

George glanced at his team; they knew not to respond to the leader's threats. The other cadets would not change their minds, regardless of who they were or what they said. The argument was pointless and would only lead to someone getting hurt. But the other team leader would not let it rest. He stood up and leaned in toward George.

Andy exploded from his seat, landing next to George. With lightening speed, George waved him off. Andy sat down in the empty seat next to George as an empty trash can in the back of the room crumpled and bent. Andy cringed, struggling for control of his thoughts. George turned and looked straight into the leader's eyes, the hatred in the other leader's mind was deep. Then he smiled and planted a seed of peace and compassion in the leaders mind. The leader jerked back from George with an odd look on his face.

"They are not worth our time," he said, sitting back down in his chair.

Major Gatte entered the room the instant the Calshene team leader took his seat.

"Coincidence?" Sara signed.

"Not here," Emily signed.

"A test?" Gus signed.

"Yes, it was a test," Emily signed, nodding.

"Open your 3D projectors and call up the Calshene sector of space. Display the galaxies above your tables. Based on the information on your pads, identify at least twenty-four of the trader outposts in this sector. Identify how you would approach each trader outpost administrator to obtain landing clearance. Begin now," he said kindly.

Major Gatte walked around the room, looking at the cadet team's projections and the notes they were typing into their pads for each trader's outpost. Anna was fast and she, Emily, and Sara were nearly complete by the time the Major made his way to their table.

"Well done, Anna, Emily, and Sara. I hope George, Andy, and Gus are paying close attention," he said, calling them by their names.

"How, un-Calshene," Andy thought.

"Yes, sir. Thank you, sir. They have even made several suggestions, sir," Anna answered, smiling cheerfully.

"Keep them learning, Anna, you have a gift to share," he said, nodding. Anna glowed. Gus was sure she had a soft pink aura around her.

"Well played, George, well played indeed," Morja Gatte said, dipping his head to George.

"Thank you, sir," George answered, dipping his head in acknowledgement.

The Major walked to the next group of cadets. Andy looked at George and smiled. He knew the Major was pleased with Anna, Emily, and Sara's work; however, he also knew they had reacted well in dealing with the team next to them and that it had not gone unnoticed. Andy still thought things should be plainer; however, he was happy he understood more of what was going on at Asteria station.

Anna pointed at their completed 3D holographic projection and Major Gatte nodded. Anna saved the program and brought up the star charts from a few weeks earlier.

"There is something we are missing," she said, bringing up the file they had created.

"The lines, they reminded me of something," Anna said, spinning the galaxies around.

"You are right, this is so familiar, but why? What are we missing?" Emily whispered.

She knew if anyone was going to make the cryptic connection, it was going to be George. Yet, George seemed a little weirdly distracted at the moment.

"Class dismissed," Major Gatte said kindly.

Anna shut down their file and the cadets stood up.

"What's wrong, not done yet?" one of the other cadets taunted.

"We are never done with our studies," Anna replied with a smile and snap click of the table projector.

The cadets left Major Gatte's classroom and headed for the dining hall. Andy signed back and the cadets lowered their heads and pressed hard against the corridor wall as two cadet sector guards and a CORE officer ran past them, entering Major Gatte's classroom. The cadets backed into an empty classroom, holding the door open. A few minutes later the cadet sector guards and the CORE officer were leading away the cadets that had taunted their team during class.

"We're not going to lunch. Are we?" Gus whispered, half sighing.

Andy signed, and they stepped out of the classroom doorway and into the corridor. Emily threw a tiny star-shaped tracking marker at one of the cadets as they were paraded by. It skidded across the cadets back and hit the wall falling to the ground and spinning to a stop. Emily's face fell.

"Now what?" Andy signed as the officers and cadets disappeared around the corner.

"I can track them," Gus whispered, grinning.

"How?" Andy asked.

"I put a tracking star on the lead cadet when I flipped him in Colonel Moawk's Sport training a while ago," Gus replied, beaming.

"Why?" Anna asked.

"I wanted to know if he was near us. I didn't trust him," Gus whispered.

"Well done," George said, patting Gus on the back.

Gus brought up a tracking program on his pad, and the team followed along slightly behind them. Soon the guards, the CORE officer, and cadets entered the CORE sector corridors.

"They are going to the detention area," Andy signed.

Emily raised her hand, but George caught her hand in mid air. He swung her hand gently around, stopping her from removing their stripes.

"Not this time, we need to find another way," he said softly.

Anna smiled and an archway appeared on one of the corridor walls. Emily twisted her free hand and opened the door. The air in the corridor gently filled the cave.

"There really is another way," Sara whispered.

The caves had become their hidden pathways around the cadet stations. What had once been forbidden and terrifying was now commonplace for George and his team.

Gus waited for Andy to enter first. He had gotten used to Andy entering first and figured out that he wasn't pushy. To Andy it was his position to take the risk first. Gus didn't agree, but he had gotten used to the idea. Andy slipped silently inside and the others followed. Anna slid her pad down from her sleeve, held it next to Gus's pad and seemed to motion it to talk with Gus's pad. Soon, she smiled and pointed the direction through the cave. The others ran along behind Gus and Anna. She raised her hand and they came to a stop.

"They are here, on the other side of the cave wall," Anna signed.

"Where are we?" Andy asked, looking around the cave.

"This is the detention area, the brig," Anna signed.

"Are they alone?" Andy asked, looking at Anna and then George.

George was quieter than normal. Something wasn't quite right, and yet, Andy couldn't put his finger on it. The concentration to hide the cadets' knowledge of the officers' library scrolls was beginning to take its toll on George. He was weakening and the trouble with the other cadets in Major Gattte's classroom had only weakened him faster. Gus touched George's shoulder and made a link. Andy joined, sharing his energy. Emily put her hand on the cave wall.

"Their minds are being beaten like Pete's and the others were," Emily said sadly, pulling her hand back from the wall.

The cadets stared at each other in disbelief.

"Like what the scanners on Mahadean do?" Anna asked. Emily nodded.

"I don't care if they were plotting to destroy us, violence is not the way," Sara whispered, frustrated with the CORE officers' choice for punishment.

They all nodded. With the new knowledge they possessed, they were reading others' thoughts like the Viceroys.

"George, who are you connected to?" Andy asked quietly, trying not to worry the others.

He was sure something was going on with George, and he was worried it was a stealthy mind invader.

"I don't know, I only know that for a thousand years there has been too much hatred and suffering. It needs to end or our universe will not survive," he said cryptically, not understanding Andy's question.

"Then we need to rescue them," Gus said, thinking that George was talking about the other cadets in the detention cell.

"And the plan is?" Sara asked.

"The art of distraction," Andy replied, giving George time to think.

It was becoming one of their favorite ideas.

"And where will we hide them once we get them free?" Sara asked, not worried that they could free them from a CORE detention cell!

"The cooler, of course!" Gus said, piping in quietly.

They all wanted to laugh; however, they smiled instead, holding it in for another time. The plan would be to rescue the cadets now and beg for forgiveness later.

"Emily, can you open and close the brig door from here? I mean, not one of Anna's cave doors but the door inside?" Andy asked.

"Hmm, an interesting challenge," she said as Gus put his hand on her shoulder.

Emily placed her hand on the cave wall and seemed to tell a lifeless bit of rock what she was going to do. The door inside the detention cell opened and then closed and then opened again. The CORE interrogator and guards stopped, ran out of the room and then ran back inside again.

George placed "invader" in the CORE guards' minds and Emily opened the door again. They all ran out into the corridor this time and Emily closed the cell door, locking the interrogator and guards out of the detention cell. Anna made an archway and door into the cell from the cave and Emily opened the door. Andy, Gus, George, and Sara ran inside. Anna kept their door open as Emily opened and closed the other doors in the detention area.

They lifted up the cadets, carrying them from the cell into the cave. Anna released the door and the archway disappeared. Emily locked all of the detention cells and corridor doors so they would not open.

"Ten minute delay. Tops," Emily whispered as she picked up a cadet from the cave floor and flipped her over her shoulder.

George nodded as he picked up the lead cadet. With a cadet over each of their shoulders they took off, running through the cave. Anna nodded the direction as they ran, leaving the detention cell as far behind as they could.

"Ten minutes?" Gus asked, still puzzled.

"In ten minutes the CORE computer programmers will have all the detention doors working again, Gus. We have ten minutes to get to your cooler before the guards know the cadets are gone," Andy replied, actually translating cryptic for Gus.

"That was good, Andy," George said, nodding to Andy.

"What? Oh no, you're the cryptic translator, not me," Andy mumbled on until Anna signed "stop" and pointed at the cave wall.

She made a door and Emily opened it as Andy hurried through first into a large kitchen. Emily opened the cooler door with the twist of her wrist on her free hand. Quickly, the cadets ran into the cooler as the cave's archway door closed silently. Gus stopped at the cooler controls to turn down the temperature on the cooler before he entered.

"We aren't going to make that mistake again," he muttered, closing the door.

They all huddled in the back of the cooler, breathing hard. Gus laid his cadet down. Carefully, he and Andy pushed some of the shelves at diagonal angles toward the cooler door.

Sara looked down at her cadet. "How could they have done this to them so quickly?" she whispered.

"They were plotting to destroy us," Andy answered, reminding her who they were as he sat down.

"And beating their minds will prevent that—how? Retraining, perhaps; however, beating only reinforces the hatred. It does nothing positive," Sara said, making a small yellow glowing sphere over her cadet.

"Are you sure you want to do that?" Gus asked, raising an eyebrow.

"I will not let them die, Gus. Not for a crime they didn't commit. Besides, thinking it doesn't mean they would have really done it," Sara replied seriously.

"Yes, yes, we all agree," George replied, nodding for them to share their energy with Sara.

Gus connected everyone to the new link, and Sara's yellow healing sphere grew. One by one Sara healed the cadets. Gus slid out rations from one of the cooler shelves and bottles of water for everyone. He slipped a few extra into his backpack. When Sara was done healing each cadet, they ate their rations while holding their cadets close to keep them from getting cold.

In the middle of a bite Andy signed silence, and the group dropped down low. George concentrated and they all disappeared.

"Click" went the latch. Two guards walked in and looked around. Gus's shelving arrangement made it difficult for the guards to walk to the back of the cooler and look around.

"This one's stuffed with food. No one is in here, let's check the next one," the guard said.

George did not uncloak. The door closed and then quickly reopened again, a standard trick. Again, the door closed and the guards left. Andy bumped George and they reappeared.

"How'd you do that, Earther?" the lead cadet asked, regaining consciousness.

"My name is George and this is Andy, Emily, Sara, Anna, and Gus. Who are you?" George asked, never answering his question.

"I'm Mills, and this is Cain, he's my second. There's Lilan, Bowx, Mits, and Kara. You rescued us from the detention cell, why?" he asked bluntly.

"They would have beaten you until your spirit was broken or you were dead, and we can't have that because of us," Emily said, handing the cadets bottles of water.

"What?" he asked, not understanding her words.

"They knew you were planning to destroy us. The officers were going to stop you one way or another," Anna said, handing them rations to eat.

"The cadet sector officers don't want any destroyed cadet issues on their station," Andy repeated rather matter-of-factly.

"That's not true. We never planned to destroy you," Mills replied abruptly.

"You're lying to get us beaten!" Cain yelled.

"Yes, it is true. Please don't lie to us again," Sara said, staring at Cain, her eyes narrowing.

"How do you know what we were thinking?" Mills asked.

"Because you don't hide your thoughts very well," Emily replied.

"The Colonels and Majors simply read your plans in your minds and the rest, you know," Anna said, and shook her head.

"Then, why did you rescue us?" Bowx asked.

"You did nothing; you only had thoughts and ideas. You didn't act on your thoughts," Sara replied.

"The CORE officers beating you for your thoughts and not for your actions was wrong," Emily answered seriously.

"First, you free us from the detention cell. Then you hide us and heal us from wounds that most likely would have destroyed us and all the while you knew we were planning on trying to destroy you," Cain said, not believing them.

"What do you really want?" Mills asked, speaking for his team.

Andy shook his head and smiled. "Nothing."

"And you expect us to believe that?" Cain asked.

"Yes," Andy replied, drinking his water.

"You are fools, the officers are going to beat you for saving us and so we win," Bowx said, laughing with the other cadets.

"Maybe, but I don't think that is what the training is all about," Emily said.

Suddenly her face went blank; she paused. She shook her head, smiling a 'gotcha' kind of grin. Andy and the others laughed.

"We walked right into it!" Andy said out loud, grinning.

"What are you talking about? What?" Mills asked rudely.

"It was really easy, and Sara was able to heal them with only a little energy," Emily said cryptically, not answering Mills question.

"The CORE officers set us up, I can't believe we fell for this one," Gus said, sighing. He understood the cryptic words.

"What?" Mills pressed.

Andy looked at George, "I'm not the translator."

George smiled and turned toward Mills. "They took your team to see what we would do. Would we let you suffer or would we take on the responsibility to rescue you and move the punishment off of you and onto us," George said seriously.

"I hate it when we do something good and then get caught at it, everyone thinks we are so wonderful, yak, yak, yak," Gus said, whining a little.

"They're here," Andy signed mid-way through Gus's whine.

They helped the other team up, and George moved the shelves apart with a simple raise of his hand. The other cadets stared at the shelves and then at George.

"How did he do that?" Cain asked, but Andy didn't answer.

"Who's here?" Mills asked; however, George only shook his head and lowered it.

George's team followed his lead. Mills team did not. They sneered and pushed through George's team as the cooler door opened. Mills' walked directly into Viceroy Petrosky, Pete's dad, and two Inner Circle officers.

"You should have listened to them, Cadet Mills," the Viceroy said firmly.

"But they," Mills started to say when the Viceroy cut him off.

"They what?" the Viceroy shouted.

"Nothing, sir. Nothing at all, sir," Mills said, coming to attention and lowering his head. His team followed his lead.

"Take them from my sight," the Viceroy ordered firmly, waving his hand.

"No, sir. Please, sir, spare them. They made a foolish mistake. That's all. It was only a foolish mistake of youth, sir," Emily said quickly before George or the Viceroy cut her off.

The Viceroy turned to Mills.

"Even now they plead for your lives, when you plotted to destroy them, and they rescued you from the CORE officers. Are they strong or weak, Cadet Mills?" the Viceroy asked.

"Weak, you destroy your enemy," Mills replied abruptly.

"Are they your enemy or fellow cadets?" the Viceroy pressed.

"They're Earthers, sir!" Mills said bluntly.

The team's hearts fell. The Viceroy motioned and the two Inner Circle officers walked out of the cooler with the cadets.

"Please don't beat them again, it will not change their minds, sir," Sara said, pleading.

"They need retraining, sir," Anna added quickly. The Viceroy raised his hand.

"They will not be beaten. We tried it this way, now we need to try it another way; however, retraining will be a large part of their life from now on," he replied.

"Thank you for letting us try, sir," Emily said, smiling a little, letting him know they had figured out the officer's plan had been intentional.

"How did you find us, sir? I turned the temperature down, sir," Gus asked quietly.

"Oh, there is this pie-eating grandfather," he said and winked. "However, right now you need to get to the cadet dining hall before a particular captain explodes," the Viceroy said, hinting in a most un-Calshene way.

"Yes, sir. Thank you, sir," Andy said.

Each cadet shook his hand as they walked out of the cooler. George was last.

"Sir, I have to ask you for help. I need Max and I cannot seem to find him. I know he and grandfather do not exactly get along," George said and then paused.

"Max is resting right now, I'm sure he'll be back soon enough," the Viceroy said, not understanding the urgency of George's request.

Chapter 23

BEINGS OF WHITE LIGHT

George nodded and hurried to catch up to his team.

"What's up?" Andy asked. He had lingered a little out of ear shot, yet he never actually left George.

"Andy, I need Max and soon. The Viceroy said he is resting. Maybe we can find another of his kind," George whispered, not wanting to worry the others. Yet, his hand was shaking at his side again.

"There are others? Why didn't I think of that? I'll work on it. You concentrate and don't think about Max. I will find a way to get help," Andy replied confidently, trying to support George.

Andy was beginning to figure out what George was trying to tell him. George was acting weird. However, he wasn't in a link with a stealthy invader, he was blocking everyone's minds and thoughts from invaders and from themselves, preventing them from seeing the knowledge of the library scrolls they had read. If Max was a being who appeared with a glow of white light, then there had to be others of his kind. Andy had to find them and get help for George. Quickly, they hurried to catch up to the others so no one would be the wiser.

As the Viceroy had said, Pete was pacing outside the dining hall when they arrived. His father, the Viceroy, had said not to worry, but Pete wasn't so sure. When the cadets arrived they weren't sure if he was happy to see them or angry for their rescue. He looked like he was going to explode.

"Sir?" Andy said as they arrived at the door.

"First dinner, then report," Pete ordered in his captain's voice.

"Yes, sir," they replied as they entered the dining hall.

Andy grabbed Pete's arm as he entered last, spinning Pete around so Andy was now facing toward the rear of the hall.

"We need Mid or Sid after dinner, sir. George is starting to struggle and I am having a hard time helping him. We need Max and there is only one place we can go that will be safe," Andy said cryptically.

"Max cannot come right now," Pete replied, staring at Andy.

"Then we will need to call for another, sir," Andy said, nearly begging.

"Another what?" Pete pressed, not understanding his cryptic request.

"Please, sir, do not ask me to explain, not here," Andy said, pleading—not his standard blow-it-up style.

"I will make the arrangements," Pete answered, having no idea what was going on with the cadets.

Andy hurried and caught up to the others. Emily held George's hand to stop it from shaking as they sat down at their table for dinner. Pete stared as his cadets now eating quietly at their table. Nick bumped Pete's arm as he ran into the red cadets dining hall.

"What's up?" Nick asked, looking around the room.

Like Andy, Nick was always tuned into what was happening around them. He knew something was bothering Pete.

"I don't know, something is not right with George. Only Andy answered my questions. George never spoke. Get Sid or Mid right away," Pete said seriously.

Pete never took his eyes off his cadets as Nick ran from the room.

After dinner George was weaker, not stronger. Andy was now walking next to him, supporting him. He was pretending they were having a deep conversation. In the corridor, George folded over. Oddly, Pete was nowhere in sight. Andy looked up, and Gus was already making the link.

"No matter what, you must not look inward toward your own thoughts. Everyone must think only calm thoughts and focus on George getting better. Promise me no matter how curious you get, you cannot look inside to your own thoughts, promise," Andy said seriously, flipping his hand over to reveal a small reddish-yellow sphere.

Each cadet shook his hand. The red sphere was small and did not burn them, only stung their skin to remind them of their focus. Pete and Nick ran down the corridor.

"I can't get the Viceroys; however, Mid will be here soon," Pete said, reaching for George.

Andy quickly flipped his hand over and a new red sphere grew, glowing red hot. Pete jumped back.

"No, sir. You cannot know, sir. Please don't make me, sir," Andy said, pleading as his red sphere glowed brightly over his palm.

Pete and Nick backed away. The wall rumbled and a slit appeared. It was Mid. Nick held open Mid's slit as only the cadets stepped inside. Gus carried George inside, and Andy set his red sphere in Nicks' hand.

"Thank you, sir," Andy whispered.

Mid's slit closed. They disappeared. Pete and Nick ran for the Viceroys.

"Take us to safety," Andy asked, holding George up with Gus now.

He hung between them as if he was unconscious. Mid took off quickly, and the cadets had to fight to keep their balance.

"Mid wants to thank us for taking care of their children while they were detained," Emily thought.

"It is us who should be thanking Mid for her children taking care of us. They are very brave kids," Gus said, tickling Mid with his free hand. He was beginning to understand how many creatures were protecting them as Mid glowed a warm red.

Mid sped along quickly, slowing down only when entering the tunnel hog cave where they slept. Sid was there with the two little hogs when the cadets stepped out of Mid. The girls hugged the hogs while Andy and Gus carried George into the other cavern.

"Did you notice, they hide this place and yet never come inside," Sara said, following Andy into the second cave.

"It's a map room or a communication port and probably a lot more. That's why we don't feel good inside it, you're not supposed to. It wants you to leave. Everyone stand in the center. Slide out your pads and project the 3D map we saw at the end of class today. Anna, overlay war and peace and the rest of the lines," Andy said, giving commands like George.

"Andy, how do you know all of this stuff?" Emily asked puzzled and worried that George was no longer speaking.

"George is telling me, don't ask me how; but he is telling me," Andy said, staring at George who was hanging between himself and Gus. "What was it? The one thing Major Gatte said we could not do?" Andy asked as Anna rotated the projections on everyone's pads.

"Go to the center where all the lines crossed," Emily replied.

"Then this is how we get there, to the center where all the lines cross or how they come to us," Andy said.

"They who?" Sara asked, staring at Andy and then at George.

But Andy didn't answer her question. Instead he continued to repeat George's words.

"Think of that space where all of the lines cross, everyone," Andy said and concentrated.

They stood in a small circle in the center of the cavern and concentrated, thinking only of the space where they could not go. Time seemed to slow down as they focused their minds. Moments later, bursts of white light formed a circle of glowing, white light beings around the cadet team.

"Calm and focused we shall be," Gus whispered over and over.

The cadets stood in the center of the cavern as if in a dream. All around them the room was lit by bright, glowing white light beings. One shimmering white light being glided forward toward the cadets. Shifting, the light took on human form.

"Welcome. Why have you come here, children?" the eldest shimmering light being asked.

Andy and the others stared at the glowing being in human form. They did not lower their heads as the Inner Circle officers, Viceroys, and Senior Viceroys did when the beings of white light appeared. Instead they stared at them as teachers. They were beings like Max, who helped and guided them with kindness and respect.

"George carries within him the truth of the prophecy, the truth for each of us and the truth of the existence of Max and the others like him and you. He blocks from us the words from the scrolls and books of the Calshene officers' library that we read. We are not able to stop this knowledge within us from being taken from us and used to hurt others. We were seeking Max to have the knowledge and truths taken from us. However, we were told that Max is sick; and we assume he is dying, or he would have come. So now, we have come to ask for the knowledge of your existence and these truths to be taken from us by the ones who are like him and to ask for Max's life to be healed," Andy said, his voice cracking as he pleaded, repeating George's words.

A second being of white light stepped forward and solidified, staring at the young cadets.

"Please, help us. Somehow our connection to Max has hurt him, and we have unwillingly caused him great harm. He has sacrificed much, and we cannot allow him to pay such a severe price for helping us," Andy added, nearly begging.

He may have spoken the words; however, the others knew they were George's words.

"And as payment of all of these things that you ask? What do you offer in exchange?" the eldest being of white light asked.

Andy turned and handed George to Gus to hold up. He stepped forward toward the eldest white light being. With his last step, he knelt down on one knee and looked up.

"I freely offer you my life in exchange for Max, George, and the others'. It is not much payment for what I have asked of you; however, it is all that I have of any value," he said, lowering his head in respect.

That was not the deal George had told to Andy, but he was too weak to stop him. A third white light being shimmered, taking human form and walking toward the cadets.

"The one you call Max is right about you," the third white light being said, waving a glowing arm over the cadets.

Gently, the cadets slipped to the ground in the center of the cavern, asleep.

"You are indeed most remarkable examples of your species," the second white light being said.

"One member falls and the next takes his or hers place," the eldest white light being added.

"You cannot take this young child's life," a fourth white light being said, shimmering and taking shape and form next to the cadets.

"I know; however, I wanted to know its commitment," the eldest white light being replied.

"Their lives are so fragile, and yet, they give freely all that is precious. They sacrifice their limited lives for each other and for, what did they call him, 'Max' without hesitation," the second white light being said sympathetically.

"They do it not for admiration or reward. It is out of respect for each other and their compassion and caring. It is to make a difference while they can before their limited lives end," the fourth white light being added.

"The one called George knows who we are, and yet, his concern is that somehow they have caused harm to us or will cause harm to us in the future. He wants the memories of us removed from their thoughts, so no one can harm us," the second white light being said, worried about the young cadets.

"Perhaps, he does not really understand?" the fourth white light being replied.

"No, I think it is precisely because he understands that he makes the request," the third white light being said and then turned toward the eldest white light being.

"George, your requests are granted. All will be done," the eldest white light being replied.

The small cavern started to glow a brilliant white light. The energy pierced the cavern walls and filled their sector of the universe with peace once more.

The cadets awoke in the tunnel hog cavern squished in between Kid and Bid early the next morning. George pushed Andy, and he rolled over, falling off Bid and splatting onto the cavern floor. A swirl of dust wafted up and he sneezed. If tunnel hogs could laugh, George was sure Bid and Kid were laughing. George laughed for them.

"What are we doing here?" Andy asked, hugging Bid and rolling up onto his back again.

"I'm just happy we are alive," Gus said, rubbing his stomach.

"We must have found them, the other beings of white light like Max. You did well, Andy," George said, dipping his head.

"Yes, well. It took me some time to figure out what was really going on. You were so weak. Then when you showed me what you were blocking in our minds, I knew we needed help faster than what the captains thought you had asked for," Andy replied quietly.

"How did you figure out the tunnel hogs' cavern was a map room?" George asked, sliding off of Bid and scratching his dry dusty skin as Bid wiggled.

"I didn't, you told me," Andy replied, staring at George and sliding to the ground next to Kid.

"I didn't tell you. Well, I don't think I told you. However, I do remember you broke out of our link for awhile, Andy. Why?" George pressed, raising an eyebrow like Pete.

"Don't you remember?" Andy asked, hoping he wasn't going to have to tell George what he had done.

George shook his head. "What did you do, Andy? What did you say? You didn't trade your soul to the devil, so to speak?" George asked, suddenly worried.

"I traded my life for yours, Max, the others', and for all of our memories. You were too weak to object. It seemed like a fair trade," Andy said, bracing to be yelled at by George.

George paused and stared at Andy. Andy had once made him promise that if it ever came down to his life or George's, then George had to let Andy do what he was meant to do. How much Andy had grown this rotation. How could he ever repay such an amazing friend?

"Then it was a wise decision, my friend," George replied most unexpectedly. Andy grinned.

"Look, look the light," Anna said, pointing into the other cavern. The other cadets slid off of Kid and Bid and ran into the other cavern.

"Max!" Emily, Sara, and Anna screamed, running to the center of the cavern nearly tackling him to the ground as they all hugged him at once.

Max hugged the young cadets as a proud grandparent hugs his grandchildren. George, Andy, and Gus were equally happy to see him; however, they greeted him in a more dignified kind of way without actually knocking him to the ground—instead, they lifted him up.

"Max, you're here. Are you OK?" Emily whispered.

"Yes, yes, I'm fine, thanks to all of you," he said and wrapped his glowing white arms around the cadets, solidifying as he walked them back to the other cavern.

"Max, how old is this cavern and its writings?" Anna asked as they walked.

"Since the dawn of your time. You are the first to understand its meaning and use it for that purpose," Max replied, choosing his words very carefully. They sat down on the floor of the other cavern near Kid and Bid.

"How, Max? Why are we alive?" George asked.

"What happened?" Gus asked.

"We found the other beings of white light, and then it is all a blur," Andy said.

"We have so many new questions," Emily said hopefully.

Max grinned and looked at Andy for a minute. "Andy, don't touch the fungi. It will bite and then it will be sad because it can't help itself. Emily, ask the fungus to retreat to the walls again and Gus can give it some more of his purple liquid later before you leave," he whispered.

Emily smiled and touched the cavern ground and the light green glow faded from the ground.

"Max, are you really OK?" Sara asked, holding his hand and sliding a small yellow sphere over it.

Max smiled. "Yes, I am fine. Stop worrying, children."

"Tell us what has really happened," Anna said kindly.

"Tell us about this place. Please, Max," Sara asked softly, closing her hand as her glowing yellow sphere faded.

"Your grandfather will not be happy if I tell you," Max replied seriously, looking at all of the cadets.

"It is OK, he will not be angry," George said, staring off in space.

"What? How do you know that?" Andy pressed.

"I don't know. It's a feeling I got when I thought about Emily's question. Like I needed an answer and he told me," he replied, a little confused by his own words.

"You know, George, you all know. Open your minds to the possibilities around you. All things are possible; however, some are simply more probable given the time we have available. George, you did well in blocking the prophecy and scrolls from everyone and blocking their other thoughts as well. The knowledge of the prophecy has been removed, you might say, as has the knowledge of the books from the officers' library," Max said before George could ask.

"But we still know you, I mean, we know about the people of white light, Max," George said hesitantly.

"And I cannot forget the feeling of the white light people," Sara added, nodding her head.

"Us, too!" they all chimed in together.

"They are kind," Emily said wistfully.

"They care so much," Anna added, smiling at the warm thought.

"Then it was left intentionally as a memory for you," he replied kindly, yet with a more serious tone in his voice.

"Why?" they all asked simultaneously, staring at Max!

Max rolled back and laughed. He laughed so hard tears rolled from his eyes.

"George, Andy, Emily, Anna, Sara, and Gus, think. Why would the people of white light, as you call them, leave the memory of this place, these ancient symbols, and knowledge of them buried deep within your minds, think. Why?" Max pressed, trying to get them to look past where they were and open their minds to the possibilities.

"Because they like us?" Gus said, guessing.

"Well perhaps, Gus, however, not what I think their only intention was," he said, pressing for more.

"So if something ever happened, we would know how to find them again," Gus answered again.

"Yes, now you're getting it. Excellent," Max said, patting Gus on the back.

"Max, you are one of them, one of the people of white light, aren't you?" Emily asked.

"Yes, Emily; however, you have known that since the first time you asked. Open your minds and thoughts, children, see past the burden of the day, and see the possibilities that surround you with a little bit of work and effort," he said kindly.

"Grandfather says that," Emily replied, smiling at the thought of Pete's grandfather.

"On that, we agree," Max said kindly.

"Max, are there caverns like this one across our universe?" Anna asked.

"Yes, Anna, there are some other caverns across your known universe. Good observation," Max replied, patting her on the back.

"How did you know?" Gus asked Anna.

"Do you know where they are?" Andy asked curious to see what she had found.

"I don't know how I know. I just know they are there and I know I can find them if we need them," Anna said, pulling up a 3D projection of the galaxies in their sector.

The projection filled the center of the cavern as George leaned over closer to Max.

"I'm worried about Andy controlling his red energy spheres that destroy, Gus converting the red sphere energy to keep us alive, Sara's healing and nearly dying to save injured people, Anna losing herself in the navigation, and Emily's deadly computer programs and viruses. The conflicts within them are so strong. At times it seems to tear them apart," he whispered.

"Yes, they, too, are each worried about each other and about you. They worry that you support them so well, that you will sacrifice yourself for them," Max replied gently.

"They're right. They're all right. I would die for them," he answered firmly.

"And they for you; however, we need to prevent that from being the only option available to you and your team in the future. Your grandfather has a plan. You must listen to his voice and hear his words," Max whispered. "Will you do this?"

George smiled.

"Yes, we will, sir," Andy replied formally, leaning back and then returning to Anna's 3D projection.

"Yes, sir," George replied with a grin. "Max, why do you help us? Don't say it is because of the words of the prophecy ,and it's not just to annoy grandfather. It is something else. What?" George asked, hoping Max would tell him the truth.

"You asked me from the depth of your hearts and minds, you might say from within what you call your souls—your compassion," Max replied quietly.

"But Pete and Frank asked you to be a part of their teams before us," George pressed a little.

"Yes, they did," Max replied and nodded.

"You're not going to exactly answer this question. Are you, sir?" George said, lowering his head.

"I answered your question. The rest of the mystery you will need to discover on your own," Max whispered.

George paused. What did Max say that he had not heard?

"Will you always be with us?" George asked.

"Why? Do you want a replacement?" Max replied, teasing him.

"No, sir," George said, stumbling a little.

"Your grandfather is looking for you. It is time for you to go," he said, looking around the cavern.

"Max, does Grandfather know? I mean about you and the others and this place?" he said, looking for a quick answer.

"He knows more than most; however, he has never found this place or any like it. That is something that only your team has done. Now you must go. Answer his call, George," Max insisted.

George concentrated, and Andy put his hand on George's shoulder. George thought of Grandfather, and in his mind's eye he could hear his voice clearly.

"We are fine and will be in the tunnel hog terminal shortly," George said calmly.

"Very well," Grandfather answered, quietly knowing Max was with them and that whereever they were, they were safe.

George and Andy turned around, and Max was gone. George and Andy smiled, locking arms and pulling each other up.

"It's time to leave, Grandfather is looking for us," he said quietly.

"Is he angry?" Anna asked, a little worried.

"No, he only wants us back safe and sound," George replied, trying to keep them calm.

Sid rumbled into the cavern and a slit appeared in his side, waiting for the cadets.

"Wait!" Gus yelled frantically as George and the others walked across the cavern floor to Sid.

He opened his backpack and pulled out two large bottles of purple liquid—bottles he knew he didn't put in his backpack. He ran over to one wall and then to the other wall. He poured out every drop of purple liquid on the edge of the florescent green fungi. Finally, he slipped into Sid, and the tunnel hog glowed a warm red.

"Sid, says thank you from the fungi," Emily replied.

Gus hugged Sid back. Sid rolled from side to side in the empty cavern, flipping the cadets over. They fell to the floor inside Sid, tumbling and rolling. Soon the cadets were flying through the air inside of Sid. Sid was stronger than the other tunnel hogs, so having a little fun with the cadets was always an option, although not often permitted on Asteria station.

With the cadets all tumbling around, he sped off for the main tunnel hog station, bouncing the cadets inside as he gained speed. Soon, Sid was skidding into the tunnel hog station to stop. He sent the cadets inside rolling and tumbling again. By now, they were all laughing so hard, they could hardly stand up. Sid wiggled, and Pete popped his head inside to find all of his cadets heaped up in the back of the tunnel hog laughing.

"If you are all done with your joy ride, we have places to go, cadets," Pete said, using his captain's voice.

"Yes, sir. Yes, sir." they all replied, standing up. Thanking Sid for the ride and everything else, they slipped out of Sid.

"Sir...," George started; except, Pete waved him off.

"You will report later. Right now, you're late," Pete replied seriously, motioning for them to follow.

However, George knew Pete was happy that they had all returned alive and well. Yet, Pete was worried, they had been gone for a week. Even though his grandfather had said not to worry, he knew something important had happened; and they had changed. He needed to know where they had gone? Where did they think safe was?

Chapter 24

SPORT FINALS

They walked at a quick pace through the corridors of the station, weaving in and out between the cadet teams on their way to training. George and the others wanted to ask Pete how he and the others were. It now seemed as if it had been ages since they had spoken with Pete, Frank, Toma, and the others. However, protocol training prevented them from speaking up as they followed along in silence.

Pete stopped at a classroom. The cadets followed him inside and took their seats in the back of the classroom. Pete walked to the back of the classroom and brought out trays of food for the cadets.

"Pancakes dripping with syrup, sweet milk, and juice," Gus said practically, drooling.

"How did you ever manage?" Sara asked, her eyes as big as saucers.

"Eat quickly. Your class will be starting soon. I will not be back this evening; however, I will see you in the morning," he said, and with a nod he turned, heading for the classroom door.

"Where will you be, sir?" George asked for the team as Pete opened the door.

"Think about it, you already know the answer," he replied and slipped out the door.

"Riddles, more riddles. It's nearly the end of our third rotation, and I still don't get most of the riddles," Andy said, stuffing an entire pancake into his mouth.

Emily, Sara, and Anna shook their heads.

"What? I'm hungry," Andy replied, stuffing in another pancake.

Gus and George would have said something in Andy's defense; however, they had stuffed whole pancakes in their mouths without cutting them up, which seemed like a good idea at the time to them so they nodded and grinned in support of Andy instead. Soon the cadets were stuffed to the brim with pancakes. George and Andy stacked the trays on the counter in the back of the classroom as the other red cadets started to enter the room.

The room filled quickly with red cadets. Noticeably absent was the team that had taunted them in their last stellar navigation class. One of the other red team leaders leaned back towards George as Major Gatte entered the room.

"Thanks, we don't know what you all did, but it worked, we haven't been beaten up for a week," the lead cadet said, and his whole team nodded in agreement.

"What? Who?" George whispered.

"Them, they're gone. It's great," the leader said, pointing to the empty table on the other side of George and the others. George and Andy smiled and nodded as if they had a clue as to what was going on.

"We were gone for a week?" Anna signed.

"Cadets, if you are finished! Can we begin training today?" Major Gatte spoke sternly.

"Yes sir, sorry sir," George replied dipping his head to the Major.

"Bring up your 3D holographic projectors. Display the known universe," the Major ordered.

"We can't do this," Anna whispered quickly.

"Why, Anna?" Emily asked.

"It's too big for our individual projectors," she answered.

"Then we must all work together," George said, leaning back and whispering to the team behind him.

Andy and Gus followed his lead as Emily and Sara walked over to two more teams and whispered the plan to them. Major Gatte sat at a desk in the front of the room, pretending to be working on his computer. He grinned as he watched the cadet teams work together to build the known universe, one sector at a time. Emily powered up the desks of the missing cadet team, and Anna added the coordinates for their sector. Soon the entire room was filled with star clusters, nebulas, supernovas, black holes, and voids of the known, all expanding and growing universe.

"Where is the beginning of the known universe?" the Major asked, without looking up from his computer.

The teams started walking around the room, pointing and calculating on their pads.

"Here, sir. It is here," the first team to answer said point to the geometric center of the known universe.

Anna crinkled her face and slowly shook her head.

"Do you all agree?" the Major asked, not getting up from his chair.

One-by-one the other teams finished their calculations and came to within one light year of each other, agreeing that the beginning of the known universe was the geographic center of all galaxies and star systems displayed.

"Cadet Hawkins, does your team agree?" he asked loudly, knowing Anna would disagree.

The class suddenly snapped their heads toward the back of the room and stared at George and his team.

"I defer my answer to Cadet Jhang, sir," George replied formally, knowing the Major's question was not for him.

"Cadet Jhang, does your team agree?" the Major asked again.

Anna was pleased George valued her judgment on stellar things and allowed her to lead their team when needed. All of the cadets in the classroom were now staring at Anna.

"No, sir. Our team does not agree, sir," she replied formally, holding Gus's hand behind her back for courage.

George and the others did not even bat an eye. Anna had disagreed with all of the cadet teams' findings, and George was sure Andy, Sara, Emily, Gus, and himself included had no idea why. Only that if this was Anna's decision, then it was the right answer, and they were there to support her. The cadets' heads snapped back, all staring at Major Gatte to see his reaction. The Major smiled and nodded.

"Why, Cadet Jhang?" he asked seriously, dragging the class along so they would learn.

The cadets' heads snapped back again, facing Anna and waiting for her reply. Anna smiled, squeezed Gus's hand, and walked to the center of the universe displayed on the 3D holograpic imagers in the classroom.

"It is true that this is the geographic center of the known universe," she said, pointing to the same point the others teams had discussed. "Mathematically it is the center of the universe, as it has expanded. However, it is not the point where the universe began. Some people believe the universe was created by a higher being and all of the physical evidence is simply the remnant of that theory. Others believe that the physical evidence is the true story and there is no higher being that created the known universe. Both or neither theory may be true, that is not for me to decide," she said calmly.

She paused and took a deep breath. "If we look at the gravitational constant of the universe and assume it is a universal constant, then the beginning of the universe is not the geographic center, it is here. The place where all of the paths between the home worlds cross. It is the one place Major Gatte has said we cannot go," Anna said, pointing off to the side of the geographic center of the universe.

"Excellent work, Cadet Jhang. How did you know?" the Major asked, looking up from his computer with a grin.

"It is the one place all of the mathematic equations collide. Gravity is wrong, and it's not a black hole. Every single path crosses the same point, as if they are spokes on a wheel. All of our charts plot space jumps around that sector of the universe when it would be quicker to pass through that sector of the universe. I assume trial and error has cost many ships and lives in the exploration of that part of the universe, and so today all ships are banned from going there, sir," Anna replied as if an equal with the Major.

"A wise and learned answer, Cadet Jhang. Class dismissed," the Major said, standing and motioning toward the doorway.

The cadets stood still, stunned. They couldn't believe what they had just heard. They chattered loudly as they left the classroom, staring and pointing at Anna and then at Major Gatte as they headed to the dining hall for lunch.

"That was amazing, Anna," George said as they walked through the door and into the corridor.

"Thanks," she replied, blushing and grabbing onto Gus's hand.

Slowly, her nerves calmed—speaking to large groups made her uneasy.

"How did you know what you said was right?" Andy asked, staring at Anna.

"How do you make your red hot energy spheres?" Anna asked, not answering his question.

"I don't know, I just do," he said, grinning.

"Me too. I just knew it. It all made sense, like the pieces of a puzzle fitting together," she answered as they walked.

"Are you all sure we should go to the dining room for lunch? I mean, you know, every time we do something bad happens. I'm not against a good lunch or anything. It's just, well, ya know," Gus said, waffling.

George and the others laughed.

"Gus, you worry too much," Anna said, giggling and feeling better as she wrapped her arm over his shoulder.

"Sure, you say that now, but just wait, it's been quiet for at least four hours," he added.

They all laughed even harder. It was funny in a weird way, and they all knew Gus was right. Gus really was looking forward to lunch in the dining hall.

"I need a door here," he said, stopping and staring at the corridor wall in front of them.

"Here we go again," Andy whispered.

"No, really, I need some supplies, that's all. Remember the cereal this morning," Gus said as seriously as he could.

They all moaned.

"We are going into a kitchen, right?" Emily asked hesitantly.

"Yes, yes. We are going to the dining hall for lunch. I need supplies, that's all," Gus repeated, smiling a huge grin.

Anna made the archway and door. Emily opened it with a simple twist of her wrist. Emily waved her hand, and their stripes disappeared as they walked into the kitchen.

There were a few cooks and kitchen staff hurrying around. They hardly gave the cadets who now look like officers a second look. Gus went from cabinet to cabinet gathering this and that for his backpack. He nodded to George and Emily opened the door again. She turned them back into red cadets as they entered the corridor again.

"Where are we going now?" Andy asked, staring at Gus.

"To eat in the dining hall!" Gus said, shaking his head.

They walked on and entered the dining hall to sit at their usual table. They sat and ate for the entire period and nothing happened. Andy kept looking around as if there was going to be an explosion.

"No boom-booms today, Andy!" Sara said, teasing him.

"Maybe, it's just so nice in here. Everyone is so nice today," Andy whispered, twisting his head and waiting for something to happen.

"And this is bad—how?" Emily asked and crinkled her face, looking silly.

"I have to agree with Andy, everyone actually seems happy, very un-Calshene," Anna said and grinned a little.

"True enough; however, I prefer it to Andy's booms," Emily replied and chuckled.

Soon the cadets started leaving the dining hall, heading for their next training assignment.

"So where do we go now? I don't even know what day it is," Gus said, trying to look happy.

"Gus, we are going to flight training," Anna said, hugging his shoulder.

"I like flight training," he said, smiling.

They followed other cadets in the navigation class through the corridors to the flight training cavern doors. They entered the space cavern in the usual way with a flash of white light.

"The flash of white light is training, isn't it?" Sara asked.

"It must be to get cadets used to seeing it, because they could have as easily walked to the flight cavern at any time," Anna replied.

"Everything seems to be training," Gus whispered.

Anna and Emily nodded as they lined up in their standard columns as if getting ready to jump into a training glider and take off for parts unknown. Major Pennelo entered the cavern and waved her arm for the red cadets to sit. She seemed to float around the cavern effortlessly as she spoke. A quick wave of her hand and a large holographic screen appeared in front of them, floating in the air.

"Today we will review the control systems on the basic fighters and transport ships," she said, beginning her lecture.

Gus had spoken too soon. The cadets all moaned and groaned.

"Major Gatte must have talked to her," Anna whispered.

It was as if every bad science film they had during the school year on Earth were replaying out in front of them. The topics may have been different; however, the effect was the same. One by one the red cadet teams fell asleep. George shook his head and held his hand out behind him, signing to his team. Gus touched Emily's shoulder, and soon they were all in a link.

"We are being scanned," George thought to the others.

"There are half a dozen officers behind us," Andy added.

"They must want to know where we were hiding," Gus whispered.

"Pay attention, concentrate on the training, only on the training," George thought back.

They squeezed the shoulder of the person in front of them until they reached George. Message understood.

Andy and Gus listened intently. Anna, Sara, and Emily took notes on their pads. George kept focused and concentrated on blocking the officers' attempts at reading his team's minds. After having blocked the street scanners on the Mahadean planet for nearly two weeks, these CORE officers were easy to block. Only the best of stealth invaders could make it passed George now.

"Major Pennelo, sir, where are the weapons controls?" Andy asked.

The Major was surprised anyone was even awake to ask questions. Emily, Gus, Sara, and Anna took Andy's opening and asked question after question about the two ships. They were focused and wanted to share the dull discussion with the Major and the scanning officers for as long as they could. Eventually, it became a game—a battle of wits. Finally, Major Pennelo raised her hand to stop them.

"Enough, cadets!" she said, nearly exasperated.

"Yes, sir?" they chorused happily.

"Cadets, dismissed!" Major Pennelo said and left the cavern in a huff as the CORE officers stepped back into the shadows.

"I don't think she likes us today," Anna said with a mischievous little smile.

"I don't suppose she does. We need to wake everyone up," George replied and nodded toward the sleeping cadet teams.

They stood up and started to shake the other red cadets, sleeping on the cavern floor. Soon, the teams of cadets were up and heading for the dining hall for dinner.

"It was not as bad as I thought it was going to be," Anna and Emily said, smiling.

Cal was waiting for them when they reentered the red corridor after the flash of white light. He smiled and signed for them to follow him. Cal was not so good at English, and the Thorean whistle language was not allowed because his holographic projector bars made him look like a Calshene captain.

"Where are we going, sir?" they asked all at once; however, Cal only grinned.

They walked out of the red cadet sector and into the food court. Emily thought there were more colors on the walls on the Calshene station than there were on the Indus and Jupiter station corridor walls. Soon, Sheta and the other Thoreans in their triad joined George and his team. They greeted the cadets and hugged them, draping their arms over their shoulders—a point not missed by George.

Cal looked at Emily, then pointed toward her red stripes and shook his head. Cal pointed at Sheta's yellow stripe next. Emily lifted her hand and turned their red team into yellow. Cal smiled—well, kind of smiled—as best he could. Emily seemed to change their stripes so easily. George wondered how she did it, yet he was sure she didn't actually know. Like Sara's healing and Andy's red spheres, Emily just did it—how was still a mystery to them.

They stood in the food court, as if trying to decide what they wanted to eat. George started to ask where Toma was, even though they were in public; hunger was beginning to cloud his thoughts.

"Focus," Toma ordered, walking up behind the red cadets. Toma had no issues with speaking English.

Emily, Sara, and Anna spun around and ran to him, hugging Toma as he walked up. His arms spread wide to hug them back. Gus, Andy, and George nodded.

"Yes, sir. Why, sir?" George asked.

"Final game, you will need to keep your minds focused," he said firmly.

"I knew it. I knew it," Andy blurted out.

"What?" Gus asked.

"They are both in the finals. Aren't they?" Andy replied, his eyes wide with excitement.

"Yes, they all are. We must hurry or we will miss the start. Stay focused, remember where you are," Toma warned, wrapping his arm around George's shoulder and walking through a small corridor archway and out into the Sport arena.

Cal and the other Thoreans followed Toma's lead, each taking a cadet to protect.

"How can Frank and the others play here?" George asked.

"They cannot," Toma said, cutting George off. "No, they are not rested enough; however, it is their right to enter and compete," Toma said, finishing George's comments. "Remember where you are, or we will leave," Toma warned again.

Toma was the most serious of the captains in their triad and George didn't want to press him further. He lowered his head and nodded. The others followed George's lead. Gus raised their link a little and joined Toma's team into their link to reinforce their focus. Toma led them through the crowd to seats about mid-way down in the middle of the yellow section. They looked around—no red cadets in the crowd.

A few minutes passed and the crowd roared. They looked down at the Slugamie on the floor of the Sport arena and watched Frank's green team enter first. As before, their uniforms were all green, and they had only a thin white stripe on their sleeves. The green captains and officers went wild, whooping and hollering. The Slugamie was hard and firm as they walked; however, it turned into a lumpy mess after the last player passed. It seemed like the only time the Calshene captains and officers were ever loud and noisy was when they were at Sport.

George could hardly believe Frank, Niels, Kate, Maria, Lucita, and Sven were strong enough to compete in the Sport semi-finals, nor strong enough to have won and made it into the Sport finals. Especially to be able to be in the finals of Sport on the Calshene station—they knew the Calshene beings were physically stronger than the Earthers.

George's team looked OK. However, he would never have said they were ready to play at this level of competition. George's head started to hurt, someone was trying to break into their link. Instantly, Andy and Cal raised red spheres in their link, and the invader backed down. Toma smiled and pointed toward Frank and the others, waiting to climb the vines hanging in the Sport arena as if nothing had happened.

The second team entering the Sport arena was Pete, Nick, Rachael, Karmen, Han, and Jennifer. Their deep blue uniforms glistened under the bright Sport lights. Again, the cadets were surprised they could play at this level. Pete's team walked across the floor of the Sport arena to their chosen vines as the blue captains and officers screamed and yelled, cheering them on. George leaned forward over the edge of the seats and looked up. However, he could not see the Viceroy in the box.

"So who do we cheer for, George?" Andy signed.

"Both, I guess?" George signed as Toma pulled George back and shook his head.

The captains roared louder, and the cadets focused on the arena again. Colonel Moawk slid down a vine in the center of the dome and stood between the two teams. He held the brown Sport ball, about the size of a basketball with handles, in one hand. The teams turned and waved to the captains and officers. Then they faced the high box. The Viceroy stood up and the Sport arena fell silent.

"Players, ascend your vines," boomed the Viceroy's voice.

The players ascended to different levels and then held their positions. Some were high and some were low. Gus was his typical self, waving his arms wildly. Emily, Sara, and Anna giggled and looked away to hide their smiles from Gus. Pete, Frank, and the others glanced over and nodded. They did not even seem surprised to see George, Andy, and the others. Gus was happy and sat down.

"Teams ready?" boomed the Viceroy's voice.

The arena fell silent. The teams replied with a single unison clap of their hands.

"Centar Comen," boomed the Viceroy's voice, and all the captains and officers cheered again.

Colonel Moawk flung the ball high into the air, and the blue team dove for the catch. The green team countered with a wild vine snap and Niels snatched it from their grasp just before he ran out of vine a few feet above the ground. George and the other captains were on their feet. There would be no sitting down during the final Sport match this time. For the first time, George and the others were not in the Viceroy's box for the final match. They could yell and holler, bend and flow with each hit and miss of the two teams.

Pete's team was fast and Frank's team was methodical when running their plays. Nick dove for the ball as it ricocheted off of Sven's shoulder, catching the edge of one of the handles and deflecting the ball toward Pete. Maria swung in, catching the ball and flipping over Karmen, defending the blue team's goal. She stuffed the ball in the goal as she flew by. Niels caught her just before she went headlong into the arena support.

"One point green," the announcer called as the captains and officers roared.

Colonel Moawk appeared in the small hole at the top of the arena and dropped the ball. Pete rushed in for the grab, not seeing Frank do the same thing. The two team leaders collided in the center of the arena. The crowd flinched, feeling their pain as the two captains fell, spinning helplessly to the floor of the arena. The Slugamie swirled around the captains and they disappeared.

Han caught the ball as all eyes were on the two falling lead captains and threw the ball with such force and speed into the green team's goal that it caused the wall to groan from the impact of the ball.

"One point blue," the announcer called.

The crowd yelled and cheered; however, most had missed the point as they had been watching the two lead captains fall.

George smiled.

"What's up?" Andy whispered.

"Grandfather says, now we'll see," he whispered.

"Is he here?" Andy signed.

"No. However, he is close enough," he answered.

"Focus," Toma thought into their link; however, he was happy the Senior Viceroy was helping protect them in such a public place.

Colonel Moawk threw the ball up from the floor of the arena. Niels and Nick dove for the ball this time. Nick pulled up just as Niels caught the ball.

Nick flipped on his vine and stripped the ball from Niels. Karmen was wait-ing below to catch the ball as it fell. Maria swung by like a circus trapeze artist and snatched the ball in mid-air. She tossed the ball to Lucita and she flipped over, dropping the ball to Sven.

Sven spun and rocketed the ball to Kate who was waiting near the blue team's goal. She hung out on her vine and launched herself forward to tip the ball in for five points. Rachael dropped from her perch on the ceiling beam support and caught Kate's tip, preventing the five point score. The captains in the arena went wild. Play after play, the teams caught, spun, threw, and bounced the ball across the arena. Sven dove and missed his new vine, land-ing on Jennifer's vine.

"Player disqualified," the announcer called.

"What happened?" Emily asked as Sven slid down his vine into the wait-ing Slugamie.

"You can't land on an opposing team's vine. You can land on one of your team's vines to stop your fall; in fact, you can't stay long, only a few seconds, or you can be disqualified just as if you had landed on the opposing team's vine," Sheta whispered.

Andy hardly blinked, not wanting to miss any of the action in the arena. Green was now one team member short and Sven was their team member with the rocket. Colonel Moawk dropped the ball from the top of the arena to restart Sport. With Sven gone, Nick and Han double-teamed Niels. It was a mistake.

Karmen swung with wicked speed toward the falling ball. Maria flipped up out of the way and Karmen collided with Jennifer, clipping her in the shoulder and sending her falling into the Slugamie below. Kate caught the falling ball and with every ounce of strength left in her, threw the ball across the entire arena at great speed, hitting Lucita's arms and stopping with a loud thump! To everyone's surprise, she caught the ball. With a twist of her shoul-ders, she reached out her graceful arm and stuffed the ball into the blue team goal as the buzzer sounded, ending regulation play.

"One point green, green wins!" the announcer yelled over the wild roar of the crowd.

The captains and officers went wild, screaming and yelling. Very few cap-tains could rocket a ball across the entire length of the arena. Most often it was the lead captain or the second that had the physical strength to throw a ball hard enough and fast enough to make it all the way across. Yet, Kate had done it and it won them the Sport final.

The officers started chanting, "Kate, Kate, Kate," in honor of her amazing throw. She took it all in stride, swinging around her vine and waving as she descended gracefully to the ground. Then she walked over to Lucita and raised her arm high into the air with hers. It was an equally amazing catch!

The captains and officers cheered as the two teams left the field. In a few minutes they all reappeared in the Viceroy's box. The box slid out into the arena and Frank and his team stepped forward as the officers cheered. Pete's team stood behind them cheering them on. The captains came to the Viceroy's box to collect their champions and carried the green and blue captains away for their celebration. George, Andy, and the other red cadets wanted to join Frank and Pete and the others; however, Toma shook his head.

The arena was emptying as Toma, George, and the others made their way back down the corridors to the red cadet sector. Toma nodded and Emily changed their sleeves from yellow to red when Toma's sleeve changed to red as they entered the red sector.

"Get some rest. You will need it," Toma whistled, once they were inside their sleeping room. "The last few days of training are grueling on Asteria station. I'll see you in the morning," he said, slipping out their door and heading back to join the celebration.

Gus was pulling out rations when George and the others turned around.

"We need to eat!" he said, pouring purple liquid and water into six silver cups.

"How much more grueling can it be?" Andy asked as he sat down for a bite of ration.

"Don't say that, Andy. You know what happens when we do," Sara said, adding a few drops of orange liquid on everyone's ration.

Chapter 25

HONOR REWARDED

They slept easily that night. George's mind seemed to travel the galaxy in his dreams. In the morning, Toma was sitting at their table, handing out bowls of dark brown cereal.

"Gus, you wouldn't happen to have any sugar in your bag of food would you? I only want a few grains to sweeten this stuff," Andy asked.

Gus shook his head. "I'll see what I can find if we stop in a kitchen on the way back from training today," he replied.

Emily bit into the cereal. "I can't, I can't. I hate this stuff. It is like eating dirt. No, I have eaten dirt, this is worse," Emily pleaded, staring at Toma.

"Look at your bowl, Emily. What do you see?" Toma whispered kindly.

"Dirt, with a few lumps of rock on the side," she said sadly.

"What do you want to see, Emily?" Toma asked his voice soft and low.

"I want a bowl of sweet oatmeal with a swirl of brown sugar on the top and a ring of cool milk around the edges," Emily replied wistfully.

"Then imagine that is what is in front of you in your silver bowl," Toma said, his voice low and soothing.

Emily looked down and saw her sweet oatmeal with the swirl of brown sugar and warm milk on the edges. She tasted the cereal and smiled.

"How did you do that? We couldn't do that before!" Sara said surprised.

"No, you couldn't, now you can," Toma said.

Sometimes he could be even more cryptic than Pete.

"Can you do that?" Sara asked Toma, while staring at a hot bowl of her grandmother's potato cereal.

"Yes," he answered with his best Thorean smile.

"So on the Mahadean home world, the others were imagining," Andy said, looking for more answers.

"Their favorite food, like my mom's sweet winter soup with crispy bites on the top," Toma replied wistfully, while cutting off Andy's question.

"And they didn't tell us?" Gus whined.

"You didn't ask them. Besides I'm not sure you or they could really have done it then. Everyone was pretty weak," he replied as the cadets ate.

"Now you know you can," Toma said when they had finished their cereal.

"So let me see, we learned something, and we are not even in a training class yet," Andy groaned, his head falling on the table as it melted into the floor.

Toma shook his head. "How is it that the simple things seem to fly over their heads while they are able to decipher the complex," he muttered as they left their sleeping room and walked along the corridor to Colonel Moawk's training dome.

"I'll see you after training," he said, leaving them in the corridor.

George never had the opportunity to ask where Pete was as they entered the dome. The cadets lined up inside the dome with the rest of the red cadets. The vines were gone, the room looked bare without them. Andy glanced up and George caught his eye. Andy looked at George and shook his head.

"Everything is fine," he signed in their new sign language.

Colonel Moawk walked into the dome behind the cadets.

"Today you will begin your formal Chen Lo training," he said, walking up to the center of the dome.

With the clap of his hands six orange captains descended from the supports high in the dome.

"That's what Andy had seen earlier as they waited for the Colonel. No wonder he wasn't concerned," George thought.

"Each team will follow the movements of one of the orange captains in front of you," the Colonel said and motioned the cadets forward toward each orange captain.

Emily's face twisted; "Six captains and seven teams today?" she whispered.

"Cadet Hawkins, bring your team this way," the Colonel said as the other teams lined up with the orange team captains and started their training.

George and the others followed the Colonel over to the small dome on the side of the main training dome. A Senior Viceroy was waiting inside for them when the Colonel entered the smaller dome. George dropped his head and stopped at the door, waiting to be motioned inside. The Senior Viceroy was taken aback at first by their formality and then seemed pleased they had respected protocol. The Senior Viceroy nodded; and George, Andy, and the others entered and lined up behind George in the small dome. The Colonel nodded and left, returning to the main training dome.

"My name is David Lu, you will address me as, sir. From now on I will be your Chen Lo instructor. Cadet Hawkins, step your team through each level of Chen Lo you know. I want to assess your progress. You may begin," he said formally.

George nodded to the Senior Viceroy and then turned, holding his arm out to Andy.

"I release command to Cadet Penteado, sir," George said, dipping his head and stepping back.

Andy stepped forward and the others took their places around him as the officer raised his eyebrow and stepped to the side of the dome to watch. Andy started the team out on level one and over the next few hours brought them up to level ten easily.

All the time they laughed and smiled when they slipped or fell, helping each other up as if in fluid motion. They jumped, rolled and flipped as one. Their minds cleared as they focused and concentrated on nothing but the moment. By the end of the eleventh level, the cadets were breathing harder, yet not as hard as the first time. Andy slowed them down and stopped, facing the Senior Viceroy.

"Dismissed," he said, turning around and lowering his head.

The cadets lowered their heads and raised their arm to their chest. Turning, they left the small dome. The large dome was empty and quiet.

"Listen, do you hear it?" Emily asked, smiling.

"Hear what?" George asked.

"The walls and caves are happy again," she whispered.

George swung his arm around Emily's shoulders. "You really need to get out more," he whispered softly.

They left the dome and headed for the dining hall. Senior Viceroy Petrosky, Pete's grandfather, appeared in the small dome after the cadets had left.

"What do you think, David?" he asked.

"They are ready. However, I have never seen this level of focus in cadets so young before," David replied.

"Can you teach them the focus and control they will need?" the Senior Viceroy asked.

"Yes, I can teach them; however, I am worried they will not understand what they are being taught," he replied and they disappeared in a flash of white light.

Toma was in their sleeping room the next morning when the cadets woke up.

"Where were you? We missed you at dinner last night, sir," George said.

"I was held up. One of the orange captains was to walk with you after class. Why, what happened?" Toma asked, changing to his captain's voice.

"We were late in leaving and must have missed the captain, sir," George said, staring at his bowl of cereal and imagining his mom's pancakes with maple syrup dripping down the sides.

"Late? What did you do? What happened? Report!" Toma said, getting excited and worried.

"It's OK, sir. We're not in trouble. We are training on Chen Lo with another officer, sir," Emily replied, sitting down close to George.

"Why, what did you do? Who was the officer?" Toma asked with worry in his voice.

"Nothing, sir, really. We're not in trouble, sir," Emily added, smiling and thinking of the Senior Viceroy.

"He's very nice, sir," Anna added kindly.

"We have reached level ten and Senior Viceroy David Lu is now our instructor, sir," Andy said, quite proud they had achieved level ten.

Toma's mouth dropped open. "He retired many years ago," he said, hardly believing them.

"Well, he's back and training us, sir," Andy said proudly.

"I hope you appreciate him, he is an excellent teacher," Toma said, standing up. He still could not quite believing the Senior Viceroy was back; Pete and Frank would need to be informed.

The cadets finished their cereal and slipped their bowls into the cabinet. Whispering quietly, they followed him out the door and down the corridor to Colonel Moawk's training dome again.

"We were here yesterday, sir," Gus said, wondering if Toma was confused on what day it was.

"It is the last week, and you will be sent to where they think you need the most work before the end of your rotation," Toma replied, leaving them in the corridor and disappearing down the corridor quickly as if he, too, was late for training.

The cadets entered the training dome and lined up as before. Colonel

Moawk appeared again and the orange captains descended from the dome supports again. George and his team were led to the small dome off the side of the large training dome. Again they waited until they were allowed to enter. The Senior Viceroy David Lu seemed pleased with their respect. The team thought it was the least they could do, as he had been brought back out of retirement to teach them.

This time the cadets lined up with Andy in the lead position. The Senior Viceroy walked across the small dome and stood in front of the cadets.

"We will begin with level ten and see how far we get today," he said, speaking directly into their minds.

The cadets nodded and thought nothing of someone talking directly in their minds. It was like a link of sorts, except they were only listening. He turned around and started their warm-up movements.

George thought the team was more fluid today. Yesterday they had started out awkward and stiff. Today they were moving as one sooner than before. The Senior Viceroy announced the level and then started the basic moves within the level.

He named some moves when he connected two or more moves together. They looked like fluid motion. Andy, George and the others rolled, spun, leaped and nearly flew through the air in the small dome. The eleventh level flew by and then the twelfth level. The cadets were as one, focused and smooth.

At the twelfth level they felt as if they were in rhythm with the galaxies around them. George lost himself in the sounds of the galaxies. He flipped and dove without effort. Soon the cadets were being slowed down by the Senior Viceroy. Before, George, Andy, and the others were often out of breath at the end of their training. This time they were breathing no differently than when they had entered the small dome.

"Sir?" Emily spoke up when they had completely stopped.

"Yes, Emily," the Senior Viceroy replied, without turning around.

"Sir, we're not tired or out of breath today. Why, sir?" she asked softly.

"How did you feel when we made the Chen Lo motions today?" he asked.

"In harmony with the galaxies, sir," she answered wistfully, spinning around.

"Are the galaxies tired and out of energy, Emily?" he pressed.

"Why no, sir," Emily replied, laughing.

"Then why would you be tired if the galaxies are not tired?" he asked kindly.

The cadets stared at each other. Pete and Toma may be cryptic; however, they were nothing compared to the Senior Viceroy. He was downright spooky. They had no idea what the Senior Viceroy had said.

"We'll ask Grandfather, he'll know what Senior Viceroy David Lu means," George signed to his team to calm their questions.

"Dismissed," he said, turning around to face the cadets again.

The cadets bowed and left the small dome. George turned and looked back at the Senior Viceroy as he stood in the doorway of the small door. The Senior Viceroy nodded.

"You can ask; however, he will not tell you the answer. You must figure it out yourself," he replied in George's mind.

David Lu had shown them how to use the raw energy of the universe with Chen Lo, they simply did not understand yet! The door closed, and Senior Viceroy Petrosky appeared in the small dome behind David Lu.

"They are an amazing team," David Lu said, still staring at the closed door before turning around and facing Senior Viceroy Petrosky. "They remind me of another group of wild, untamed cadets many, many years ago. They are even more focused then your team was, Alexander," he said.

"I have a plan, walk with me," Senior Viceroy Petrosky said, and they disappeared in a flash of white light.

Pete met the cadets in the corridor outside the training dome. They were happy to see him again.

"Where have you been, sir, and where's Toma, sir?" Sara asked.

"We must hurry or we'll be late," Pete said and started to run down the corridor, not answering Sara's question.

As they ran through the corridors, Pete's team joined them, lining up on one side of the cadets. A few more corridors and they entered the green captains' sector, and Frank's team joined them, one team member at a time coming out of classrooms and lining up on the other side of George and his team.

They ran in columns with George, Pete, and Frank in the first row; then Emily, Jennifer, and Kate; followed by Gus, Han, and Sven; and then Anna, Karmen; and Maria; followed by Sara, Rachael, and Lucita; and finally Andy, Nick, and Niels. A few more turns and they were in the yellow sector, and Toma appeared as a Thorean. He, too, joined the run, and one by one his team lined up next to Pete's team.

Their triad was complete. George could feel the strength, focus, calm, and unity. The thunder of their run echoed through the cadet and captain sector corridors. The captains and cadets opened their classroom doors to see the commotion in the corridor. Soon hundreds of captains and cadets were following them.

To the rhythm of their footsteps, Pete spoke, "Peace is our path;" and their triad answered, "It unites all beings."

Frank was next, "Courage is our character;" and again, their triad answered, "It joins us as one."

Toma spoke, "Harmony is our nature;" again they answered, "It connects us to the universe."

George followed with,"Strength is our will;" and they answered, "It protects us all."

Together the three captains and George then finished; "Four parts come together to heal the fear of the past and present," to which their team replied, "To start anew with

Once spoken, they repeated the verses and this time the cadets following them joined in the verse. The captain and cadet sectors rumbled with their footsteps and verse. Pete turned their teams into a large archway and they entered the Sport arena on the ground level. Inside the arena only standing room was left as other captains and officers already filled the seats. The officers stood and roared, cheering as Pete, Frank, Toma, and George's team entered the arena. George thought every officer, captain, and cadet on Asteria station was crammed into the Sport arena. The sound was deafening.

Pete led them on a lap around the floor of the arena and then stopped in the center. The cadets backed up and made a circle around them. The stamping of their feet in rhythm thundered around the arena. High above them in the Viceroy's box, Pete's grandfather, the other Senior Viceroys, and the entire Galactic council appeared in a brilliant flash of white light. The cadets, captains and officers gasped, and the arena fell silent.

The older officers lowered their heads as a sign of respect, and the younger cadets followed their example. Frank, Toma, and George, with a little push from Pete, dropped down on one knee. Andy and the others in their triad followed. It was the protocol thing to do as most cadets and captains rarely, if ever, see Viceroys and Senior Viceroys and never the Galactic council.

"Triad,arise!" boomed Senior Viceroy Petrosky's voice.

They stood up and all eyes moved to the Viceroy's box. The Senior Viceroy continued, his voice echoing around the arena.

"The Galactic council has been most recently reminded of the value of honor, courage and compassion in the face of overwhelming odds. The red team of George Hawkins, Andy Penteado, Emily Millar, Anna Jhang, Sara

O'Conner, and Gus Reiter and their triad are the teams that have reminded the Galactic council of these fundamental values," the Senior Viceroy said firmly.

The whispers in the arena fell silent and the cadets and officers stood in awe of the red cadets and captains.

"Their list of accomplishments is astonishing not only for this, their third rotation, but also for the previous two rotations as well. They completed their triad, set the new cadets fighter record and earned the award for outstanding courage and compassion in the face of great danger and personal risk. This award has a field of red which symbolizes courage when confronted with a relentless enemy. The white star laid over the field of red symbolizes compassion to share what you have to save the lives of others," he continued.

"In this year's rotation, they have brought hope to a planet devastated by slavery and compassion to a bureaucracy ruled by fear. For these accomplishments they are awarded one of our highest awards. It is for compassion and honor; the field of yellow symbolizes honor, the giving of your life to save others. The white star laid over the field of yellow symbolizes compassion to share with others all that you have!" he said proudly.

Senior Viceroy Petrosky waved his hand in the air, and the awards appeared on the team's suits. The Senior Viceroy knelt down on one knee and lowered his head as a sign of respect. All of the Galactic council members, Viceroys, Inner Circle officers, and CORE officers followed his lead. As one massive team, the arena thundered with sound of the captains and cadets also kneeling on one knee.

George and the others always thought they did what they did because it was what was right and not because they wanted the fame, although at this moment in time the fame wasn't too bad. The cadets and captains seemed to glow with a reddish-white aura.

The Senior Viceroy stood up, and the arena followed his lead again. Then he started to clap his hands together, and the arena roared to life. The cadets cheered and yelled. One of their own teams had a huge, immense, enormous award; and they were ecstatic. George and the others smiled and waved to the cadets and officers. As he waved, he started to recite the words they had said in the corridor on the way to the arena.

"Peace is our path, it unites all beings.

Courage is our character, it joins us as one.

Harmony is our nature, it connects us to the universe.

Strength is our will, it protects us all.

Four parts come together to heal the fear of the past and present.

To start anew with peace, courage, harmony and strength."

Soon the entire arena was saying the words. The cadets on the ground rushed forward, lifted the cadets and captains high into the air, and paraded around the arena. The Senior Viceroy clapped his hands and the floor of the arena changed into a hard floor and silver tables and chairs grew up from the floor.

The arena was transformed into an immense banquet hall. The officers and captains streamed down from the arena seats onto the main floor to congratulate the cadets and captains before making their way to the tables for dinner. The arena seats folded back into the cavern walls as more officers and captains streamed onto the ground floor to congratulate the triad. When everyone was seated, Pete, Frank, Toma, and George stood up and raised their cups for a toast.

Pete yelled, "The young do not always do as they are told."

"To the irreverence of youth," Frank replied, yelling back.

Toma yelled, "Our elders have rules and regulations, guidance and focus."

"To the wisdom of age, may it not elude us," George replied, yelling as Frank had done.

The Viceroys and council nodded and in a flash of white light disappeared. The cadets, captains and officers relaxed. They ate and talked in the arena late into the night. In time the cadets, captains and officers said their good evenings and drifted off to their sleeping rooms. Toma nodded and the teams knew it was time to go.

They left the arena and walked out into the corridor to return to their sectors. Emily moved her hand across the cadets and their award disappeared.

"Why?" Pete asked, yawning as they walked.

"We are cadets, we have been honored, now it is time to return to being who we are, cadets on our third rotation," she replied seriously.

Pete looked at George.

"Don't look at me, sir. I'm not going to disagree with Emily," George signed, grinning and wrapping his arm around her waist.

Pete looked at Andy next.

Andy shook his head. "I am many things but dumb enough to cross Emily when she made a decision about something isn't one of them, sir," Andy signed.

"Don't you want to bask in the glory," Frank asked, grinning and walking all weird and wobbly, gesturing with his hands.

"I am tired and even I know this is a trick question. Either Pete will beat us tomorrow for getting big heads or Emily, Sara and Anna will. Personally, I'd take Pete's beating over Emily, Anna, or Sara being mad at us, any day," Andy whispered back to Frank, Toma and Pete.

They looked at each other and laughed out loud.

"Laugh all you want, sirs. Like you three would ever cross Jennifer, Kate, or Sheta," George whispered over his shoulder.

"Oh yes, point well taken," Pete replied, and they all laughed together.

Frank, Toma, and the others slipped off, and soon Pete and the cadets were alone in the corridor. They were all tired and walked on in silence.

Their third rotation had nearly come to an end. Soon it would be time to return to school for their junior year. As he walked down the red cadet corridor on Asteria station, George wondered what school he, Andy, and the others would attend, or if they would return to Earth at all.

The End